# LICKED CLEAN

'You'd better sit down, I suppose,' Severe drawled. 'God, you're a pathetic-looking specimen. Coz told me you were a bit of a weed, but I didn't realise what a soppy worm he had to put up with. Luke! What sort of wormy name is that?'

Luke flushed. His first reaction to her cruel words was to rise stiffly – in every sense – make a frigid excuse, and withdraw. Yet, settled in a lumpy leather armchair, with his risen cock grotesquely obvious, he reasoned that any attention was better than none. To his horror, his cock throbbed harder at her cutting remarks. To be touched by her verbal swordblade was better than not being touched at all. She was so blasted gorgeous in her icy, aristo way, as if, secure in the citadel of her own beauty, she despised not just him, but the whole world.

She lifted her leg, letting her short skirt slip high up her thighs, and propped her foot on the arm of his chair. He stared at her upper legs quite revealed: the stocking tops, clamped by lemon satin garter straps, the lacy lemon sussies and, nestling in its frame, the matching sliver of panties, covering a mound swelling to burst. His cock swelled, until he felt his trousers could scarcely contain the erection. What thrilled and maddened him was her utter disdain for his presence; she exposed her intimate flesh as though he wasn't there, or as if his gaze meant no more than a pet dog's.

# LICKED CLEAN

*Yolanda Celbridge*

This book is a work of fiction.
In real life, make sure you practise safe, sane and
consensual sex.

First published in 2005 by
Nexus
Thames Wharf Studios
Rainville Road
London W6 9HA

Reprinted 2009

*www.nexus-books.co.uk*

Typeset by TW Typesetting, Plymouth, Devon

Printed and bound by
CPI Antony Rowe, Chippenham, Wiltshire

ISBN 9780352339997

# Contents

You'll notice that we have introduced a set of symbols onto our book jackets, so that you can tell at a glance what fetishes each of our brand new novels contains. Here's the key – enjoy!

cp (traditional)

cp (modern)

spanking

restraint/bondage

rope bondage/hojojutsu

latex/rubber/leather/enclosure

fem dom

willing captivity

medical

period setting

uniforms

sex rituals

# 1

# Bare Bottom Shame

Poldipple Hall, set amidst pretty lawns and flowerbeds, and washed in the fresh breeze from the River Tamar, evoked the familiar sensation of prickly dread, as Luke Redruth's footsteps crunched on the remaining few steps of gravel driveway. The taxi, having noisily deposited him before the portico of the great house, roared away into the distance, towards Saltash, and he bit his lip, as his last chance of freedom was gone. He could have ordered the driver to return to Aunt Amy, then stamped his foot, and insisted that at eighteen – just – he had no intention of putting up with her mediaeval ideas of 'discipline', especially for such a trivial crime.

What on earth had he done wrong? He had just been playing around. A hot day, a lazy lunch al fresco, a couple of glasses of wine, and his Aunt Amy had taken a nap. It was her fault if she'd let a pair of her panties fall from the laundry basket. Naturally, like a well-brought-up boy, he picked them up; his nose had been assailed by their rich female perfume, his eyes entranced by the lacy pink whorls and curls, the swooping high cut and the narrow, delicately stained gusset that had embraced her holy of holies. For whom did Aunt Amy wear such a divine garment? How did it feel? Luke had to know.

In a moment, he had been nude, and had slipped the tight silk flimsy over his own balls and buttocks, straining the fabric to the limit. It had clung so gorgeously, tight to

1

the point of pain. And then . . . and then . . . why did Aunt Amy have to wake up, to catch him, just at *that* moment? To laugh, and call him the vilest names, her insults the more deadly for her lack of anger, the cool, calm tone of her voice, the almost humorous insistence that he pay for his offence in the interests of justice. He had said he was sorry, but she had replied that there was nothing to be sorry about. It was simply that a smutty boy must suffer for his pleasure. How could that be justice? Especially as she wasn't even his real aunt, just some blasted umpteenth cousin.

What absurdity, to take a taxi to a flogging! Yet, apart from his bicycle – too demeaning by far – he had no other means of transport to the traditional 'seat of punishment' as his guardian aunt impishly put it, where Commander Standish Compaigne, RN, another cousin, infinitely removed, would yet again attend to his errant bottom with bluff naval homilies about the cane 'making a man of him' and such rot. Aunt Amy would have had a fit before allowing a stranger to lay a hand on her beloved Luke, or so she said, but 'family' was all right. The bitch was always so coy about the thing, never referring to the flogging, which she knew was the object of visiting Poldipple, but coyly ordering 'a talking-to' from the beefy commander, with a note, penned in violet ink.

Luke knew full well her notes contained the most vicious and intimate details of his punishment, usually six or eight stingers on his trousers, drawn as tightly as possible over his buttocks, with no chance of a stuffed magazine or extra shorts escaping the commander's eagle eye.

Aunt Amy, when she felt particularly unkind, made him show her his bare arse, so that she could count the welts, and made him tell her how it hurt, and whether he had cried out, and all that sort of cringe-making stuff, which was almost worse than the beating itself; at least that was a manly, nothing-personal affair, and over quickly. Women were such a strange mixture of love and cruelty.

Curse Cornwall and its extended families! Aunt Amy *was* truly a bitch. A youthful, tennis-honed thirty, she wasn't that much older than him, and she could very well have caned him herself – an awful, shivery notion – but she murmured coyly that such things were not women's work. Luke had an image, as so often, of her golden arm muscles tensing, with some sort of blasted cane over his stretched trousers, her frilly tennis skirt whirling, bum bouncing and pert titties wobbling, as *she* thrashed him. And it would be so like her to invite her snotty-bitch tennis friends, to watch him, as he squirmed under his tanning.

The image of ladies eagerly watching him caned excited him in some stomach-clutching and disturbing way, so he rapidly suppressed it, as always. Suppose Amy found him wearing her panties, and made him take the panties clean off, in front of jeering women, to cane him on ... on his *bare buttocks?* That caused Luke's cock to stir, which terrified and shamed him.

He wasn't supposed to think of Aunt Amy's titties as pert, or her bum as big, although they were. He knew that if he ever got a girl naked, after years of hopeless fumblings and frustrations, and finally *did it* – lost his cursed cherry – well, the girl would be *miles* better than Aunt Amy, quite different, in fact, and her smooth, creamy girl meat would raise him to heights of ecstasy he could hardly dream of, and ... and all that kind of thing, and he would spurt and spurt and spurt into a really tight, wet, young girl's quim. At thirty, for heaven's sake, Aunt Amy was a proper wrinkly! Yet those panties were like a teenage girl's. Blast it, Aunt Amy was a girl.

Meanwhile, there was nothing to be done but grimly accept fate. Any hopes of freedom at leaving boarding school – what a dreary bore *that* had been – evaporated when Aunt Amy made it clear his residence at Clear House – her inherited pile – depended on his helpfulness, cheerfulness and willing obedience in the most trivial chores: mucking out and mucking in, fetching, carrying, shopping, sweeping, all things the bitch was too lazy to do herself. It seemed to give her pleasure to sit with a gin and tonic, bare

3

legs crossed, and tennis skirt hoisted almost rudely to bare most of her golden thighs, while she watched Luke stripped to his shorts and sweating, as he forked dung, weeded, mowed and carried, like some blasted serf.

She didn't seem to mind his glances at her bare thighs, with sometimes a crotch-tingling glimpse of a sliver of pink, blue or lemon panties, as she crossed her legs, or at her titties spilling from her blouse, with only a few buttons fastened, and then the inevitable swelling in his shorts. In fact, she seemed to enjoy it. She was the executrix of his late uncle's will, with all that money tied up in some impenetrable trust fund, which meant that if he failed to please Aunt Amy, the trust fund would remain locked, until his twenty-first birthday. Blast, and triple blast!

All around him, butterflies fluttered in the July sun, the clouds were serene and puffy white in the blue sky, and the Tamar flowed, sparkling, on its way to Plymouth Sound. Nature seemed at peace, except for Luke Redruth. Clutching his note, damp from sweat, he trudged the last few steps as slowly as possible, and clanged the antique brass doorbell. There were steps: not the commander's thunderous tread, but a light, girlish prancing. The door swung open, and Luke gasped.

Greeting him was not the commander, but a blonde girl his own age. She was dressed in a school uniform of a grey pleated skirt that exposed her knees, which were encased in lemon nylon stockings, which shone, stretched on long, coltish legs; a white blouse and a blue-and-yellow-striped tie, severely knotted; and brown court shoes on dainty feet. Her heels were only of medium height, yet she stood as tall as Luke. The uniform clung tightly to her body; her long blonde tresses cascaded, as if only just released from the bondage of a hairslide or pin, over her full breasts, straining under the cotton blouse, which was damply translucent with sweat and allowed him to see her bra. It was one of those sheer, scalloped ones, scarcely a bra at all. The small clinging skirt seemed made for a girl years younger, hugging her bottom, so as to emphasise her rippling thighs and the ripe, amply swelling glands of her buttocks.

Luke's heart started to pitter-patter, and he cursed himself, for here, in the flesh, was a living doll of fantasy, and his cock could not help stiffening, uncoiling in his grey flannels like a blasted snake. The girl looked him up and down, with utmost scorn on her curled lip, as only a teenage girl knew how.

Luke's legs seemed to turn to jelly, even as his heart pounded, yet a way out seemed to present itself: what if the commander was not at home? He could truthfully tell Aunt Amy he had delivered the note, then rub his bottom a bit and, with luck, she would not demand his assurance that he had indeed been whopped! He smiled hopefully at the sneering girl. The girl yawned. Her big firm breasts rippled, as she put all her teenaged female contempt into that yawn. Luke felt like a worm.

'Commander Compaigne . . .?' he stammered.

'Coz is at sea,' she drawled, her voice as fresh and clear as cowbells. 'For three weeks.'

'I'm . . .'

'I know who you are,' she snapped. 'You have a letter to deliver. I hurried back from school to be here. Tomorrow's the last day of summer term. We're a serious school, at Saltash Gentlefolk, and don't break up for summer until much later than plebby schools.'

'Well, the letter's for the commander, miss.'

She snatched it from him, and a shiver went through him at the touch of her skin on his. 'It's for "S Compaigne",' she said.

'Commander Standish Compaigne, you see,' he said.

'I am S Compaigne. S for Severine, but I'm called Severe for short. You address me as "miss", or "Miss Severe".'

'I think it's meant for the commander, really, Miss Severe,' he blurted.

'I'll be the judge of what "really" means. What's meant is what's written.'

She tore open the envelope, and quickly scanned the letter. As she did so, her lips puckered and, when she raised

5

her head, she looked Luke full in the face, with a lop-sided smile.

'You'd better come in,' she drawled. 'Don't forget to wipe your feet. I get *very* cross with smutty boys who forget to wipe their feet, and it seems *you* are a *particularly* smutty customer. Quite the beastly little oik, in fact.'

Blushing, and his face contorted in shame, Luke wiped his muddy shoes with extra care, then crossed the threshold, following her like a puppy into the musty coolness of the vestibule, hung with words and portraits of mariners gone by.

'If the commander's away, I can always come back.'

'No time like the present,' she said, with a smile that was half coy and half mischief.

'I mean, miss, really –'

'The R word again,' she said irritably. 'How you bore me. Stop talking about my coz. He's my guardian, in loco parentis, but I'm eighteen now, and may think for myself. He's a seadog, so I take charge of things when he's away dogging at sea.'

That seemed to amuse her for she tossed her mane, threw back her head and trilled with laughter. Luke stared at her creamy throat, and her breasts bobbing, as if trying to break free from their constraining cloth. The teats were sharply outlined, and he saw her left nipple, plain as day: a massive strawberry, plump and stiff and jutting from her trembling breast flesh.

His cock swelled to full erection, and he began to walk in a sort of hobble, crossing his thighs and hoping she wouldn't notice. Of course, she did notice. Girls always noticed anything to embarrass a fellow. But she said nothing, as they entered the drawing room, contenting herself with an impish glance, and licking her lips, with a flash of her starry white teeth, like a tiger's.

What on earth did Severe want? Feverishly, Luke imagined some dream seduction – the girl gagging for and helpless to resist his cock, whose enormity Luke felt should be appreciated, rather than mocked by his schoolfellows'

6

smutty jibes about splitting girls open with his monster, which, given his virgin state, were sadly untrue. A *girl* – now *she* would appreciate his nine-incher ... except that girls always seemed to look at his blushing face, awkward hands, everywhere except the place he wanted them to. He looked at girls' bums and titties, as they intended, didn't he? So why was the honour not returned? Dream seductions, he concluded glumly, only happened in dreams.

'You'd better sit down, I suppose,' Severe drawled. 'God, you're a pathetic-looking specimen. Coz told me you were a bit of a weed, but I didn't realise what a soppy worm he had to put up with. Luke! What sort of wormy name is that?'

Luke flushed. His first reaction to her cruel words was to rise stiffly – in every sense – make a frigid excuse, and withdraw. Yet, settled in a lumpy leather armchair, with his risen cock grotesquely obvious, he reasoned that any attention was better than none. To his horror, his cock throbbed *harder* at her cutting remarks. To be touched by her verbal swordblade was better than not being touched at all. She was so blasted gorgeous in her icy, aristo way, as if, secure in the citadel of her own beauty, she despised not just him, but the whole world.

She lifted her leg, letting her short skirt slip high up her thighs, and propped her foot on the arm of his chair. He stared at her upper legs quite revealed: the stocking tops, clamped by lemon satin garter straps, the lacy lemon sussies and, nestling in its frame, the matching sliver of panties, covering a mound swelling to burst. His cock swelled, until he felt his trousers could scarcely contain the erection. What thrilled and maddened him was her utter disdain for his presence; she exposed her intimate flesh as though he wasn't there, or as if his gaze meant no more than a pet dog's.

Taking a cigarette from her packet of Dunhill's, she placed it between her lips, then, without looking at him, snapped her fingers. Luke bounded forwards, lit a Swan Vesta match, and held it, trembling, to her mouth. She

7

puffed in the ebbing flame until it was almost down to his skin, smiled to herself, and nodded, as he retreated, rubbing his stinging finger. Quite unconcernedly, she plucked at her garter strap, which left an ugly red imprint on her thigh flesh.

'It's no use,' she said thoughtfully. 'I really must change into something more comfortable, or I shan't do a good job. A girl's things are always so beastly tight, aren't they? But otherwise, she wouldn't feel pretty.' She patted her skirt back into place. 'It's Coz, you see,' she said, looking at him, as if only just noticing him. 'He's so frightfully stingy. He absolutely refuses to buy me a bigger uniform to replace this one, because I've only another term to go. Men!'

'Why, miss, I think your uniform is . . . is awfully nice,' Luke blurted.

She shot him a venomous glance. 'Wrong thing to say, worm,' she spat. 'I think I'm actually going to enjoy this job.'

She blew a contemptuous plume of smoke in his face. Luke went a little pale, pondering her words. Job? What job? Surely she didn't intend to . . . to beat him herself? No, the idea was absurd. Yet, she had accepted the letter, with its customary instruction; had invited him in. Thrashed by . . . by a *girl*! The utter shame! His stiff cock throbbed mercilessly.

Severe left the drawing room, and Luke heard her footsteps scampering up the stairs. In the distance, a telephone rang, and was answered. He heard her voice, warm and cooing, then a male voice at the other end, rather abrupt; then, Severe's voice sharp, querulous; shrill, unbelieving; and the phone slammed down.

After several minutes, she reappeared, her face scarlet and her eyes moist. She had been crying. She wore a white gymslip, with a delicious little frilly skirt that scarcely came over her bottom, and no apparent panty line; the bodice of the slip was as tight as her school blouse, but this time, evidently, with no bra: her massive titties jutted hard and full without the need of one. Her long brown legs were bare, and her feet were in white fluffy socks and gleaming laced-up tennis shoes. A red ribbon knotted her lush blonde mane in a ponytail. Luke rose, and said rather awkwardly that if he was in the way, he had perhaps better go. His words twisted her face with rage.

'What do you mean, in the way, you beastly worm?' Severe spat, her breasts and ponytail bobbing furiously. 'Of course you're in the way. Snivelling tykes like you are in the way anywhere on earth. But I've a job to do on you, and I mean to do it.'

Trying to take his eyes from her stiff, massive nipples, topping her bouncing breasts, naked under the thinnest of cotton covering, Luke blurted that it didn't seem fair to accuse him of snivelling, as he hadn't yet had an opportunity to snivel. No sooner were his words spoken, than he regretted them, groaning inwardly. They seemed to cheer her, in a chilling fashion. Her lips creased in a smile, and she licked the tips of her teeth.

'I'm sorry if I've said the wrong thing, miss,' he said.

'Oh, you've said the wrong thing, all right,' she snarled. 'At this stage, anything you say would be the wrong thing. I expect you eavesdropped on my telephone conversation.'

'Why, certainly not, miss,' he replied.

'Liar. You men are all liars. I intend to go extra hard on you for that. You must have heard what that . . . that absolute bastard Justin was saying, the . . . the absolute *bastard*!'

'No, miss, I assure you,' he blurted. 'I have no idea who Justin is.'

'That's it, take his side. You men always stick up for each other. Well, I'll show you.'

She opened the sideboard, where Commander Compaigne kept a row of shiny wooden canes, leather dog-whips, and gleaming braided riding crops. Seeing them, she began to caress them, one after the other; her breathing calmed, and when she turned round, she was smiling.

'Don't gape like a ninny,' she said amiably. 'You've seen this lot before.'

9

'Certainly, miss, but ... I mean, surely you don't propose to ...'

She snatched his aunt's note, and thrust it in front of him, ordering him to read.

' "Bearer insolent again",' he read, in a faltering voice, ' "this time with my own soiled panties. I needn't go into the disgraceful and obscene details. If boys will be boys, they must suffer severely for it. Please punish accordingly." '

'That is just what I intend to do,' she drawled, smacking her lips. 'Isn't it a splendid morning for swishing a boy's horrid insolent bum? We've a good two hours before luncheon, so I intend to make a hearty meal of you first. You'd better strip off.'

'I ... I beg your pardon, miss?' His voice quavered.

'Are you deaf as well as repellent? I said strip off. Disrobe completely for your punishment. I find that nudity brings a proper sense of shame, in addition to the actual physical pain. You don't need to be shy, for there's no one else at home. It's the maid's day off.'

Unconcernedly, she selected the longest, most vicious riding crop from her guardian's collection. Luke had felt it only once, when he took six of the best for getting the wrong sherry from his aunt's wine merchant in Saltash, and knew it stung abominably. His heart was in his mouth.

'Riding crop is more painful than cane, isn't it?' Severe murmured dreamily. 'Although learned opinion differs. At any rate, it makes a much more satisfying noise: a real thud, instead of a whistle. You can really *hear* the bare flesh sizzle.'

*Bare flesh?*

'Miss, I don't think I understood you. I'm to be caned – I accept that, even from a girl – but strip off? I mean, your coz always canes me on the trousers.'

Now she was angry again. ' "Even from a girl"? Especially from a girl is more like it. You think Coz canes hard? You've a lot to learn about girls, young master. I never cane less than a dozen, and on the bare bottom.'

'Oh, no! Completely bare, miss!' Luke exclaimed, trembling. 'Not a dozen!'

'A whole dozen, and *always* on the bare. Does a horse wear trousers when you whop his flank? A clothed caning is no more than a gnat bite, so strip, you petulant little worm. I shan't tell you again.' She stroked the riding crop, flexing it, and pressed her lips to the shiny leather. 'So lovely and hard,' she said. 'Fibreglass underneath, and soft leather outside. Skin on skin. You won't be so cocky when this blisters your naked buttocks, although it's not as if you have never been spanked on the bare, is it?'

'Of course I've been spanked, pants down, miss,' he blurted, 'but surely spanked is different. Aunt Amy has often paddled or spanked me, bare breech, but when I was old enough, she began to send me to your coz for a man's punishment.'

'A man's best punishment is from a girl's hand,' she snorted. 'Although you're nowhere near a man: you're an abject, whining boy. A real man, like Justin, wouldn't make such a fuss.'

Luke's cock throbbed, and his heart raced, as, numbly, he began to disrobe. His eyes blurred with sweat, in which the white-clad girl shimmered, his goddess of terrible revenge. Whoever Justin was, Luke wanted to sort him out for getting him into this. He wondered if she had ever dealt the same punishment to Justin, whipping him on the bare, and was suddenly filled with envy.

'Coz favours the brisk naval chastisment,' she purred, 'but I'm only a weak little girl, and take my own lazy time – long and slow. Gosh, am I going to enjoy skinning you.'

Removing his shorts, Luke turned coyly, presenting his buttocks, but concealing his throbbing erection.

'Shy, worm?' she sneered.

'Yes, miss,' he said wretchedly.

'Never been nude in front of a girl?'

'Of course I have. Matron at school, and Aunt Amy used to bathe me, until I had hairs on my ... you know where.'

11

'Hairs?' she said, wrinklng her nose. 'How beastly. The rest of you is nice and smooth, which is the only point in your favour.'

'A chap can't help having hairs down there, miss,' he said feebly.

'Never heard of a razor? Justin's completely smooth, and he's older than you, little boy. Why, I expect you're a virgin.'

'There's no shame in that, miss,' he retorted, jerking round, and baring his huge erection.

Her eyes widened, and she gasped, allowing Luke some small pride. 'You mean that dreadful, obscene ... *thing* has never been inside a lady?' she blurted, swallowing hard.

'No, miss.'

'It's disgusting. How dare you insult me with that monstrosity? I've a good mind to tell Coz or your aunt. How the poor lady must suffer from your beastliness! On second thoughts, I'll punish you myself. Give you *extra* slices, that is. I'm so cross! I'd like to whip every beastly boy in the world.'

Luke stammered that he accepted Severe's caning, on the bare, and a dozen, and fully understood her anger – which made her more angry – but offered to serve her a cup of coffee beforehand, as he did so wish they could deal with his caning amicably. Her eyes brightened.

'That's the first sensible thing you've said, whelp,' she drawled, fishing in a drawer of the sideboard, and pulling out a frilly white apron.

Perhaps 'whelp' was a little better than 'worm'.

'Here, put this on,' she commanded. 'It seems you like wearing girls' things.'

'No, miss,' he blurted.

'Do you disobey?' she hissed, her breasts heaving in rage.

'No, no – I can't disobey you, Miss Severe.' He fastened the short skirtlet around his waist, and blushed scarlet, for his cock erected the fabric like a tent.

'You do look funny.' She giggled. 'Scamper into the kitchen, maid, and make the coffee strong. It's absolutely the most expensive and exclusive Brazilian – Coz has interests there – so *you* can't have any. You'll find some chocolate digestives somewhere; they are my favourite. Don't walk with big boyish strides, either. I want you to mince, like a girl, so that I can laugh at you.'

He put his feet together, and did his best to roll his thighs and wiggle his bottom, like a girl, as he went to the kitchen, at which she chortled and clapped her hands, making him blush fiercely; he exaggerated the wiggle of his buttocks even more, hoping to embarrass her, but she clapped her hands again. He made the coffee, savouring its rich, almost overpowering aroma, which, curiously, seemed to suggest wanton sensuality, bare girls' bodies under the tropic sun, the perfume of laughing brown girls' breasts and lips and bottoms and wriggling painted toes.

Placing everything neatly on a silver tray, his erection as stiff as ever, he minced back to serve the girl, who was sprawled in the armchair, with her leg draped over the arm. He caught a glimpse of her thigh under the white skirt, and her cleft, and the moist lips of her quim! The bulging mons was shaven – smooth and hairless – with the succulent quim lips gently writhing beneath, like the mouth of some giant pink salmon. He poured her coffee, and she sipped, with a sigh of satisfaction. Crunching a chocolate biscuit, she asked Luke quite casually if he had been looking at her slice.

'Miss?'

'Down here. My quim, twat, gash, *cunt*, whatever you filthy boys call it.'

He reddened. 'I may have glanced, without meaning to, miss. I apologise.'

'Thought so,' she said, tucking into another biscuit. 'I'll have to adjust your punishment accordingly. Let's see, failure to wipe your shoes properly, telling lies, earwigging my phone call and now peeking up my skirt, like some horrid little masturbator. I suppose, with you being a virgin, that applies? You frig your pego shamelessly and gush your spunk at the merest sniff of a girl? Or her panties?'

Luke blushed crimson. 'I really don't think, miss . . .'

'You wouldn't, being a boy. Well, as I'm in a good mood, with a juicy bare-beating to enjoy, I'll let you have some coffee before your caning, whelp.'

Severe poured coffee into her saucer and set it on the floor by her feet, then ordered Luke to kneel on his hands and knees, and drink with his snout. He obeyed, cock rigid at his humiliation, and feeling her eyes on his upthrust buttocks, as he slurped the coffee. Crooking her leg, she inspected the rubber sole of her tennis shoe, then, abruptly pushed it into his face.

'Lick me clean, whelp,' she drawled. 'Every inch.'

Whimpering in giddy, frightening excitement, he obeyed the humiliating command, and licked the rubber sole clean, although there was nothing to remove but some dust. She repeated the process with her other shoe, then rose, stretched and grasped her riding crop. She ripped off his apron, and cast it aside, licking her lips as she eyed his cock, and sneered unpleasantly.

'A boy who gets hard before a girl's beating, eh?' she murmured. 'I'll have to ensure you don't actually *enjoy* your two dozen.'

'What? *Two* dozen, miss?'

'I told you – extra strokes for your other misdeeds. Now, where shall I take you? Over the chair back I suppose. Bend over, grasp the arms, put your face down in the cushions and spread your legs wide, so that each ankle is against the foot of the chair.'

'You make it sound so cold and clinical, Miss Severe,' Luke moaned, as he rose, and obeyed.

Splayed naked, with his balls dangling between his spread thighs, stiff cock wedged against the leather chair back, and buttocks thrust in the air, he felt terribly vulnerable. He could smell her body – the fragrance of her sweat and the aroma of her bare quim – as she padded around him, gloating, smacking her lips and swishing the crop in the air.

He trembled in every tensed muscle, dreading his flogging, yet wishing it, for this imperious girl would at least pay him some attention, however painful. And there was a terrible glory at baring himself most shamefully to a woman, being totally in her power, knowing she could make him suffer at her slightest, cruellest whim. He was helpless, not because he was trussed, but because he *wanted* to be helpless. He jumped as something touched his bottom, but it was only her fingertips, soft and cool, as she rubbed some liquid on his skin.

'I'm going to give you an oiled beating,' she purred. 'It's so much more painful when the skin is moist.'

'Yes, miss. Thank you, miss,' he heard himself croak.

Yet, the touch of her fingers, stroking his bare bum, made his cock rigid, the sperm churning in his balls.

'I shouldn't thank me too soon,' she said. 'Your bum's going to look like a side of raw beef when I'm finished with you.'

'I'll . . . I'll thank you, whatever you do to me, miss,' he gasped.

'Cheeky scoundrel!'

'No, miss . . .'

'You've earned another dozen for *that* insolence. By God, your bum is going to have some tramlines.'

He heard the rustle of her gymslip as she raised the crop high over her head. 'Yes, miss,' he moaned, cock rigid, and heart racing, with a stranger thrill than he had ever known. 'Thank you, Miss Severe.'

# 2

# Vain for Weals

Vap!

'Ahh!'

Glinting in the lazy sunlight, the schoolgirl's riding crop flashed, whistling, as it descended to lash the boy's naked fesses. It stroked him squarely and deeply across the central buttocks, which clenched tight, almost at once, then lingered for a fraction of a second in the instantaneous pink weal, before sliding from the quivering bare arse flesh, to be raised again over Severe's head.

Luke's eyes misted with tears, and his gorge rose, as searing fire stroked his exposed buttocks. The pain was dreadful, worse than he had ever known, seeming to grab and claw him, like the pincers of some maddened beast. It throbbed, biting his whole bottom, with waves of agony shooting up his spine, until his head was filled with only that hideous smarting in his croup. He felt his knees buckle at the shock. Despite himself, he clenched his cheeks tight, as if that would ward off further assault, and squirmed pitiably to try to dissipate the agony.

His breath came in hoarse gasps, then easing, as the pain reached its plateau and began to ebb, yet his eyes were still moist and his heart pounded in terror. The shame of his nakedness, helpless before a cruel woman, seemed to compound his pain. That was only the first stroke! His squirms died down, his legs stopped trembling and, at that moment, she stroked again. Vap! She thrashed him hard,

17

her breasts bouncing inside her flimsy gymslip, which deliciously rubbed her big strawberry nips, and her skirt twirling above her rippling bare thighs to reveal, for an instant, the bare peach of her own golden, unpantied bottom.

'Ooh!'

The agony of the first stroke was nothing to the second. Ripples of pain filled his whole body, and he clenched his teeth, as hard as he clenched his buttocks, with his eyes screwed shut to try to stem the tears. He panted harshly and rapidly, like a puppy. Vap! A third took him lower, on the taut skin of the underfesse.

'Oh! Oh! It hurts dreadfully.'

'I forgot to tell you, worm, there is a penalty for whimpering like a girl. Every time you cry out or snivel, the beating starts again from stroke one.'

'God, you're cruel.'

'Now you've got the hang of it. Do your whimpering before the flogging starts, worm.'

Severe Compaigne gazed at the naked boy's clenched bare bottom, and licked her teeth, conscious of her moistening quim, and the tense stiff domes of her nips, with an electric tingle in her clitty making the nubbin stiffen and tremble quite deliciously.

*So thrill-making, to call a boy a worm, and watch him take the shame. They are worms, all of them, and must be punished for it, on their lovely juicy bare bums.*

Vap!

'Ohh!'

Vap!

'Ahh!'

Vap!

'Oh ... oh ... oh ...'

Luke wept, his flogged bottom already wealed crimson, and squirming tight. Severe pursed her lips, gazing proudly at the naked buttocks, glowing with her stripes. The arse pears were taut, muscled and smooth, apart from the crusts of the crop weals: a boy's bottom as it ought to be –

18

luscious, bare and twitching under a girl's power. The glistening olive oil made the glow of welts that much more lurid. Her teeth bared in a rictus. Any boy with an arse as juicy as that deserved to suffer.

*Is that what my own bum looks like under cane? It must . . . and does my whipper feel the same pleasure? A cruder one, certainly, with his big cock stiffening to gristle, not like the dainty swelling of my adorable clit. Boys are not artistic, except when their bums squirm.*

Yet the whimpering boy's cock was so big and bare and hard for her. Even thinking about such a monster, let alone gazing at it, made her knees weak; just the image of it penetrating her hole, filling and pounding her, made come pour from her slit. In unconscious sympathy with the wealed boy – consciously, she desired only to make him smart as dreadfully as possible – she rubbed her own bottom, bare under her gymslip, which was clinging with sweat. She rubbed her naked thighs together, startled at the squishy sound, as the lips of her quim squelched, and drips of come oozed from her twat.

She *was* sopping, down there, in her pulsing squelchy slit, with heart aflutter, clitty and nipples tingling stiff. She brushed both nipples, and gasped, as electric pleasure flooded her belly, spine and quim. Smiling fiercely, she lifted her riding crop over the boy's succulent bare croup. Vap! Her crop scythed the air, lashing him low on the underfesse, which jerked, and the whole arse clenched horribly tight, squirming at the same time. She heard his anguished hiss of breath, but this time he did not cry out. Vap! She took him on the tender top bum, its thin skin a most painful target, and saw the buttocks jolted to wriggle helplessly. Short, sharp pants burst from his lungs, but not loud enough to constitute a squeal.

'Ah . . . ah . . . ah . . .' he gasped.

'Don't worry, Luke,' she purred, 'you *will* get used to it. I know it seems a tall order, and you must be hurting so very badly, but after a while, your bum will adapt. Trust me.'

Vap!

'Ooh!'

Vap!

'Oh! Oh! Miss!'

The boy was close to tears. After ten strokes, with his agony prolonged by pauses of a good half-minute between each cut, she paused, panting, and caressed his welts with her fingertips. Moisture squelched in her quim, and her fingers trembled, ever so slightly.

'You are blistering well,' she panted, 'with some really nice colour – a particularly deep shade of crimson, with tinges of purple, and I think that'll go to black after not too many more cuts. That's why a proper flogging is always on the bare – there is absolutely no point in hiding the rod's artistry. And no matter how much a boy can conquer his pain, he cannot escape the delicious humiliance of being caned naked. You'll have something to be proud of when you look in the glass. I think we're both going to enjoy a nice long, slow session, while I skin you alive.'

'*Enjoy* it, miss?' he gasped.

'You know what I mean. Your cock is ramrod stiff. I can't say I'm displeased, in the circumstances.'

'I . . . I . . . it's a nervous reaction, miss.'

'Tch! You fibber.'

She tapped his most livid weal, across his top fesses, raking it with her fingernail, and he shuddered, letting out a long choking gasp of agony. Tears sprang to his eyes.

'You *are* cruel,' he said with a sob.

'That statement is true. But I'd rather you didn't remind me. Take it in silence like a man, and let me guess how much I'm hurting you. We girls love a puzzle. You understand *why* you must suffer, I hope. I must hurt you for the crime of being a beastly, filthy, smutty boy, and making me cross with you.'

'Y-yes, Miss Severe, I understand.'

'Good. That's the main thing.'

Vap! Luke's flogging recommenced. His head buried in the chair cushions, he panted, in a hoarse, choked rhythm, as the crop lacerated his wriggling naked fesses. She took him past the dozen, past two dozen, while his buttocks bruised deeper and blacker. Severe's quim dripped juice; it trickled down her thighs and into her socks, which made her toes all squishy, as she whirled to flog. At each stroke, her skirt flew right up, but, in the hot, humid air of the drawing room, she welcomed the cooling air on her bare bum and cooze.

Her titties were more of a problem; unfettered beneath the skimpy slip, they bounced quite dramatically, flapping and thudding against her ribcage, so that she wasn't sure bralessness had been such a good idea, except that it got whelps properly frustrated to see a girl's naked breasts. Anyway, the feeling of her titties slapping against her was exciting in itself, as evidenced by the quite gigantic stiffening of her strawberries.

'Uhh . . . uhh . . .'

'Heavens, whelp, you sound like a steam engine.' Severe chortled. 'Not many to go. I'm sure you can manage it.'

He raised his face, which was contorted in anguish. Tears glazed his cheeks. 'Oh, Miss Severe,' he said sobbing. 'I'm not sure I can. I've never been whopped so hard. Please have mercy.'

She trilled with mocking laughter. 'Here's your mercy,' she said.

Vap! A vertical cut took him right in the arse cleft, lashing the anus, and the tip of the crop scorched his perineum, a hair's breadth from his balls.

'*Ahh!* Ooh! Ahh!' he cried, leaping up and stamping his feet on the floor. His hands clutched his bare bottom and began a frantic kneading.

'Hands down, sir!' she rapped. 'This instant!'

Groaning, he resumed his position, burying his head in his cushions, and his flogged arse wriggling like two whipped red jellies. He snivelled. Severe licked her lips, shuddering, as little tweaks of electric pleasure surged from her rock-hard clitoris, and a gush of come sluiced down her rippling bare thighs. *So* wise not to have worn panties, which would have been utterly spoiled by her gash juice. Yet, at the sight of that helpless bare, she could no longer resist caressing herself; did not wish to resist.

Her fingers crept under her gymslip and kneaded her breasts, squashing and mashing the stiff nipples, then moved down the muscled slab of her belly, poking her navel. She shivered at the waves of delight, as she stroked her own flesh. Then her fingers moved over the bulging, satin-smooth mons to the swollen wet gash flaps, until she gasped, as she touched her clitoris, flooding her body with pleasure. Her belly and titties heaved as she masturbated; a few touches was all it took to send her into a convulsed spasm, her quim pouring come, her legs giddily trembling, and her rock-nippled breasts flapping wildly. She raised the crop once more. Vap!

'Ooh! Ouch! You cruel lady, you're enjoying this,' he said, sobbing.

'Why, you cheeky . . .'

Vap! Vap! Vap!

'*Ahh! Ahh!*'

Luke's bruised bottom squirmed frantically at three deep, savage cuts to the tender top fesses.

'You know the rules, worm,' she said, panting and squelching her thighs, wet from her flowing come. 'After that disgraceful outburst, the beating starts over again from scratch.'

His wail of misery was music to her ears. *The worm called me a lady.*

'Another three dozen,' she said, gloatingly. 'I hope you're ashamed of yourself, putting me to such trouble. This is hard work.'

He did not respond. His naked buttocks maintained their poise, presented for her crop, legs splayed rigid, and those absurdly large balls dangling like tight red plums between his thighs, as if taunting her, inviting her lash, with that beastly – that *insolent* – tool stiff as a flagpole against his belly. How *dare* he? Severe's hand clasped her soaking twat, her palm filling with hot gushed come; her

22

thumbnail sliced her clitty, and began to rub hard. Titties quivering and the gymslip cotton rubbing with excruciating sweetness against her swollen stiff nipples, she gasped, as she masturbated. The crop crashed against his bum flesh. Vap! The purpled buttocks writhed, his feet rose and fell, kicking the floor, and a choked, gasping moan filtered from beneath the cushion.

'Ohh, Miss Severe, I really cannot take it!'

'But you must.'

'Please, miss! Have pity, I beg you! My bum's on fire. I've never, ever felt such pain. I'm doing my best to be a man, to do my duty, and accept my punishment, but I'm afraid I'll . . . I'll panic, and lose control of myself.'

Severe frowned, with a thin smile, at his glowing bottom. She stroked her chin. 'There is a way,' she said slowly. 'But it's quite a privilege. I'll have to place you in restraint, so that you can't struggle. You'll be able to take your thrashing quite easily, when you've no choice.'

'Anything, miss,' he said with a sob.

'Very well. I'll strap you to the tuning fork, only you'll have to fetch it from the barn. It's part of Coz's collection of . . . ephemera from the history of Poldipple Hall. I'll let you up, and you can put on your apron, but no rubbing your bum, understand?'

'Yes, miss,' he said wretchedly.

Erect cock bobbing behind his frilly apron, the sobbing boy followed Severe out to the barn, where she indicated a mysterious trestle table, amid piles of frames and artefacts: yokes, braces, stools and miniature gibbets, along with a collection of fierce leather whips – the entire collection, fragrant with old wood and leather, apparently destined for the corporal punishment of humans. Severe said that the Cornish peasantry were a rough lot, in centuries past, and responded best to frequent flogging, especially the girls.

'This one was primarily for errant milkmaids,' she said, licking her lips, as she watched the pulse of Luke's wealed buttocks, while he puffed to bring the 'tuning fork' into the house.

The device was a waist-high table, in three parts, matching human legs and torso, and forming a 'Y'. When it was in place, Severe ordered her 'maid' to dust it, then remove her apron – folding it neatly – and straddle the table, belly down and legs splayed. Luke's arms and torso occupied the main board, while each leg stretched on a sharply angled arm of the 'Y'. Ropes dangled from each extremity, and she knotted Luke's ankles and wrists tightly to the board, while chatting casually.

She told him that milkmaids who erred, that is, by spilling milk or being lazy, were strapped to this very same tuning fork, and given a lashing on the bare buttocks. It was all accounted in the archives of the manor, and, over the centuries, her coz had found a direct relation between the number of floggings given and the estate revenue, from milk, timber or animal hides. In brief, the more floggings, the higher the productivity.

Domestic servants, such as scullery or parlour maids, were not immune to corporal punishment, and even wayward footmen or valets might be stripped and beaten on the bare, to the amusement of the female servants gathered to watch. Far from objecting to such punishments, or running away, the servants accepted and even welcomed them, appreciating a firm, no-nonsense master, and always ready to thrill at the distress of a bottom whipped naked, except, Severe presumed, when it was their own turn, although she suspected a healthy milkmaid rather enjoyed the thrill of baring her bottom for a tingling dozen on the naked fesses.

'Just as we loved a beating at school,' she said. 'The sight of another girl's bottom, caned crimson, never failed to thrill us, lustful devils all, and our own bare-beatings were made tolerable, even exciting, by the acclaim we expected, upon displaying our bruises. With our skirts up and panties shamefully at our ankles, we exposed our naked buttocks for the dreadful, swishing cane, winced and sobbed and panted, knowing that soon, cool fingers would rub our bare bums in admiration. How vain girls are, even

24

vain for weals! We never really escape our schooldays, do we?'

A wide rubber sheath was draped and tightened around the small of Luke's back, pinning his belly. She looked under the board, where his stiff cock protruded, and made a disapproving noise.

'Miss!' he exclaimed. 'What are you doing?'

'Isn't it obvious?'

He began to moan and thresh in his bonds, as Severe fastened several lengths of copper wire around his erect cock, at the base of the shaft, just above his balls, then applied a similar restraint to the cock shank beneath them. His tool bulged, fiercely crimson, but his erection did not soften. She clicked her tongue in annoyance.

'That should have tamed your monster,' she said with a sigh. 'Well, let's hope it does when I've made your bottom sore enough. It'll have to do.' She picked up the riding crop. 'Three dozen you're due,' she said briskly. 'And, of course, an extra dozen for the use of the tuning fork, making four dozen in all, with two extra for luck, bringing us to a nice round fifty cuts.'

'Oh, Miss Severe,' Luke groaned.

'Don't worry, we have all day if we want. Now you're trussed, I'm certainly going to have my way with that arse. I shan't let you go, until you are quite unable to sit down, or even walk, without severe discomfort. Don't think you can wriggle out of your bonds. I gained a badge for knotting and lashing in the Girl Guides, you know.'

Vap!

'Ahh!'

The table rattled, as Luke's buttocks squirmed helplessly; the cruel wires enclosing his cock and balls prevented more than the slightest motion, so that all he could do was shudder against his bonds, which made Severe's slit wetter still, as she contemplated the frantic, constrained wriggling of the boy's bare bum. Her fingers delved between her swollen cunt lips, and found the stiff hillock of her clitty. Face scarlet, Severe masturbated, with come pouring from her slit, and loud squelching slurps coming from her wanked gash. Vap!

'Ooh! Miss Severe, with respect, anyone would think you were enjoying your work,' Luke whimpered.

'One must derive whatever pleasure one can,' Severe said solemnly. 'Caning *is* quite agreeable work: with small motions, the caner stays cool, while her subject gets unbearably hot. One could make a career of it.'

Vap!

'Ahh!' Luke squealed, his buttocks clenching and squirming fiercely.

'Your helplessness is as delicious for me, as it is excruciating for you. Your legs apart, bum up for lashes, and your balls in full view, a most tempting target. You must be quaking in fear that my aim might slip and lash those juicy bollocks.'

Vap!

'Ooh!'

'Careful. That was almost an exclamation.'

Vap!

'Uhh . . . uhh . . . uhh . . .'

'I haven't decided on a career, actually, save that it must make me rather rich. What sort of career do *you* have in mind, whelp? You'd be a good lady's maid.'

Luke mumbled that he had thought of a commission in the Royal Navy. Severe burst into guffaws.

'A weed, who lets his bum be flogged by a girl? Never.'

Vap!

'*Ooh!* Oh! Oh!'

Luke's face was scarlet and glazed with tears; every stroke thumped his belly against the hard board, and made his buttocks squirm fiercely, to his utter shame. Yet, Severe was right: after several strokes, the pain did not diminish – the smarting was more dreadful, if anything – but his ability to deal with it strengthened. The pain had won acceptance, become part of him, and it was no longer possible to think of his buttocks without the smarting, which seemed their natural condition.

Most important, the pain in his whipped buttocks was from a *girl*, a tall blonde girl, fabulous in her anger and cruelty, with rippling thighs and bottom and titties, and he knew he must prove himself strong, to endure whatever agony she wished to inflict. He knew that he deserved her thrashing for the insolence of his arrogant swollen cock. Vap!

'Ooh! Ahh! I . . . I don't think you're entirely fair, miss, with respect.'

Vap!

'Oh! Oh!'

'Explain yourself, worm.'

'Well, you've remarked on my . . . my erection. That's scarcely the sign of a weed, surely?'

'You arrogant swine.'

Vap! Another stroke took him straight in the arse cleft, perilously close to his balls. He gasped, in a wretched squeal, and his whole body jerked stiff, with the whipped anus pucker winking, as his buttocks clenched rapidly over it. Severe's lips gaped slack and drooling, her nostrils flared and her eyelids were heavy with lust, as she masturbated her dripping cunt.

'Perhaps you're not wrong,' she gasped, squelching her fingers in her slit. 'Insolence can be exciting . . . it's a challenge to whip that beast soft.'

'Miss, you'll never do that, as long as you are so beautiful,' he croaked.

'Why, you cheeky –'

Vap!

'– wicked –'

Vap!

'– beastly –'

Vap!

'– scoundrel!'

Vap! Vap! Vap!

'*Ahh! Ahh!*' he screamed, his flogged bare bum squirming madly, and tears flowing from his eyes.

Not an inch of unwealed skin remained to him; the entire croup was a mass of interlaced welts, with their myriad hues of black, crimson and purple forming a lattice of ridges and crusts, elevated to wrinkled escarpments above the crimson valleys of bruised skin. Luke's pain was a giant throbbing vice, its brutal prongs gripping his bottom, and firing the stiffness of his cock. All his male being was in his seared buttocks, flogged by a cruel woman. She placed her face close to his, her teeth bared in a rictus.

'I don't want you to like me,' she hissed. 'I want you to fear me.'

'Then you have your wish, Miss Severe,' he said with a sob. 'I hate you, and fear you.'

'That's better.'

'*Because* you are so cruel and beautiful. Your beauty is terror. How can I resist? My cock will always stand for you.'

'You . . . you *fucking whelp*,' she snarled. 'By God, I'm going to skin that arse raw.'

Vap! Heat from his wriggling buttocks flowed to Luke's trussed balls and cock, making the tool throb rigid, as though about to burst its bonds, burst its skin itself. He had never felt so helplessly virile. Vap!

'Ohh! That shall be my honour, miss,' he said, through his tears.

Severe's expression of fury slowly changed to a sly smile. She caned him another six, and, while he writhed and moaned, she paused to mop her brow. Her gymslip was sodden with sweat, showing every inch of her naked body beneath, and useless as a concealment. Placing herself in front of Luke, she nonchalantly raised her dress over her thighs, then her belly, revealing the smooth-shaven bulge of her satin cunt hillock, then the huge, jutting melons of her bare breasts, and finally stripped it off altogether, to stand before him in the nude. His eyes goggled.

'We've a long way to go,' she said, 'so I might as well be at my ease. You're no problem, Luke. A real man would escape from his bonds, and overpower me, but you're just a worm.'

28

Resting her bottom on a padded stool, Severe propped her left foot on the tuning fork, before his lips. 'My, aren't these summer days getting hotter? I think I'd like to be barefoot, for my total comfort. You will please oblige, maid. Undo my laces.'

Taking her shoelaces between his teeth, Luke tugged, to unravel the knot. Directly above him, Severe's wet gash winked crimson. Without ceasing to grin at him, she casually placed her finger in her gash, parted the lips, to show her wet pink slit meat and erect, gleaming clitty. With a loud squelch, she began to masturbate for his gaze. Luke got the first shoelace undone, and was then obliged to pull the tongue of the shoe, until it fell to the floor.

'Sock, now, worm,' she panted, wanking hard, with Luke's eyes fixed on her gaping wet cunt, and the streams of come streaking her rippling bare thighs.

Taking her sweat-moist white sock between his teeth, he managed to pull it from her foot.

'Pooh! What a smelly girl I am. You won't mind licking my toes clean, Luke, will you?'

She reached over him with her crop, and positioned the tip at the cleft of his buttocks. Vap! Vap! Vap! Three cuts popped like gunshots, as she flogged his top bum, just under the spinal nubbin. He gasped, squirming and weeping silently, and applied his quaking tongue to the cheesy spaces between her toes, then licked the sole and upper of her foot, finally taking the whole set of toes into his mouth, and sucking them, swallowing her sweat and toe yeast. Vap! Vap! Vap! Another flurry of cuts made his arse squirm. Luke moaned.

'Enjoying yourself?' Severe purred. 'Isn't it frustrating to watch me wanking off at your pain, while you suffer and serve? A girl must enjoy her work, and a beastly boy's bare bum striped is a most thrilling satisfaction.'

His wide eyes, glazed with tears, stared at her, and he nodded bitterly, as he sucked her smelly toes with the devotion of a puppy. The performance was repeated with her right foot, until she was totally barefoot, with each foot by turn plunging between his eager lips, to be licked and sucked. Swivelling, she stretched her belly, bringing her cunt within a tongue's distance of his mouth, and poked her toes under the flogging frame, where she began to flick his swollen glans with her big toe, then tickle his balls. Luke began to moan.

'Oh ... oh ... miss ... I'd rather take a hundred canings, than be tortured like this. You feel how stiff I am ... you must know how I long to ... to ...'

'Say it,' she whispered, rubbing his swollen glans between her toes.

'To spurt, miss,' he cried wretchedly.

Her big toe caressed his peehole. 'Yes, you're ready, aren't you?' she cooed. 'I can feel all that seething spunk in there, begging to be released. How strange and simple boys are. All they want is to pour that flood of cream into a girl's hole. Mm ...'

Clitoris swollen between thumb and forefinger, she wanked, inches from his face.

Vap! Vap! His buttocks jerked.

'Uhh ... uhh ...'

'My thighs are all wet. Lick them dry, worm.'

His tongue slid across her come-soaked thighs, licking and swallowing her cunt's fluid. As fast as he dried the rippling smooth skin, she wanked more come, to soak herself anew. His tongue strayed within a hair's breadth of her outer gash flaps, where a bead of crystal come dripped onto it. Vap! Vap! The crop's tip lashed his anus bud.

'Ooh!' he squealed, his bum writhing in agony.

Tears dripped from his eyes, to pool with the come glazing her thighs. Her toes pressed his naked balls, harder and harder, until he panted, moaning, his eyes wide in fear. She stopped the pressure, when his balls were snugly locked between her toes.

'Beastly brat,' she hissed. 'Your tongue nearly touched my twat. Don't you *ever* ...'

Vap! Vap! His arse wriggled, as she lashed him on his most jagged weals.

'Oh! Cruel Miss Severe,' he groaned, 'I am yours. I promise to obey. But please ... please ...'

'What is it, worm?'

'Please let me spurt into your toes. Just a touch, a flick, a caress ... I promise to be your slave forever.'

Severe appeared to ponder this. 'You disgust me, you smutty little oik,' she drawled. 'You'll take your full fifty, first. It's nothing. Why ...' She turned to show him her naked bottom, and he gasped at the intricate patchwork of pretty weals, faded to mauve, which criss-crossed her taut, muscled bum flesh. 'You're not the only one,' she murmured. 'Girls can be naughty too.'

While Luke's tongue shuddered on her thighs, Severe dealt the remainder of his strokes, until his naked bottom was a glowing moonscape of black, purple and blue. During the chastisement, Severe masturbated twice to orgasm, squashing her naked breasts and pinching her nipples to white, while increasing her flow of come to a torrent, which Luke tearfully swallowed. After the fiftieth stroke, firmly on his bumhole, he sobbed, threshed, groaned and finally lay still, his lips and nose pressed to her skin, smelling the fragrance of her wanked cunt.

'Please, cruel miss,' he whimpered, 'let me spurt, let me worship your feet with my spunk ...'

'God, you are pathetic,' she said, lighting a Dunhill with a Swan Vesta match, which she flicked out on his blackest bum welt, making him squeal. 'I've a better idea.'

# 3

# Up a Girl

Bruised and sobbing, Luke consented with utmost docility to his release from his table of pain, to be trussed once more, for his lady's pleasure. Severe made him stand, forbidden absolutely to rub his whipped buttocks for relief, and roped his wrists behind his back. Then, she fastened a dog leash around his neck.

'You've been my maid, now you can be my puppy,' Severe said. 'Isn't it a glorious day? Smell the lupins and honeysuckle, and the gorgeous scent of damp grass. How wonderful, to be in England in summer.'

She strode to the French windows and flung them open. Outside stretched an immaculate lawn, and the sparkling turquoise waters of a kidney-shaped swimming pool. She forced Luke to crouch, flicked his leash, and he hobbled after her on all fours. By the swimming pool, she tied his leash to a wrought-iron seat, and dived in, to poise upside down, with her legs and naked quim in the air. Luke gazed, his cock throbbing and his balls longing for release. After splashing for several minutes, she emerged, to drip all over him, then lifted her leg, and perched her foot on his neck. He gazed at the lips of her cunt, as liquid spurted from the naked, writhing slit. An acrid stream of piss splashed his face.

'Drink, doggy,' she commanded, and he obeyed, swallowing her hot wet piss.

She giggled. 'Most owners take their dogs for a walk, so

that the dog can pee,' she said. 'I take my pet so that I can pee. Was it refreshing?'

'Yes, Miss Severe,' Luke said with a sob.

'I expect you've been ogling my bum? Answer truthfully.'

'I couldn't help it,' he moaned. 'You are so beautiful. It is cruel of you to tease me.'

She clapped her hands. 'Which is exactly why I tease. Isn't it terrible, you may not touch your tool, and relieve yourself?'

'Miss, I would never do such a thing,' he said, blushing hotly. 'Not in front of a lady.'

'But you *do,* don't you?' she sneered. 'All boys do. Smutty swine.'

She stood behind him holding a garden hose, and sluiced him down with a powerful jet of icy water, aiming the spray at his balls and cock, which had him hopping and squealing. Still, his cock stood ramrod stiff. She inserted the nozzle of the hose into his anus, and laughed, as he yelped and pranced, his rectum and colon filled with water. After the irrigation, water squirted from his anus in a fierce jet, as he wept, squirming in pain.

'Well, I never,' she said. 'You virgins are amazing. I'll have to teach you another lesson.'

She led him back into the drawing room, placed an antique wooden washboard on the armchair, and made him sit down. He groaned as the sharp wooden slats lacerated his arse weals. Hands behind him, he lay back, his wired cock and balls standing above his belly like a tree and its bulbous roots. From the barn, Severe fetched a three-foot-long plank, with an ankle slot at each end, and into these slots she fitted his feet, locking the cuffs, so that his legs were stretched wide, and his feet immobile in the hobble.

'I must say, I'm surprised you haven't softened,' she said affably. 'That cock of yours must be simply aching to spurt.'

'Miss Severe,' he whimpered, 'haven't I been punished?'

'Yes, you have, but not enough. Remember your note – "at convenience"? I've a bit of a grudge to take out on you, Master Luke. I was looking forward to a lazy afternoon, free of school, but you've put me to such hard work. And then Justin, that *bastard* . . .' She snuffled, and wiped a tear from her eye. 'A girl needs it, you see, and I'm no longer going to get it from him. So you'll have to do, worm though you are.'

She squatted in front of him, and prised her buttocks apart, stretching her perineum, so that her anus pucker winked at Luke's goggling eyes. She caressed her buttocks, drawing fingertips over all her faint bum weals, and sighing.

'It does a girl good, to have her bottom heated,' she whispered. 'Makes her want absolutely oodles of wanks.'

She stroked her perineum, from the wet, swollen cunt lips, until she reached her anus bud – leaving a smear of come – then slipped a thumbnail inside, and poked and tweaked for the anus to admit her entire thumb.

'Ooh, that's good,' she gasped.

She began to frot her clitoris, holding a teacup under her quim for the copious come to drip, tinkling, into the china.

'Mm . . . mm . . .' she crooned, wriggling her naked buttocks inches from Luke's face.

She clapped the cup to her gash, and her belly tensed as a spurt of piss filled the cup, with steam hissing between her thighs, as if from a geyser. When the cup was brim full with liquid, she stirred it with her forefinger, and gave the finger to Luke to lick. He obeyed, taking her finger an inch into his mouth, and sucking hard.

'No biting, doggy,' Severe said, playfully smacking his bell end.

She pressed the cup of mixed girl piss and come to his mouth, and he drank, swallowing every drop.

'Now you're ready,' she hissed.

She placed her feet on his ankle hobble, forcing his feet to the floor, and balanced her weight on the arms of the chair. Bending forwards, she wiggled her bottom nearer

35

and nearer his cock, until his peehole brushed the crinkled plum of her anus. She wiped her hand in her cunt, and oiled her anus with come.

'What?' Luke gasped. 'I don't understand.'

'You must be very slow-witted, even for a boy.' She grasped the shaft of his cock, and thrust his glans between the lips of her anus, which expanded to admit him. 'Time for you to lose your arse virginity,' she whispered. 'I *suppose* you're an arse virgin. Who knows, with you boarding-school fellows?'

'That's dirty,' he squealed. 'I've never done anything like that. I admit some of the fellows – low types – well . . .'

'Just wanking games, then? All those bare cocks and arses, having a bit of slap and tickle in the showers? Or dreaming of girls' naked titties and bums when you steal their panties? I know what beastly boys get up to.'

'No, I don't, I mean, only a bit – blast it, you've tricked me! Well, what's wrong with that? It's better than bumming. Ugh! That's too horrid to think about.'

'You're going to have to do more than think about it, sir,' she snapped. 'You are to perform. Unless that filthy stiff cock suddenly wilts, which seems unlikely. I may assure you, very little is better than bumming.'

'But up a *girl*? It'll never fit in there. It'll hurt. You'll skin me alive, miss.'

'Just what I intend,' she said, licking her lips. 'Anyway, how do you think I feel? Look at my tiny bummy, how do you think *she*'s going to like a poking from such a horrid great knob?'

She waggled her bottom, clenching the scarred cheeks on his glans, trapped in her anus, then abruptly lowered herself to engulf his cock two inches inside the anal elastic. He squealed.

'Ouch! Oh, it hurts. Please, no.'

She began to knead his cock, contracting her sphincter and squeezing his knob in her anal elastic, which was swimming with arse grease. The arse grease began to drip onto his balls and cockstem, until his cock squelched loudly as she raised and lowered her buttocks, moving it up and down in her channel, with longer thrusts at each slam of her rump. He moaned, as his cock sank further into her bumhole.

'Oh! It's so tight. You're skinning my prepuce right back, and it really hurts.'

'You've *never* been up a girl before?' she panted. 'I want it to hurt you, as much as it hurts me. You're in my rectum now – feel how I squeeze you?'

With a fierce thrust, her buttocks slammed down, squashing his balls, as his cock penetrated her to the hilt, and she squealed, squirming in delight.

'Yes ... right to my colon,' she gasped. 'God, that's good. My belly's bursting. Now I'm going to give you such a fucking, Luke, you'll be too sore to walk.'

She began to twirl her stretched bottom, slowly, up and down, with a sinuous writhing of her back and waist muscles, reaming his trapped cock and, every so often, slamming her bum onto his balls, to thrust the tool right to her arse root. There were no sounds, save Luke's whimpers, and Severe's determined panting. Her naked back, arse and thighs rippled like waves in a pool.

'Oh ... oh ...' Luke moaned. 'I think I'm going to spurt.'

Severe reached under her buttocks, and seized the glazed shaft of his cock, just above his balls, then squeezed it hard. He squealed in dismay; after a minute's pressure, she released him, noting that his cock had softened ever so slightly. A sucking pressure from her rectum, with the soft elastic of her anal wall squashing his bell end, restored him to full rigidity.

'Going to spurt?' she asked playfully.

'No ... not now, I don't think so,' he mumbled.

'Good.'

Severe's fingers frotted her clitty, out of Luke's sight, but he could hear the squelching slurp as she masturbated, and feel the hot wet come which sluiced from her gash, over his balls, already covered with her copious anal grease. As she wanked off, her thrusts grew harder, with more and more direct plunges to his balls, making him fuck her. After a minute, she began to gasp and mewl.

'Oh ... oh ... yes, I'm there! Fuck me, Justin, bugger my bum with your big stiff cock. Fuck me, make me squirt ... yes ... oh ... *fuck me!*' Severe exploded in orgasm, showering Luke's balls with a flood of come and arse grease. 'Urrgh ... ooh,' she moaned. 'God, that was so *good.* It's a pity a mere male cannot know the pleasure of a girl come, with a stiff cock in her hole, and the cock still stiff, for another spurt.'

'*Justin*'s cock,' Luke said bitterly.

'Did I say that? You poor lamb, how mortifying for you. If it's any consolation, you are *almost* as big.'

Her laughter a peal of cruel pleasure, Severe began to wank again, although she was still sighing from the intensity of her orgasm. Come sluiced from her cunt to soak Luke's balls; repeatedly, she applied stiff pressure to his cockshaft to retard his spurt.

'Miss Severe, *please* let me come,' Luke begged. 'I'll do anything for you. I'll be your maid, your slave, I'll bare my bottom to your whip. Oh, please. I *must* spurt.'

'Does it hurt?'

'Unbearably! My cock is really raw and my balls ache terribly.'

'How lovely! You have "blue balls". It must be awful for you,' she panted, her naked arse globes squirming on his belly. 'Still, that's part of my fun. And you'll have such a big spurt when I'm finished with you, gallons and gallons of lovely hot spunk in my bumhole. God, I must wank harder, I'm so hot just thinking about it ... oh ... yes ... *yes!*'

Titties flapping, Severe writhed in climax, showering Luke's cock and balls with copious come.

'Oh, miss, why do you wish to make me suffer?' he whimpered.

'What girl wouldn't?'

His torment continued, until his balls truly ached, and he wished for the sting of the crop, rather than the awful pressure of his sperm, begging for release. His stiff cock, pounded by her colon and squeezed by her ravenous rectum, was numb and raw. The slightest pressure on his delicate bell end made him wince and whimper, especially when she stroked his peehole with her devilishly agile colon. He lost count of the number of Severe's wanked and buggered orgasms; finally, with the sun dipping in the blue summer sky, she said it was time for him to spurt.

'Thank you, miss, oh, thank you.'

'But I'll keep you to your promise. You're to attend me as my maid, as my slave, and accept bare-bottom whipping whenever I'm in the mood. Agreed?'

'But . . .'

'You gave your word.'

'All right, blast it! I promise.'

'Wherever and whenever.'

'Now, wait . . .'

'I can keep you here, stuck up my bumhole, while I wank and wank, young master Luke, and your cock is in worse agony than your bottom. So, are you going to keep your word as a gentleman?'

'Yes,' he said with a sob. 'Anything.'

She slid her hands beneath his buttocks, her nails clawing his welts, and he cried out. She pressed his buttocks tightly, locking her own bum on his balls, with his cock penetrating her tripes, his peehole nuzzled by her sigmoid colon, and the glans half inside that fleshy tube. Luke gasped, then squealed, as she began to milk his cock with a powerful sucking of her rectum and colon.

'Come on, Luke, give me all the lovely spunk from your balls,' she cooed. 'Hot creamy spunk, filling my belly, making me come. Fuck my arse, Luke, make me squirt all over you.'

Luke groaned, panting, and Severe squealed in delight, as the first droplets of sperm jetted from his squashed peehole into her colon. He panted, whimpering, as his cream spurted into her rectum in a long powerful stream.

'Oh, yes! I can feel it, so hot and wet and creamy! Do me, fuck me, bugger me, fill me with spunk. I'm going to

... yes, I'm there ... ooh!' In the midst of his spurt, she shuddered in her own. 'Oh ... oh ... oh ... Justin!'

She withdrew, his cock leaving her anus with a sucking plop, and at once sat on his face, pushing her come-soaked anus to his mouth. 'Suck me clean, slave,' she commanded.

Her naked buttocks squashed his face, and he could not reply; instead, his cock, semi-stiff, hardened again to full rigidity, as he felt the weight of the naked girl's buttocks squatting on him.

'What are you waiting for?' she demanded crossly. 'Most boys like a girl's bum sitting on their face. Suck my bumhole dry, slave.'

He obeyed, getting his tongue an inch into her spunk-soaked anus and sucking the sperm and arse grease from the moist, elastic chamber. He swallowed it noisily. As he sucked, her fingers were on his cock, teasing and nipping the bell end and peehole, until he was throbbing again, his tight balls filling with new cream. Severe masturbated herself, as she wanked Luke's cock, and he groaned, wriggling against his hobble. He squashed his nose into her reeking bum cleft, while his tongue stabbed her anus, and come dripped from her wanked cunt over his chin. The sperm welled in his balls, crept into his cockshaft, and he groaned, his bellows vibrating through her anus, as his spunk flowed in a second copious torrent, over her soft, strong fingers, and into her palm. Severe squealed, come spraying from her frigged gash, as she climaxed with him.

Finally released, but still forbidden to rub his smarting bottom, Luke had to kneel, and lick Severe's hands clean of his own spunk. She lay back in the sofa, thighs apart, with her quim dripping, and idly played with her distended clitty. She lit a Dunhill and leaned to extinguish the lighted match, with a sizzle, on his come-soaked balls. He winced, shutting his eyes, and made no sound other than a gasp.

'I've no further use for you today,' she drawled. 'However, I'll summon you for further correction if I feel you have been naughty. Remember, you've promised to be my slave, wherever and whenever.'

'Miss Severe, you can't be serious about a promise extracted in the heat of the moment.'

'All moments are hot. Break your word and you'll never see me again. Is that what you want, *worm*?'

She opened the lips of her quim, stretching them fully, to show her wet pink slit meat, churning and gushing juice over her wanking fingers, with the clitty a bright swollen bud, pinched between thumb and forefinger. Luke gulped, as his cock stiffened rigid. Severe looked at his throbbing tool and licked her lips, grinning like a cat.

'Well?'

'I'll . . . I'll be your slave, miss.'

'*Mistress.*'

'Yes, mistress.'

Severe commanded him to lick her sweaty feet clean, and he obeyed, crouching, while she masturbated.

'Don't think you're getting your cock up my pouch,' she purred. 'I'm a pure virgin, and mean to stay that way. A girl has her slit cherry and her bumhole cherry, with every good reason to lose the second, and keep the first.'

Luke saw teeth marks at the top of the tuning fork, the table of his suffering, but they were certainly not his; furthermore, there were bright blonde tresses stuck in the hinges, and those hairs were not Luke's.

'Did Justin, or Commander Compaigne, punish you, then, mistress?' he asked timidly.

Her face darkened. 'Out of my sight, slave,' she hissed. 'When I next summon you, *if* I choose to summon you, it will be to punish *that* impudence.'

Luke was in a foul mood, as he started down the driveway. Pride would not permit him to ask Severe to telephone for a taxi, so he faced a long walk home to Clear House. Above the chirp of birds and the hum of insects, he heard a faint tapping sound, coming from the room of his chastisement. Frowning, he retraced his steps – on the grass to avoid crunching gravel – and looked through the voile curtains. There, straddling the tuning fork, was the nude Severe Compaigne, beating her bare bottom with the back of a silver hairbrush, in the shape of a warship. Luke watched, his cock stiffening, as her wriggling naked buttocks reddened, then turned to purple. She gave herself over a hundred slaps, her face twisted in agony and tears streaming down her cheeks, but with her free hand squashed between her thighs; Severe was masturbating, as she thrashed herself.

Grimacing, Luke turned away, for the walk home. His arse throbbed and smarted, and his raw cock ached, as though Severe had skinned him alive. How strange girls were! A deceitful breed, intent only on their warped pleasures, and their love of pain, at a fellow's expense. Yet he had promised as a gentleman to be her slave, and come when she called. 'Wherever and whenever' – there must, in all reason, be limits to *that*. As he approached his own home, he thought with shivering excitement of being a lady's naked slave, to be flogged at her imperious, disdainful whim – her regal indifference adding to his voluptuous, submissive pleasure.

His cock stiffened fully, throbbing, a bulge in his trousers, to his disgust. A grown-up boy, fully eighteen, whimpering and bleating and baring his bum to some snotty schoolgirl for a rotten hard whopping. And then being used to service her perverted lust in that smelly bumhole, and having to suck up his own spunk afterwards. He cringed at his willing humiliance. What could he have been thinking? Bloody women: they teased you and sneered at you, and made you burst with frustration, then took advantage of your good manners to make you say things you couldn't possibly mean, and shame you in the most painful way. He should have put the toffee-nosed slut over his knee, and spanked her bare arse. Having witnessed Severe thrashing her own bottom, he knew what bitches *really* needed.

Aunt Amy was in her blasted tennis things, showing a lot of bare thigh and breast.

'Really, Auntie, must you charge around the house half-naked?' he growled.

'It's my house,' retorted Amy. 'My, we *are* in a grumpy mood. I suppose the commander was extra-harsh on that poor bottom of yours. Let me see.'

'Must I?'

'You certainly must. Bare up, and show me the damage.'

Blushing, Luke unfastened his trousers, turned, and dropped them, to show his welted bare buttocks. *There I am, obeying a blasted female again.* He heard his aunt gasp, then felt her cool fingertips tracing his bruises, and her touch made his cock stiffen. He tried to hide it, but, with his panties down, it was quite impossible, and he knew she was gazing at his throbbing erection. She caressed his welts for an awfully long minute, tweaking the furrowed ridges, and making him wince, while cooing in sympathy, and all the time staring at his rigid tool; laughing at him, enjoying his embarrassment, the rotten cow.

'You poor boy. What a licking you've taken! Those weals are quite an artwork, so deep and crusty, you must have taken them on the bare.'

'You know very well I did,' Luke snapped.

'How squirm-making. I suppose I'd be grumpy if the commander had thrashed me so hard.'

Luke stopped himself from telling her the truth, thinking there was no need to compound his shame by telling her he'd been so heartily whipped by a mere girl. He picked up a gaudy picture postcard from the Welsh dresser. It showed a ship, garlanded with flags, in a sunny harbour. Amy tried to snatch it from him, but he eluded her.

'That's not for you,' she said, with feigned gaiety.

'Well, well,' he said. 'All the way from Gibraltar, postmarked four days ago. "I'll be shipside in Gib for the next two months. Miss my wriggly bunny, slaps and tickles from Standy-poo." So, Aunt Amy, you knew the commander wasn't there when you sent me for thrashing. You *knew* "S Compaigne" was that bitch Severe, and she would thrash me on the bare.'

Amy blushed. 'What if I did? You deserved your whipping.'

43

'You are a naughty girl,' he murmured.

Coolly, he dropped his trousers, and stepped out of them. He kicked off his shoes, removed his socks, and then, grinning sweetly, took off his shirt, to stand in the nude before the gaping girl. She blushed, and her fingers flew to her lips, but her eyes could not leave his swollen, erect cock.

'Luke, what . . . what are you doing?' she blurted feebly.

'You wanted to see, so look. Are you wearing knickers?'

'What a question to your aunt! For heaven's sake put your clothes on. You're not decent.'

'You're not my aunt, you're only some umpteenth cousin, like your bitch friend Severe. You're scarcely more than a blasted schoolgirl.'

'Really!' She pouted, but her eyes fluttered at the compliment.

'Answer the question, Amy.'

She blushed hotly. 'No, I'm not wearing knickers,' she murmured, 'as if it's any of your business.'

'It is my business, because, in the absence of knickers, I shall be obliged to whip you on the bare.'

'*What?*'

'You heard.'

'You'll do no such thing. This is quite scandalous.'

'Was it scandalous when you used to spank my bare bum, not so long ago, and watch me stiffen? Then peek at me afterwards, for you knew I'd be so excited, I'd have to wank off?'

Amy reddened. 'There's no harm in a girl's curiosity, Luke darling. We girls like to watch . . . you know. A boy excited is so . . . well, exciting. And girls wank off, too, especially at the sight of such an impressive pego standing to attention.'

'Then you can gratify *my* curiosity. I want to know how your bottom responds to the lashing you've richly earned, miss. Will you bend over, or do I have to make you?'

She bit her lip. 'So I'm a miss? This isn't fair, Luke. You're much stronger than me –' her eyes fixed on his stiff cock '– in every way.'

Luke grabbed her by the waist.

'Ooh! What are you doing?' she squealed, legs flailing the air. 'Put me down this instant, sir!'

Luke forced her down across the rosewood dining table, and ripped up her skirtlet, to reveal her naked quim and buttocks. The bulging mons, carpeted in a jungle of matted pubic hair, glistened with sweat, which dripped into the swollen red gash lips, pouting beneath the unkempt cunt forest, whose tendrils dangled down below the pendant cunt flaps and clung to her bare inner thighs. The army of hairs almost engulfed her navel, and marched deep into her arse cleft, where its creepers caressed her anus bud.

'Luke – careful – mind the candelabra – you'd better move it.'

Luke did as he was told, while Amy clung to the sides of the table, snuffling and whimpering, but making no move to escape. He seized a dusting brush, snapping off the bamboo handle, nearly three-feet long. He pinned Aunt Amy's neck to the table, and lifted the makeshift cane over her bottom. The end was jagged, sharp bamboo splinters jutting where he had snapped off the broom. Amy twisted to look at the cane, and blanched.

'Oh, God,' she gasped. 'It's been so long since I took it with a splitter. Please go easy on me, Luke. You're a man, and so strong.'

'Present your bum, miss,' he ordered. 'I'm sure you know how – my wriggly bunny.'

Vip! The bamboo lashed Amy's naked buttocks, which clenched at once, with a pink stripe appearing.

'Oh,' she whimpered.

Vip!

'Ooh!'

Vip!

'Oh! Ouch! You're hurting me, Luke.'

Vip!

'Ooh! Gosh, you're a real man.'

Vip!

'Ahh!' she cried. 'Go easy, I beg you.'

45

'No,' he said coldly.

Luke watched, as come began to trickle from the woman's squirming pussy. The nude boy continued to flog her, placing the splayed tips of the bamboo right at the end of each cut, and leaving a livid purple gash where the jagged ends struck. Vip!

'Ahh! Ooh! That hurts awfully. You are a beast, Luke. You're making me frightfully fruity.'

Amy's breasts heaved, and her breath came as a hoarse rasp, as her naked bottom squirmed and wriggled under the tight bamboo cuts. Vip!

'Ooh! God, you cane them tight!'

'Like Standy-poo?' snarled Luke.

Vip!

'Oh! Oh! If you must know, yes. He does spank me in play, sometimes.'

'And what else?'

'Mind your own business, you rude boy. I'm taking your punishment – I admit, I played rather a sneaky trick – but you've no right –'

Vip! Vip! Two lashes took her right in the bum cleft, stroking her anus bud, which swelled and bruised crimson from the cuts. Amy's bare writhed madly, her ridged crusts glowing purple, around the new crimson in the taut bum crack.

'*Ooh!* You absolute swine. I can't take much more.'

'How many does the commander give you, then?'

'A dozen, with his sword flat, or a nice whippy ashplant, never more than two –'

'Two dozen it'll be, then.'

'Damn you, Luke, for tricking me!' she cried.

Vip! Luke held his aunt's face pressed tightly to the table, misted by her harsh, panting breath, and her knuckles were white, as she clung to the table's sides. As he flogged her, tears rolled down her face, her bare buttocks squirmed, and she panted hoarsely. Vip!

'Ooh! Luke, you're so strong. It's not fair. And with my bum nude . . . why, you've a much easier delivery.'

'You aren't naked with Standy-poo?'

'That's quite out of order.'

Vip! Vip! Her cleft took a further double, bruising it to purple, with the crinkled prune of her anus bud swollen to a walnut.

'Ah! Ooh! Oh, *please* stop, Luke,' Amy gasped.

'No.'

Vip!

'Ahh! That splitter is quite lethal. What will my poor bum look like?'

'It looks very pretty, like a bowl of melted raspberry-ripple ice cream.'

'Flatterer.'

Vip!

'Ooh! Stop, oh stop!'

'No.'

Vip!

'Oh! God, I'm going to lose control. Stop! Stop!'

'Ditto.'

Come poured from Amy's juicing cunt, forming glistening rivulets down her rippling bare thighs, which slammed rigid at each cane stroke. She craned her head, to stare, through tear-glazed eyes, at the erect cock of her chastiser.

'Luke,' she whimpered, 'I'm terribly frightened – not of my beating, which I deserve, although you are terribly strong, but of that awful monster wobbling from your balls. You're right – all this time, I've pretended to be in charge, but I'm really just a soppy little girl, who needs a man's firm hand.'

Luke did not reply, but dealt the final cane strokes, covering both haunches, with top and lower fesses, until her arse was a mottled mass of crimson, black and purple weals.

'Oh ... oh,' she moaned, grinding her cunt hillock against the table, which was shiny with her oozed come. 'Oh! Do me, whip my arse, you vile beast. Ahh! Yes!'

Vip!

'Oh ... oh ... *ohh*!'

Come sluiced from Amy's quaking cunt flaps, as her feet thumped the floor, and her titties and tummy heaved in orgasm. Her spasm had not yet ebbed, when Luke pronounced the beating complete, grabbed Amy's hips, and pushed his erect cock between her glowing wealed buttocks. His peehole nudged her anus bud.

'No,' she said with a sob, 'no . . .'

With a grunt, Luke inserted his cock into her anus, and pushed, until his glans disappeared, engulfed in her anal elastic.

'Ooh!' she squealed. 'Luke, anything but that, not in my bumhole. It makes me so sore. Fuck me in the cunt, look how wet and warm she is, for that gorgeous big cock . . .'

Luke thrust again, and his cock was swallowed by her anus, right to his balls. He began to bugger her, with powerful, slamming thrusts, and the slap of his balls on her buttocks echoed in the parlour.

'The shame,' she wailed. 'Oh God! It's so good! Fuck me harder, Luke, bugger me to ribbons, fuck me raw.'

'That's disgusting,' Luke panted. 'I never thought to hear an English lady utter such filth.'

'Didn't Severe say it, this afternoon, when you were up the girl?' gasped Amy.

'You bitches,' he snarled. 'You're all in this together.'

'Oh! Ooh! You're hurting me,' squealed Amy, as he buggered her with fierce, smacking thrusts. 'God, right up me, that's good. Fuck my bum, fuck me hard, don't stop.'

Her rectum squeezed and sucked Luke's cock, making each exit from her anus a struggle; his tool squelched out, with a sucking noise, until his peehole nuzzled the lips of her bumhole, before he rammed it up her again, right to the colon. She twisted, writhing like a fish on his impaling cock, while her cunt mound rubbed against the come-soaked rosewood table. Luke groaned, as the spunk surged in his balls, to jet from his peehole; his sperm overflowed, bubbling from her squirming anus, as he spurted his creamy load at her sigmoid colon.

'Yes,' she gasped, 'fuck me to pieces, burst me, split me, give me all your spunk, Standy-poo! Ohh ... I'm coming ... *yes!*'

Amy's bum jerked up and down, milking Luke's tool of his spunk, and she banged her breasts on the table, rubbing the stiff nipples, in her own climax. Luke sank onto her back, his fingernails clawing her bum weals, which provoked little sighs of pleasure from his flogged and buggered aunt. He reached to the sideboard, and helped himself to one of her Gauloises Blondes, lit it with a Swedish kitchen match, then stubbed the glowing match in her deepest purple cane weal. She winced, with a shudder, and her fingers flew to her cunt.

'Oh! God, that hurts,' she panted. 'I shan't stop wanking for ages, you beast. That's the best seeing-to I've ever had. You whip and tool so expertly, Luke, like a real grown man, who's come to the age where he understands what a girl really needs.' She groped for a cigarette, which Luke lit for her. 'Severe must really have floated your boat,' she purred, exhaling lazily, and openly squelching her clitoris. 'She and I aren't really in this together, but, given your talents, we *could* be.'

# 4

# Slave of Severe

Amy made no further mention of the whipping episode, but was as cheerful and aunt-like as ever. Over breakfast, the day after her thrashing and buggery, she walked with a rather exaggerated hobble, but did not wink or smile, as Luke expected, although her face wore the glow of a satisfied masturbatress. She made a point of reminding him she controlled his purse strings, and that he owed her absolute obedience, until his twenty-first birthday, three long years away. Meanwhile, being far too lazy to go to university, Luke would enjoy his allowance: enough money to go to the pub with his friends, or to go up to London, or Wales, or even take his bicycle on the ferry over to Brittany, but just enough money for such humble pleasures.

'Unless,' she trilled, pouring him another cup of fragrant Brazilian coffee, 'you want to get a *job*,' pronouncing the word with a pout, as if referring to an infestation of slugs; Luke hastily assured her that such a thing was far from his mind.

She worked Luke harder, devising pointlessly strenuous tasks for him, outside in the sun, while she watched from her parasol, sipping sherry and smoking a Gauloise Blonde. The only difference was that now she allowed, or obliged him to work in the nude, while she herself wore the scantiest of skirtlets, T-shirts without a bra, and crossed her long bare legs frequently enough to remind Luke that she was knickerless. It was hard not to notice the curly, flowing tendrils of her cunt forest, which seemed to creep down her bare thighs, and absolutely everywhere around her bum and cooze; impossible for Luke not to get stiff as he saw, smelled or even thought of her lush hairy quim haven.

'Why, Luke,' she drawled, 'you've shaved. How sweet, and so much more hygienic than all that horrid hair. I'm just too lazy to shave! Someone must have set you a good example. I wonder who?'

Luke blushed, but did not betray Severe's confidence, his cock stiffening, as Amy smiled, looking at his smooth-shaven cock and balls. Then, as always, it was rare that he did not rise to throbbing erection, and he gazed back at Amy, coolly scrutinising his body and tickling herself quite blatantly between the legs, with a large wet stain on her skirt.

This went on for some days, with Amy's self-pleasuring growing less and less modest, as she stared at Luke's rippling muscles and erection brushing his belly. She began to expose her naked quim, at least her naked bush, with the cunt lips hiding underneath; then, to play with herself quite openly, so that her swollen clitoris peeped out. Eventually, with a coy smile, she would blatantly wank herself to gasping, moaning orgasm.

'My, you are strong,' she gasped, one day, as she openly masturbated, pushing her skirtlet aside to show her wet pink slitmeat, gushing come, and her thumb mashing her swollen clitoris, staring at Luke like a dragon's eye.

He threw down his watering can, and, smeared with mud from the flowerbed, swept Amy up in his arms. Her skirt fell flapping back, baring her cunt, and her legs flailed helplessly, as he put her over his shoulder and carried her into her bedroom.

'Ooh! Stop! I forbid you,' she squealed. 'What are you doing? You'll get mud all over my carpet.'

'You know what I'm doing, you teasing bitch. Go and fetch the bamboo.'

52

'Luke, please, no.'

'Fetch it!' he cried. 'You may go on all fours, and bring the bamboo back in your mouth.'

'Well, mind your boots, please.'

Luke scraped the mud from his wellingtons, and smeared it all over her bed. When Amy returned, hobbling at the crouch, with the bamboo between her teeth, she gasped, dropping the rod, as she saw the filthy bedspread.

'What have you – urrgh!' she squealed, as he flung her face down on the bed, and began to wipe her breasts, cunt and thighs in the mud, until she was covered in dirt.

He put his wellington boot on her hair, and pressed her face into her muddy pillow, then lifted the bamboo, and began to thrash her naked bottom.

Vip!

'Ooh!'

Vip!

'Ah! Stop!'

Vip! Vip!

'Oh! Oh! You're getting me all excited, you foul brute.'

Amy's hand disappeared under her mons, and she began to masturbate, as the split ends of the bamboo raised welt after purple welt on her squirming buttocks.

Vip!

'Urrgh! No, no, please no, I'm so wet . . .'

Vip!

'Ouch! Ooh! You cruel beast, I'm coming!'

Vip!

'Ahh! God, it hurts! No more, I beg you!'

Vip! Vip!

'*Ahh!* Ah . . . ah! Have mercy! You'll thrash me to ribbons. I'm spurting, I'm all wet! God, don't thrash me so, Luke, please don't shred my bare arse. Not my *bare*, it's so shameful. *Ahh!* I'm all wet, my quim's gushing, you cruel, cruel master! Ooh . . . yes!'

Luke continued to flog Amy's wriggling nates, as a pool of come spread from her frigged cunt, and she writhed, gasping, in orgasm. He did not cease beating her bottom, until it was a glowing patchwork of ugly purple weals and gashes, with numerous strokes to her quivering thighs, criss-crossing the skin with black-and-blue stripes. Thigh cuts seemed to cause her most distress, for she wriggled and howled like a demon, as he whipped the soft skin below the fesses, causing him to deliver more and harder cuts to that defenceless thigh flesh. Vip! Vip!

'Ahh! Ooh! Not fair, not my thighs!' she squealed, sobbing, as her tears and pussy juice gushed.

After her orgasm, Amy continued to masturbate, with Luke working on her quivering haunches, and drawing loud screams also, whenever he lashed the tender skin of her top buttocks, just below her wriggling spinal nubbin. In a minute, her torrent of come was wetting the bed again, forming a slimy pool with the mud from the flowerbed, with Amy's belly and titties squirming in the filth. She gurgled in shame and pain and fear, fingers squelching, as she wanked her cunt. Tears streamed down her face. Vip! Vip!

'Ahh! God, it hurts! You cruel, beastly monster,' she said, sobbing. 'Oh, please, Luke, darling, haven't I had enough? You are far harder on me than the commander.'

Luke's teeth bared in a rictus, his cockpole bobbing, as he lashed the woman's helpless naked bottom, squirming beneath him. Vip! Vip!

'Ahh! Ooh!' she gasped, masturbating herself to a second climax. 'Oh! Oh! Yes . . .'

Luke threw aside the bamboo cane. He grasped her flogged buttocks, and parted them wide, exposing her crinkly anus bud, his nails clawing her weals; she squealed, squirming.

'Oh, no. Don't do me there. Don't bugger my bumhole, Luke. Haven't you hurt me enough? I can't bear your monstrous stiff cock fucking my tripes to agony.'

'You foul-mouthed slut,' he snarled. 'You'll get what all sluts deserve.'

He rammed his glans an inch into her anus, and she howled; the cockshaft plunged an inch more, and she began to wriggle, sobbing uncontrollably.

'Oh ... oh ... oh. God it hurts,' she said between sobs. 'Don't put it up me any more. I can't bear arse-fucking. Why not fuck my lovely cunt, all hot and wet for your tool? *Ooh!*'

Luke slammed his cock into her rectum, right to his balls, which slapped her churning wealed arse meat, as his cocktip touched her colon. His shaven pubes slithered against her wriggling buttock weals, as he bum-fucked her brutally, slamming hard thrusts to the colon, then withdrawing to the neck of his glans, before plunging his entire throbbing cock anew into her squirming tripes. Holding her hips, he pressed her arse to his loins, preventing her escape, until, after a minute's fucking, he felt her buttocks rise to meet his thrusts, her rectum tightening on his plunging cock to milk him of spunk.

'No ...' she moaned, as her clinging sphincter squeezed his tool, and her bare bum danced in the rhythm of her buggery. 'Please don't fuck my arse, Luke, it's so absolutely shameful. You're hurting me awfully. I can't bear a cock spurting hot spunk up my colon, please don't spunk up my bumhole, anything but that, Luke, please ... ooh! *Ohh! Yes ...*'

Luke grunted, as the first droplets of sperm oozed from his peehole, mashing her sigmoid colon; then the full force of his spurt erupted in her belly, his jet of hot spunk filling her rectum, and overflowing, to dribble from the mouth of her cock-stretched anus. Thwap! Thwap! Luke's tight balls smacked loudly on Amy's shuddering bare buttocks, as, scowling furiously, he slammed hot cream into her thirsty colon.

'Yes!' she squealed.

A gush of glistening come spurted from her cunt, as Amy writhed, groaning, in another orgasm, her titties and cunt smeared with mud and come. The bedside telephone rang; without decoupling, Luke picked it up and answered it. A girl's voice cooed from the earpiece.

'Yes, mistress,' Luke blurted. 'At once, mistress.' He hung up.

'Ooh ... ahh ...' Amy groaned, sobbing, as Luke fetched his clothing. 'Gosh, my arse hurts, Luke. I just hope Severe pays you back in spades for my scandalous treatment.'

Luke returned, tucking himself into his grey flannel trousers. Above, he wore a white shirt and green-and-yellow striped tie.

'You wanted it,' he sneered.

Amy smiled coyly, fist between her cunt flaps, thighs spread wide, masturbating. 'I know,' she purred. 'And I got it. My bum's smarting dreadfully, and my colon just drank up all your lovely spunk, and I'll have to frig and frig, till I stop tingling. You'll get what *you* need from that cruel girl.'

He blushed. 'It's not a question of need,' he retorted. 'I made her a promise, and a gentleman keeps his promises. I promised to obey her commands. Hence ...'

He grimaced coyly, as he slipped on his black school blazer, with yellow piping. Amy clapped her hands, with a loud smack on her bare bottom.

'How wonderful!' she cried. 'You must dress as a smutty schoolboy. You look awfully sweet. I can't say I'm not a teensy bit jealous, but I'll have some lovely wanks, thinking of *your* naked buttocks squirming under her lash. I imagine she can't wait. Take the taxi money from my purse.'

'Well, thanks, Auntie. Miss Severe has sent a taxi for me already.'

'You'll pay, of course. Good luck, slave of Severe,' she said, blowing him a kiss.

Amy picked up the telephone, and pressed a button.

Severe Compaigne stood nude before her looking glass, running her fingertips over her swollen cunt mound and heavy, jutting teats. Her hand caressed her buttocks, while she flexed her sphincter to tighten and relax the rippling arsemeat. Her fingertips traced the fine spray of faded weals that graced the taut satin bum skin. There was –

already! – a tiny trickle of come from her slit, moistening her bulging red gash flaps. Her blonde tresses, ironed flat and held with an amethyst slide in a side parting, cascaded over her breasts. Head cocked, she murmured into her telephone, wedged between chin and shoulder.

'Mm-mm ... yah ... if you want ...' She burst into giggles. 'No, honestly ... yah ... that would be super. I'm getting goosy already. You know the way in ... yah ... ciao.'

She turned to her armoire, pursing her lips, as she selected her clothing. From the stocking drawer, she took a pair of lemon-yellow hose in sheer nylon, sat on her bed, and raised her right foot to draw the nylon over her toes, which she wiggled against the smooth fabric; then she rolled the stocking slowly up her calf and thigh, until its frilly top clung inches below her naked cunt. She did the same with her left leg; then pranced, pouting, before the glass, with her hand covering her shaven mons, and dipped her fingers in the come seeping from her gash. She gasped, touching her throbbing clitoris, which poked from the fleshy slit, but removed her hand, wiping it on her bottom.

She returned to the armoire, and selected a lemon-yellow silk suspender belt, the lacy pattern matching her stockings, and strapped it to her waist, before clipping the four garter straps to her stocking tops. Next, a pair of matching lemon silk panties, in a very high bikini cut, and the gusset so narrow as to make them no more than a glorified thong. She pulled them up tight over the sussies, looking down, and licking her lips, as she noted the stain darkening the cunt-silk, which clung to her fesses and mound, clearly outlining the arse cleft and gash. She rubbed her thighs together, and smiled, hearing her panties squelch. Under or over the sussies? A point hotly debated among eager schoolgirls, but for the moment the 'overs' had won.

The matching bra slid over her trembling breasts, the big pink nipple domes already hard as new plums, and snugly encased the globes in see-through satin: a conceit, offering no support to firm teats that demanded none. Then, the covering of a white cotton blouse, short-sleeved for summer; the haunches encased in her pleated school skirt of fine grey wool, its hem swirling seven inches above her nyloned knees; brown court shoes, a blue-and-yellow striped tie, and Severe's school uniform was complete.

She lit a Dunhill, parking it in the corner of her mouth, as, hands on hips, she contemplated herself, smiling cruelly, in the glass. She lifted her skirt up, to show her panties; touched herself quickly on the clearly swollen clitty, and gasped, with a nod of satisfaction to her reflected image; then she lowered her skirt, as the doorbell rang. She went into the drawing room, and poured herself a glass of sherry from the crystal decanter; sipping, she allowed herself a minute to finish and extinguish her cigarette, before going to open the front door.

'You're late, worm,' she spat at Luke, who was trembling, in his own school uniform. 'Didn't I order you to wear your short trousers?'

'Why, mistress, I don't think so,' he blurted, 'and they'd scarcely fit me.'

'You mean they would be painful and embarrassing,' Severe snorted. 'Exactly what a worm like you deserves.'

With a curt nod, she bade him enter. While she lounged, smoking, and sipping her sherry, he was made to stand with his hands behind his back for her inspection. Casually, Severe crossed her thighs, with a generous slither of nylon, and let her skirt ride up, so that he could see her stocking tops and the moist sliver of lemon panties peeping between her smooth bare thigh tops. She repeated this manoeuvre until she was satisfied with the bulge that sprang at his crotch, and the blush suffusing his cheeks.

'There is the matter of punishment for your offence upon your last visit,' she drawled.

'Yes, Miss Severe,' he murmured.

'I dare say you know what to expect.'

'Yes, mistress,' he said, gulping.

'Any objections?'

'N-no, mistress. I am yours to command.'

She leered. 'I know *that*, worm. Try and limit your pathetic bleats to something I *don't* know. For example, you could enlighten me as to why you have a disgusting bulge in your trousers when you know very well I'm going to blister your bare bottom with my cane.'

'I can't explain it, Miss Severe,' he replied wretchedly.

'Does the prospect of pain excite you?'

'Mistress,' he blurted, 'anything from you excites me.'

'Another thing I know already,' she said, yawning. 'You bore me, worm. I think we may proceed to your chastisement. Beating is the only way to lick filthy boys clean of their impure thoughts. Perhaps your arse, properly blistered, will bore me slightly less. We'll have those shoes and socks off, to start with.'

Luke obeyed, then, biting his lip, and grim-faced, he unbuckled his belt, and bent over, touching his toes.

'We'll liven you up with an apéritif,' Severe drawled. 'A school beating – a brisk dozen.'

'A dozen, Miss Severe?' Luke gasped. 'A school beating is surely only a sixer.'

'Are you a miserable coward,' she hissed, 'or unaware that at *my* school, girls are always caned a dozen? You cannot even take what a sixth-form girl takes, with her skirt up, panties at her ankles and buttocks naked?'

'If a girl can take it, so must I,' Luke mumbled.

'That's right. Girls are anyway braver than snivelling boys. Hmm . . . perhaps being a girl would help.'

'Mistress? I don't follow.'

'You will. Now, for the moment . . .'

With a flourish, Severe ripped his pants down to his ankles, baring his fesses, and swiftly knotted his shirt over his ribs, explaining it was to allow herself a wide expanse of target skin.

'Legs apart, and hang onto those toes,' she commanded. 'This set is really going to sting.'

Humming, she sauntered to the cane cabinet, and selected a long yellow wand, with a crook handle. She swished it in the air, while Luke blanched at its vicious whirr, and pronounced herself satisfied that this rod would cause him maximum pain.

'Gosh, you do look pathetic, with that horrid meaty tube and those silly pods dangling. But I'm glad to see you've shaved the beastly things. Ready?' she cooed.

Without waiting for an answer, she lifted the cane in a swirling motion, and lashed him squarely across the centre of his naked, tensed buttocks. Vip!

'Ooh!' he gasped, his fesses clenching in and out, with a long pink stripe darkening the flesh.

Tears moistened his eyes, and his face reddened. Between his legs, the massive cock began to stir. Vip!

'Oh!' he cried, his flogged buttocks beginning to squirm, as he clenched.

Vip! Vip! She lashed two rapid forehand and backhand strokes.

'Ahh!' he squealed.

His scarlet buttocks wriggled fiercely, as tears coursed down his cheeks.

'Enough howling,' she spat. 'You'll take that double stroke over for your blasted girly insolence.'

'Oh, please, I beg you, don't be so cruel, mistress,' he whimpered. 'The commander never beat me this hard.'

'You don't get it, do you?' Severe sneered. 'Amy sent you to Coz for punishment, as a gift, so that he would lash *her*, and, of course, fuck her, too. Coz rather likes whipping people. I've always been caned, bare bum.'

'Did . . . did Justin cane you?'

'Of course. There is no love without whipping.'

'The beast!'

'That's what a girl looks for in a man. A girl's bum is made to smart, I'm afraid. But my revenge is sweet.'

Vip! Vip!

'Uh . . . uh . . . uh . . .'

His breath came in hoarse, rasping pants, while his cock trembled, half-erect. Severe prodded the peehole with the tip of her cane.

'What's this? Stiff? How rude,' she snarled in disgust.

She stuck the cane tip into the peehole, and reamed it, making him squeal.

'Ooh! Ooh!'

'Hurt, does it?'

'God, yes.'

'I like hurting you,' she purred. 'But you'll take your punishment in total silence from here.'

His cock sprang to full stiffness. She ripped the cane from his peehole, swung it in an arc, and lashed him across the top buttocks. Vip! The cane left an ugly crimson welt, aslant to the previous weals. Luke panted hoarsely, but did not cry, although his whipped nates were squirming hard, and his legs trembling rigid, as he clutched his toes. Weeping, he heard his cruel mistress express her distaste for his – quite monstrous! – erection, and decree further punishment, for what she could only deem an insult.

'I can't help it, mistress,' he said, sobbing, as his bare bottom danced in pain. 'You are so beautiful, so powerful, and your perfume of cruelty is so irresistible, I can't help stiffening. And . . . and . . . you look divine in your school uniform.'

'You impudent cur!'

Vip!

His reddened bare buttocks squirmed, like two whipped jellies.

'That concludes your *first* set,' she panted, 'for I ordered silence, whelp, and you disobeyed. Your punishment is far from over.'

'Yes, mistress,' he whimpered. 'I understand.'

'I don't think you do. I'm going to play with you until you're blistered and weeping, out of your mind with pain, and cursing the day you called me "mistress". Do you still want to remain my slave?'

'I promised, mistress,' Luke said.

He obeyed, without protest, when Severe ordered him to strip nude; nor did he protest, save for a whimper, as she fastened his nipples and the loose skin of his balls in separate pincers, all attached to a single chain leash.

Flicking the chain and swinging her riding crop at her haunches, she led him, wincing, out onto the lawn, her bottom waggling playfully before the tethered boy, under the swirling pleats of her school skirt, and her nylons glinting in the sun.

'Happy, slave?' she asked.

'You're hurting me awfully, mistress,' he moaned.

'But are you happy?'

'Yes.'

'Always start a slave session with a good crisp beating, you see,' said Severe thoughtfully. 'It tames him, breaks him for the pain to come. He'll whimper and scream, of course, but he won't *resist*.' Her fingers clasped his balls tight, and he winced; she faced him, glaring into his eyes. 'Do you understand, slave?'

'Yes, mistress.'

'Liar. You'll never understand.'

'I don't understand, Miss Severe, how you can be so cruel, and yet accept the whip on your own body.'

She shrugged. 'A girl has things done to her. If she's lucky, she does them to someone else.'

She stared at his stiffened cock, stroking her chin, and licking her teeth. Slowly, she unbuttoned her blouse, and pulled the cloth aside, to reveal her brassiered breasts. He goggled, as she pushed aside the soft fabric of the cups, and showed him her bare teats, with her fingers squeezing and caressing her nipples. His cock throbbed rigid.

'That's better,' she said. 'You *are* filth.'

She tucked away her breasts, smoothing her blouse and carefully replacing her striped school tie. He groaned, as Severe produced a length of copper wire, then pulled his prepuce fully back, and bound the wire tightly around the neck of his glans. She fastened the other end of the wire taut to his nipple tongs.

'Crouch, pony!' she ordered.

He got down on hands and knees, with a moan, as his leash was stretched tight. Severe mounted him, like a horse-rider, the chain leash drawn over his shoulder and across his back. Vip! Vip! He jerked, as two cuts from her riding crop lashed his bare buttocks, and she tugged on the chain, pulling his nipples and ball sac.

'Giddy-up!' she cried.

Whimpering with pain, he hobbled around the sward, with Severe's nylon stockings, sussies and wet panties slithering on the small of his back, crushed under her weight, her crop savagely slashing his wealed flanks and arse, and the silence of the summer's day broken by his choking sobs, as he groaned and wept.

'Coz is too stingy to buy me a real pony,' she confided. 'I suppose you'll do.'

Vip! Vip! She lashed his haunches.

'Ooh!'

'Be quiet, you noisy brat.'

Vip! Vip! She cut him right in the deepest weals of mid-fesse, gouging new crimson welts on top of the blackened ridged skin, crusted from his caning. Luke's flogged bottom squirmed frantically, as he reared in agony, toppling his mistress to the grass. Her skirt flew up to show her panties, stained at the gusset, by her seeped come. Luke leapt to his feet, and grasped her arm to help her up. Angrily, her eyes like red-hot coals and breasts heaving, she slapped him away, while smoothing down her skirt over her trembling thighs.

'You'll pay for that, slave,' she hissed.

'I'm sorry, mistress,' he wailed.

'You will be.'

She gave a savage jerk on his chain, and led him, hobbling and whimpering, to the barn. She pinned his leash to a tall, oaken whipping post, then bound his wrists in front of him, her arms brushing his stiff cock as she knotted him tightly. On her command, he raised his wrists, and she tied the binding to a nail, stuck in the whipping post.

A leash, fastened to his ball and nipple tongs, was anchored taut to a floor bolt. Severe picked up a leather stockwhip; as Luke watched, gasping, she lifted her skirt, and slid the thick whip between her thighs, across her panties, several times, drawing the thong back and forth across her cunt lips and sighing with pleasure. She brought it out, gleaming with pussy juice.

Placing herself behind Luke, she raised her whip. The thong whistled. Whap! It crashed, streaking fire across Luke's bare back and making him jerk in pain, his wriggling back tugging his ball and nipple tongs to cause fresh agony. He gasped, moaning and drooling, but forced himself not to cry out, however hard she whipped him. Whap! The flogging assumed a dreadful, steady rhythm: the whistle, the crack and the searing pain on his naked back, then the hot slither of the thong, like a snake, as she deliberately caressed his weal, before raising the whip again.

'Whipping's more shameful than caning, I suppose,' she panted. 'For a boy, at least. You are so delightfully helpless, my brave, juicy young seaman, flogged at the mainmast. What a lovely conceit.'

Luke twisted his head to stare at her, his face a mask of agony and streaked with tears; through blurred eyes, he saw Severe's skirt raised, and her fingers delving into her wet lemon panties. His mistress was masturbating, as she whipped him. With a cry of anguish, he let his head sink to his chest, only to jerk up again, as the next whip stroke lashed his back.

'Oh!' he panted. 'Oh, God, it hurts.'

'Careful, slave,' she warned.

Whap!

'Uhh . . .' he drooled, his head shaking from side to side, and his whole body wriggling, as the leather striped his back.

On and on the whipping went, amid dappled sunlight and gently swirling eddies of dust, the barn musky with sweat, leather and naked pain. As she flogged the boy, Severe masturbated to moaning, gasping orgasm, then, eyes bright and teeth bared, she put the whip aside. Luke was groaning. He had taken thirty strokes to his bare back, stippling it in livid purple bruises. She untied him, and replaced his leash by a much longer rope, which she formed into a noose, and threw it up to loop over a rafter.

The blonde schoolgirl attached Luke to the rope by a wrist-brank, securing his arms behind his back. Then she slowly tightened the noose, shortening the rope, and forcing his arms up behind him, *in strappado*, while the leash tautened, wrenching his clamped balls and nipples. Luke panted hoarsely, sweat and tears pouring from his face, and his cock throbbing stiff. Each ankle was cuffed – the metal cuff attached to a rock, as deadweight, and the two rocks placed wide apart, so that Luke's legs strained, stretched painfully, with his tight balls dangling, fully visible between his trembling thighs.

Severe stepped back to admire her work, smacking her lips at the trussed boy, who was unable to move and ease his distress: trying to lower his arms would pull more painfully on his nipple and ball tongs, and vice versa. She touched the protruding slabs of his bare, wealed buttocks.

'What juicy flogging balls,' she murmured.

Luke heard a rustling; the schoolgirl's skirt came clean off, followed by her sopping wet panties. She wadded the panties, and told Luke to open his mouth wide. She stuffed the panties into his mouth, pushing them right to the back of his throat, and said it was for his own comfort, as the next treatment would really make him squeal. She cupped his balls, stroking them tenderly, and told him he would hurt most dreadfully, but he wasn't to mind; then, she gave his balls a gentle squeeze, making him wince and moan.

He felt his fesses parted and a hard object nuzzling his anus bud. He strained to look, and saw Miss Severe, skirt pinned up, and her buttocks and cunt basin nude, save for a huge ribbed tool strapped to her crotch by a lattice of rubber thongs, like panties. The tool was the shape of a stiff cock, much bigger than his own, and gleaming in hard black rubber, with a pair of giant gourds pendant beneath. Smiling, Severe called it her cruellest *godemiché*.

'Mm! Mm!' he gasped, into his wet panties gag, with a frantic shaking of his head.

Severe bared her teeth in a rictus of amusement; her hips jerked, making her titties bounce in their sweat-damp blouse, and she thrust hard.

'*Urrgh!*' Luke squealed, deep in his throat, as the tool entered his anus.

His arse squirmed, but could not stop her strapped-on dildo penetrating his rectum. With a few powerful thrusts of her clenched bare buttocks, the schoolgirl drove the monstrous black tube deep into Luke's arse, until it sank in to the gourds, and the boy was whimpering and gurgling, writhing in pain and fear. Severe withdrew a few inches, the cock squelching in Luke's rectum, and drove in hard, as she impaled him.

Her body rippled, bum dancing and clenching, as she fucked him with hard, slamming strokes; the whimpering boy wriggled like a skewered fish. Drool trickled through his panties gag, and his nipple and ball clamps flapped, as his body vainly tried to resist Severe's merciless arse-fucking. His cock bobbed, rigid and shiny, at his squirming belly. The blonde schoolgirl panted, sweat pouring from her belly, into the come which squirted copiously from her cunt, wetting the shaft of the dildo, as it plunged again and again, remorselessly, into the boy's squirming arse.

'*Mm . . . mm . . .*' he squealed.

'Nice?' she asked.

'Mm . . .'

She picked up the stockwhip, flicked it, and expertly sent it curling around the boy's rigid cock. As she fucked him, she began to tug on the cock-coiled whip, the thong pulling and caressing his glans.

'Mm . . .'

Severe began to gasp, as come flooded her cunt, and her belly began to heave. 'Yes!' she gasped, pulling harder on the whip.

'Mm . . .' Luke groaned. 'Mm . . .'

A bead of white cream appeared at his peehole, followed by a powerful jet of spunk, spurting into the leather coils of the caressing whip. Severe panted and groaned, as orgasm wracked her cunt, and her fucked boy sobbed, as his sperm poured into the leather that had flogged him.

Concealed behind a heavy wooden gibbet of fourteenth-century provenance, Amy panted harshly, as she watched Luke's buggery. Skirt up and panties at her knees, she masturbated her bare wet cunt. As she watched Severe writhe in spasm, and the boy's cream spurt, she brought herself off, to a shuddering, gushing orgasm, wetting her quivering thighs and nylons, and sluicing her knickers with come.

'Fuck the blasted boy,' she moaned, her eyelids fluttering, fixed on Luke's spurting cock. 'Ooh, *yes* . . .'

# 5

# Tough Titty

'Please, mistress,' Luke murmured, 'you haven't disciplined me lately. Have I displeased my mistress?'

It was late in the summer. Slanting rays of the lowering afternoon sun illumined the drawing room, where Severe, lounging in her armchair, sipped sherry.

'You've never pleased me, worm, so I don't see how you can displease me,' drawled Severe, smoking a Dunhill. 'Why are slaves such a nuisance? I suppose it'll take a dozen stingers on bare to stop your beastly whining?'

'Whatever pleases you, mistress,' Luke blurted, blushing. 'I've done all the scrubbing and laundry, and everything, and I must have made some errors.'

'If I caned you for every error, you wouldn't have any skin left,' said Severe with a sniff. 'Perhaps I haven't felt like it. You look too demure. However, I'll beat you extra hard for your impudence in demanding it.'

'Thank you, mistress.'

Luke wore his mistress's school uniform of grey skirt, lemon stockings and sussies, white blouse and translucent brassiere – the ensemble painfully tight on his boyish frame, especially at the groin, where his erection tented his tight girl's panties, and the lacy white petticoat that peeped below his skirt hem. Severe wore the same, as she lounged, thighs apart, on her armchair, except that she was unpantied, and her shaven cooze hillock, with cherry gash lips pouting below, glistened in the slanting sunlight. Mechanically, he continued to flick a feather duster on Severe's furniture, until she nodded for her cane. He crouched, and fetched it on all fours, carrying the wand between his teeth.

'Take off your skirt, slave, and bend over,' she drawled, slipping off her court shoes, and wriggling her toes in her moist lemon nylons.

She loosened her school tie, and then, with a smirk, undid two buttons of her blouse, showing creamy bare teat flesh and the lacy top of her bra. His stiff cock quivered.

'Petticoat up, well above your hips, and panties lowered to your knees. Legs well apart, so that I can see your bollocks. I like to watch you cringe in fear that I might miss the arse.'

Luke obeyed, assuming position, with his fingers touching his stockinged toes. At the test swish of Severe's cane, he shuddered. His cock throbbed to bursting, despite the wires knotted around his glans and scrotum, and the heavy brass weights dangling from the wires, between his legs, forcing him to walk, thighs apart, in a girlish mince.

'Mistress, may I say something?'

'I suppose so.'

'It's Aunt Amy. You've summoned me so often, these last two months, I think she might suspect something's going on.'

'Hmph!' she snorted. 'You are a smutty, snivelling slave, who needs regular discipline, that's all.'

'Discipline!' he blurted. 'Whipped and caned on the bare, racked, pinned, buggered, dressed as a maid or schoolgirl, ridden and lashed like a pony, made to do laundry, even fry bacon in the nude, for a heartless, cruel mistress. It's been more than discipline, Miss Severe.'

'And hard work for me. Why should Amy suspect? Unless you show her your bruises, and that girly's bumhole of yours, stretched to a proper sailor's shilling.'

She glared at him, and he blushed, lowering his head.

'You *do*, don't you?' she exclaimed. 'You've being doing it with Amy! Well. She didn't tell me *that*, the smutty slut.

I thought her main interest was wanking off. She has told me how much she likes masturbating, watching naked boys.'

'You know Aunt Amy, mistress?'

'You *are* a fool. But you shall mind your own business, slave. Your impudence has displeased me, and I'm in the mood to correct it. I propose to blister your bare, until you howl for mercy.'

'Yes, mistress. Thank you, mistress.'

Vip! Severe lashed Luke across the top buttock, and he jerked, with a loud gasp. Vip! The second took him on the underfesse, and he sighed in contentment. Vip! A stroke to the haunch made his bottom squirm, with his eyes shut and a twisted smile on his face. Vip! Vip! His bare buttocks clenched and wriggled, as the welts flared in livid crimson streaks.

'Ooh!'

'Tight, eh?'

'Yes, mistress,' he gasped. 'You whip superbly.'

'Tell me the whole truth, slave, about you and Amy,' she drawled. 'You'll take unlimited cuts, until your words please me, and your bottom is in real agony.' She spat on her cane tip, and smiled, a feline with her prey. 'I've a long, lazy afternoon to cane you raw.'

Over fifty cane strokes lashed purple stripes on Luke's squirming bare buttocks, before he finished sobbing his story: the shame and confusion of his double life, to return from slavery to his beautiful, icy mistress, and become the master of Amy, who needed thrashing and the cruellest buggery.

Vip!

'Uh . . .'

'Confusion is for girls, you fool,' she spat.

Vip!

'Oh! It hurts,' the boy moaned, as his flogged arse wriggled.

'*That*'s not confusing, I hope.'

Vip!

71

'*Ahh!* No, mistress.' He gasped. 'It is so wonderful to feel pain from you, whom I adore. I feel you want me. Dressed as you, I feel I *am* you.'

'Impudent wretch,' she hissed.

Vip! Vip!

'*Ooh!*'

'You silly fucking slave, nobody wants you.'

'I . . . I can't believe that.'

'Not believe your mistress?' she snarled. 'By God, you do ask for pain.'

Vip! Vip! Vip! Three savage cuts sliced his arse cleft, lashing his swollen anus bud, and striping his flesh within a hair's breadth of his pendant balls.

'*Oh! Ahh!* Yes, mistress.'

She took his beating far beyond the edge of his whimpering and tears, while openly and contemptuously frotting her clit, as she whipped his arse to purple. Throughout the ordeal, his cock stood rigid. The dry cracks of the cane echoed in the silent sleepiness of the sunlit chamber, broken only by Severe's wanked panting and the whipped boy's hoarse gasps and whimpers.

By the end of the set, Severe's thighs and cunt were wet with the come of three orgasms, while her flushed face, flared nostrils and slit eyes, indicated her lustful readiness for more. Groaning, Luke rose, his stiff cockpole tenting his girl's skirt. Severe gave him the rod to kiss, and he crouched at her feet to obey, taking the hot cane tip into his mouth. Then she plunged his face into her sweat-stinking stockings, to lick and suck the moisture from her nyloned toes. Her lip curled, in amused disgust.

'You filthy cur,' she murmured. 'Well, I've a surprise for you.' She snapped her fingers. 'Amy, you may join us.'

'What?' Luke blurted.

The curtains opened at the side of the French windows to reveal Amy, pulling up her white lacy bikini panties, which gleamed wet with come. Amy licked her glistening fingers, and smiled at Luke.

'I hope you don't mind our little deception,' she purred. 'I have had such gorgeous wanks, watching you suffer.'

She tripped to Severe's side, and embraced her, bussing her long and hard, full on the lips. The girls' tongues squelched in a wet, passionate kiss. Amy put her elastic bootee on Luke's nape, and pressed his face into Severe's feet. Her hands delved beneath the schoolgirl's skirt, and began to caress her bare bottom, while Severe remained aloof, allowing her tongue to stab Amy's mouth, and taking Amy's nipples, braless, under her thin blouse of tight brown silk, to tweak the buds hard and painfully, so that Amy's breasts heaved, the nipples stiffening, as she squealed in her throat. The girls disengaged, Severe leering, with Amy flushed and panting.

'Severe, darling,' she gasped, 'do let's show him a thing or two.'

'Strip, then,' Severe ordered curtly. 'Everything off. I want to see you nude.'

Amy hastened to obey.

'The way this worm sees you,' Severe added drily.

'Oh . . .' stammered Amy, blushing. 'Yes, of course . . .'

She stood, nude and trembling, before the uniformed schoolgirl; her nipples were stiff plums, her naked titties quivered, and her massive pubic bush glistened wetly in the rays of sunshine, slanting across the carpet, above little trickles of come from her pouting cunt lips.

'You never told me he was doing you,' Severe said.

Amy's blush deepened, suffusing her breasts and belly, and the trim, erect points of her wine-red nipples. Her lush pubic mane quivered, right up to her navel, where its exuberant thatch crawled, covering her lower belly; the copious pubic hairs dangling below her cunt flaps, stirred, dripping with her wanked come. Severe jerked Luke to his feet, and ripped off his skirt and petticoat, then the blouse, until he stood nude, but for stockings and sussies, dominated by the huge bare cockpole. Amy gaped at the boy's throbbing red tool, and she pressed her fingers to her lips.

73

'It's your bottom the boy sees mostly, I take it,' Severe drawled, flicking her cane. 'Doing it doggy?'

'Yes . . . I suppose so.'

'Well, then. Bare up, you slut.'

'I . . . I beg your pardon?'

'You heard.'

'Really, Severe!'

Vip! Severe thrashed the cushion of the leather sofa, then pointed, with her cane. 'You, boy. Sit here. You, bitch, bare up, cheeks wide. I shan't tell you again.'

Luke lay back on the entire length of the sofa, his cock piercing the air. Trembling, Amy clasped her buttocks, and pulled the cheeks wide, exposing her naked anus bud, as wrinkled and stretched as Luke's own. She licked her lips, swallowing nervously.

'Squat,' Severe commanded.

Amy straddled Luke's balls, with the tip of his cock brushing her anus bud. Her face screwed tight and eyes shut, she moaned softly, as she sank onto his stiff cock, the glans penetrating her anus to its neck.

'Ouch! He's so big,' Amy gasped.

'You knew that already.'

'It seems larger. Must I?'

'You must.'

'Ooh, it hurts,' Amy wailed, lowering her thighs, until his cock impaled her fully, with her bare buttocks squashing his balls. '*Uhh!* He's up my colon. I'm bursting.'

'Fuck him, bitch,' rapped Severe.

Come poured from Amy's cunt, as, groaning and sobbing, she bent forwards like a racing cyclist, and, propping her hands on Luke's ribs, began to lift and lower her cunt basin to engulf the giant cock in her anus. Her parted thighs exposed her split cunt, amid her dripping jungle of cooze hairs, straggling down her perineum to her anus and thighs. Her bouncing nipples slapped Luke's chest, as she rammed his cock up her rectum, with loud squelching, and her come dripped heavily onto his cunt-squashed balls.

Luke began to thrust, plunging his cock right to her root; Amy drooled, head lolling, but with her powerful thighs and buttocks pumping of their own accord, and screamed softly at each smack of his peehole to her colon. Come poured from her sluicing wet cunt, coating his balls, already glazed with a copious drip of arse grease from her fucked bottom.

'Ooh! Ooh! It's too big! He's hurting me, Severe.'

'It hurt all those times before.'

'But I felt so guilty, feeling your weals on his darling arse, and I needed to be punished . . . to atone.'

Severe lifted her cane. Vip! The wood slapped savagely across Amy's pulsing bare arse globes, raising a thick red welt.

'Ooh! Severe!'

Vip!

'Ahh! No!'

Vip!

'You'll atone, bitch,' hissed Severe.

As she flogged the buggered woman, Severe stripped, dropping her skirt and blouse, until she was nude, but for stockings and sussies. Thighs apart and cunt dripping, Severe masturbated vigorously, as she whipped Amy's naked buttocks to a tapestry of livid weals. At the thirtieth stroke, a stink of come and sweat wafted from Severe's furiously wanked cunt. Amy squealed, her buttocks writhing, as Luke continued to bugger her, and her belly tensed, with her pulsing thighs powerfully slapping his balls.

Amy sank onto Luke, her titties squashed against his collarbone; one hand crept to her cunt, which gurgled, as she wanked, rubbing her stiff nipples against his chest. Vip! Vip! The stinging rhythm of the cane on her arse followed the rise and fall of her buggered anus, drawing Luke's slimed cock out of her hole, right to his tip, before, with a groan, and a little dribbling scream of agony, she slapped her belly once more on his, thighs clasping his balls and anus sucking his cock, to make the massive stiff tool slam her colon.

Wanking, Severe gasped, as her belly fluttered in a come, which spurted rivulets of cunt juice from her gash, over her rippling thighs, and drenching her lemon stockings with its dark stain. As her cunt pulsed in orgasm, she slapped herself on the buttocks and shaven cunt hillock, until bare mons and fesses glowed pink. Her cane thrashed the enculed arse of Amy, who was snivelling and weeping, as she smacked her buttocks on Luke's balls. Vip!

'Ooh! Ahh!' Amy shrieked. 'God, it hurts, you bitch.'

Vip!

'*Ooh!* I'm coming! Luke, fuck me harder, split me open, hurt me, give me all the lovely spunk from your balls, right up my bumhole. Fuck me, fuck me, fuck me . . . *ahh!*'

Come sluiced from Amy's writhing cunt, as she orgasmed, shrieking in tortured little gasps. Luke grunted, and began to spurt inside her rectum, with his powerful flow of cream spilling past the lips of her distended, squirming anus, to glaze his balls. As Amy's spasm ebbed to a whimper, Severe wrenched her hair, and pulled her from Luke's cock, which left her anus with a loud sucking plop.

'Ouch!' squealed Amy. 'What are you doing?'

Severe embraced her with a deep, lustful kiss, her tongue stabbing the buggered girl's mouth.

'Mm . . . mm . . .' gurgled Amy, embracing her whipper, and squashing her bubbies against the schoolgirl's.

The pair sank to the carpet, tonguing, with hands squelching their wet cunts, and withdrawing, to smear the writhing bare buttocks. Their teats and bellies squirmed, pressed tight.

'Poor darling Amy,' gasped Severe, 'did Severe hurt you, while that boy's monstrous cock spurted all his horrid spunk up you? Let Severe kiss you better.'

The blonde schoolgirl brushed a tress from her brow, swivelled, placing her lips at Amy's cunt, and began a vigorous gamahuche, swallowing the girl's gushing juice. Her mouth embraced Amy's anus, still dribbling Luke's copious sperm, which Severe sucked and swallowed, getting her tongue an inch inside the bumhole, and tickling

76

her, to the gamahuched Amy's squeal of delight. Amy wanked her clitty, while applying her lips to Severe's swollen nubbin and taking the schoolgirl's hard, swollen clit fully into her mouth.

'Ooh! Ooh!' gasped Severe, nuzzling the stinky fold of Amy's arse cleft, and her hips and bum squirming, with her cunt oozing come, as Amy sucked her clitty.

Luke gasped, his cock rising to new stiffness, as he watched the tribades gamahuche each other to orgasm, rubbing nipples, while kissing their cunts and bumholes with voluptuous sucks and slurps. At last, they disengaged, and rose to stare at the erect Luke, their hands caressing naked buttocks, and licking their lips, dripping with arse grease, spunk and come. The oily rivulets soaked their heaving bare breasts, nipples stiff as ripe young plums. Severe rubbed the grease into her belly and teats, pinching her big nips hard, and working a coating of the oily fluid over her taut pink buttocks and cunt hillock, glowing from her own spanks.

'Mwah!' Severe kissed Amy's nose, taking it into her mouth, and licking it. 'The boy is stiff again,' Severe said with a snort. 'What's to be done, Amy, darling?'

Amy looked at Luke. 'He'll have to be despunked,' she said, thoughtfully.

'Agreed.'

'But *my* hole's far too sore.'

'Tough titty,' Severe sneered.

Amy paled in anger. 'Oh! You cow,' she hissed.

She grasped Severe's arm, twisting it savagely up her back, and Severe stumbled and howled, as Amy forced her to a crouch.

'Stop it!' Severe squealed. 'You're hurting me!'

Amy squatted, with her arse and cunt basin inches above Severe's head. She drew both the schoolgirl's arms up into a tight full nelson, pinioning her face to the floor, with her knees stamping the carpet and her buttocks writhing. She ripped the belt from Luke's discarded trousers, and deftly wrapped Severe's wrists, buckling them in a tight cinch, while continuing to pinion the wriggling schoolgirl.

'Luke, give the slut some of her own medicine.'

'I can't,' he whined. 'She's . . . she's my mistress.'

'It's what she needs,' said Amy with a snort. 'If you don't give her what you give *me*, you can pack your bags and leave home without a penny.'

'Urrgh! Mm!' squealed Severe, chewing the carpet.

Trembling, Luke seized the cane, and positioned himself over the schoolgirl's buttocks.

'Exactly what you give me,' purred Amy.

She held Severe's wrists effortlessly, with one hand, while the other slipped between her own thighs, to stroke her clitty, peeping from swollen cunt flaps, already spewing come over Severe's hair.

'I'm sorry, mistress,' Luke stammered. 'I have no choice. You must blame Amy for her cruelty.'

'Mm! Mm!' squealed Severe, shaking her croup.

Vip! The cane lashed the squirming schoolgirl in the centre of her bare buttocks.

'Urrgh!' Severe howled, her face reddening, as a pink stripe wealed her bum flesh.

'Harder, Luke,' urged Amy, licking her teeth, with her fingers powerfully diddling her dripping cooze. 'Whip the bitch's arse raw.'

Vip!

'Ooh!'

Vip!

'*Ahh!*'

Vip!

'Oh! Oh!'

The schoolgirl's whipped bum globes quivered, clenching and squirming, at each dry slap of the wood on naked flesh. Severe's anus was exposed, as the buttocks stretched tight, then hidden by the cheeks slamming together, and squeezing the arse cleft to a thin furrow. Come poured from the blonde girl's wriggling cunt, as Luke flogged her arse a deeper and deeper crimson, until her bruises merged one with another in a jagged tapestry of crusted dark ridges.

Fingers deep in her sopping cunt forest, Amy masturbated with coos of pleasure; at the fifteenth cane stroke to Severe's squirming bare, she paused in her frig to release a steaming jet of piss all over Severe's blonde mane. The pinioned, flogged schoolgirl sobbed in helpless, frustrated shame, as Luke's naked cockpole swayed over his cruel mistress's ravaged fesses. Vip! Vip!

'Urrgh! Ooh!' Severe gurgled, her face soaked in Amy's piss, and her voice muffled by the carpet. 'Stop, you filthy cunt, stop . . .'

Come spilled from her twitching gash flaps, soaking her wriggling thighs, and dripping to the carpet, between her knees.

'The dirty slut,' panted Amy, wriggling, as she masturbated. 'Not content with foul language, she's wetting Coz Compaigne's carpet.'

'You must be punished, mistress,' Luke said. 'You, especially, will understand. I'm going to stripe your whole bottom, from thighs to haunch to spine.'

Vip!

'*Ahh!* Ooh! Bastard! Fucking cunt!'

Luke's teeth bared in a rictus. 'I'm truly sorry to hear such vileness from your lips, mistress,' he panted.

Vip! Vip! Vip! Twisting the cane, he laid three savage cuts in her squirming bum cleft, darkening the flesh to crimson and slashing her squarely on the anus bud.

'Ooh!' Severe howled. 'Swine! Dirty bugger!'

Luke caned the bare bum to 37 strokes, until Severe was well striped, with numerous cuts to her tender thigh backs and top buttock, while her haunches were blistered with livid bruises. As her flogged bottom squirmed, the schoolgirl wept and whimpered, drool cascading from her lips and tears flooding her eyes.

'Stop,' she said, sobbing. 'Luke, my darling, please stop. You're hurting your mistress awfully. Do anything, I beg you, but not this.'

'I must obey your command,' Luke gasped, throwing aside the cane.

79

Squatting, he dragged her hips towards his cock, and mounted her.

'Wait! No!' Severe squealed.

With a savage thrust, Luke's cock was inside her anus.

'Ahh!' she screamed.

He thrust again, his cock sunk halfway in her hole, and penetrating her rectum.

'No! No! Not that!' the trembling schoolgirl shrieked.

'You said *anything*,' Luke panted.

A further thrust plunged his cock fully to her colon, with his balls squashing her buttock meat. Luke lowered himself to straddle and crush the writhing bare girl, as he began to encule her bumhole in rapid, powerful buggery. Severe's sobs and squeals filled the gentle summer air.

'I can take nine inches of cock meat up my hole,' said Amy scornfully. 'Can't *you*, bitch?'

Amy masturbated herself to fluttering, shrill orgasm, her cunt dripping come over Severe's piss-soaked hair, then released Severe's wrists. As the schoolgirl wriggled helplessly under Luke's cock, which was pounding her arse root, Amy rose to fetch the giant rubber dildo and strapped it at her cunt. She squatted behind Luke, and oiled the dildo with the come dripping from her cooze, then placed the tip at Luke's anus. She ordered him to pause, and he obeyed, allowing his cocktip to rest at the schoolgirl's mashed colon, just long enough, so that Amy could sink her dildo into his own bumhole. He groaned, and continued to bugger the sobbing schoolgirl, while Amy, adapting to his rhythm, buggered the boy, her hips slapping Luke's arse, with the dildo plunged deep, slamming the boy's colon.

'God, that hurts,' he gasped, his face twisted in pain. 'You'll suffer for this, Miss Severe.'

He began to spank her bare buttocks, as he buggered the girl, turning her squeals and whimpers into screams. Come poured from Severe's cunt, into the carpet, sodden with piss. Luke's cock squelched in the schoolgirl's copious arse grease, dripping onto his balls from her stretched anus.

Amy vigorously fucked the boy, while masturbating, with her fingers plunged deep in her forest of sopping cunt hairs, and tweaking the engorged clitty, peeping from her slit.

'Is that good, Luke?' panted Amy.

'Yes, yes,' he moaned. 'I hate you. God, it's wonderful. Fill me, Amy, fuck my arse, split my bum, bugger me senseless . . . oh, please, miss, fuck me harder.'

'Oh, yes,' Amy groaned, slamming her cock between the boy's buttocks. 'Spurt in that bitch's hole, Luke, give her all your spunk, right up her. I'm coming . . . *ooh!*'

Spunk squirted, overflowing from Severe's arse lips, as Luke washed her colon in a bath of hot spunk. Severe squealed, writhing in her own orgasm, with a torrent of come from her flapping gash soaking her thighs and feet, and pooling on the carpet, with her arse grease and drool, amid Amy's piss. There was a click, then a bang, as the door crashed open.

'Well!' boomed Commander Compaigne. 'What's this, Amy? Fun and games on the lower decks?'

With a plop, Amy withdrew the dildo from Luke's anus. 'Commander!' she cried. 'How lovely! I've missed you so.'

'I see. Buggery amongst the tars, eh? That's a whipping offence.'

'They are a smutty crew,' Amy gasped, kissing the commander's lips, and rubbing the swelling bulge in his uniform trousers. 'I'm sure you are up to punishing them.'

She slipped her hand under his waistband, and began to massage his naked cock; then, she unbuttoned his naval fly, and extracted the stiff cockpole, which gleamed erect, a full ten inches. Amy opened her mouth wide, and got her lips around the massive glans, which she began to suck vigorously. Luke tried to withdraw his cock from Severe's anus, but the squeezing pressure of her sphincter was too strong for him.

'No . . . no,' mewled the enculed schoolgirl. 'Don't leave me . . .'

'Can't disobey a lady, Luke, my boy,' breezed the commander.

Shooing Amy away from his cock and tucking himself in, the commander ordered her to fetch ropes from the barn. Blushing and sweating, Luke lay on top of Severe, whose buttocks clenched his tool in a vice. When Amy returned with a selection of ropes and hawsers, the commander lashed the two prone bodies tightly together, with ropes around waists, teats, balls and thighs, so that Luke's cock was quite unable to escape from the school-girl's anal embrace.

'Please, sir, it was all my fault,' quavered Luke.

'Nonsense, Luke,' said the commander, chortling. 'It's landlubber talk that the gent is always in the wrong. In the navy, the female is the beast of the species, and must be soundly punished for it. The carpet's a mess and someone must pay. Amy, my dear, as senior rating present, you will mount the table and take number-three position, if you please.'

'Oh, Commander, I beg you, be gentle,' she whimpered.

He picked up the cane, and swished the air, nodding and licking his lips. '*At* the double,' he barked.

Amy climbed onto the table, and lay on her back, with her buttocks at the table's edge and her legs straight up, splayed at an angle of thirty degrees. Her arms were stretched out at a wider angle, with her wrists twisted, so that she clutched the table rim. Licking his lips, the commander gazed at her exposed cunt and arse furrow.

'A lovely gash,' he purred, 'ripe for fucking. But first . . .'

He lifted the cane, and lashed her across the lower thighs. Vip!

'Ooh!' Amy shrieked.

Vip! The second cut took her on the upper thighs, leaving a dark slash, inches from her cunt. Amy's whole body jerked, her titties wobbling vigorously.

'Ohh! Ooh!' she wailed.

Vip! He flogged her on the exposed buttocks, then set to a rhythm of caning, striping the thighs and nates, to form a frame of weals around the winking wet cunt, dribbling come into her bruises. Vip! Vip!

'Ahh! Oh, please, my bum can't take it,' Amy groaned, her legs shuddering violently, but still erect, like storm-tossed masts, and her breasts shaking like jellies.

'In that case . . .'

The commander approached, and lifted the cane over her naked breasts.

'No!' Amy screamed.

Vip!

'Ooh!'

He began to whip the helpless bare titties, striping them with cruel red welts, while Amy, legs still up, screamed and shuddered, shaking her head from side to side and banging the table with it.

'No! No!'

Vip!

'*Ohh!*'

Watching Amy whipped, Luke's cock stiffened, inside Severe's rectum.

'Fuck me, Luke,' whimpered Severe, milking his rigid tool with her arse sphincter. 'Fuck me, my slave.'

Groaning in his bonds, Luke jerked his loins, and began a slow buggery of the trussed schoolgirl. The commander's cane having reduced Amy's titties to a quivering mass of crimson bruises, he reapplied his strokes to her thighs and buttocks.

Vip!

'Oh! Oh, you cruel beast, sir!'

Vip! Vip!

'Please stop! I'll do anything.'

'Girls are not there to do anything,' said the commander. 'They are there to have things done to them.'

Vip! He laid a cut straight to her cunt flaps.

'Ahh!' she howled.

Vip! Vip!

'*Ooh! Ohh!*'

The cane lashed the squirming bare gash, as Amy screamed and wept. After the fortieth stroke to Amy's purpling thighs and arse, he laid down the cane and took out his massive, stiff cock.

'Watch this, Luke,' he said. 'Sometimes, a chap fancies a bit of the exotic. Look how wet I've made your auntie.'

Come streamed from Amy's flogged gash. With a single thrust, the commander sank his cock into her cunt and began to fuck her. Luke and Severe both stared, as the huge, come-soaked tool slammed, squelching, between Amy's swollen slit lips. The commander delivered his load of spunk, and rested for a minute, without uncunting. Then, he withdrew his tool, newly stiff, and plunged it into Amy's anus, right to his balls.

'Ooh! That's a real man. Oh! Oh! Yes!' she squealed, exploding at once in orgasm, as the commander began a vigorous enculement.

'Fuck me, slave, fuck my arse,' whimpered Severe. 'I want your cream up my hole. Bum-fuck me, brat.'

Wriggling in his bonds, Luke buggered with all his force, squeezing his cocktip right into her sigmoid colon and making her squeal in pain, as his hard glans mashed the soft tissue. Luke grunted and, soon, spunk poured from his tool into Severe's writhing arse, with come squirting from her gash flaps, to smear her belly and thighs.

'Yes, I'm coming!' Severe yelped. 'God, that's good! Hurt me, fuck my hole, split me . . . yes! Oh! Yes!'

As Luke's sperm spurted from his peehole, up the schoolgirl's colon, Severe erupted in a savage orgasm, squirming so hard that she loosened her ropes. Their two slippery nude bodies parted, with a squelching smack; the commander looked round at the loud plop of Luke's cock, ejected from Severe's bumhole.

'You are a noisy fucker, my dear little Severe,' he said, with his balls slapping loudly against Amy's squirming fesses, as he buggered her.

'Yes, sir,' Amy panted. 'Fuck my bum, do me hard, split me open, it hurts so much . . . fuck me, fuck me . . . oh!'

'You too,' said the commander.

'Ah! Ah! I'm bursting . . . *yes!*' Amy gasped, and her slit spurted massive come, as she climaxed, with bubbles of spunk drooling from her anus, as the commander's load of spunk overflowed her wealed buttocks.

'Now,' the commander said amiably, 'I think, Severe, you will don your maid's pinny, and make us all a nice cup of my favourite Brazilian coffee, before I proceed to *your* chastisement.'

'Yes, Coz,' panted Severe, curtsying.


At Clear House, no mention was made of the scene at Poldipple, and Amy comported herself with complete ladylike decorum. In the days that followed, as the summer mellowed to autumn, so too did Amy's attitude to Luke mellow. She no longer watched him, stripped, at his work, and in fact neglected to give him much to do. Frequently absent, without explanation, she would return somewhat flushed and tousled, and drop ominous hints that it would soon be time Luke got a job. Luke, for his part, moped, unsummoned for chastisement by Severe, his mistress, and fearing she no longer wanted his submission.

Matters came to a head one evening, when Amy made some slighting remark about the much greater virility of older men, which Luke chose to take personally. He accused her of being in the thrall of Commander Compaigne, and ordered her to take her pants down for a thrashing. She sneered that the summer of lustful fun was over, and it was time for Luke to leave her home and support himself.

'I've put Clear House up for rent,' she said. 'I'm moving in with my master, the commander. He has no objection to my friendship with Severe. In fact, there's plenty of room for everybody, except you. Severe herself told me that. She wants nothing further to do with submissive worms.'

Enraged, Luke grabbed the squealing Amy, ripped off her skirt and panties, and pinned her to the table, with her bared bottom wriggling and her legs kicking. He administered a caning of 44 cuts, reducing Amy's buttocks to a squirming mass of striped flesh, with weals all over her naked thighs and bottom. She lay, weeping and cursing him, and he thrust his cock into her anus, making her scream in pain, to give her a particularly hard buggery, which she complained was the most savage he had ever given.

'But your cock is too small,' she spat, before his spunk washed her arse root, and she seethed, in her own painful climax. 'Even your arse doesn't squirm under cane like a real man's. Severe says so.'

'You're lying,' he cried. 'I'm going to have this out with her.'

'Don't come back, you perverted swine,' Amy said with a sob. 'You're finished in Cornwall.'

Luke rushed into the night, and ran to Poldipple Hall, tears streaming down his cheeks. He rang the bell, repeatedly, until Severe answered. She was wearing a diaphanous nightie, which exposed her nude body underneath; it was covered in cane weals and bruises to the breasts, belly, thighs and fesses. Her hair was dishevelled, and her eyes were red from weeping. She listened to him beg, from his knees, that she should take him back, and inflict the most dreadful punishment she cared to.

'Don't you remember, mistress, I swore to attend you as your slave, wherever and whenever? Surely you owe me my submission?'

'Get up,' she sneered. 'I owe you nothing. My God, you're pathetic. Even your stupid *name*'s pathetic. *Luke!*'

A male voice echoed from within, but it was not the commander's. 'Severe, you lazy sow, get your blasted arse back in here,' it drawled, with aristocratic nonchalance. 'My blasted decanter's empty. I've a good mind to give you another bare-bum thrashin'.'

'Coming, Justin,' she called, her face flushing with happiness. 'Now there's a *real* man.' She slammed the door in Luke's face.

# 6

# Naked Licks

'Of course, you've no qualifications on paper, but that's not the main thing, for a physical education teacher, is it?' said Miss Tupper brightly. 'You look strong, but not too, um, *butch –*' she simpered '– lithe body, really quite pretty, with a nice tight bum, if I may say so. Girls always notice a chap's juicy bottom, as I'm sure you're aware. It gains their respect. And I sense you are a gentleman. You're a games player, I take it?'

Outside, bare-legged girls in frilly skirtlets batted balls on the Oxfordshire sward.

'Why, yes, miss,' Luke said.

'The only thing our girls have in common is a love of games,' said Miss Tupper, 'sometimes the most sly, nasty, girlish games, especially where males are concerned. That, and being stinky rich. You've never been ... *poor*, have you?'

'Gosh, no, miss,' Luke blurted.

'Thank heaven for that. You see, rich people are different, especially girls. They are spoiled, pampered, used to getting their own way, and having everything they want. That's why they come here at seventeen or eighteen, to give them a lick of discipline, before they invade the world as full grown-ups, to wreak havoc in men's hearts. Our girls are chosen for physical beauty, too. Rich *and* beautiful girls are quite unmanageable, and that is why Licks is the most expensive school in England, apart from Crushards, our associate boys' school, down in Berkshire. They have a similar policy – that if unruly boys have to bare up for shameful lashing by females, their desire for vengeance will make them go out and conquer. So we have gentleman as well as lady teachers to *try* to manage the girls. You are familiar, I hope, with the usual tools of corporal punishment, the basis of a girl's training here. The code of rules is deliberately strict. So, a miscreant girl is sentenced to "licks a half 'un" – that is, six cuts – or "licks a dozen" or even "licks at discretion", which is jolly tough, and the thing the girls most dread. Minor offences are punished by beatings on panties, pyjamas, gym shorts or nightie, but serious licks are on the naked bottom, which is "naked licks". You went to a top-class school, of course, so your own bottom will be no stranger to the cane.'

Luke was aware of the school's curious predilection for traditional punishment, but tried to sound as casual as the young headmistress, herself seeming scarcely older than a sixth-form girl, in discussing the question. Inside, his lust for vengeance simmered, a hot glow of desire, to make each and every female squirm in agony and shame, as she – *they*, the filthy, cruel sluts! – had made him squirm.

'No, miss. I have been beaten on my buttocks. I may say, I hope without indelicacy, that I have often been flogged on the bare.'

'Capital! Smarts like the dickens, eh?'

Luke made a face, but smiled. 'Very much so. Therefore, I think I can bring a knowledge of the matter to any necessary discipline.'

'These girls understand discipline precisely when it is *not* necessary,' Miss Tupper declared. 'That's what keeps them submissive – the fear of capricious caning. Our schoolmasters must be thoroughly dominant, motivated by a healthy desire for power over a gaggle of giggling, vicious and froth-headed young belles. A real man always has the hareem instinct. Have you, Mr Redruth?'

'Very much so, miss, I must admit.'

'Excellent. As your bottom is accustomed to receiving the cane, I dare say your wrist is no stranger to wielding it?'

'Happily, I have plenty of experience in that department, miss,' Luke said, rather smugly. 'Cane, strap, riding crop, even the whip, on particularly recalcitrant bottoms.'

'Any experience in thrashing the female of the species?'

Luke blushed, crossing his legs to conceal the rising of his cock. 'As it happens, yes, miss,' he replied smugly.

Miss Tupper pressed her palms together. 'I trust you didn't feel any namby-pamby sympathy,' she purred, licking her lips, 'to prevent you from doing the job, and delivering a jolly hard thrashing to a girl's naked bottom?'

Luke's cock was straining stiff. 'No, miss. I feel that a vicious miscreant, whether boy or girl, earns punishment. A girl's buttocks are just as tough as a boy's, and can take it on the bare.'

'The right answer. Girls need blistering just as hard as boys, probably harder, as they are far more wicked. Here at Licks, we don't school them in computer rot or any other fancy modern nonsense, but in ladylike deportment, and sweetness of smile and demeanour, with plenty of hard exercise, cold showers and crimson bums. Thus, they are fit to succeed in the world as ladies always have, by bending men to their wills. Of course, the way a properly submissive girl enslaves her man is by baring her bottom to his cane, so that he can't do without her. You won't object, if I put you to an immediate test?'

'Why, no, but I don't quite see . . .'

Miss Tupper rose, and strutted from her desk, her long legs quivering in their sheer nylons with a sheen, on wobbly stiletto heels, placing her at an inch taller than Luke himself. She was wearing a short grey skirt over blue nylon hose and a white blouse, so that she looked indistinguishable from a schoolgirl, especially as Luke computed her age at no more than thirty, like Amy's. Miss Tupper seemed from the same stable as Amy: trim, tan, with firm, bulging buttocks and heavy, jutting teats, bouncing perkily, under the too-tight cloth, with no apparent need of restraint, although the head-mistress was wearing a rather obvious scalloped sheer bra, with her big plum nipples visible through bra and blouse. Over that, her glossy chestnut hair bobbed in a flick, like some cute, all-American film actress of the 1950s.

The teats and buttocks quivered, as she stood on tiptoe to open her high cabinet door, and reveal a rack of shiny canes. Her long legs stretched fully, and her skirt rode up, exposing her scarlet sussies and panties – a mere thong, wedged deeply in the crack of her firm bare arse. She held her exposed position for almost a minute, while Luke, heartily erect, feasted his eyes on her bared flesh and skimpies, then looked round, blushing slightly.

'Have to keep them up here or the blasted girls will be at them,' she said, without explaining why a girl could not reach as far as she could.

'You mean . . . you wish me to cane a girl here and now?' Luke stammered.

'No time like the present. Have you any preferences?'

There was a supple, whippy-looking ashplant; a gleaming, crook-handled willow; a sturdy hawthorn; or a long, viciously thick rattan. Luke gulped.

'I think I should leave it up to you, miss,' he said. 'You are going to summon a girl, just for me to cane her?'

Desperately, he tried to conceal his erection. He was sure Miss Tupper had noticed. She picked out the ashplant, purring that it was nice and springy, and always raised good, coloured welts on a bare bum, then looked him straight in the eye. She allowed her gaze to slide down his body, and fix on his bulging groin. She licked her lips, and laughed, a smoky chuckle, deep in her throat.

'Why, no, Mr Redruth,' she said. 'If you will be so kind, you are going to cane *me*.'

She handed him the cane, accidentally on purpose letting the tip brush his erection, then the handle stroke his balls; she twirled round, bent over her desk and lifted her skirt, tucking it neatly into her belt, and baring her buttocks, framed in the frilly scarlet sussies. Arms outstretched, she gripped the far corners of her desk. Her legs strained, quite far apart, so that the arse cheeks were taut, and, beneath the minuscule loop of her thong, Luke could espy her anus bud, and the outer lips of her cunt, wreathed in heavy pubic thatch, whose shiny chestnut curls seemed to straggle across her bum cleft and upper thighs – in fact, everywhere. His erection throbbed painfully and rock hard.

'I ... I ...' he stammered, blushing.

'Don't be shy, Mr Redruth,' trilled Miss Tupper. 'You're a man of the world, and have seen many girls' bare bottoms, I'm sure.'

'I couldn't cane my superior, miss.'

'Why, you have caned girls, and I am one, am I not?'

'Yes, miss, and a most ... most ... an awfully nice one. I couldn't possibly cane *your* bottom.'

'Are you suggesting there is something wrong with my bottom? That I am abnormal? That I couldn't bear it?'

'No, no, of course not. It's just that – please don't think me silly – I'd be afraid to incur your displeasure, and that in revenge, you would order me to bare up, take my trousers off and present *my* naked buttocks, you know, um, for a really severe swishing, the cane raising dreadful crimson welts on my skin, making my bum squirm most shamefully to your lovely eyes, and the horrid, smarting agony in my fesses making me weep, like some abject slave.'

Miss Tupper laughed, her eyes twinkling, and glanced at his bulging crotch. She licked her lips.

'You are awfully sweet, with quite a poetic imagination. The girls you caned – I assume, with a vigorous young man like you, Mr Redruth, it was "girls" in the plural, and always on the bare?'

'Yes,' Luke gasped hoarsely.

'So much the better. Technically, I'm wearing panties, but, as you can see, this thong is a panties only in name, and dashed uncomfortable it is too. What a girl must do to feel pretty! So it's naked licks – just my luck, eh? Your cane will lash me on my bare cheeks, and I do hope you'll lash only on skin, and be careful to avoid ripping my sussies and panties. It's such a bore to have to take them off for each caning. I'm feeling a bit shivery, for you are a strong young man, and I am only a helpless girl, shivering, with my buttocks naked for the cane. I may tell you that I'm not looking forward to it.'

'I shall obey your instructions, miss,' Luke said with a sigh, 'but please tell me how many strokes, and how hard?'

'No, no, that is for you to decide, Mr Redruth. The aim, d'you see, is to instil terror into puppyish girl brats and, for the moment, I am one of them. I'm feeling so trembly, so scared, and afraid I'll wet myself – please don't laugh – and that is *just* the way you must make a miscreant girl feel.'

'Very well,' said Luke solemnly. 'I shall give you six of the best, Miss Tupper – licks a half 'un.'

His heart thumped, and his cock throbbed.

*That luscious peach, bare for stripes . . . if only it were my arse, and Miss Tupper waling me. Stripped to her undies, her titties bouncing, and thighs and bum rippling, as she thrashed my naked buttocks to ribbons. Then, through my tears, to kiss her feet, lick her soles and take her toes in my mouth, begging her to forgive her slave . . .*

He frowned, in a grimace of anguish, putting the ignominious desire from him.

'Six of the best. Ooh,' she whimpered.

'Very hard,' he murmured, flexing his cane.

'Oh. But why, sir?'

'Well, um, for your misdeeds.'

'But I've said I'm sorry, sir,' she wailed. 'All the girls lift their nighties up to masturbate, and I was caught by pure bad luck. If that rotten old bat Miss Tupper let us have boyfriends, we wouldn't need to masturbate, or frig each other's quims. I think I'm going to cry.'

Miss Tupper's ripe fesses began to tremble, like peach jellies, with a distinct gleam of moisture at her pendant gash lips. Luke frowned.

'You insult Miss Tupper? Why, that is a vile crime.'

'Why, she masturbates all the time, more than any of us. Please don't punish me further for saying so, sir,' whimpered the headmistress, wriggling her buttocks, so that her anus bud winked at Luke, from her slithering scarlet thong. Her svelte, coltish thighs rippled in their nylon stockings, as the buttocks tensed.

'But I must,' Luke blurted. 'You shall take an extra three strokes, maid, for that insult.'

Miss Tupper's arse cheeks trembled, and her quim began to drip onto the carpet. 'Nngh . . .' she moaned.

'And a further three,' Luke spat, 'for the crime of telling lies. Miss Tupper is not a . . . as you called her. She is young and vigorous, a flower of girlhood, her body firm and curved enough to excite any male, and an example of beauty and decorum to you all. Her legs are glorious columns of muscle and flesh, her bottom, twin pears of bare delight, her feet, as dainty and delicate as can be, forced in two lovely prisons of black leather, with points, fit to stab most cruelly a male slave's body . . . the rest, the swan's neck, and full, firm breasts, are for the imagination. I'm not sure Miss Tupper herself shouldn't be baring her bottom to my cane, for a dreadful licking, as punishment for her beauty, powerful enough to enslave any male, and make him beg to be trampled by those luscious feet, crushed by those gorgeous big fesses, whipped raw by those graceful hands.'

'Nngh . . .' whined Miss Tupper, her cunt oozing come.

'That makes a dozen strokes of the cane, very hard, on the naked buttocks, miss – licks a dozen.'

'Mm . . .' she bleated.

'Do you agree to your chastisement, maid?'

'Yes!' gasped Miss Tupper. 'Oh, quickly, please . . .'

Luke took position, standing right on top of her croup, beaded in perspiration, and trembling with gooseflesh. He raised the cane and twirled it, ruffling her hair and blouse, with a humming swishy noise.

'Ooh,' moaned the girl, her arse flans aquiver.

Abruptly, he caned her full across the fleshy mid-fesses. Vip!

'Ooh!' she squealed.

Her cheeks clenched tight, hiding the trembling scarlet thong strap, and her whole bum wriggled, with her long legs rippling, as they jerked straight behind her quivering nates. A pink weal sprang livid on the naked skin. Luke waited until her buttocks unclenched, and the thong and anus were once more visible, before delivering the second stroke. Vip! This one took her high, just under her spine, on the thin, tender skin of top fesse.

'Ahh!' she shrieked, her whipped bum squirming wildly. 'Ooh! Oh! You beast!'

'Steady, maid,' he said, panting, 'there are a full ten strokes to go, and they shan't get any softer.'

'Ooh, sir!' she said, sobbing. 'You are so strong, so masterful.'

Vip!

'Ooh! Ouch! Go easy, sir, please. I can't stand it. I've never been caned so hard.'

'You shouldn't masturbate, you smutty girl. Is it true, then, that you frig a lot?'

'All the time, sir. We have no cock to pleasure us. It is dreadful. Our holes long for ramming. Miss Tupper thinks that sports and cold showers will drain our energy, but in truth, they make us hotter and wetter for cock.'

Miss Tupper's cunt dripped come, in a steady pit-pit to her carpet. Luke's cock throbbed. Vip! He lashed her thigh tops, raising a livid stripe.

'*Ahh!*'

This was revenge: for all Severe's wounds and insults, for his humiliation by women, for the brutal welts striping his naked arse, for his tears of pain and submission and pleas for mercy, as a cruel woman flogged him. *This* was what Luke wanted, Vip! He sliced the cane between her wriggling buttocks, lashing her right in the cleft and stroking the quivering crinkled anus bud.

'*Ohh!*'

94

Her legs jerked straight, raising her squirming bottom from the desk to reveal a pool of come, where her dripping cunt forest rubbed the wood.

'You're cruel,' she said, sobbing. 'I've never been beaten so harshly, sir, not even as a naughty girl.'

Miss Tupper's fesses were striped in glowing crimson weals, which, as Luke continued to lash the naked skin, puffed up to cruel blackened ridges. The drips of come from her cunt, mashed to the desk, became a flow, as the squirming girl ground her pubes and clitty against the wood.

'So you have experienced the cane before, maid?' he said, panting.

'Yes, sir.'

'On the bare buttocks?'

'Yes, sir. At my last school, I was an especially naughty little girl – smoking, masturbating under the sheets at night, and frigging between classes with other girls in the lavatory, even when I knew I should earn a bare-beating. I couldn't help wanking off, for I have such vivid fantasies, that obsess me, make my twat sopping, and I just have to relieve myself. I dream of a luscious hot boy, with his big tool, doing me, wickedly, in my bum. Pounding my tripes, and filling me with his huge hot cock, then spurting all his lovely hot spunk right up my hole. There! Am I not the vilest slut? I know I need the cane on my naughty bottom, and cheeks well glowing. The headmistress had a horrid ritual of parading a miscreant girl in her nightie, past the gauntlet of prefects, each holding her sizzler, as we called a school cane. She had to hold her nightie up at her neck, showing herself nude, and take a cut on her bare bottom from each cane; only then, when she was sobbing and her fesses were waled with nine throbbing stingers, was she permitted to bend over and touch her toes for a stiff sixer on bare from the headmistress's willow wand. How it hurt. How my hot bum stung, and how I wanked afterwards.'

'You are a thoroughly naughty maid,' Luke hissed. 'You deserve to taste *my* sizzler.'

Vip!

'Oh!'

Vip!

'Ah! Ouch!'

Vip! Another cut sliced the arse cleft, this one savagely wealing the anus pucker.

'*Ahh!*' she shrieked.

Miss Tupper's bottom rose and fell, slapping her cunt on the wet desk, then grinding her slit hard, with little sucking squelches, as her flaps mashed the surface. Between her thighs spread wide, and across the wet dangling pubic jungle, Luke could see her swollen pink clitty, mashed and frotted against the wood. Vip!

'*Ahh!* Oh! Ooh!'

'This is the last, miss.'

Vip! Her buttocks clenched and she squirmed madly, thumping her clit on the desk.

'Ahh! Ahh! *Yes!*'

Come gushed from her writhing cunt to flow onto the stained, sopping carpet.

'Ah . . . ah . . . ah . . .' she panted, in evident spasm, as her knees jerked, and she slapped the floor with her toes.

Her entire arse crack was dripping with come, the massive pubic jungle a swamp of tangled wet hairs, sopping with her cunt ooze. Luke's cock throbbed; he panted, heart racing, and could no longer tolerate the sight of the scarred bare fesses, writhing below him, with the flogged anus winking and pouting amid the glaring purple cane weals. Cursing, he stripped off his trousers and released his cock, which sprang up, rigid and quivering, inches from the girl's succulent arse. He parted her cheeks, and thrust his helmet between the buttocks, with his peehole squashing her anus bud.

'Uhh,' Miss Tupper moaned. 'I need to be punished, for I'm a wicked girl . . . ooh!'

Her arm slipped from the corner of the desk and plunged between her thighs, where she began to blatantly masturbate. Savagely, he penetrated her anus with his throbbing tool, gave another thrust and sank his cock into her rectum; a final jerk of his arse slammed his glans to her colon.

'Oh! Oh, it hurts!' she said with a sob. 'Yes, sir, punish me.'

Luke began to bugger her squirming arse, his cock slid up the squeezing anal passage, lubricated by her copious arse grease. Come sluiced from her writhing cunt.

'Urrgh . . . urrgh,' she groaned. 'It's agony. You're going to split my belly in two . . . plough me harder, fuck my hole raw.'

Luke buggered fiercely for over two minutes, until he grunted and a bead of his cream bubbled over the stretched lips of her anus.

'Yes, give me all your sperm,' she moaned, masturbating her clit. 'Fill my bum with your cream, spunk in my belly, do me. I'm almost there. Oh! I'm coming . . .'

As Luke pumped his sperm into her colon, she writhed and wriggled, drooling, in a new orgasm, more intense than her first. Gasping, he withdrew his cock with a loud plop, despite the squeezing of her anal sphincter, as if the headmistress did not wish to let him escape. He rapidly made himself decent, while Miss Tupper rose, tucked her buttocks into her panties, smoothed down her skirt, and smiled brightly at Luke.

'Well!' she gasped. '*That* was jolly good. Those were quite some stingers. You'll excuse me if I remain standing. Cripes, they smart. Of course, as a mature lady, I can take a beating, and judge it rationally, without all sorts of girly whimpers and snivels. Your stroking action is first class, young man. I think you'd be just the chap to strike terror into the sixth form.'

'I'll certainly do my best, miss,' Luke said eagerly.

Miss Tupper smiled. 'In that case, you're hired, Mr Redruth. Full bed and board is of course included in your salary package. Can you start at once? I mean, this instant?'

Luke thought of his grimy bedsitter in Reading, with its rent arrears, and his meagre, expendable belongings; he nodded assent.

'Capital. You'll be thrown in at the deep end, but you look like a chap who can handle himself.'

She rubbed her bottom, and grimaced. 'I like the way you handled *me*. But not a word to anyone, especially Matron. If the girls found out, there'd be hell to pay. They are a jealous and vengeful bunch, the beastly little sluts.'

It was the matron, Miss Rhona Cluster, who showed Luke to his quarters: a spacious and airy apartment in the school's north tower, with a balcony overlooking the lake, coppices and playing fields. He had a washbasin, with a shared bathroom at the end of the corridor. Miss Cluster was a trim, pertly titted blonde, her hair bunched in a luxuriant bun, on which perched a jaunty white nurse's cap; she seemed even younger than the headmistress, with a swaying carriage of long, white-nyloned legs, and jutting round buttocks, beneath the tightest of starched white skirts, which Luke sensed was meant to tease.

'I know boarding-school chaps are usually terrified of Matron,' she chirped, at Luke's coyness, 'for she whops their bums. But you mustn't be in awe of me, unless you need an enema, which I'm rather good at. A clyster from Cluster, the girls call it. I shan't whop your bum, unless you absolutely want me to. I'm a healer, not a wealer.'

She burst into a musical, tinkling laughter, which made her plum-nippled breast cones bounce in their clinging white blouse; Luke smiled politely, trying to pass that off as a joke, but a sensuous glint in Miss Cluster's eyes suggested that in certain circumstances, it might well not be. He tried not to stare at her long, coltish legs and rippling thighs, encased in white sheer nylon, under a skirt quite brief for a medical officer. Instead, he gazed at her slender feet in their white leather slingback shoes, with pointed toecaps of burnished brass, and her long, dainty toes outlined under the soft leather.

He looked up, grinning rather sheepishly, and hoping she would not notice his cock stiffening, as she explained the daily maid service, arrangements for laundry and the like. Miss Cluster opened his wardrobe, and he saw an array of canes, like Miss Tupper's. The matron giggled, at his surprise.

'Those are your most important tools,' she said, po-faced, 'I mean, scholastic tools, of course. But don't think you'll practise on my bum, sir! I saw you eyeing my fesses.'

'I assure you, I wasn't,' he stammered.

'Why not?' she demanded, frowning, in what seemed genuine puzzlement. 'Don't you find them ripe?'

'Oh, wonderfully ripe, miss,' he murmured, blushing.

She chucked him under the chin. 'You wouldn't lie to me.'

'No.'

'Good. If I thought a fellow wasn't scanning my behind, and dreaming of spanking me, I'd be awfully cross. Why else do we girls have arses?'

A bell clanged, and Miss Cluster said it was time for luncheon. Luke followed her through winding oaken corridors, scented with antiquity, into the low, raftered refectory. The girls were already sitting decorously at tables, and all heads swivelled to scrutinise the new master, with a buzz of whispers and giggles, until Miss Tupper, at high table, rapped the floor with her cane.

While Miss Cluster joined one of the senior girls' tables, Luke took his place at high table, amongst the other staff, who nodded their polite greetings. Miss Tupper, at the head, made introductions. There were two other males, among the staff of seven: Tim Playfair, a hulking, cheerful, muscled fellow, of craggy brow, no-nonsense crew cut, and crushing handshake; and Martin Morton, with thinning hair plastered to his scalp, a straggly nicotine moustache, a bookworm's watery eyes, behind big horn-rimmed glasses, and a shabby brown suit, stained with cigarette burns, flapping on his lank frame. One taught 'arts', and the other 'science', although Luke quickly forgot which. He was more interested in the four schoolmistresses: Misses Joly Goosnaugh, Irena Trench, Arabel Stiffence and Liliane Lupus.

All were young, in their twenties, their long hair lush and shiny, but modestly swept up or back, and dressed very much in the manner of the girls, save for the black gowns draped over their backs: white blouses, with striped silk ties, grey pleated skirts, hemmed high, to show, in each case, long legs, topped by ripe fesse pears, and powerful thighs, rippling under a variety of pastel-hued nylons.

Joly and Arabel had their pleated skirts hitched quite impudently up, so that Luke could not avoid seeing their stocking tops and sussies, pink and baby blue, respectively, and the sliver of pink panties at Joly's groin, while, in Arabel's case, he espied a triangle of creamy, shaven cunt flesh. Miss Stiffence (needlepoint, ancient history, physical geography and conversational French) was wearing no knickers. Every mistress had hard, bright eyes, like Severe Compaigne's. His cock swelled, and the svelte blonde Arabel met his eyes, with a mocking, flinty twinkle of her own.

Over their tomato soup with croutons, Tim Playfair held forth. The only thing these damned girls respected, he assured Luke, was tough love: the slaughter on the hockey field or netball court, the route march, the hour's running on the spot, the hundred press-ups, the freezing cold shower and sound sizzling on bare bum, with rod or strap.

'Tame them and shame them. The cane's the only lingo they understand. You look like the bloke to give it to them. I like the cut of your jib, Luke, old chap.'

Martin Morton smiled wanly. Thin slices of rainbow-hued roast lamb were served by teetering stiletto-heeled schoolmaids in rather daring frilly French costumes, with black fishnet stockings, high frilly skirtlets, permitting a view of their full sussies and minuscule white nylon panties, scarcely covering their otherwise fully bared buttocks. Their lacy caps were set rakishly, threatening to fall off on the exposed portions of their bottoms, where fresh cane stripes glowed a sullen mauve.

'At the slightest hint of rebellion,' Tim expounded, 'you give them licks, old boy. A giggle – the cane! A smirk – the cane! Dumb insolence – the cane! A filly doing nothing at all, that's suspicious – the cane! You have to impress them with the force of personality. I'm sure Morton agrees.'

'Oh, yes,' muttered Martin Morton, chewing disconsolately on a piece of lamb.

'We ladies agree too,' murmured Arabel.

Suddenly, Luke felt a pressure at his groin. He reached down to scratch, and found himself clutching a stockinged toe, rather moist and smelly with girl sweat. Curious, he felt the moist toes, which were encased in a lady's nylon stocking, all right, but one designed like a glove, in which each toe had its own pouch. He replaced the linen table cloth, and, trembling, continued his meal.

The toe – toes, now – were rubbing his cock, in a way that allowed no misinterpretation. He scanned the faces of the ladies, all bland, and imperturbably munching. The toes performd a sensuous dance, rubbing and squeezing, until his cock throbbed so hard, he felt it should burst from his trousers. Arabel dropped a fork.

'Silly me,' she trilled, and slid under the table.

Luke started, as he felt a hand clawing at his crotch, unzipping his flies. Cool, nimble fingers pulled out his naked cock, and he gulped, as it was plunged in a hot, wet throat, which licked and sucked him, for an instant, before withdrawing.

Across the table, Arabel emerged, clutching her lost fork, and smiled sweetly at him, with dazzling white teeth amid wide pink lips, which she licked, with viper flicks of her glistening tongue. His exposed cock strained, and he gasped, dropping a piece of meat with a splash, into his mint sauce, as his bare glans was squeezed between two nyloned toes, which began a gentle frottage.

The conversation continued, over the squeals and laughter of the schoolgirls below, but Luke contributed with nods, gasps and grunts, scarcely able to fork the food to his mouth, as the deft nyloned toes expertly frigged him, passing from glans to cockshaft, to a luxurious tickling of his balls, between two nyloned soles. For afters, the frilly maids sullenly served roly-poly pudding, slathered in a lake of custard; Luke stabbed helplessly at the plate, as spunk surged in his balls.

'I take it you agree with Mr Playfair, Mr Redruth,' said Arabel, 'that the hard approach is necessary?'

'Why, yes, miss,' Luke mumbled, dribbling crumbs.

'A schoolmaster can never be too hard, where girls are concerned,' she added.

'I know Mr Morton agrees,' said Joly, and the ladies simpered.

Martin Morton blushed slightly, and concentrated, with trembling fingers, on his pudding. Suddenly, he gave a brief gasp, and his eyes narrowed, with his breath harsh, as if in duress.

The nyloned toes were up at Luke's glans, as if sensing his impending spurt. The soft fabric swirled on his peehole, caressing the neck of his glans, his tingling, sensitive frenulum and corona, sending shivers of ecstasy through his balls.

He groaned, as the first drips of his come moistened the frotting toes, then gritted his teeth, shutting his eyes briefly, as ecstasy flooded him, and he spurted a full flood of sperm over the nylon toes rubbing his glans and peehole. His hands shook; pudding fell from his fork, splattering his shirt.

'Gosh, Mr Redruth,' purred Arabel, 'you've spilled your custard. It's a licking offence for a schoolgirl, but since you are a new boy, we will overlook it, just this once.'

# 7

# Nude Basting

'Well, Arabel?' asked Joly Goosnaugh. 'What do you make of the new master?'

The two ladies squatted on adjacent lavatory bowls, the doorless cubicles filled with the melodious tinkle of their pee. Tapping their shoes on the tile floor, Liliane and Irena awaited their turns.

'A nine-incher, I'd judge,' said Arabel. 'So much cream! It made quite a mess of my stockings. And such a darling shudder, as it spurted, like a stallion trying to break free of his reins.'

'Question is,' said Liliane, 'who's going to be the first to fuck him? Oh, do hurry, Arabel, I must poo.'

Arabel wiped her wet slit, and stood up. 'It was so dreamy, toe-tweaking the stud,' she drawled. 'Do you know, I think he's tamable. I sensed submission. Gosh, I need to wank.'

Nonchalantly, she lifted her foot to the washbasin, reached to her quim, parted the moist, shiny gash flaps, thumbed her swelling clitty, and began to masturbate. Liliane swooped to the lavatory seat, her skirt up, with knickers ripped to her ankle, and sighed, at her steaming plop-plop of dungs.

'Ooh, that's better.'

Joly vacated, and was replaced by Irena.

'I suppose we all want to be the first,' Irene said, as her pee flowed. 'Let's make it a competition.'

The girls agreed.

'And the winner's prize?' Liliane drawled.

'She gets naked licks twelve, on the others' bares,' murmured Joly, licking her teeth.

'Why not naked licks at discretion?' Irena suggested impishly. 'It's been a while since my cane striped any of your rotten bums, and I'm bound to win.'

'*You*'ll squirm when I win,' said Liliane, pouting.

'Well, are we agreed?' drawled Arabel. '*I*'ll make the lot of you wriggle, and wish you'd never been born, or at least, never with a bum bare for licks.'

The girls agreed, rolling their eyes in mock agony. Arabel's fingers made loud squelching noises, echoing in the white-tiled powder room, as she eagerly wanked her cunt.

'I say, Arabel, you're making me fruity,' said Joly.

'You had Morton's lunch-time load,' said Arabel, panting.

'That's just it. He scarcely fits between my toes, the brute. I want so badly to come. Double diddle?'

'All right.'

The two girls faced each other, each with her fingers in the other's cunt, and mutually masturbated, gasping, while Liliane and Irena squatted at stool. The two peeing girls exchanged glances.

'Shall we?'

'Why not? Those two lustful wankers are.'

Each reached between the other's thighs, and began an enthusiastic caress of her friend's dripping cooze.

'We haven't had a spankathon for absolutely ages,' said Irena, panting.

'Have we time?' purred Arabel. 'I'll gladly redden your lovely bum, Irena.'

'Blasted classes too close,' grumbled Liliane.

'With a few pocket beatings to keep us fruity, till the next wank,' said Joly with a sigh. 'It's not fair, the chaps getting all the really juicy canings. I'd like to lick that bitch Sonia Pewte, I mean really hard, with a rattan, in the nude, quite starkers; whip her bum and thighs, and tits and tummy and everything. God, I'm going to come just thinking of it.'

'Cane her twat,' gasped Liliane. 'The sizzler, squelching and hissing between her gorgeous big wet cooze lips. Mm!'

'Yes! I'm coming any second, you beast,' squealed Joly in delight.

There was a bang, as the door clattered open, and Luke burst into the chamber. The four schoolmistresses stared coldly at him, but without ceasing to masturbate blatantly.

'Oh! I'm terribly sorry,' he blurted.

'The gentlemen's convenience is three doors down,' said Arabel, fixing him with her eyes, as her fingers slopped in Joly's cunt.

She spread her thighs wider, treating Luke to an unabashed panorama of her own frigged gash, the naked pears of her bum, and her pert anus bud, winking at him, as she squeezed her sphincter. Luke goggled; his cock rose at once.

'Invading the ladies' loo?' Arabel murmured, while thrusting her shaven cunt hillock against Joly's tweaking fingers. 'You've committed a grave offence. Any schoolgirl would have her bum licked purple for such an affront. I hope you realise that, sir. We could overpower you, rip your pants off and thrash your horrid arse, this instant, should we choose.'

Luke's cock throbbed rigid. 'No, wait! I . . . I'm sorry, honestly.'

She shrugged, tossed her head, and sniffed. 'They all say that.'

'I'd better go,' Luke blurted.

'Yes, you had. Meantime, I shall be thinking of your punishment. As a master, you deserve something more subtle than mere whopping.'

Luke coloured crimson. 'Now, look here . . .'

Still masturbating the squirming Joly, Arabel reached down, and clasped his swollen cock and balls. She began to stroke his cock on the peehole.

'Uhh . . .' he whimpered.

'Not a very *impressive* sex organ, compared to *some* –' the other girls tittered '– yet stiff, appallingly rude to us ladies – an insult! Do you deny it?'

'No, miss,' Luke squealed. 'Oh, please . . . ooh, what are you doing?'

Arabel rubbed him for a minute, while he panted, then, abruptly, released his stiff cockpole. 'You shan't be punished just yet, sir,' she said, 'for I can't work out what chastisement would be suitable.'

'I suppose I should thank you,' Luke said, his caressed cock throbbing.

'Not really,' she whispered. 'I'm going to wait until *you* suggest it.'

'Please do, sir,' gasped Joly, belly fluttering, in her approaching spasm.

'I'd love to see that bum redden,' said Liliane, panting. 'Ooh! Yes! I'm off . . .'

'Ah! Ah! Yes! *Ohh* . . .' crooned Irena, orgasming.

'Mm! mm . . .' gasped Arabel, her eyes blinking furiously, as her wanked quim spurted come, and her buttocks and belly heaved in climax.

Cock rigid and balls fruity with spunk, Luke fled the laughter of the schoolmistresses. He found the gents' washroom, and urinated copiously, though not enough to still the longing in his balls, caused by Arabel's expert manipulation of his trousered cock. Then he made his way to Tim Playfair's classroom, where, as his introduction to the academic regime of Licks, he was to take part in 'team teaching', followed by a session with Martin Morton.

His new black gown swirled at his ankles, with his springy ashplant cane swaying beneath, and he began to feel quite proud, deciding it was better to leave the episode in the ladies' loo unmentioned, and *certainly* to conceal his spurt at the luncheon table, from that minx Arabel's pliant toes.

He entered Tim's classroom and the class of a dozen eighteen-year-old girls stood as one, skirts rustling over crisp panty lines and stockinged legs, to curtsy to him, but not without lips creased in crafty simpers. Luke felt a surge of power in his balls, still fruity with the spunk Arabel's cock-frot had summoned. The girls wore standard school uniform, of course, but each had adorned herself with coquettish individuality.

Mouths were smeared in the lightest pastel lipstick or plain gloss; there were manes in bobs and plaits and ponytails, ribbons and brooches of silver, red, blue, pink and yellow; snowy petticoats peeping under daringly high skirts; high shoes, daringly pointed, and with not-quite-legal spiked heels; smooth sheeny nylons, with a delicate lacy or flowered pattern, or an inexplicable, sluttish rip at knee or calf, as if inviting punishment; bras that pushed big titties into thunderous, menacing cones, the tips of the nipples pointed like bullets; skirts pleated so high on the leg, and so tightly, that they clung to the bottom, revealing every detail of haunch and bum cleft, with the panty line often a mere string, etched like an engraving.

Their pert, full bodies, faces with sleepy eyes, and wide sensuous lips, pouting impishly, had the same arrogant languor Luke remembered so well in Severe, the same lazy, voluptuous selfishness he saw in Amy. He licked his lips, curled in a sneer. These luscious young bitches were teasers and coquettes, sluts all! And he was permitted, indeed required, to exact vengeance on them – on *all* women – by caning their naked bottoms.

According to Miss Tupper, he, as schoolmaster, was expected to flog at least two girls' bottoms every day. It went without saying that the miscreants' buttocks would be nude, not pantied, for *his* canings. Luke rubbed his hands, leering at the quivering, full-fessed maids, who mistook his leer for a smile of approving flirtation, and twittered eagerly, with some girls blushing and crossing their legs, in a collective, moist slither of swishy, scented nylon.

*Luscious bitches. Superb, snobbish, superior, cruel, beautiful bitches, and they'll pay for it. I'll make every slut's bum smart.*

Tim, wearing a tracksuit to emphasise, as he said, the athletic, no-nonsense method of teaching girls, introduced Luke, and led the class into some mathematical textbook, which Luke gloomily felt he understood as little as any girl. The air was heavy with the cloying perfume of lustful maids' bodies, girl sweat, and the stink of their toes in damp nylons, wriggling free of shoe straps. Several times, an exasperated Tim had to call for silence, with a rap of the cane on his desk. Luke gazed at the maids, their breasts thrusting in their skimpy school blouses, and some with a button or two surreptitiously undone, under their ties, to show creamy bare teat flesh; his cock would not stay still.

He stiffened, crossing his legs, and wincing, at his stiff groin pole. He tried covering himself with his gown, but feared drawing attention, and looking silly; besides, the gown fell away, unless clutched. One of the girls began to stare at him; she was big boned and ripe titted, with a long blonde mane, cascading over impishly bared top breasts – a younger version of Arabel Stiffence. She began to lick her pencil with long slurping strokes, gazing unashamedly at Luke's erection, which made it throb even harder.

Tim bounded around, muscles rippling, and booming in his stentorian voice. He made the dry lesson a show of athleticism, yet was unable to stop the girls murmuring, giggling or passing scribbled messages. Smiling deliberately at Luke, the blonde girl slid her hand under her desk, and parted her thighs, with a swishing of cloth. Luke watched, blushing, and his cock throbbing, as her arm began to move rhythmically up and down, like a piston in her groin. There was no doubt that she was masturbating, as she watched Luke's stiff tool, and that she wanted him to know she was masturbating. She licked her lips, pouting and winking at him, and Luke felt sperm churning in his balls.

'And so the square on the hypotenuse equals . . . can you go on, Bonita?' Tim looked at the blonde girl, who did not notice either scrutiny or question. 'Bonita?'

No answer. The schoolgirls began to giggle, looking at Bonita frig, with blushes and popping eyes.

'Bonita Spear, what *are* you doing?'

Flushed and smiling dreamily, the girl turned to Tim, who was red with anger, a few feet away.

'I'm having a wank, sir, if you please.'

'Ooh!' gasped the schoolgirls, in tremulous delight.

'I *beg* your pardon?' he stammered.

'I'm masturbating, sir,' she drawled. 'Don't all we girls frot our clits to pass the time in these interminably dreary lessons?'

She smiled sweetly, and her tongue peeped through her lips.

'Why, you . . .! That means licks, my girl. Come up here at once, and bare up for the cane, with your knickers at your ankles.'

'Shan't.'

'*What?*'

'You'll have to make me.'

'This is an outrage!' Tim exclaimed, glaring at her.

'What's wrong, sir? You're a big strong male, and I'm only a helpless girl. You can sweep me over your shoulder, carry me off and ravish me. Gosh, that thought's making me even wetter. Your big stiff cock, spurting its spunk up my hole. I'll have to finish my wank, now.'

'You cheeky, impudent . . .' Tim lifted his cane, and slashed the air in frustration. 'I'll tell you for the last time, miss,' he said coldly. 'Present yourself at my desk, bend over and touch your toes, with your skirt knotted above your croup, according to school's regulations, and your buttocks bared, with legs apart, and panties across your ankles, as tight as they can stretch. You've earned not six, not twelve, but naked licks *at discretion.* Otherwise, I'll . . . I'll report you to Miss Tupper, who'll . . . who'll take a very dim view of the matter.'

'Boohoo!' wailed Bonita suddenly, pretending to cry. 'You horrid bully.'

'Now, wait, Bonita,' he blurted. 'You know I'm just doing my job.'

The class began to seethe. 'Bully. Cad,' the girlish voices murmured.

'Let's give the bully a taste of his own medicine.'

'Up, girls, and at him.'

'No, please!' Tim cried, as a wave of snarling schoolgirls overpowered him. 'Redruth! Help!'

Luke shrugged helplessly, as Bonita Spear directed three of her friends to pinion him, while she unzipped his trousers, and pulled out his quivering stiff tool. The girls made wide eyes, and collectively gasped, 'Ooh!'

Bonita seized Tim's cane. 'Strip him, girls,' she ordered.

'Wait,' Tim wailed. 'I'll . . . I'll comply.'

Skirts rose, and girls' dainty hands began frotting their wet panties, as he removed his clothing.

'Every stitch,' snapped Bonita.

Tim stood nude and trembling, covering his balls with his hands. Vip! A cane stroke whipped them away to reveal his tool stiffly erect, and the girls, eagerly frigging, simpered with laughter.

'Bend the cur over,' Bonita drawled. '*He*'s for naked licks.'

Tim was pinioned, with his chin on the desk rim, hands clutching the corners, legs apart, and back and buttocks in the air. He nodded sagely at Luke, assuring him that this was part of his teaching plan. Bonita threw the cane to a sultry raven-haired girl, who caught it, flashing dazzling white teeth.

'You whop him, Mabel. The beast caned you most abominably last week, so it's time for your revenge.'

Mabel placed the cane between her teeth, and slowly stripped off her school uniform, carefully folding her skirt and blouse, and sliding out of her nylons and sussies, until she stood only in a skimpy scalloped peach-coloured bra, exposing the dark plates of her nipples on her sultry tan breasts, and peach thong panties, which left her lush bum pears almost totally bared, with the gusset snaking invisible between her massive, clinging cheeks. Luke recalled the envious mentions of Mabel Otrifice, in the staffroom; she came from an old Anglo-Brazilian family, whose plantation produced the most expensive coffee in the world.

110

'That's better,' Mabel said. 'Stretch him tight, girls. Yes, now I can *really* skin the wretch. Nude basting of a juicy male arse, gosh, my cooze is wet just *thinking* about it. It's *too* wank-making.'

Tim groaned and whimpered, his buttocks taut as a whip. Bonita knelt at Luke's feet, and began to lick his peehole, her eyes twinkling into his. As she delicately fellated Luke, her fingers gurgled, masturbating her come-soaked cunt. Luke groaned, as his cock bucked.

'Please, no,' gasped Tim, his buttocks quivering, as he struggled helplessly. 'Don't cane me, Mabel. I'm sorry! There, I've said it.'

'Silence, worm,' snarled Mabel. 'I'm going to blister that arse black and blue. Licks at discretion.'

She licked her lips, touched herself at the gusset of her panties, and shuddered, with a little mewl of pleasure. The gusset, rapidly staining dark with come, outlined her heavy swollen cunt lips, and stiffened clitoris, bulging within. Breathlessly, she rubbed her clitty through the panties, trembling and moaning softly, until trickles of come soaked the soft bare skin of each inner thigh, below the panties. She lifted her finger, and sucked her come off it.

'Now I'm really in the mood for bare-beating a man,' she murmured.

'Please, no, Mabel,' Tim pleaded. 'The shame. At least thrash me with my shorts on, for modesty. Not the wood striping my bare bum. The horrible weals, the dreadful smarting, and my tears, as I weep and squirm and wriggle. I can't bear the thought of it.'

'You won't have to bear the *thought* of it, sir,' hissed Mabel, lifting her cane over her head to the full exent of her arm, 'for you are going to enjoy the real thing.'

Vip! She lashed him across mid-arse, leaving a vivid pink streak across the bum skin.

'Ooh!' he shrieked, his cheeks clenching tight, and his whole arse wriggling, so that his weal danced like a worm.

Vip! The second stroke took him in the same weal, deepening it to crimson.

'Ahh!' he screamed. 'Stop! No more!'

Vip!

'Oh! Ahh! Oh!'

Vip!

'Ooh! Ahh! Please stop, Mabel, I beg you.'

Tears poured from his eyes; his back and thighs rippled, straining helplessly against the powerful girls' wrists that clamped him.

'You fucking cissy,' said Mabel, panting. 'You gave me no grace when you gave me licks last week. I begged you to stop, my bum wriggled, maddened with pain, I pissed myself in agony, yet you took me to tariff.'

Luke watched the naked buttocks flogged, with Bonita's lips and tongue expertly fellating his cock: licking and teasing, and, every so often, making him gasp, as she plunged to take the whole cockshaft to her throat, and caress his balls with her lips. Luke's balls squirmed under Bonita's mouth, as Tim's arse squirmed under her friend's cruel cane. Vip! The sweating, half-naked whipper girl bared her teeth in a rictus, as she delivered stroke after stroke to the bruised and darkening bare buttocks.

Tim howled, sobbed and squealed, his arse wriggling, as if each fesse wanted to disappear into the other to escape its frightful pain; remorselessly, the welts grew to ridges, black and jagged, across the tight, clenched fesses. The whole arse flesh was caned crimson, with the weals stretching from underfesse to top bum, the haunches cruelly striped in criss-cross lashes. His chin banged the desk rim, as his croup jolted at each cane cut. Drool trickled from his gasping mouth, and tears coursed from his eyes, yet, as his naked buttocks wriggled, his cock swayed, ramrod stiff. Vip! Vip!

'Uhh . . . uhh . . .' he moaned.

'You dirty fucking swine,' said Mabel, panting. 'Your tool's proud. How dare you?'

She thrust her fingers inside her come-soaked panties, and began quite blatantly to wank.

'I can't help it, Mabel,' he groaned.

112

'You find it exciting, to be flogged by a girl?' she spat. 'For shame!'

'No ... no ... please stop.'

Vip! Masturbating vigorously, Mabel sliced the cane between his cheeks, in the arse cleft, lashing his anus, with the tip whirring near his balls.

'*Ahh!*'

Vip!

'Oh! Oh!'

Vip!

'*Ahh!* I can't stand it,' he said, sobbing. 'I'll do anything, just stop the pain.'

Without doubt, Bonita's ardour was fuelled by the sight of a male being flogged. Luke clasped the schoolgirl's hair, pressing her head to his cock. Her hand squelched in her dripping cunt, as she wanked off, sucking his throbbing tool, and he knew he could not hold back his spurt much longer. The cluster of maids around the flogged teacher all had their hands in their wet panties, with skirts immodestly up, and were frigging, with little coos of pleasure, showing their swollen, come-stained gussets, as they inspected the darkening stripes on the male's squirming bare buttocks. Vip!

'Ooh! Mabel, please, enough!'

Mabel leapt onto the desk, and sat with Tim's head flat on the desk rim between her thighs, and her long legs stretched, so that her stockinged feet caressed his balls. Wrenching him by the hair, and pressing his nose to her sopping cunt, she jerked his head back and forth, while masturbating her clitty with his nose.

Come streamed from her writhing slit, into his mouth. She ripped off her bra, and began to squeeze her naked breasts, pinching and kneading the nipples, until they stood hard as apples. She continued to flog his buttocks from the vertical, with every stroke lashing his cleft, now purple with bruises. He gurgled, swallowing her come, and then his lips bubbled with a steaming jet of hot piss spurting from Mabel's twat, straight into his throat. Her swaying nyloned toes kicked his cock and balls, as she writhed in the pleasure of her pee.

'Urrgh . . .' he moaned, as a droplet of cream appeared at his peehole.

Vip! Vip!

'Ooh! Ahh!'

His cock bucked, and began to spray sperm over Mabel's stockinged feet, which were rubbing his balls.

'You filthy worm,' she snarled, mashing his face to her cunt, and wanking her breasts and clit harder. 'Yes, I'm coming . . . Oh! Oh! *Yes* . . .'

Mabel's belly heaved, and come spurted from her gash, along with the golden remnant of her pee, into his gasping mouth, and Tim swallowed her whole spurt, while his spunk splattered her stockinged toes and ankles.

Bonita's tongue curled, licking furiously, around the neck of Luke's glans, with his peehole squashed at her palate, and he groaned, as her lips clamped his cock, sucking and milking him of the spunk which spurted powerfully into her throat.

'Ooh . . . ooh . . . sweet . . .' Bonita panted, wanking herself off, with a flood of come slopping her stockings.

Mabel made Tim lick her stockinged feet clean of his spunk, before she permitted him to rise. The bell went, signalling the end of class. Mabel and Bonita dressed, and surged out with the others, clutching their books, and giggling.

Tim rose shakily to his feet, and wiped tears, piss and come from his sopping face.

'Ouch!' he groaned, gingerly rubbing his welted arse. 'I say, am I awfully damaged, old man?'

'You do look a bit the worse for wear,' Luke murmured.

Tim climbed into his tracksuit. 'Still, it's all for the good, isn't it?'

'I'm sorry?'

'You saw how I kept the bitches quiet? Showing yourself tougher than them, why, it's the only way to get respect. They don't dare mess with Tim Playfair, that's for sure.'

Luke said he was due to attend Martin Morton's class. Tim frowned. 'I hate to say this, old boy, but Morton – fine chap, but he just can't keep order, you know. The girls simply don't respect him. Don't say I didn't warn you.'

Luke was not too surprised to find that Tim's prediction proved, at first glance, less than accurate. It was a different class of sixth-form girls, but the dozen school-uniformed beauties who greeted him with shy pouts of their glistening red lips, presented the same various adornment as Tim's class: hair, skirts, blouses, stockings, shoes and often visible underthings, all pleasingly individual. The girls deferred most respectfully to Martin Morton, rising, to curtsy politely, with a swishing murmur of skirt on nylon, when he introduced Luke as the new teacher of 'PE and sundries'.

Sitting at the front of the class, Luke found Martin's exposition of Caesar's Gallic Wars just as dreary as Tim and his geometry, so scanned the faces and bosoms of the eager schoolgirls, mentally selecting those he most looked forward to thrashing. The girls' pencils scratched on paper, without any murmuring or giggles; they seemed in awe of their teacher, whose low, monotonous voice droned about praetors and legions and Gauls. Martin had a long caramel-coloured rattan cane fixed at the side of his pulpit desk, but made no allusion to it, and did not tap it, or meaningfully nod, for the girls were as good as gold, all except for one. Martin whispered that she was Sonia Pewte, and Luke should be careful.

Sonia was blonde, her hair more of a honey blonde than Bonita Spear's dazzling corn yellow, and cascaded over her swelling breasts, like a waterfall over boulders. Her body was, if anything, even more lavishly curved than Bonita's. The bosom was massive, yet firm as rocks, jutting from her slender ribcage with only the sheerest, flimsiest see-through nylon bra for unneeded support, and the huge strawberries of her nipples poking aggressively through her clinging school blouse. Her shiny nyloned legs, crossed, with the already short skirt slid almost up to her panties, were bunched against the desk, as the rippling thighs and calves, leading to dainty, narrow ankles, were too long to be contained.

Her waist was pencil thin, swelling to buttock mounds whose ripeness and girth Luke could easily guess, with a thrill, as he contemplated caning the girl – such an imperious, sullen beauty must have done *something* wrong – making the haughty siren wriggle and squirm and squeal, with breasts heaving in her agony, and tears dripping into her shivering blouse, with Luke, the avenger, striping the naked riches of those succulent bum flans.

He stared at her, feeling his cock stiffen; in a certain light, as dusty sunbeams splayed through the classroom, she was the image of Severe Compaigne! His cock rose to full, throbbing hardness. Sonia's sultry eyes flickered, glancing at Luke, and a haughty smile creased the corner of her lips.

'Sonia, will you please translate the paragraph beginning "*Cum puellis . . .*" ' Martin ordered.

Stifling a yawn, Sonia slipped a stick of chewing gum into her mouth. Luke looked at Martin, to see if he had noticed this impertinence; evidently he had, for he frowned.

'Sonia,' he said resignedly, 'are you misbehaving *again*?'

'Yes, sir, I'm afraid so,' drawled Sonia.

'Then I must correct you. You know how much I hate doing so.'

'You caned me yesterday, on the bare, sir,' Sonia murmured, still chewing, 'and the day before. My bum's quite crimson.'

'With your record of disobedience, anyone would think you actually enjoy the cane,' Martin said mildly.

'It's not unheard of,' she said, smirking at her classmates. 'Your cane is more of a tickle, sir. It doesn't really hurt. You're rather a softie, in fact.'

Martin sighed. 'You're not making things easier for yourself, or for me,' he said.

He opened the lid of his desk, and extracted a birch sheaf, a good 45 inches in length, and wide of spray, whose twigs made a dry, crackling sound, as he swished the air in front of Sonia's breasts. The girl's eyes widened a fraction, and her smile grew, while a shocked murmur rippled through the class.

'The birch, sir?' she drawled. 'Gosh, how pain-making.'

'Perhaps you'll think me less of a softie,' he replied drily. 'Come up here, Sonia, and spit out your gum, then present yourself, bared up, over the stool. You know the drill.'

Sonia rose, and slouched, simpering, to the front, where a small flogging stool stood in readiness. She spat out her gum, which missed the waste basket, and landed on Martin's shoe. He paled in anger.

'You try my patience, girl,' he said. 'You may lick my shoe clean.'

It was Sonia's turn to pale. 'I beg your pardon, sir?'

Vap! The birch lashed the seat of the flogging stool.

'Lick it off, you cheeky bitch,' he hissed.

'Y-yes, sir. At once,' Sonia mumbled.

The blonde girl crouched, buttocks up, to show her shiny mauve bikini panties, sussies and frilly stocking tops, in dark-purple fishnet nylon. She picked up her chewing gum with her tongue, and flicked it to the waste bin.

'No need to rise, girl,' said Martin. 'Assume position on the stool. Sussies off, panties at your knees, and thighs spread. In fact, for birching, I think it best you disrobe completely from the waist down.'

'You are going to birch me in the full nude, sir?'

'You may keep your blouse, but knotted securely halfway up your back. I don't wish to spoil your rather pretty stockings, but I want a good field of fire across your thighs and haunches. Most disciplinary birches have quite a wide circumference of spray, you see.'

'I know, sir,' she murmured. 'I've taken the birch before.'

'On the bare?'

'Of course, sir. From my boyfriend, Justin.'

There was a delighted, shocked gasp from the girls.

'He's so *cruel*,' Sonia murmured, licking her lips. She snapped open her garter straps, and rolled down her

117

stockings, caressing her bare satin legs, under the teacher's gaze. 'He really knows how to make a girl squirm, with her bum all crimson and smarting. He says mere caning doesn't tame me, even on the bare. Justin *loves* a nude-birched bottom. You can ask Mabel Otrifice.'

Martin smiled. Luke's cock stood rigid, and he saw the beginning of a bulge in Martin's shabby brown trousers. With a slow, slinky wiggle of her hips, Sonia slid down her panties, exposing the swelling firmness of her naked cunt basin and buttocks, the cheeks coquettishly clenched, and the cooze mound shaven alabaster pure. She slipped her stockings off her toes, and waggled them, caressing her bare ankles, soles and toes with sharp, purple-polished fingernails.

'Mm,' she said, 'It's so cool. Are you sure you wouldn't prefer to nude-baste me, sir? I'll take my top and bra off, if you like. Please? It would make me so much more comfortable.'

'All right, then,' Martin said. 'But I warn you, Sonia, it will hurt.'

'I expect it to, sir,' she murmured.

Sonia licked her lips, as she unfastened her blouse buttons, then reached behind her back to unhook her bra. The girls gasped, as her massive breasts sprang naked. Martin merely smiled, making no attempt to conceal the swelling at his crotch, unlike Luke, who, rock hard, crossed and recrossed his legs in some embarrassment. Nude, Sonia put her hand blatantly between her thighs, and began to stroke herself, with her mouth gaping open and her tongue dangling over her lower lip.

'Will you go easy on me, sir,' she whined, in a little girl's voice, 'although I've been so terribly naughty?'

'Do you really want me to?' asked Martin affably.

'Not really, sir,' she purred, crouching, with her naked bottom upthrust for the birch. 'I'd feel awfully sorry for you, sir, if you didn't enjoy yourself.'

# 8

# Morton's Fork

The classroom was deathly quiet, with the schoolgirls' breasts straining to hold their shocked breath, as Martin's birch rose over Sonia's straining bare buttocks. The girl perched, kneeling, on the stool, with the soles of her naked feet up and her back arched, its muscles tensed and rippling. Her trunk sloped sharply down and she was resting on her hands, which were splayed on the floorboards. Her thighs were well parted, displaying her entire bum cleft, with the crimson prune of her anus winking nervously, as her sphincter tensed and dilated, and the heavy folds of her naked cunt lips swayed pendant and aquiver.

Her head jutted up awkwardly, and her blonde tresses cascaded over the tips of her erect red nipples, brushing the floor. Martin brought the birch sheaf down. Swish! The twigs crashed across Sonia's croup, masking it entirely, before slithering from her skin, leaving a mass of delicate pink weals, like a porcupine's bristles. Sonia's buttocks clenched tight, and she gasped, with a low, agonised hiss of hoarse breath.

'Ooh!'

Swish! The birch whipped again.

'Uhh!'

Sonia's bottom began to squirm tightly.

Swish!

'*Ohh!* Ouch!'

Her whole body jolted, thighs tensing and rippling, her back and flogged buttocks squirming, and her head swayed from side to side, sweeping the floorboards, to which each birch kiss mashed her nipples. Swish!

'*Ohh* . . . that's tight! I say, steady on, sir!'

'They'll get tighter, Sonia. That's what you earn for being a cheeky brat.'

'Don't you call *me* –'

Swish! Martin dealt an uppercut, lashing Sonia full in her bum cleft, with the twigs swishing her inner thighs, anus and cunt.

'*Ooh! Ooh!*'

Sonia's flogged buttocks wriggled in torment. Her face was contorted and she was weeping, with tears flooding over her cheeks and soaking her hair. From her writhing twat oozed a trickle of limpid come, to wet her squirming thighs. Her knees rose from the stool in frenzied little jumps, pat-pat-pat, as her buttocks squirmed. Her choked, gasping sobs of agony filled the classroom.

'Ooh . . . ooh . . . please, don't hurt me any more.'

Swish! Martin lashed a second uppercut.

'*Ahh!*' Sonia screamed, from deep in her throat. 'Oh, God, stop!'

Swish! A third uppercut reddened her bum cleft, until the cunt lips and anus bud were no longer discernible by colour, amid the wealed crimson skin.

'*Ahh!* Ahh . . . I can't bear it. I can't take this! Oh, please stop, I beg you, sir.'

Sonia's whole body trembled, as in a St Vitus's dance, her bottom, thighs and titties shaking uncontrollably, with sweat and tears pouring from her face, and come spurting from her whipped gash folds. His cock rigid, Luke stared at the pussy juice streaming from her cunt, in shiny rivulets down her thighs, and he saw that all the girls were watching, too. The girls began to shift in their seats, many blushing and reaching down between their legs. There was a gentle rustling, like butterflies' wings, as the girls stroked and teased their panties, under lifted skirts. Swish! Martin delivered a top-down stroke, splayed across her top buttocks and spinal nubbin.

'Oh God!' she said, sobbing and writhing.

'Hurt much?' he asked.

'Gosh, yes.'

'You've taken eight, and should be getting used to it.'

Swish!

'Ooh! Yes, I rather think I am. My bum feels really blistered and smarts horribly, but it's all tingly and warm and yummy, under the smarting. My ... my coozy-poo is rather wet, sir. I'll need a jolly good wank after you've finished with me.'

'If I ever finish with you, smutty bitch. According to King's Regulations, a hundred years ago, twelve strokes of the birch was the maximum permitted for juveniles under the age of fourteen, but those over fourteen could receive up to thirty-six strokes. You are eighteen, Sonia, so I propose to award you two strokes for every year of your age. For maximum correction, I'm going to treat you to a slow birching, with the cuts on the thirty seconds. That gives you just enough time to absorb the pain, and just when you think you have it mastered, another cut comes to drag you back into agony.'

'No, please, no! That's cruel!'

Swish!

'*Ahh!*'

Sonia's nude-birching continued for another half-hour, with the flogged girl screaming and sobbing, as her skin blackened with weals; yet, after the twenty-sixth cut, her cries became muted to a drooling moan, fluting sometimes into eerie gasps of pleasure. Her thighs glistened with a torrent of pussy juice, spurting from her wriggling bare cooze lips, and, as the cuts fell, she squashed her erect nipples to the floorboards, rubbing and mashing them, with a sensuous undulation of her spine.

Swish! Twigs flew from the birch, and fell to the floor with a clatter. The watching girls squirmed in delight, fingers busy, quite blatantly, at their cunts, as they masturbated under their desks, with much sighing, gasping and licking of lips, at orgasms achieved or awaited.

'Only nine to go, Sonia,' said Martin amiably. 'You are taking it well.'

'Oh, you can birch me all you want, sir,' she gasped. 'I can take it. You cannot crush me. Only my boyfriend can do that.'

Martin frowned. Over the next four minutes, he took the birching to her tariff, and laid down the tool, half denuded of twigs.

'Is that all?' said Sonia, defiantly, with tears streaming down her face. 'I need more than that to tame me. You're not much of a bircher, are you, sir? This is what I think of you.'

A heavy jet of acrid golden piss spurted steaming from her cunt, splashing over Martin's feet. The masturbating girls' come-soaked fingers flew to their lips, gaping in horror.

'You'll have to lick all of that up,' said Martin quietly. 'But first . . .'

He unbuckled his belt.

'No, sir,' moaned a girl at the back of the class. 'Have pity on her.'

The chorus rose.

'Have mercy, sir.'

'She didn't mean any harm.'

A lone voice rose in contradiction: 'Give it to her, sir, she deserves it. Give her Morton's Fork! Make the pig squeal!'

Emboldened, other girls joined in.

'Do her, sir. Make her cry, shame the slut!'

Soon, every girl was urging Sonia's humiliance. Martin raised his hand, commanding silence, and the classroom magically hushed.

'I'm sorry, Sonia, but it must be so,' he said. 'You have proved yourself untamable by any other method. I want you to know that this will hurt me, as much as it hurts you.'

He dropped his trousers, allowing his erect cock to spring free.

'Ooh!' the entire classroom gasped, hands at their lips, before each girl's fingers flew back to her cooze, and began vigorous masturbation.

Luke gaped; Martin's cock was enormous, or, more than enormous, grotesque. He could not imagine such a tool, outside some freak show. Sonia twisted her head, her jaw dropped and her tongue hung down, with drool gushing from her lips. He parted her welted, glowing arse cheeks, and his monstrous bell end nuzzled her anus. Reaching under her drooling cunt lips, he collected a palmful of her come, and used it to lubricate his naked glans, a shiny battering ram, with its prepuce fully stripped back.

'Wait,' she stammered. 'I'm sorry, sir, I didn't mean . . .'

'Too late, Sonia,' he murmured.

His hips jerked, and his cock sank an inch into the girl's anus.

'*Ahh!*' she screamed, her back and buttocks jerking wildly.

He thrust again, and his cock plunged halfway into her rectum.

'Oh! Oh no! It's agony!' she squealed, drool foaming at her lips. 'I can't take it!'

A final thrust sank his cock in her bumhole, right to his balls. The lips of her anus were white, distended to the size of a grapefruit.

'*Ahh! Urrgh!*' she shrieked. 'You're splitting me in half. Oh, birch me again, sir, birch my naked bum a thousand cuts, but don't bugger me, not with that horrible giant monster of a tool. I beg you, have mercy.'

Imperturbably, Martin began to fuck her. Her bum wriggled and squirmed around an anus horribly distended, and by now stretched wide enough to admit a girl's arm. Ramming her bumhole, his cock made loud, squelching slurps; his thrusts were punctuated by sharp squeals of '*ahh!*' from the enculed girl, as his helmet slammed her root, over the hard slapping thwack of his balls against her

123

arse meat. Sonia's buttocks, gouged in a myriad of dark birch welts, whirled in a glinting kaleidoscope, as she gasped, crumpling, under Martin's savage buggery.

'No! Ooh! Stop! It's agony!' she screamed. 'You're bursting me!'

Implacably, he fucked her for two, then three minutes, with the squirming girl weeping, sobbing and screaming, but with copious come gushing from her writhing twat lips and wetting her thighs and ankles. Her legs glistened with oozed come, bathing Martin's balls as he fucked, so that the slap of his balls on her flesh became a wet slurping crack.

The schoolgirls masturbated vigorously at the spectacle, their faces scarlet, and their fingers squelching inside their panties, to the accompaniment of sighs and gasps of pleasure. Luke's cock was painfully stiff against his bursting trousers. He gazed at Sonia's widened arsehole, wondering how anyone could take such pain.

'Urrgh . . . urrgh,' the buggered girl snivelled, drool cascading from her lips. 'Oh, yes, split me, fuck me harder, fuck me, do me, I'm your bitch, give me all your spunk up my hole, make me come.'

Martin grunted, and a bead of cream plopped from Sonia's anus, followed by his full load, as he spurted inside her.

'Yes! Hot spunk! I'm coming!' cried the girl. 'Fuck me, fuck me, fuck, fuck fuck, yes . . . Ah! Ah! *Ahh . . .*'

Come sprayed from her cunt, as she shuddered in long, squealing orgasm. With a plop, Martin withdrew his cock, scarcely softened, and replaced it in his trousers. Still erect, he faced the class, and said he hoped they had learned a lesson from Sonia's distress. Sonia hobbled back to her seat, clutching her flogged and buggered arse, with a beam of triumph.

The rest of the lesson proceeded in absolute, obedient silence. By the time the bell rang, and the girls' books had slapped shut, Caesar had satisfactorily come, seen and conquered. The girls curtsied to Luke and Martin, gathered their books and scooped Sonia up to carry her shoulder-high from the classroom.

'Thank you, sir,' they murmured, cherry-faced, to Martin. 'Thank you for a lovely class.'

Cheering, they announced to the school that Sonia was their heroine for she had taken Morton's Fork! Martin said he needed to take a leak, and Luke accompanied him to the washroom.

'You see the problems I have keeping order,' Martin said with a sigh. 'I wish I was tough, like Playfair, then it would be easy.'

They unzipped, pointed and sprinkled. Luke hoped a pee would relieve the pressure in his cream-filled balls. He noticed that Martin stood far back from the urinal and pointed his cock like a cannon. He looked down.

'Cripes, Morton!' he exclaimed, 'I thought I packed a wallop, but yours . . .'

Morton looked up, with a shy, resigned smile. 'Yes, I know,' he said. 'It's a blasted nuisance, sometimes, to be dangling thirteen inches. How long's yours?'

'Just nine.'

'More than enough,' said Martin glumly. 'Girls expect such a lot of a fellow. They call mine Morton's Fork, the cheeky minxes. That was after Chancellor Morton, under King Henry VII, who had a rather brilliant jape for getting taxes from people. If you looked rich, you had to pay tax to the king, but if you looked poor, then you were obviously concealing your riches, so you had to pay even more tax. Sort of, damned if you do, and damned if you don't.' He sighed. 'It's the same with having a big tool. If you perform, you are a sex monster, but if you don't, you are a spoilsport.' He shook it, or rather, wrestled with it, and put it away. 'Trouble is, in this place, full of bitches on heat, I have a job for life. Because of *that*.'

Martin went back to tidy up and lock his classroom. On the way to the common room, Luke met Arabel, who pointedly looked at his bulging groin.

'Well!' She smiled. 'You must have enjoyed watching Sonia's little escapade. It's already the talk of the school.'

125

Luke shivered. 'It was more than an escapade,' he mumbled. 'It was dreadfully brutal, yet she seemed to like it. I can't understand.'

'You seemed to like it, too,' she purred, clasping his cock with her palm, and caressing his balls.

'Uhh!' he gasped.

'You're hard, Mr Redruth. Full of naughty spunk. I expect you'd like a despunking?'

'Don't mock, miss,' he replied hoarsely.

'I wouldn't. I know how awful it is for a chap to have his bags full of cream, without relief.'

'Since you put it like that,' blurted Luke, blushing, 'yes, it is rather frightful. Your touch on my balls is so heavenly. I'd give anything for relief, just now.'

'Then follow me,' said Arabel, licking her lips. 'You may have coffee with us in the ladies' common room.'

Arabel led him through winding corridors, scented with old wood and leather, and the pervasive perfume of girls' sweaty shoes, panties and stockings. They entered a cosy, book-lined sitting room, with a picture window, looking out on lawn and lake. Instead of a carpet, it had a tiled floor, like a bathroom, with runnels and sinkholes, and various shower attachments on the wall. The floor was covered in throw rugs. Joly, Irena and Liliane were there, and Luke was served pungent, almost erotically aromatic, coffee. He nibbled on a custard cream, while the ladies looked at him, smiling crookedly, as if sizing him up, but carried on chatting about clothes, film actors and diets.

They sprawled on comfortable chairs, crossing their legs to let their skirts ride up quite shamelessly, with their frilly stocking tops, sussies and knickers well on show. Luke's cock throbbed in his trousers and, in view of Arabel's promise, he made no attempt to conceal it. At last, Arabel put down her teacup, licked her fingers of crumbs, and spoke.

'Would you like a tit-wank?' she said in a loud voice. 'I've already given you a shrimping, and I know a rampant boy like you has plenty more cream.'

'It was *your* toes . . .' Luke blurted.

'Of course.'

Arabel kicked off her shoes, and flexed her stockinged toes, each in its nylon sheath. Smiling and licking her lips, she slowly, coquettishly, opened her blouse, letting the sides fall away, to expose her breasts, trembling in their skimpy bra, an obvious size too small for the massive smooth teats. She snapped the hook, and her bra fell away, allowing the titty globes to jut naked. They quivered slightly, with the big pink domes of her nipples swelling to coy erection. She peered down at her nipples and tweaked them between her fingers.

'See?' she said. 'You've got me all excited. Get your kit off – all of it.'

Arabel closed the curtains; Luke simpered, and obeyed. He had to kneel on the table, presenting his stiff cock to the lounging Arabel's breasts. She enfolded his tool between the massive soft teats, and began to rub him, while her palm caressed his balls. He moaned at the expert pressure on his glans, enfolded in her breast. The other girls had their skirts raised fully and their fingers played at their moist panties.

'I say, no peeking, you smutty pup!' shrilled Joly.

Arabel slapped his face, hard. 'You voyeur! You peeked at us in the ladies' loo, you brat.'

'I didn't! I – ooh!'

She slapped him again. 'Lying hound! Mr Smarty-pants thinks he can come here for free coffee and tit-wank, because of his enormous cock. Well, you're going to pay the price of your impudence. Seize him, girls.'

Luke could not resist the weight of four girls pinning his nude body. Whimpering and crying, he gasped for breath, as Arabel's moist-pantied anus ground into his nose, with her buttocks crushing his face. Joly sat on his thighs, with her stockinged feet clamping his balls, while Liliane and Irena pinioned his arms and legs.

'We know about Miss Tupper and her tests. I suppose you think Licks is all about satisfying your filthy male lusts

127

on innocent girls' bottoms. This lesson will teach you otherwise. The male is there for a girl's pleasure and nothing more.'

'Urrgh!' Luke squealed, as Arabel's panties writhed, squashing his mouth and nose.

She raised her buttocks a fraction, allowing him to gulp air. 'That's just a taste of what we are prepared to do, sir. Do you promise obedience, and to take punishment like a man, on your word of honour?'

Joly's nyloned toes began to caress Luke's balls, flicking and teasing the defenceless sac. Arabel's buttocks slammed down on Luke's face for a further minute, filling his nostrils with her arse's pungent perfume. Arse grease and come seeped through her panties gusset, wetting his lips, before she lifted her croup again.

'I promise,' Luke gasped.

When he rose, trembling, his eyes widened in dread, for each girl carried a raised cane. Reminding him of his promise, Arabel ordered him to bend over and touch his toes. Liliane kicked the throw rugs aside, so that Luke stood on cold bare bathroom tiles. Luke assumed position; a pressure of Arabel's cane tip on his balls obliged him to part his legs, until his arse cheeks were spread taut; his erection nudged his belly, as he bent over.

'I didn't mean any harm,' he bleated.

'Silence, you pathetic worm,' snarled Arabel.

Vip! Her cane cracked across his bare nates, followed by three more vicious cuts from Arabel's colleagues. Vip! Vip! Vip!

'*Ohh!*' Luke gasped. 'Oh, God, that hurts!'

'Silence!' Arabel thundered. 'You'll take your punishment like a man, not like some pathetic cringing girl. Unless you'd prefer that, and wear girly things?'

There were coarse chuckles.

'Let's dress him,' said Irena. 'He can wear my knickers.'

'No, mine,' shrilled Joly. 'They're tighter.'

'Please! I'll take my punishment naked,' he blurted.

'You'll take what you're given, slime,' hissed Joly.

Vip! Again, four cuts in fast succession lashed his buttocks, rocking Luke on his toes. His fesses clenched and wriggled furiously; his gorge rose, and tears sprang to his eyes at the hideous smarting pain.

'Uhh . . . Uhh,' he whimpered.

Vip! The canes rained on his helpless arse, streaking his skin with liquid fire, which set his buttocks squirming and his teeth chattering, as he wept and panted in shame. The beating continued, with cuts on the ten seconds and, after three minutes of chastisement, Luke babbled that he had done nothing to deserve such agony. Arabel snarled that he had a cock and balls and that was crime enough. Vip! Four canes lashed him on the vertical, between the spread buttocks, right in his arse cleft, and struck his anus, making him howl and squirm.

'*Ahh!*'

'*Will* you be quiet?'

Vip! The girls' canes whipped him for a further two minutes, by which time Luke's arse was striped with the livid gashes of over fifty cane strokes. His body seemed on fire, consumed by the smarting, throbbing pain of his cane welts. Weeping, he lay face down on the tiles, and heard the slither of undone skirts and panties. He moaned, as he felt hot trickles of girl piss stinging his weals, then cruel fingers rubbing the piss into his bruises. When three girls had pissed on him, there was an odour of vinegar; suddenly, he screamed, writhing in agony as wet fingers mashed his smarting arse.

'Just a little chilli pepper sauce,' crooned Arabel. '*So* health making.'

'You cruel monsters,' Luke said, sobbing.

He groaned, as he was obliged to turn over on his back to rub his seared, stinging buttocks against the cool tiles for some small relief from his arse's agony. Through eyes glazed with tears, he saw Arabel's bare bottom and twat, thighs spread, descending, to squat inches from his mouth. He gurgled at the hot jet of piss which steamed from her cunt into his throat.

'He must have sausages with his coffee,' said Joly.

'The expense!' retorted Arabel.

'Go on, it's such fun.'

'See to it, then.'

Joly retreated, and Arabel ordered Luke to raise his thighs over his belly, with his knees up to his neck, and hold his buttocks apart, in what she called the chicken position. Groaning, he obeyed.

'No,' he moaned, as Arabel stood over his balls, wearing a hideous black dildo, just like Severe's, strapped at her cunt.

The dildo's smaller, secondary shaft, a clitty-tickler, was lodged in her quim, which she squeezed on the false cock, to massage her erect nubbin. The schoolmistress openly masturbated, with wide streams of come glistening on her rippling thighs, as she curled her lip, contemplating the helpless male. He banged his elbows on the tiles.

'No, please,' he whimpered.

'The strap-on is always much more fun when you can see its effects, face up,' Arabel purred. 'How does it feel to submit, helpless, with your hole exposed, just like all those innocent girls you've fucked?'

She dropped, knelt, and slammed the dildo into his bum cleft. Pulling the arse cheeks so taut that he squealed, she forced the huge rubber cocktip into his anus, at which Luke squirmed, screaming even louder.

'Ahh! It hurts!'

A further thrust, and the giant dildo filled his rectum, its cold, hard tip squashing his colon.

'Oh, no, please no,' he said, sobbing.

Arabel's belly squashed Luke's, sandwiching his stiff cock, as her buttocks began to rise and fall, in a savage arse-fucking. Luke wriggled, squealing, as he was buggered, clutching his knees and spreading his thighs wide to open his hole for the girl's tool. His nostrils filled with the smell of frying sausages.

'Oh . . . you're splitting me,' he whimpered. 'It hurts so dreadfully.'

'Be glad it isn't Morton's Fork,' Arabel said, panting, as she slammed the huge cock into his arse.

Come squirted from her slit all over his balls and buttocks, so that his cheeks squirmed in a pool of her pussy juice. He began to move his arse in the rhythm of her thrusts.

'You cruel bitch,' he said, tears streaming down his face. 'Yes, do me . . . it's so good, it hurts so much. God, I hate you. I'm your slave. I need to be fucked. Do me, fuck me, miss, fuck me full . . .'

Beside him, Liliane and Irena stood nude and masturbated, with come from their wanked cunts spraying his face. Joly padded back to join them, and the smell of cooking became overpowering. The wanking girls giggled, with hisses, as they peed, and then Luke's view was blotted out by Joly's smooth bare buttocks, squatting over his face.

'Eat your sausages, sir,' she sneered. 'I hope you like them spicy.'

From her straining anus, a dung-shaped brown tube appeared, glistening with girl piss and arse grease. She forced it into his mouth, and he bit, tasting sausagemeat. Joly perched, squatting, on his knees, while Arabel continued to encule him. When he had eaten Joly's arse-load, Liliane took her place and excreted another sausage into his mouth, followed by Irena, who delivered herself of two whole sausages, fragrant with her juice.

'Oh! Ahh! Yes! *Ooh . . .*'

The buggering Arabel gasped in orgasm, spurting come all over Luke's bum and belly, and then transferred her dildo to Joly, while she squatted over Luke's face, for her own anus, between dripping buttocks, to excrete another sausage into his mouth. Joly bum-fucked him, until she climaxed, then Irena and Liliane took their turns with the strap-on dildo, gasping in repeated comes, until the groaning, weeping Luke had been buggered solidly for fifty minutes.

'That blasted cock is still stiff,' snorted Arabel, masturbating, while squatting over his face and squirting come into his mouth. 'The arrogance of males.'

'You did promise him a tit-wank,' said Joly, masturbating vigorously. 'I'll do it, if you're too scared.'

'Lay off, bitch,' hissed Arabel. 'You heard him. He's my slave.'

'The worm belongs to all of us,' spat Joly.

In instants, the two nude schoolmistresses were writhing, gouging, scratching and clawing on the floor.

'Ahh!' screamed Arabel, as Joly kneed her in the cunt, and responded by biting savagely on Joly's left nipple.

'Ooh! Stop!' Joly whimpered, lowering her head to take Arabel's cunt lips between her teeth, and chew them.

Arabel groaned, weeping, and clawed Joly's clitoris with her sharp purple fingernails. Writhing under Liliane's buggery, Luke saw the nude bodies, a slippery, sweaty thresh of limbs, and heard the frenzied squeals of the two girls in merciless combat. Joly sat on top of Arabel, straddling her with crushing buttocks and forcing her face into the pool of come and girl piss on the tiles. Arabel screamed and wept, struggling and kicking, but could not prevent Joly from seizing a cane and beginning a vigorous flogging of Arabel's naked arse. Vip! Vip!

'Ooh! Ouch! You pig!' Arabel shrieked, as her squirming bare bottom reddened with weals.

Come sluiced from Joly's pussy, as she rubbed her swollen pink clitty on Arabel's writhing back, while flogging the girl's buttocks.

'Oh! Oh! Enough!' Arabel squealed. 'Pax!'

'All right,' Joly said, panting. She slithered off Arabel's back, with her hand wanking her distended clit.

At once, Arabel leapt on her, biting her nose and titties, and delivered a stiff pummelling to Joly's cunt, forcing her thighs apart, then biting the lips and clit, before raining punches on the wet hole.

'Urrgh!' Joly shrieked, her bruised twat writhing. 'We said pax!'

'Stupid bitch,' grunted Arabel.

She seized the cane, still hot from her own buttocks, and pinioned Joly's neck to the tiles, with the girl's face squashed in a pool of piss. Vip! Vip! She flogged Joly's squirming bare arse, until the girl sobbed and whimpered, begging for mercy. Luke groaned under Liliane's fierce buggery. As Joly collapsed into a whimpering heap of wealed flesh, Arabel flung aside her cane and squatted over the weeping girl, pissing in her face. She ordered Joly to lick her cunt and anus clean, and, with Joly's tongue flicking in and out of Arabel's holes, Arabel spreadeagled herself, plunging her face between Joly's thighs. She began to gamahuche Joly, with her tongue and lips on the girl's come-soaked twat.

'Joly, darling, let girls be friends,' she purred.

'Yes, let's,' Joly gasped, swallowing Arabel's copious come.

Luke whimpered, as his arse was seared with the pain of Liliane's buggery. Bum-fucking hard, Liliane began to gasp, as her orgasm approached; Luke watched the writhing girls gamahuche, until Irena, masturbating powerfully, squatted on his face, crushing him with her buttocks, and a fresh jet of girl piss engulfed his mouth.

Come from Liliane's cunt splashed his balls, as Irena's piss and wanked cunt juice filled his nose and mouth, and she began to moan at the onset of orgasm. Joly and Arabel groaned, as they tongued each other to come; Liliane buggering Luke, and Irena crushing him, both writhed in orgasm, and Luke gasped, as his own spunk jetted powerfully from his cock, splashing high all over Liliane's belly and teats.

'You smutty brat,' snarled Liliane, 'spunking all over my bubbies like that. I didn't offer you a tit-wank.'

'He's my slave,' gasped Arabel. 'I'll make him pay.'

She seized the cane, turned Luke over and, with the other girls sitting on him, dealt ten stingers to his flaming wealed buttocks, while he whimpered, squealed and cried. Freshly caned by his mistress, Luke had to kneel and lick Liliane's breasts clean of spunk, then apply his tongue to each cunt in turn, as the schoolmistresses knelt before him to demand thorough cleansing of their grease-oozing bumholes, and cunts gushing come.

Only then did Arabel consent to give her slave the promised tit-wank. She took him between her breasts, cooing sweetly, and licked her lips, as she rolled her heavy naked teat flesh over his rigid cock, engulfing him from balls to glans in her massive bubbies.

In moments, Luke spurted a powerful stream of sperm over her face and breasts. Lips and eyes smeared in his spunk, Arabel wiped her face with her fingertips, licking and swallowing all the trickling spunk, and twisted her breasts up to her face to lick the creamed bubbies clean of Luke's copious ejaculate. At last, Arabel told him to dress, and rid them of his obscene presence.

'In future, you'll come when I summon you, slave,' she drawled. 'That's the way we do things at Licks.'

She picked up her discarded panties and wiped them around her cunt basin, stuffing the gusset into her cunt and anus and cleaning herself of all her fluids. She sniffed the panties, wrinkled her nose and smiled. 'To remind you of your obedience,' she drawled, 'here are my panties for you to wear until I permit you to take them off.'

Luke slid into her moist, smelly bikini panties, pulling them up high at her command, although they were painfully tight on his cock and balls.

'How can you be so cruel?' he said with a sob.

'You like it, don't you?' Arabel sneered. 'We know your sort, you submissive wretch. You'll be back for more.'

Luke's face was wet with tears; his arse smarted with fearful welts; his cock was sheathed in humiliating, stinky girl's panties; his enculed bumhole was agony.

'No!' he blurted. 'You're beastly! You've flogged me, and buggered me, and tit-wanked me, like some pet animal, and made me wear shameful girly panties, and I hate you. I'll never submit to such humiliation again.'

Arabel tapped his stiff cock with her cane. 'On top of that, we've made you a liar,' she said.

# 9

# Crushards

Severe Compaigne adjusted the fastening of garter strap to frilly stocking top, pulling the sheer blue nylon over her skin, until both skin and nylon were satin smooth. She patted her nurse's white skirt into place, its hem a good six inches above her knees. As the new matron of Crushards College, she had to look smart for her duty of inflicting corporal punishment on sullen boys, then dressing their bum weals with ointment. Caning ripe young boys on the bare bum, every day – what a wonderful job for a girl so young!

She had the commander's connections to thank, of course, as well as her Girl Guides' first aid badge, and also the one for knotting and lashing. After Justin – *the absolute swine!* – had abandoned her – *for some common little tart from the jungles of blasted South America!* – she needed to get away, and restore her self-esteem by earning her own crust. Being matron of a school for senior boys was a wonderful opportunity to achieve closure, by venting her rage on every bare arse presented for correction.

When she crossed her legs, a sliver of cream panties at her crotch was visible in the mirror. She adjusted her nurse's bonnet to a cocky angle, and undid the top two buttons of her shirt, exposing bare breast skin, and a strip of cream bra cup. She touched her left nipple, and let out an involuntary gasp; the plum was hard, and sent tingles up through her spine and clitty.

135

Cautiously, she raised her skirt and touched herself between the lips of her cunt, which were clearly outlined by the tight panties. Her fingertip brushed her clitty, swelling hard, and she gasped again. Her panties were moistening at the gusset, with a seep of come from her gash. She touched her clit with the tip of the whippy ashplant cane, draped across her thighs, and moaned in pleasure, as her clit stiffened to rock.

She looked at the clock; a few minutes past ten, and a queue of boys waiting outside with their pink punishment slips. Well, they could wait, while she got herself properly primed. No need to take her panties down, a touch under the cloth would bring her off. It was the same every day: she began her duties, as juicy as could be and, after caning several bottoms, ended up even juicier.

Sighing and licking the trickle of drool that seeped from the corner of her mouth, she slipped her fingers beneath her panties, slid them across the bulging silken mound of her shaven cunt hillock, and parted her quim lips. Her fingers penetrated her wet pouch and pressed the swollen clitty. Gasping with pleasure, Severe began to masturbate.

She gently frotted her clit and wet gash, her fingers making a puddling sound between the slit lips, sluiced with fast-flowing come, which quickly soaked her panties gusset. *My panties will be in a state. But then, they are always in a state.* She thought of all the muscular buttocks awaiting her cane, just beyond her oaken door, then of one arse not present, that of the whelp Luke Redruth.

She thought of his naked buttocks, squirming and wealed, as she flogged him; of his giant, thrill-making tool, bursting her own panties, which she obliged him to wear; of her dildo wrenching his rectum, and his squeals of pain. It would be nice to enslave a fresh young male. Quickly, efficiently, Severe orgasmed, her cunt spurting come into her panties. A good wank, but she wanted more. Breathing hard, Severe pulled up her panties tight, feeling the clammy wet stain of come at the gusset, smoothed down her skirt and pressed the button which lit up the ENTER sign at her door.

A tall young boy, with an unruly blond coiffure, and a trim, muscular body, stepped shyly into the surgery, and, bowing, handed Severe his pink slip. She scanned him with professional interest: a well-muscled arse and – she licked her lips – the beginnings of a bulge at his crotch.

'Well, Mr Julius Puncknowle,' she said, crossing her thighs to allow the newcomer to glimpse her panties, 'this is the first time I've seen *you*.'

His eyes flickered, as he saw her moist panties, and his crotch bulge increased healthily. Reading the pink slip, Severe smiled. 'It seems you've been a *very* naughty boy, Julius.'

'Y-yes, miss. I ... I don't know what came over me, miss.'

'But I think you do,' said Severe, tapping her cane. 'Sheer, perverted beastliness, that's what. Happily, I have the instrument to beat it from you. It may take quite a while, though.'

Julius gulped and began to shiver, with his cock still firming. Severe learned that only one other boy awaited punishment, Duddy of the sixth.

'He's a regular customer,' she said. 'Due his usual sixer, for smoking. Not on bare, unfortunately. The beastly tyke is clever enough to incur only clothed beatings. How I'd love to cane his bare, and see his fesses twitch. You won't mind if I deal with him first, Julius? Then I can give *you* the time you deserve. I trust it won't upset you to watch.'

The smirking Duddy swaggered in, bowed to Severe, and dropped his trousers, keeping on his shorts. She gave him a short homily on the evils of smoking, during which he stifled a yawn. Without bidding, he bent over her battered old leather sofa, clutching the sides, and pursed his lips, with a wink at the trembling Julius. His clothed buttocks shone in the sun's rays streaming through Severe's bay window.

Severe lifted her cane and dealt him six stingers on the rump, with Duddy's arse clenching a little, but not squirming, even as her cane sizzled, wrenching his arse cloth. Severe caned so hard that her breasts bounced furiously and she panted in her exertion. Julius gazed, as though petrified, at the nonchalance with which the boy took his strokes. When she lowered her cane, Severe's panties made a loud squelching noise.

'Phew!' Duddy gasped, when the sixer was complete. 'Those were right sizzlers, miss. Like getting the horsewhip from my governess, on my dad's ranch in Brazil. Except she whipped me in the nude – me, not her, worse luck. I'd say you were practising for gaucho beating, miss.'

He winked again at Julius, whose face was pale; yet Severe saw that Julius's cock stood rock hard, with a bulge too large to ignore. When the insolent Duddy had sauntered out, Severe turned her full attention to Julius. She ordered him to lock the door, then she sat and lit a Dunhill. She puffed plumes of blue smoke in the boy's direction, while he stood, shame faced and erect, with his head lowered and hands behind his back. His crotch bulge stood out obscenely, Severe thought with satisfaction.

'Miss Firgate requests me to go hard on you,' she said slowly. 'From her report, I see no reason not to. A vile crime, indeed.'

He blushed crimson.

'It will be a lot harder than a sixer, you realise, and, of course, on the bare buttocks.'

'Y-yes, miss.'

'Whatever possessed you to steal Miss Firgate's soiled panties from her laundry basket?'

He opened his mouth, but she held up her hand, advising him that, on second thoughts, she preferred not to know. She clucked her tongue and pointed at his cock tent.

'I'm afraid that erection compounds your offence,' she murmured. 'It is an insult to me, and you shall have to pay for it, with additional strokes.'

'I can't control it, miss,' he blurted, his eyes moistening.

*The poor lamb. How fruity I am for tanning his bare. Just as when I first thrashed the whelp Luke . . .*

She pressed the handle of the cane to her lips. 'Then my ashplant will help you. Right, to business, young Julius. You're to take twelve strokes for your crime to Miss Firgate, and a further six for your erect cock. That makes eighteen in all. You may strip off for you'll take your beating in the full nude.'

Julius paled, but obeyed her command. Severe bit her lip, as she watched the stiff tool emerge naked, standing like a tall tree at his thighs, and the tight bare slabs of his arse. She ordered him to turn and show her his buttocks, then to part the cheeks slightly, so that she could see his balls, pendant beneath the taut arse cleft. Her panties were sopping with come, seeping ever faster from her tingling cunt.

She commanded him to face her, with hands at his buttocks, and she licked her lips, staring icily at his rigid cock. Panting, she crossed her legs, with a loud, wet slither of nylon, and paused, to expose her wet panties for several seconds; the boy's eyes locked on her crotch. Severe sprang to her feet, scything the air with whistling cane. The boy shuddered.

'Were you peeking up my skirt?' she hissed.

'No, miss. That is, I couldn't help . . .'

'You vile pervert! I should report you to the head.'

'Please, no, miss. Anything . . .'

'Now I really want to punish you. I suppose it would make that disgusting cock soften if I stubbed out my cigarette on your balls?'

His cock seemed to stiffen more. 'If it pleases you, miss,' he stammered. 'I'll take what punishment you decide.'

'You'll take extra strokes, then.'

He nodded miserably.

'Eighteen plus six makes a nice round two dozen,' she purred, extinguishing her stub in the waste bin.

'Twenty-four cuts on the bare, miss?' he gasped, his face a mask of anguish, yet his cock fully stiff. 'I've never even been caned before. I know it's the whole point of Crushards, but I thought just the threat of caning would make me behave. I never dreamed . . .'

'A cane virgin,' said Severe, her nipples and clit throbbing, and her cunt gushing come. 'Let's fix that right away, Julius. It's nice and early, so I have all morning to skin you.'

Bent over the sofa, Julius shuddered, as Severe tapped his balls with her cane tip and ordered him to spread his legs wider. He obeyed, and sprawled, naked and shivering, with his limbs splayed across the leather sofa. Sunbeams illumined his buttocks. Severe lifted her cane, and brought it down in a slashing arc on the boy's defenceless arse meat. Vip! Julius groaned, his fesses clenching, with a livid red cane stripe right on their central portion. Vip! Severe's cut took his arse aslant, making a neat cross on the skin. Julius began to wriggle, clenched tightly, and his breath came in hoarse, sharp pants.

'Oh . . . ooh,' he gasped, tears moistening his eyes.

'Tight?' asked Severe, panting.

'You bet, miss. It hurts awfully.'

'It's supposed to,' she replied. 'You'll note I'm spacing the cuts every twenty seconds. That's to let you have full time to absorb the pain, and then, just when you think you can manage it, the next cut tops it up and hurts even more.'

Vip! The wood sliced his tender top buttocks.

'Ohh!'

The boy's arse began to squirm violently, livid with weals, and Severe touched herself between the legs, emitting her own little gasp, as pleasure throbbed in her stiff clitty. Her panties were soaking with come. Vip! She lashed savagely in the arse cleft, slicing the boy's anus bud.

'*Ahh!*' he squealed. 'Ooh! Oh!' His blistered buttocks writhed and clenched, and he danced on tiptoe, with shuddering thighs. 'How can you be so cruel, miss?' he asked, sobbing.

'Because I'm paid to,' she said. 'You're not taking it too badly, Julius. It should ease off after the tenth; that is, your bum will get used to the pain, although I don't expect you to like it. At least you're no longer a cane virgin, so that's a plus. Tell me, are you a virgin in the other sense?'

'Well, I . . . I've had plenty of girlfriends, miss.'

'Answer the question. Had that cock ever been up them? Have you "had your hole", as I believe filthy boys say?'

'N-no, miss. But I've had my fingers, dozens of times.'

'Smutty pup!'

Vip!

'Ahh!'

There was a timid knock on the door. Clicking her tongue, Severe went to open it.

'I'm sorry I'm late, miss,' blurted a boy's voice.

'Can't you see I'm busy?' she snarled.

'Oh! Yes, miss.'

She snatched the pink slip from him, scanned it, and smiled. 'Mr Matthew Morden, another naughty boy,' she drawled. 'Well, you'd better come in. I'll see if I can accommodate you both. Dear me, Matthew. Eighteen strokes for groping one of the kitchen maids. How perfectly loathsome. You don't mind a tandem flogging, I hope. I'll just give Julius here his sixth.'

Vip!

'Ahh!'

Julius squirmed, with the newcomer staring, ashen-faced, at his wealed croup, yet trying to avert his eyes from the stiff tool between the beaten boy's legs. Severe said that they were now equal, each with eighteen to go, and Matthew should strip off completely. Shyly, the boy stripped, while Severe ordered Julius to shift up on the sofa and make room for her new victim. She assured him he would be much cosier, having a friend in durance.

Matthew covered his crotch with his hands, until Severe tapped them away with her cane to expose the boy's cock, almost as large as Julius's, blossoming into erection. With her eyes on the rising cock, Severe's cunt seeped come into her wet panties, and she said in an innocent voice that she really didn't understand why boys became rampant when faced with caning. Matthew's pallor turned to deep scarlet, and he mumbled that he was awfully sorry, but he couldn't explain his condition, save as a nervous reaction to fear of the rod.

141

'To be beaten bare bum is shameful, miss,' he blurted. 'Caned on the trousers, or even pyjamas, it smarts no end, but it's not as painful to your dignity as a naked thrashing.'

'Oh, good,' purred Severe.

Sighing, the boy stretched himself beside Julius, with an exchange of 'sorry' as they wedged themselves into position. Severe thrilled, her cunt a churning maelstrom of come, as she surveyed the two bare male bottoms, raised for her caning pleasure: the one cruelly striped, the other pale, deliciously tense and shivering. She said she would lash each in turn, on the twenty, so that she would cane one stroke every ten seconds. Thus, the boys could expect their beatings to last six minutes. Both shuddered and exchanged woeful, embarrassed glances.

Severe raised her arm and dealt Matthew his first stroke. Vip! The cane left a sharp weal on his underfesse, and he trembled, gasping, as his cheeks clenched, but made no other sound. Vip! Julius's seventh stroke renewed his low squealing moan. With drool seeping from his lips, he turned his eyes away from his companion, to hide their misting of tears. His bum squirmed hard, while Matthew's merely quivered.

As the caning progressed, Matthew's naked buttocks soon came up to speed with his fellow's, wriggling under each savage cut, until the blistered arses glowed with equal welts. Now that they were partners in pain, their eyes were able to meet. At each stroke to his fellow, the other nodded in sympathy or admiration.

'Tight one, my man.'

'Yes, a bit.'

'Well taken.'

'No talking!' Severe snapped.

Faces wrinkled in agony, yet smugly defiant, they stared at her, as if despising the uncaned. She began to lash uppercuts between the thighs, between the arse cheeks and perilously close to the pendant ball-sacs, which made them hiss with pain. They danced on their toes, which thumped the floor, as their buttocks squirmed, making their stiff cocks wobble. Severe's twat squirted come into her squelching panties, and she longed to take them off. Vip! Vip!

'Ah . . . ah . . .' the boys panted hoarsely, in a chorus of torment.

'Tell me, miss,' said Julius with a sob, after a fierce stroke across his left haunch, 'are *you* a virgin, by any chance? Is that what makes you so cruel?'

Matthew tittered.

'Why, you filthy cur,' Severe exploded. 'You'll take an extra six for that outrage.'

'You *must* be a virgin,' said Matthew.

'Six extra for you, sir!'

Severe forgot her twenty-second agenda, and began to flog them rapidly. Her breasts pumped, as her arm rose and fell like a metronome, and her stockings were soaked with her flowing come. The buttocks were covered in welts and crusting ridges, so that scarcely an inch of unblistered skin remained; Severe lashed them across their backs and shoulders, provoking them to ouraged gasps and sobs, yet no protest. The cane cracked across their rippling muscles, creased under the impact of the wood that laid broad stripes on the boys' wriggling shoulder blades.

They took the stripes, groaning, with teeth clenched, and heads hung low and shaking from side to side. Their buttocks still clenched, even as the cane fell on the back. Severe whimpered, as her hand flew under her skirt to grasp her sopping panties, and begin a frig. The merest touch to her clit brought her off, without disturbing the rhythm of her cane; yet she could not stop masturbating, her throbbing cunt demanding further relief, and she slipped her fingers inside her panties to caress the naked gash.

She penetrated her gushing pouch, and reamed the slit walls, as her thumb pummelled her stiff clitty. She panted harshly, bringing herself to orgasm twice more, in an unbroken wank and without ceasing to flog. She dropped her cane and stroked the boys' naked flesh.

143

'That's enough,' she said, panting and masturbating harder, as her fingers caressed the deep weals on their bums and backs. 'You've taken it like men.'

The boys gasped their thanks, lifting their heads, to see Severe's skirt lifted, and her wet panties pumping in her wank.

'Why, miss, you're diddling,' Julius blurted.

'Smutty mot,' Matthew said.

The boys rose, grimacing, and each rubbing his welted buttocks. They wiped the tears from their eyes, and stood, looming over Severe, with shy grins at their massive, stiff cocks.

'You couldn't thrash us soft, miss,' murmured Matthew. 'I don't think you really wanted to, did you?'

Severe's fingers squelched from her panties, and dangled at her side, dripping come onto the carpet.

'You wanted to wank off,' said Julius. 'Using us for your pleasure.'

'I, your matron, masturbate? How dare you,' retorted Severe, flushing. 'Caning miscreants is a disagreeable duty. I take no pleasure in it.'

Julius's hand darted between her thighs to clamp her wet cunt. 'This says you do,' he hissed.

'Ouch! Stop this outrage!' Severe cried, her belly squirming, but she was unable to escape the pressure of the boy's fingers on her twat.

Leering, he began to frig her, squeezing her cunt like a lemon, until he withdrew his sopping hand, and smeared Severe's face with her own come.

'Ooh! Urrgh!' she spluttered.

Julius reached under her blouse and pinched her titties, kneading and clawing her stiff nipples.

'Your nips are all excited,' he said. 'I think she wants a seeing-to, the cow. Otherwise we'll tell the head on her, won't we? Ogling boy's tools, stiff nips, wet cooze and wanking off. Not too good on your CV, miss.'

'You wouldn't tell,' Severe whimpered. 'Please. We can arrange this, surely?'

Matthew picked up the cane, hot from the boys' arses. He swished the air, making a loud whistle, and licked his lips.

'A taste of her own sizzler,' he murmured. 'Bend over, bitch.'

'I shan't – you've no right –'

Matthew slapped her face. 'Now,' he snarled. 'Over the sofa, skirt up, panties down and legs apart.'

Snuffling, Severe obeyed. She groaned, as Julius ripped off her panties, baring her bum, and, with rough, poking fingers, forced the cheeks wide. Her cunt dripped come and it trickled all over her spread thighs.

'Hold her down, Julius, there's a good fellow,' Matthew said. 'Look at that fucking arse. It's so big and tight and meaty: a fucking masterpiece, ripe for blisters.'

Julius pinned Severe's face to the sofa cushions, with his foot on her neck. She moaned and wriggled, her bum flailing, as Matthew took aim. Vip! The cane streaked her bare buttocks pink.

'Urrgh!' she squealed, into the cushion.

Vip!

'Mmph!'

Vip!

'Nngh!'

Her buttocks writhed and flapped, like whipped red jellies. Julius wrenched her head up by her hair. Severe's face was streaming with tears and flushed scarlet.

'You bastard,' she said, sobbing.

'Shut your mouth, girly,' Julius snarled.

He thrust his erect cock between her lips.

'Ooh! Urrgh!' she gurgled.

'Suck on this, bitch,' he commanded.

Vip! The cane rose and fell, with powerful strokes, as Matthew lashed Severe's squirming bare. Convulsed with sobs, the flogged girl sucked Julius's tool, her tongue licking all around the neck of the glans and flicking his peehole, before diving to his balls to take his cock to the back of her throat. She squeezed and sucked vigorously, as she shuddered, with small choking gasps.

145

While Severe fellated Julius, Matthew caned her to twenty strokes, in the space of a minute. Her buttocks were a tapestry of pink, black and purple weals, the savage blisters already crusting to deeply gouged valleys and ridges of blackened skin. Tears poured down Severe's cheeks, as come sprayed from her cunt.

'Dirty bitch, juicing all over the carpet,' said Matthew, panting.

Vip!

'Ooh!'

His cane lashed between the thighs, right on the cunt flaps, striking her clitoris and anus. Severe danced in agony, her mouth slurping drool over Julius's balls, as she frantically tongued his swollen cock. Matthew stroked her four more cuts between the legs, each of which made her wriggle violently, and her gurgles of pleasure, at the stiff tool in her throat, were broken by choking sobs of pain. Matthew lowered his cane, and pressed his cock to her bottom, stroking her welts with his glans tip. He said that haughty cows needed bumming.

'Mm . . .' Severe moaned.

His cocktip nuzzled her pucker.

'You like one-eye, miss?' he asked, drooling. 'Cock up your hole?'

'What . . . no! Please!' Severe squealed.

Parting her cheeks, he plunged his cock into her anus.

'Urrgh!' she squealed.

He thrust again, and got his cock up her rectum, right to his balls, then began to slap her buttocks in vigorous buggery. Her lips writhed on Julius's cock, and the boy groaned in spasm, squirting such copious spunk into her throat that it bubbled from her lips and down her chin. He withdrew his cock from her mouth, and wiped it clean with her hair, then sat on her head, pressing her face into the cushions, while he watched Matthew's pumping tool, smeared with the enculed girl's arse grease. Matthew buggered her for three minutes, his balls slapping on her churning buttocks, which rapidly adapted to the rhythm of his cock-thrusts. Severe's arse bucked to take his tool in her bumhole.

'Uhh ... you bastard,' she whimpered. 'Yes, oh yes! Plough me raw, do me, take me up the arse, split my bum, shoot your spunk up my hole ...'

Matthew's spunk jetted into Severe's colon and frothed at her anal lips.

'Yes, yes,' she whimpered, 'I'm coming ... ooh!'

Come spurted from her cunt, and Julius's cock stiffened again at the spectacle of the helpless, trussed girl bum-fucked to orgasm. He leapt up to take Matthew's place. Easily plunging his tool into her spunk-soaked, arse-greased anus, he began to slam her colon in fierce buggery, while Severe wept and squealed, with her head crushed by Matthew's arse. Matthew lit one of her Dunhills and smoked contentedly, as his cock stirred and stiffened; from time to time, he flicked cigarette ash into her hair.

'Julius, you are so cruel,' she whimpered. 'Ooh! It hurts so! Fuck me, fuck me hard.'

Suddenly, Julius withdrew his cock, with a sticky plop, and grasped her wealed bum cheeks. He sandwiched his glans between the cheeks, pressing them hard, with his fingernails clawing her welts, making her shriek in pain. His peehole was wedged against her deepest, most livid blister, its flesh a glistening dark purple, and he began to fuck the welt, squeezing the bum cheeks against his cock and balls, as his glans stabbed the tender wound.

'Ahh! It hurts! Ooh!' Severe screamed, her buttocks clenching to squeeze the cock. 'Oh! Yes! I'm there!'

Come squirted from her cunt, as the agony of Julius's bum-wank drove her to climax; in an instant, sperm spurted from his cock, over her gashed buttocks, bathing her wounds in hot cream. Matthew seized her ripped panties, and ordered her to wipe her arse clean. Then he stuffed the panties in her mouth, and told her to suck and swallow all Julius's spunk from them. Sobbing, she obeyed, her throat jerking, as she engorged the boy's fluid. Julius ripped off her nurse's skirt, and tore it into long strips, while Matthew held her, crouched on the sofa, and spanked her sopping arse with his hand.

'Urrgh,' she groaned, behind her panties gag, shaking her head frantically. 'Uh. Uh.'

The boys bound each hand to its ankle, locking her in her crouch, with her bum up. They took turns to cane and bum-fuck her, pausing only when she released a long, noisy stream of piss all over the sofa; she was ungagged, and had her face pressed in the pee-soaked cushion, until she had sucked it dry. Gagged anew, she had to endure buggery and the cane, until her arse was striped in a livid fresco of welts, and her flogged cunt spurted constant come.

The boys amused themselves by whipping her nipples with a belt, until the plums were raw, then binding them in copper wire, until the buds swelled to tight little balloons of flesh, upon which they were whipped again. Her twat spraying come, as she was buggered, she begged for relief. Julius frotted her clitty with his boot, bringing her to whimpering orgasm, with a flood of her come drenching his toecap. Her reward was several hard lashes of Julius's belt, between the cunt flaps.

The luncheon bell rang, and the leering boys dressed hurriedly.

'Not a *word*, miss,' hissed Julius, waggling a finger in her face.

'No ... all right ... I won't tell, if you don't.'

'Deal,' said Julius, smacking her bottom.

They departed to leave the sobbing matron in her bonds. Straining, Severe began to chew at her skirt ribbons, until she had freed herself.

'The fucking bastards!' she shrieked to her empty surgery.

Her hand slid to her bruised sex, and she began to masturbate vigorously, rubbing and pummelling her cunt, with loud wet slaps.

*Those bastards ... they knew how to turn me on. I shall have my revenge on them, on every blasted boy.*

She imagined a row of suspended boys, strung naked and wriggling, screaming helplessly, as their bare skin mottled with her lashes from a bullwhip. After a few moments, she climaxed, yet continued to wank off, until three more orgasms had convulsed her belly and cunt basin. The sofa beneath her thighs was soaking in piss and come. Sobbing, she fetched her spare uniform and dressed slowly, as she trembled and wept. She had no fresh panties, so had to go bare cunt.

Minutes later, the ladies at the teachers' table turned their heads to see Severe strut to her seat.

'Why, you're late, Miss Compaigne,' said Miss Leach. 'The soup's almost cold.'

'I'm afraid I had two portions,' said Miss Firgate, blushing.

'Sorry,' said Severe, with a smile on rosy lips. 'I was caning a pair of scoundrels, my two portions.'

She smiled radiantly.

'Bare bum, I hope,' purred Miss Toffe.

'Is there any other way for real satisfaction?' said Severe coolly.

The ladies agreed that there was not.

'You know how it is,' Severe drawled, 'when you have juicy bums to whip, and a really satisfying session. You forget all about soup.'

'It looks as if you've already spilled some,' said Miss Toffe with a sniff.

Severe gaped below, and saw a large wet stain spreading over her white nurse's skirt: her cooze was still dribbling come.

'Oh, that,' she said, smiling nonchalantly. 'Girls will be girls, I suppose.'

'They *must* have been juicy bums,' murmured Miss Toffe.

# 10

# Birch Bitch

As well as administering her own punishments, Severe, as
matron, had to heal the wounds inflicted by the other
mistresses. She rapidly became adept at recognising Miss
Leach's, Miss Firgate's, or Miss Toffe's caning style, from
the stippled or striped bruises on the boys' blistered
buttocks. She rubbed cool zinc ointment into their flesh,
letting her fingers stray accidentally to tickle their balls,
and relished the cocks stiffening at her touch. She would
coo in sympathy that one or other of the mistresses caned
most viciously.

'Of course, I do, too ... even harder,' she would purr,
her fingers caressing the boy's tight ball sac. 'You're lucky
I haven't flogged you.'

That made their cocks harder! Especially, when her
sympathy became a sly tease: 'A boy who gets hard before
a bare-bum caning earns extra strokes, of course, but, in
surgery, it is permitted. You poor thing. So proud and stiff.
I suppose it is my girl's touch on your skin. You must be
longing to spurt between a girl's thighs, mustn't you? Her
lovely, smooth creamy nutcrackers, all rippling and powerful. Or for relief, even from my fingers, were I to touch
your cock up there? It would be such a small gesture for
me, and would give you such huge pleasure. But I shan't –
I can't have your sticky wet cream spurting all over my
fingers, can I? Or staining my skirt. What is your longing
compared to my comfort? You'll have to live with those

151

balls deliciously full, study hard and take plenty of cold showers. So there.'

She loved making the boys even more frustrated than when they arrived; loved the thought of all those stiff cocks aching to spurt spunk, and the means by which they would do so. Dozens of nude boys, cocks throbbing stiff and spurting cream up to the ceiling. Her cooze gushed at the gorgeous fantasy. With early morning surgery over, when she had anointed her complement of wealed boys, more sheepish in baring up to a nurse for treatment, it seemed, than for the cane, Severe's habit was to lift her skirt to her breasts, lower her (by now sopping) panties, and enjoy a good ten minutes of masturbation.

Rubbing the flesh of several boys' bare bottoms, superbly harrowed by the canes of her colleagues, never failed to make her cooze seep come, soaking the panties. After her elevenses wank (as she impishly thought of it) and mid-morning coffee, her own caning duty would commence, taking her through until luncheon, before which she needed to steady herself with a cold shower, and an absolutely *massive* wank. Her panties never had quite enough time to steam dry, so sometimes she found herself hobbling awkwardly into luncheon, positive, from the other mistresses' smiles, that they could hear the sloshing moisture at her quim.

Conversation, over the soup and fish, was generally about the boys they had flogged, their demeanour, submissive or defiant, and what a pest their pegoes were, always standing stiff, even at the most painful bare beating.

'Tap the glans with a cold spoon,' Miss Firgate would say. 'I always keep a spoon on ice.'

Miss Leach favoured a tight rubber band on the cockshaft, just above the balls, while Miss Toffe favoured the addition of a cord knotted on the shank below the balls. Severe murmured that one or two boys actually spurted sperm while being caned, and the ladies agreed they had all suffered that outrage.

Miss Firgate averred that those sort needed more than bruised buttocks, they needed proper slavery as well, obliged to perform the most shameful and humiliating tasks, in between regular thrashings. A wilful, spunky boy, made to wear girl's panties, and lick clean his mistress's shoes, or smelly bare feet, before a vigorous caning on his bare, soon learned submission.

Severe drawled that she had previously enjoyed the services of a boy slave, who was absolutely infatuated with her, and had imposed a regime of the most galling chastisements. She admitted that her harshest cruelty did not prevent his pego from rising, in fact, it seemed to encourage it, so she had been obliged to make a virtue of necessity, and use his cock as her anal dildo.

'Sometimes, when I'm . . . you know, frigging, I fantasise about scourging his naked buttocks, and wanking my bumhole with his huge stiff cock, you know, churning it round, right up there, at the colon, and I have the most gorgeous come.'

The others simpered, blushing mischievously, and each professed awareness of a boy slave's anal uses. Severe said she had tired of the snivelling whelp; she did not mention Justin's return. Miss Toffe recommended the birch, on a daily basis, instead of a special punishment. Miss Leach made a moue, and said she feared too much excitement from birching a boy, with her nubbin just *too* tingly, and her quim overflowing. Birching a boy, she dreaded to think how deliciously painful it was, and had to tweak her clitty at once after the flogging, or even – she blushed – during it, hoping the boy would not turn his head.

Miss Toffe said it was the worst agony in the world, and she had been birched naked, on several occasions, while a schoolgirl, usually for solitary or communal masturbation, which, like all schoolgirls, she practised incessantly. Miss Firgate asked why she had repeated her offence, knowing what chastisement awaited, and Miss Toffe coyly admitted to an adolescent craving for bare-bottom pain, and the attention of witnesses to her squirming fesses.

'Of course, you have to wank off immediately, and repeatedly,' she cooed. 'A birching lustfully stimulates the female buttocks quite beyond endurance. The self-administered comes a girl has after birching are quite extraordinary. I doubt if boys really appreciate a stout birching, though, as they are too crude, and their bottoms too insensitive.'

A week after she had caned Julius and Matthew, Severe was in the middle of a hard, delicious elevenses frig, when a timid knock sounded on her door. Severe's fingers were squelching loudly in her wet cunt, with her thumb mashing her clitty, throbbingly erect, and deep gasps of pleasure making her titties heave. To answer the door or to wank to orgasm?

She sighed, and withdrew her fingers, intending to savour the delicious frustration of a come-brimming cooze. Upon opening the door, she saw the embarrassed figure of Julius Puncknowle. She said rather crossly that surgery was over, and her punishment session not yet begun. He stammered that he had come to seek her advice on a very delicate matter, where only Miss Severe could be of help.

'Well, I suppose you'd better come in.' She sighed, closing the door behind them.

Severe left him standing, breathing rather hard, while she reclined in her leather swivel chair, thighs crossed with deliberate carelessness, to show her stocking tops, glistening moist with wanked come. She licked her lips, seeing the rise of his cock and his blushes.

'I trust my thrashing has cured you of stealing panties,' she murmured.

'That's just it, miss,' he blurted. 'I don't think it has.'

She frowned. 'I must warn you that confession may lead to another bare-bum caning,' she said, gasping quietly, at a spurt of juice into her panties gusset.

Julius's face was anguish. 'I've dreamed of just that, miss,' he said. 'I think I need more than caning. That last time, I did things which were shameful. I became a different person. It wasn't me, bumming and ... you know. Yet I've fallen into ... into self-pollution, several times a day, thinking of it. I suffer such guilt. I need real punishment, miss. I want to be licked clean.'

'Tell me about the panties,' said Severe.

'Miss Toffe was in the shower, and I sneaked in and took hers. Then, a pair of Miss Leach's. I wear them all the time. I can't help it. Even when I self-pollute. *Especially* then. It is an act of worship, miss. I adore girls so much – not just lust after them, like Morden and other beastly fellows. I long to serve and please them, be crushed between their creamy silken thighs, be cleansed of my foulness by submission to women . . .'

His babble ground to a halt, and he blushed fiercely; frowning, Severe pursed her lips.

'You have earned caning and more,' she purred. 'You realise you could be expelled?'

'Anything but that, miss, please.'

'A psychologist might see your behaviour as a cry for help,' she said, squirming in her chair, so that her skirt rode up to expose her wet panties gusset. 'As if you actually crave whipping by a woman.'

The boy gaped, his cock stiffening to full bulge.

'I, however, have no time for such claptrap. You are a vile, smutty boy, who must have his vileness thrashed from him the old-fashioned way, and a woman's cane is as painful as a male's. However, we've established that the cane is insufficient for your needs, so . . .'

'Yes, miss?' he said eagerly.

'So it must be the birch.'

'The birch, miss?' He gasped in dismay.

'Yes,' Severe said, with a sly smile. 'A birching on his naked buttocks will cure the smuttiest boy of bad habits. You will present yourself at my chamber at nine this evening, Julius, wearing only your gym shorts.'

Julius withdrew, leaving Severe to finish her wank, bringing herself off with a single touch to her throbbing clit, through her sopping panties. There were only a few candidates for caning that day, including the inevitable Duddy, and none of the sessions merited more than a brisk six or nine cuts on the clothed bottom, which exercise only whetted Severe's appetite for proper bare-bum thrashing.

She masturbated again, quickly and clinically, before luncheon; after the meal, she enlisted the help of Miss Toffe to select her rods for a whipping instrument, from the birch coppice past the lake, at the extremity of the Crushards estate. Miss Toffe rubbed her hands in glee, as they strolled towards the silvery birch trees, and quickly selected a sheaf of the youngest, springiest twigs. There were over thirty twigs in the bundle: a bushy, fearsome instrument, that crackled in Severe's hand, at the slightest motion of her wrist.

'This must cause the boy supreme agony,' Severe murmured, her cunt juicing at the thought of naked fesses squirming under the birch's kiss.

'Well, we can't be entirely sure, until we've tested it,' said Miss Toffe. 'Every birch is different, hand-crafted, and that is why the birch is such a superbly cruel instrument. Yet a virgin birch is as unpredictable as a virgin girl.'

'We can scarcely conjure up a guinea pig out here.'

Miss Toffe bared her teeth and licked them. 'I'll do,' she said.

Before the astonished Severe could respond, Miss Toffe had her pleated grey skirt up and her panties at her ankles. Her shaven cunt glistened with trickled come, and her massive orbs of her naked croup glinted in the dappled sunlight. She grasped the birch trunk, wrapping herself round the tree.

'Go on,' she said. 'I'm ready. I haven't been birched in ever so long.'

'If you're sure . . .'

The girl's quivering bare bum flans aroused hot ardour in Severe, and her cooze dripped come. She lifted the birch and lashed. Swish! The crackling kiss of the rods enveloped the whole expanse of Miss Toffe's buttocks and, when Severe withdrew the birch, the flesh was pockmarked with tiny vicious pink weals. Miss Toffe clenched her fesses hard, and gasped at the cut, but did not cry out. Swish! Severe laid another, and another, and by the fourth, Miss Toffe shuddered, her buttocks began to squirm, and she drooled, eyes closed tight, and teeth bared in a rictus of agony. Swish!

'Uhh . . .' the flogged girl whimpered. 'That's tight . . .'

'Is it enough?'

'No . . . no . . .'

Swish! Severe continued her birching, past a dozen cuts, with the girl's wriggling bare bum a mass of vicious welts, crimson darkening to purple, and interlaced like a trellis of little vines. Trickles of come glistened on Miss Toffe's rippling thighs, as she slapped her cunt against the birch bark, rubbing the lips on the gnarled wood. Swish!

'Ohh!' Miss Toffe gasped. 'Ooh, yes!'

Severe lowered her birch.

'Why did you stop?' groaned Miss Toffe.

'Your bum,' Severe murmured. 'It's fearful. Such a mass of cruel welts. I think the birch is all right.'

'Touch me,' whimpered the whipped girl.

Severe stroked the girl's wealed flesh, hard and crusted under her fingers, and her other hand crept under her skirt to her own sopping slit, which she began to rub. Miss Toffe moaned, wriggling her cunt basin against the tree trunk.

'Touch my clitty,' she begged. 'Make me come.'

'You wicked bitch,' Severe snarled, 'you've made me all fruity, like some blasted lesbo.'

She wrenched Miss Toffe's hair and forced her to the mossy ground, then pulled her own panties down, and straddled her, with her buttocks squashing Miss Toffe's face. She pressed her cunt to Miss Toffe's mouth and ordered her to suck her clitty. As the girl mashed Severe's cunt with her nose and lips, her tongue flicking on the throbbing nubbin and her lips closing to suck the clit, Severe bent across the girl's belly and plunged her face between Miss Toffe's thighs. She found the gash spurting come, and bit on the lips, then the clitty itself, making Miss Toffe howl and suck Severe's clit harder. Her own come washed the girl's face.

'Drink my quim juice,' barked Severe, and she heard the girl's throat gurgling, as she obeyed.

Severe cupped the girl's birched buttocks, and clawed the weals, making Miss Toffe shriek and wriggle in agony. Severe's teeth were busy on the girl's massive hard clitty, biting, chewing and sucking and, as Severe's belly heaved in spasm under Miss Toffe's frantic sucking of her clit, she felt the girl's belly shudder, come squirt from her bitten cunt, and Miss Toffe writhe, squealing and panting, to join her in noisy climax.

'Ah! Ah! *Ahh!*' the girls gasped together.

'What's going on?' spat a female voice.

Severe looked up to see Miss Firgate, holding her birch, with an expression of distaste.

'Miss Compaigne! You a lesbo? I never suspected,' snarled Miss Firgate. 'And taking out your brutal lusts on poor Miss Toffe.'

'No, wait . . .' Severe began. 'Ouch!'

Miss Firgate pulled her hair, toppling her onto the damp moss.

'You'll get a taste of your own medicine,' Miss Firgate hissed. 'Miss Toffe, if you please.'

Miss Toffe leapt to her feet, kicked Severe squelchily in her come-soaked groin, and, as Severe writhed, shrieking in pain, sat on her head, squashing her face in the moss. Severe's bared buttocks wriggled, the flailing of her legs hampered by the panties strung between her thighs. Miss Firgate lifted the birch over Severe's croup.

'No!' Severe shrieked. 'Please, no! It's a mis –'

Swish!

'*Ahh!*'

She squirmed, cunt on the clammy moss, as tongues of searing pain stabbed her naked bum. Swish! The second stroke was even more horrid than the first! Swish!

'*Ooh! Ahh!*' she shrieked, into the moss.

Swish!

'*Urrgh!*'

Tears streamed from Severe's eyes, and her gorge rose, sickeningly, in her throat, as Miss Firgate's savage birch continued to kiss her squirming naked buttocks. Miss

Toffe had her fingers down the front of Severe's nurse's blouse, and had grasped her bare titties to pinch, claw and scratch the nipples very painfully. Swish!

'Mmph! Please stop,' Severe bleated. 'I can explain . . .'

Swish!

'*Ahh!*'

Come flowed from Severe's writhing cunt, until the slamming of her loins into the ground, at each birch cut, made a loud squelchy thud. Agony seared not just her buttocks, but her whole body, from clawed titties to quivering toes and clit.

'That is the birch's beauty,' said Miss Firgate, panting, 'it seems to embrace you in pain, doesn't it?'

Swish!

'Ooh! Ooh!' Severe sobbed, her arse writhing helplessly.

So hard was her birching, that twigs split from the sheaf at each cut, showering Severe in splinters. Come poured from her gash, which she rubbed furiously against the lank mossy tendrils, forcing the mushy moss to creep into her slit and fill it, embracing her throbbing nubbin in their wet frondlets. Squelch! Squelch! Her bum rose and fell, slamming her cunt against the ground, until a wave of electric pleasure filled Severe's belly, and she began to whimper: 'Yes! More! Harder! God, I'm coming . . .'

Swish! Swish!

'Ahh! Ooh! Yes . . . oh! Oh!'

Severe's cunt erupted in orgasm, as the final twigs fell from the denuded birch, and the panting Miss Firgate ceased to whip her. Miss Toffe rose and helped the sobbing Severe to her feet. Severe rubbed her wealed bottom, smarting fearfully, with every single weal glowing in its own fire.

'How could you be so cruel?' she said, sobbing. 'My birch is all spoiled now.'

Miss Firgate had her skirt up, and was tickling her panties with the denuded stem of the birch. Come flowed from her twat into her stockings.

'Just have to bring myself off,' she said, her face flushed, and smiling. 'Can't birch without a wank.'

'Don't worry, Miss Compaigne,' said Miss Toffe brightly, 'I'll help you pick another for your boy's arse.'

That evening, Severe waited impatiently for nine o'clock. Her smarting bottom felt nice and warm, the hideous pain of birching soothed by copious application of her own zinc ointment. She cradled a fresh new birch, of over thirty twigs, at her expectant loins, already seeping come at the sweet prospect of revenge on Julius Puncknowle's naked buttocks. His knock came punctually, and she bade him enter.

'Now, Julius, you filthy boy,' she said, smiling frostily. 'We have all night for you to taste some of your own medicine. I'll make you weep and whimper, shame you till you wish you'd never met me.'

He stood, shivering in the nude, save for his skimpy white gym shorts, already tented by a telltale bulge at his crotch. Severe ordered him to step out of his shorts, and he did so, trembling.

'I'm ... I'm ready for my birching, miss,' he said hoarsely, trying vainly to conceal his erect cock.

'Oh, there's more to it than that,' Severe drawled. 'I've decided that the punishment should fit the crime, of course, and also that sin is its own cure. You seem to be addicted to girls' panties. Very well, you shall have some.'

She lifted her skirt to her ribs, while Julius goggled at her come-soaked panties, framed by frilly white sussies. She raised her left leg, and parked her stockinged foot beneath her buttocks, with the other stretched straight ahead of her, and her stockinged toes tickled Julius's balls. Lazily, she began to masturbate, her face flushing as she wanked her clitty with slow, voluptuous strokes.

The pool of come at her gusset deepened, and the sodden cloth became saturated with her wanked fluid, so that it began to drip on her bare thighs and her stocking tops. She ordered Julius to crouch and present his buttocks upthrust; when he obeyed, she rubbed her toes in her wet crotch, moistening the nylon, then caressed his balls and bum cleft with her foot, before inserting her big toe an inch into his anus and poking him. He moaned softly.

'You know what you did to me,' she said crossly.

'But, miss, I was another person then, quite out of myself.'

'You poor lamb. You'll be quite out of yourself when I skin your bottom with my birch.'

Julius shuddered, whimpering. Severe masturbated, until her panties were slopped with come, then, gasping at the heaving in her belly, she restrained her fingers from bringing her cunt to climax; instead, she rose, and went to her bathroom, leaving the door open. She squatted on the tiles, and there was a hissing, as she pissed in her panties. Her piss finished, she removed the panties, and returned to the crouching boy.

'I've been wearing these panties all day – I haven't wiped myself after the lavatory – they are pretty ripe and stinky, for girls *will* ooze, and now I've filled them to sopping, specially for you, Julius,' she said.

Casually, she wiped her pee-soaked cooze on his hair, then fitted the wet panties over his head, in a balaclava helmet. She ordered him to suck the panties dry of her piss and come. Julius made a loud slurping noise, as he sucked her juices, and Severe calmly removed her skirt, then knotted her blouse above her belly button. Looking in the mirror, she caressed the crusted welts of her own birching, licked her lips and touched her throbbing clitty, with a little jerk, as pleasure surged through her belly. She took off her silver wrist chain, and fastened it tightly around the shank of his balls, squeezing hard, before the clasp clicked, making him groan.

'Now you are my slave,' she purred. 'You will wear your slave bracelet at all times.'

'Yes, miss,' he gasped.

Nude from the navel, save for her sussies and stockings, Severe lifted the crackly birch; Julius shivered. He was to squat on all fours, like a dog, with his pantied head low. She lifted the birch, holding it high over her head. The only sound was the boy's hoarse breathing, as he sucked her panties. The birch scythed the air, lashing his bare buttocks. Swish! He jumped, and a choked sob came from under the panties hood. Severe withdrew the birch to observe a wide pattern of tiny red weals. Swish! The second cut stroked him, three seconds later, and his buttocks clenched tight, with his stiff cock swaying.

'Ooh . . .' he moaned.

'No unseemly wriggles, sir, or girly blubs,' she snapped.

Sliding her fingers between her cunt lips, she lifted the birch, and began to frig herself. Swish! The whipped buttocks squirmed hard, with his spine wriggling, and a quiver in his thighs, over whose uppers the birch cascaded weals. Swish! Severe masturbated rhythmically as she birched, until, at the eighth cut, gazing at the mass of red that now formed the boy's croup, she brought herself to a swift, shuddering orgasm. Come spurted from her frigged cunt to drench her nyloned thighs and feet. Muffled sobbing came from beneath her panties, rising and falling at the boy's mouth, as he sucked the smelly, piss-sodden cloth. Severe continued to masturbate, as she took the birching past a dozen cuts. Swish!

'Uh . . . uh . . .' he gasped, his breath a ragged whine of agony.

'Hurt much?' she asked, squeezing her stiff clitty.

'It's dreadful, miss. Much worse than caning. Oh, I'd take a hundred canings, rather than this. I never knew –'

Swish!

'*Ohh!*'

'Careful. No squealing, remember.'

'Yes, miss.'

'You may call me "mistress" from now on, Julius.'

'Mistress, how many cuts must I take?'

'As many as pleases me.'

'You are abominably cruel, mistress.'

'Yes.'

Swish! Swish! She began to flog harder. His bottom squirmed frantically to the music of his weeping. Swish! Swish!

'Ouch! Ooh! Oh, I say, mistress, that's enough.'

'Impudent cur,' Severe snarled.

Swish! Swish!

'Ahh! I can't take any more. Stop! Stop!'

Swish! Swish!

'Ohh! I'm in agony. You cruel bitch, I hate you.'

'You'll pay for that cheek hereafter,' said Severe, panting.

Swish! Swish!

'*Ooh!*'

By the thirtieth cut, the boy was openly weeping, his bare, bruised arse squirming almost uncontrollably, as the birch licked his wounds deeper and darker. Severe masturbated continuously, bringing herself to three more spasms, by the crack of the fortieth stroke to his shivering, wealed bare. His cockpole stood tree stiff, with his tight balls shuddering, an inch from the hissing birch twigs that scoured his buttocks. She flogged, until her birch was almost denuded, and Julius's bare glowed with the ridges of 55 cuts.

Taking him by the ear, she pulled him, at the hobble, into the bathroom, where she squatted over his whipped arse to piss copiously into his welts. His hood, licked almost dry, came off to reveal his scarlet, tear-glazed face, twisted in sobbing anguish. She stood over him, while he licked the bathroom floor clean; then, he had to lick her come-soaked stockinged toes dry, after which she majestically stripped off her stockings, and, squatting on his back, held up her naked toes for him to lick dry in turn, while she smoked a Dunhill.

'Pretty cheesy, I expect,' she drawled. 'I haven't washed between my toes for ages, so make sure you get all the grume out.'

Come dribbled from her cunt, down his arse cleft, so that when she pressed her cigarette end to his anus, it sizzled to extinction. His next task was to clean her shoes with his tongue, and suck the grume from several pairs of her soiled panties.

'That cock is still rampant,' she said disgustedly. 'I should stub my fags out on your balls, you filthy boy.'

163

'If it please you, mistress,' he blurted.

'Pah! I've a better idea to tame you. For that, I need the cock soft.'

She rose and sat on the wicker chair, then extended her feet to grasp the glans of his cock between two sets of toes. She began to rub, with a fierce grinding motion, and, in a few seconds, Julius gasped, as a powerful jet of sperm spurted on her feet and dripped into the tiles. He was obliged to lick her feet clean once more, and clean his own spunk from the floor with his tongue. His cock bobbed, soft but turgescent.

'That will have to do,' she said, frowning. 'Now, lie down on your back, with your hands behind your neck and your legs well spread. On no account must you move or squirm, while I fit your symbol of slavery.'

'Miss?' he said, timidly obeying. 'I don't follow.'

'A slave must wear visible, humiliating symbols of his slavery to his mistress,' she said. 'Your ball bracelet is one, but insufficiently bold. As my slave, Julius, you are at my beck and call, must take any punishment, obey my every whim, serve me without question or complaint. Do you wish to be my slave?'

'Y-yes, miss,' he mumbled. 'I worship you.'

'A mistress wants obedience, not worship!' she snapped. 'You will call me "Mistress Severe". What I am going to do will seem strange, but you must not move a muscle. At the end of it, you will be proud. I am going to give you a Prince Albert; that is, a brass ring through the glans of your cock. Inserting it is a simple procedure, rather like a tattoo, and relatively painless, I'm afraid.'

For fifteen minutes, Julius Puncknowle trembled, as Severe penetrated his peehole, then deftly pierced his frenulum, and inserted the heavy brass ring, two inches in diameter. Gauze, soap, and peroxide were applied; when she had finished, she permitted him to admire his ringed cock in the glass, then turn to gasp at the birch welts completely covering his buttocks. Severe knelt and fastened a slender chainlet to his Prince Albert ring, fixing the other end to his ball bracelet. The chainlet dangled between glans and balls, like a fob watch chain.

'That is your security chain to stop you being filthy,' she said. 'Comfortable enough, I dare say, but if your beastly cock stiffens, the stretching of your security chain will be most uncomfortable. They say that spurting spunk is much more pleasurable with a Prince Albert, but a slave may only spurt when his mistress permits.'

Severe decreed that it was time for bed, and Julius was to spend the night naked on her floor. He sobbed a little, as she fastened his Prince Albert to her bedpost, with a longer chain, then obliged him to crouch, with head up and mouth open, for her evening ablution. She stripped nude, caressing her bare cunt and titties, inches from his nose, and smiled at his grimace, as his cock attempted to stiffen, held back by its tightened ball chain. She cuffed his hands behind him in steel handcuffs, above his buttocks, then squatted, to piss a long, golden jet of steaming pee into his mouth, and listen to him swallow. His swollen cock was curved like a longbow, bulging, under the constraint of the tiny chain, which drew his balls tight.

'Happy, slave?' she asked, as she curled up in bed.

'Oh, yes, Mistress Severe.'

'Hmm. We'll do something about that tomorrow.'

# 11

# Squid's Throat

The sultry pears of Mabel Otrifice's bottom winked at Luke, through her translucent, skin-tight panties, which gleamed like spun sugar on caramel. The schoolgirl leaned gingerly over the armchair in Luke's study, her skirt drawn up over her back, coltish thighs rippling, and her long, stockinged legs shimmering in shiny nylon.

'Knickers down, Mabel,' he ordered.

Mabel made a face. 'Oh, sir,' she said, pouting, 'surely it's only a pocket beating?'

'For spreading vile rumours?' he snapped. 'I don't think so.'

'But I didn't, sir,' she wailed. 'At least, all the girls do.'

'That's enough, maid. It's twelve licks, bare bum.'

Luke ripped her panties down, baring her fesses. Mabel snivelled, her buttocks goosefleshed and shivering, with the panties stretched tight above her knees. She clutched the side of the chair with white knuckles.

'Please be gentle, sir,' she begged. 'Isn't it some defence, if the rumours are true?'

'You vile slut.'

Luke lifted his cane, and lashed the girl's bare buttocks. Vip! She jerked, the fesses clenching, and gasped noisily.

'Gosh, sir, that was a stinger! You *are* angry.'

Vip!

'Ooh!'

Vip!

167

'Ahh!'

Mabel began to cry. Her whipped bottom wriggled, in a kaleidoscope of red cane welts. Vip!

'*Ooh* ... Oh ... Oh,' she said, the taut slabs of her buttocks squirming helplessly, with tears cascading down her face and come seeping from her cooze, wetting her nylons and stretched panties.

Luke held his cane poised above her croup, and demanded she explain the rumours. Mabel twisted her tear-streaked face, and said, with a sly smile, that if she spoke up, Sir would surely reduce her punishment to a sixer or perhaps an eighter. She told him, licking her lips, that he was called Miss Stiffence's slave, caned on the bare by her every night, and wearing her panties by day. Luke's face turned scarlet. She blurted that Miss Stiffence shared him with her lesbian lover Miss Cluster, and watched the matron encule him with the same rubber strap-on device the two sapphists used for gamahuching.

'Why, you vile trollop!' Luke snarled. 'You'll take an extra three cuts for that vicious lie.'

Vip!

'Ooh!' wailed the squirming schoolgirl. 'You promised a reduction.'

Vip!

'Ahh!'

'Nothing of the sort, hussy.'

Vip!

'Ooh! Ahh! You cruel bugger!'

'*What* did you say?' he thundered.

Vip! Vip!

'*Ohh!* Not fair! I said, prove it. Prove you aren't wearing Miss Stiffence's panties ... *sir.*'

Coquettishly, she wiggled her weal-marked buttocks, and winked her anus bud, while her cunt lips pouted.

'There's nothing to be ashamed of, sir. Girls find it awfully exciting that a boy should wear girls' panties. It's so deliciously naughty. Look how wet my twat is, just thinking of it.'

Luke's cock was throbbing; he blurted that he was not a boy, but a master. Vip!

'Ooh! You're scared, that's what,' she gasped. 'Go on, sir, bare up, and . . . and I won't object if you want to put your cock in me. Some girls say you are bigger than Mr Morton, but I can take it.'

'You *are* an impudent bitch,' he said, panting.

Vip!

'Ooh! Ouch! We have an appetite, sir. It's from being flogged on our bottoms. We get hot, and have to wank off, longing for cock to split our bums. Ask any schoolmaid.'

Vip!

'Ahh!'

Luke gazed at the writhing bare buttocks, the cheeks clenching, with the weals dancing like livid crimson fronds, and the anus lips opening and closing like a sea anemone. His cock rose to full erection. She had taken her twelve strokes; the buttocks were well-scarred, so punishment had been effected. When Mabel reached behind her to part her bum cheeks fully, and murmur that she longed to do something about the bulge at Sir's groin, he gasped that she was a slut, a tart, a monstrous minx.

'Miss Arabel won't know, sir,' she purred, undoing his belt.

'I caution you, this will hurt far more than my cane.'

She pulled down his trousers, revealing Arabel's flowery pink panties, tented by his cock.

'Ooh! Girl's pants! How sweet!'

He slapped her buttocks, and ordered her to resume caning position, then stripped off and mashed his naked stiff cock in her bum cleft. His glans caressed her anus bud, and she shivered. She whimpered that she was afraid he *was* a cruel bugger.

'You asked for it, bitch,' he hissed, ramming his cock into her anus.

'Ouch! That hurts, sir.'

'Take that, slut.'

His cock plunged to his balls, stretching her anus lips wide, with the swollen shaft filling her rectum. She danced on tiptoe.

169

'Ooh! Ooh! Ouch!' she squealed.

Luke's hips slammed her caned buttocks, as he thrust his cock to her colon, in fierce buggery.

'Don't, I beg you, sir,' she whimpered.

'Shut it, cunt,' he said, his balls slapping her underfesses, as he bum-fucked her arse root.

'It hurts so much,' she said, weeping copiously. 'You're right at my tummy, splitting me in two. Oh, don't.'

Her buttocks began to thrust against him, matching the rhythm of his buggery, with her sphincter clenching to suck and squeeze his cockshaft. His cock and balls were glistening with her dripping arse grease, while her cunt spurted come over her rippling thighs. Whap! Whap! His belly slapped her flogged bum, while his glans rammed her soft, mushy colon.

'Ahh! You're bursting me,' she groaned. 'It hurts so. You're fucking my hole to ribbons, sir.'

Mabel slid one hand across her quivering belly to her cunt, and began to masturbate vigorously, her fingers squelching in her slit, with loud slurps.

'Do me . . .' she gasped, drool trickling from her lips, as her thumb mashed her clitty. 'Fuck my bum, fill my hole, split my tummy . . .'

Spunk spilled from her anus, as Luke spermed at her sigmoid colon, and Mabel howled in a long, shuddering orgasm.

'Oh! It hurts! Give me your spunk! Plough my bumhole! Fill me with cream! Your cock's tearing me apart, I love it!' she shrieked.

Luke fucked, until his balls were empty. Mingled come, arse grease and sticky spunk dribbled from her arse cleft into her panties and stockings, and glazed her quivering bare thigh skin. His detumescent cock plopped from her anus, and he wiped it clean of come in the weals of her right buttock.

'Gosh, I came like a hurricane,' Mabel gasped. 'That was *so* good.'

The door burst open.

'*What* was so good?' asked Miss Tupper, frowning. 'You obviously were too busy to hear my knock, so I entered . . . Mr Redruth! What is the meaning of this?'

'I was administering correction to Miss Otrifice, head-mistress,' he gasped hoarsely. 'As you can see from her buttocks, she has taken twelve licks of my cane.'

'And more, it seems,' said Miss Tupper with a sniff. 'Have you enculed the maid, Mr Redruth?'

Luke pulled up his panties, and fastened his trousers. 'With respect, headmistress, you didn't see me buggering her,' he said coyly. 'I admit I had my organ out, to . . . to settle a dispute about size. That's all . . . you cannot have observed my organ actually inside the girl's anus.'

'No, you are right, I did not,' said Miss Tupper, with a perplexed look. 'Nevertheless, you were up to *something.* The girl has been caned? She is therefore restored to innocence. You may go, Mabel.'

Mabel raised her come-soaked panties, pulling them tight, with a squelchy sound, then smoothed down her skirt, curtsied to Miss Tupper, and hobbled away, bow legged.

'What is to be done, Mr Redruth?' said the headmistress. 'This is deuced awkward. I may not have caught you in flagrante delicto, but you were in flagrante something. You must be punished, of course, but discreetly. Will you accept my judgement, with no more said, and no blot on your record?'

'I admit it looks rum, so, yes, I will, headmistress,' Luke murmured.

Miss Tupper licked her teeth. She took pencil and paper, and scribbled a note, sealed it in an envelope, and handed it to Luke.

'You may take this to Matron, and she will deal with you,' she said. 'At once, sir.'

Luke climbed the stairs to Miss Cluster's surgery with a heavy heart. His cock was sore from Mabel's clinging rectum – *the minx!* – and Arabel's nylon panties were abominably tight on his balls. *Damn all girls!* If Miss Cluster's instructions were to whip him – well, he could take that from any beastly girl – she would see Arabel's panties, and his weals from her recent caning, which still smarted, and it would be all round the school. Worse, what if Miss Cluster had heard Mabel's vile rumours, and blamed *him* for spreading them? It *was* a muddle.

Miss Cluster's reaction did nothing to lessen his confusion. In front of Bonita Spear and Sonia Pewte, sitting uncomfortably in her surgery, with their shifting bottoms indicating what they were there for, she tore open the letter, scanned it and laughed.

'It will be such fun to cane a boy,' she said. 'Girls' bottoms are too tough, and they spoil my pleasure by baring up bravely, while boys are snivelling creatures, who weep and squeal and squirm quite deliciously.'

Scarlet with shame before the smirking schoolgirls, Luke insisted he was not a boy, and would do none of those things, but take it like a man. Miss Cluster licked her lips, put her lips to his ear and cupped his balls with her palm.

'If you *are* a man, and your packet suggests so,' she whispered, 'then you must pleasure *me*, afterwards.'

Luke had to wait while Sonia and Bonita lowered their panties to receive a copious application of zinc ointment on their freshly caned bottoms, with Bonita drawling that Mr Morton was in a frisky mood. To Luke's horror, Miss Cluster ordered the girls to remain, as witnesses to his own chastisement; yet the prospect of his bare bottom caned by the matron, and watched by two schoolgirls, caused his cock to stiffen at once. He looked at their long legs, thighs slithering wetly in their nylons, their proud young breasts heaving, and their tongues licking moist red lips, as they ogled his rising cock. His erection swelled to bursting.

'It is for my own protection,' she murmured. 'Rumours get around.'

Luke asked permission to read the headmistress's note, but Rhona Cluster held it away, calling him a cheeky pup. He asked to know what his punishment was, and Rhona said he would find out soon enough, meanwhile he had to obey her orders.

'Surely you are man enough to obey a lady,' she teased, 'or so I've heard. Well, sir, we'll have your pants off, for a start.'

'Must I?'

'You must. Everything off below the waist.'

Smiling, Rhona lit a Gauloise Blonde, while Luke numbly stripped off, in an agony of doubt. To the girls' titters, he stood in Arabel's flowered nylon panties, bulging with his erection, and hesitating. Rhona stabbed the panties with her lit cigarette, and Luke jumped at the sizzle; a hole appeared next to his balls. She stabbed again, and held the glowing tip longer, at his buttocks. A large piece of nylon flared to extinction.

Sonia and Bonita giggled shrilly. Scarlet with shame, Luke ripped off his panties, and stood, with his hands cupping his balls. If he turned towards the girls, they would see his naked risen cock; if away, they would see the welts on his buttocks. Rhona decided the issue, by grabbing his tool in her hand.

'Oh! Miss Cluster! That hurts.'

She whirled him round to display him fully.

'No, really, I must object . . .'

'Do you resist, sir? It will go the worse for you. Seize him, girls.'

The startled Luke made little resistance as Sonia and Bonita leapt to obey Matron's command. Sonia ripped his shirt off, leaving him completely nude, bent over Rhona's worn leather sofa, with his bum high, and both girls pinioning his arms. His stiff cock swayed at the chair back. With chiselled fingernails, the matron scraped his weals, and he moaned, wriggling his buttocks.

'Well, well, what have we here?' Rhona murmured. 'Some lovely juicy cane cuts for my wand to deepen – and not old.' She clawed his bottom viciously, and he squealed; then, she tickled his balls, beneath the throbbing erect tool. 'What a monster! Smelling of spunk, and shiny with girl's bum grease. You've some explaining to do.'

'Oh, please, miss, don't be so cruel. I've agreed to take your punishment, but don't torment me, I beg you. Don't make me confess.'

'Confession is a voluptuous pleasure. You must tell us why you wear Arabel's panties.'

Released by the schoolgirls, on his promise of obedience, and maintaining position over the chair, Luke blurted the story of his enslavement by a haughty mistress, his daily humiliation and chastisement from her lips or cane. Few days went past, without his baring up for a licking of twelve cuts or more. Sometimes, he had to strip, and accept her dog leash, while he licked her yeasty feet clean of grume, and those of her colleagues. He had to serve coffee, dressed as a girl, in maid's uniform, yet with a cruel cord fastening his balls and cane strokes to his bare; then he had to wait for the ladies to pee into his open mouth.

At any time, he must obey Arabel's summons to lick her cunt and bumhole clean after the lavatory, or to lick her erect clitty to orgasm, drinking her come, and her piss, too, as she believed no gamahuche was complete without a pee. She strung him naked for whipping, his wrists and ankles in wooden hobbles, his balls and cock cinched by a rubber cord, with heavy weights dangling from pincers stretching his ball sac. Answering Rhona's puzzled enquiry, Luke said he had no choice but to accept for Arabel was his mistress, and he her slave.

'Yet you fucked Mabel,' snapped the matron. 'Your cock smells of her bumhole. I recognise her arse grease.'

'I know Arabel shall punish me for it,' Luke mumbled, 'just as I had to punish Mabel for slandering my mistress, and yourself, miss. Spreading rumours of vile lesbian crimes.'

'Oh, *those* rumours,' said Rhona with a sniff. 'Why, they are perfectly true, aren't they, girls?'

Sonia and Bonita coyly agreed.

'You, sir,' she snapped, 'seem a disgusting submissive, who craves pain and shame from a lady. The only cure for such a vile habit is an overdose.'

She handed a long ashplant cane to Bonita, who took stance behind Luke's quivering bare. Licking her lips, she lifted the cane, then lashed hard. Vip! Luke gasped, and his buttocks clenched, over a long pink stripe. Vip! The schoolgirl caned higher, and he whimpered. Vip! Higher still, at top buttock, just under the spine, and his cheeks began to squirm. Vip! A stroke on the thigh backs brought tears to his eyes, followed by cuts to the haunches. Vip! Vip!

'Ooh!' he gasped. 'Gosh, it hurts, Bonita.'

'Then why is your sex organ still rude, sir?' said the schoolgirl, panting.

Vip! A stroke took him in the arse cleft, smacking his anus.

'Ahh!' he groaned.

Matron ordered silence. Whimpering, Luke took thirty cane strokes on the naked buttocks, which reddened to a crimson morass of welts, Bonita's licks cleverly overlaying the existing weals from Arabel's cane. His buttocks squirmed and wriggled, clenching, as he danced on tiptoe at each swishing cut to the bare. He gazed up through tear-blurred eyes, to see Sonia and Miss Cluster, hands under their skirts, wanking each other, while their lips were locked in a full tonguing kiss.

After 24 cane strokes, Bonita relinquished the cane to Sonia, who began to masturbate vigorously, as she flogged Luke's buttocks. Bonita rolled up Matron's tight nurse's skirt, and wanked her sopping panties, while deep-tonguing her throat, in a slurping kiss. Vip! Vip!

'Ooh ...' Luke moaned, his flogged arse writhing in agony. 'I can't take it, Sonia.'

'Sorry, sir, but you must,' said the masturbating school-girl, panting. 'You see, your sex organ is still rude, so you must be caned till it isn't.'

'He's a bugger, like all dirty boys,' said Rhona, her cunt squirming wet under Bonita's frig. 'For his sex organ to soften presentably, he must bum-fuck, and squirt his spunk into some unfortunate girl's anus. I shall undertake that unpleasant duty. The pup shall attend to my squid's throat.'

Vip! Sonia ended Luke's caning with a vicious uppercut to the arse cleft, stroking his anus, and just missing his balls. As he sobbed, his arse squirming violently, Miss Cluster tore down her panties, and knelt on the floor, with her bare buttocks upthrust. Sonia guided Luke's stiff cock to the matron's bum pucker, winking and gaping pink, in the taut cleft. Rhona's heavy slit lips dangled gleaming from her shorn cunt basin, dripping copious amounts of come.

Luke gaped; Miss Cluster's buttocks were adorned with a purple tattoo. Across her buttocks splayed sinuous fronds, representing the tentacles of a squid; from above, they resembled fiery cane welts. The head of the squid was her bare cunt, tattooed purple, with an eye peeping from each gash flap, below which the perineum was inked, leading to the squid's mouth, her anus bud. The mouth opened and closed, inviting penetration, and Luke stabbed it with his cock, pushing his glans an inch inside the squid's throat, then, as Miss Cluster trembled and whimpered in pain, ramming it fully to the root of her rectum, cleaving her and mashing his balls against her striped buttocks.

As he buggered her, the squid's eyes on her cunt lips rolled, while its tentacles writhed across her quivering buttocks. Sonia and Bonita embraced, pleated skirts high, and fingers scrabbling inside their wet panties, as they tongue-kissed, and rubbed nipples. Come dribbled from their frigged panties, to soak their shiny nylon stockings, which squelched, as they slithered together in a tangle of long rippling limbs.

'Uhh!' Rhona squealed. 'You're hurting me.'

'You asked for it, miss,' Luke said, panting. 'My bottom smarts like fire, and I'll punish you for it.'

Slap! Slap! His balls smacked her writhing bum globes, as his cock slammed her colon, and the matron whimpered.

'Oh, the shame!' she gasped. 'I'm going to burst with that brutal big cock. Yes, fuck me harder, fill my bum with meat, split my squid . . . punish me, sir!'

Luke grunted, as his spunk flooded Matron's rectum, and she shuddered, in a violent come.

'Oh! Yes! Fuck my bum, fill me with spunk! Yes . . . Ah! *Oh!*'

Come spurted from her cunt, and the squid's eyes blinked furiously, while the gasps of Sonia and Bonita, masturbating to orgasm, filled the room. Panting, Luke withdrew his tool from Rhona's anus.

'Gosh, you are so big, that cock really hurt,' said the buggered matron, panting, 'but not as much as Mr Morton's.'

'Why, you cheeky ...' Luke snarled, grasping the ashplant cane.

Vip! He lashed the matron on the tattooed bottom.

'Ooh! Don't!' she squealed.

Bonita and Sonia giggled, as they rushed to his aid, with Bonita sitting on Rhona's head, crushing her face to the floor, and Sonia holding her ankles. Vip! Vip! Luke's cane flashed and whistled, as he whipped the naked buttocks, rapidly turning them crimson, so that the cane-flushed bare skin masked the writhing tentacles. Matron sobbed and squirmed, with a little piercing squeal at each cut of the cane, until her bottom was fiery crimson, and the squid tattoo scarcely visible.

Come gushed from her cunt onto the carpet; her feet wriggled helplessly in Sonia's grasp, while her cries were muffled under Bonita's crushing buttocks. Come from Bonita's cunt seeped through her panties, as she wanked off, drenching the matron's hair. Vip! Vip! Luke flogged the sobbing Rhona over twenty cuts. The come gushed in a torrent from the groaning matron's gash, and she begged Bonita to frig her clit.

'Please,' she said, sobbing, 'I must come. Bonita, you sweet girl – or Sonia, my darling – oh, please wank me off.'

'I'll wank you, slut,' growled Luke, and he delivered a swingeing uppercut, right in the arse cleft, and the cane tip thrashed Rhona's stiff extruded clit.

'Ooh!' she screamed, her slit spraying come.

Vip! He lashed her between the gash flaps, the cane making a wet slapping squelch, and striking the clitty once more.

'Yes!' Rhona shrieked. 'Ooh!'

Vip! The cane smacked her clitty again.

'Oh! Yes! *Ahh!*'

Rhona shuddered in a second heaving orgasm, as her cunt spurt come over her rippling bare thighs. Panting, Luke lowered the cane. Rhona rose, clutching her caned bottom and rubbing the welts, with her face crinkled in pain.

'That was so cruel,' she said, sobbing, 'and those beastly schoolgirls were wanking off at my shame. We must teach them a lesson, sir. A dozen licks on the bare should cure them. You girls, take position, one at each end of the sofa.'

'Oh, miss, must we?' moaned Bonita.

'Skirts up, panties down, and no whingeing.'

Sullenly, the girls obeyed, bare bums up, and heads touching in the centre of the sofa. Rhona hobbled to her cabinet, and fetched a second cane for Luke – a springy rattan, three feet long. He took caning stance behind Sonia, while the matron attended Bonita. On Miss Cluster's signal, they began to flog the schoolgirls' naked bottoms. Vip!

'Ouch!'

Vip!

'Ooh!'

Vip!

'That hurts!'

Vip!

'Ahh!'

Both bottoms squirmed helplessly under cane; the schoolgirls' faces touched, their lips met and, as their buttocks reddened and wriggled, their mouths sucked in a slurping tongue-kiss. Their swollen bare cunts flapped and writhed, spurting come on their twitching nyloned thighs, as they squirmed against the sofa, frigging their clits on the leather.

As Luke caned, his cock stirred, until it was risen to full stiffness. The last few cuts made the schoolgirls wriggle harder and squeal louder, until, as the last weal striped their bottoms, both girls mewled and gasped in orgasm, their slits spurting slime over the sofa.

'What a disgusting mess,' snapped Rhona.

Each girl was obliged to crouch, and lick and swallow the other's come from the glistening leather. As they did so, the matron knelt at Luke's balls and applied her lips to his throbbing bell-end, shiny with spunk and her own arse grease. She began to suck powerfully, her head swooping from time to time to let her mouth engulf the whole cockshaft and her lips nibble his balls. Sonia and Bonita rose, flushed from their task, and licked their lips of girl come.

'That's not fair,' said Bonita indignantly.

'The bitch is having all the fun,' protested Sonia.

They seized the two canes, and raised them over Miss Cluster's bare bottom. Vip! Vip! Skirts swirling and shiny nylons flashing, both schoolgirls began to lash the fellating matron; Rhona's bum jerked and clenched, its squid tentacles writhing, and she squealed in anguish, with her mouth clamping Luke's cock harder. Vip! Vip!

'*Ahh!* Oh . . . yes, yes, I'm a naughty girl, thrash me!'

The flogged matron pressed Luke's buttocks to her face, as she gobbled at his balls and cock, whining, while her bottom squirmed under the schoolgirls' merciless canes. Vip! Vip! Sonia and Bonita panted, scarlet of face, panties down, and wanking their naked gashes, as they caned. The surgery door swung open.

'Rhona, gorgeous, I'm dying for a wank,' trilled Arabel's voice. 'Are you in the middle of licks? You can frig me, while you cane the lucky slut.' Her skirt already raised to show her wet panties, she advanced, stopped and gaped. 'What's this?' she snarled. 'Taking another girl's licks? You dirty cheating lesbo. And that boy is *my* slave.'

Her fist smacked Rhona's face away from Luke's cock, which bobbed free, dripping with girl drool. Squealing, Rhona toppled to the floor, while her caners lowered their weapons, with shocked cries. Arabel dropped on Rhona's breasts in a wrestler's smash, and, with her buttocks writhing on the matron's squashed titties, began to pummel her exposed cunt.

'Stop! Ouch! Stop!' screamed Rhona, writhing, with Arabel's fist descending on her naked gash, in fierce squelching thuds.

She clawed at Arabel's back, then got her fingers under her skirt and ripped it down. Panties bared, Arabel alternated punches with rakes of her claws, straight down Rhona's exposed quim flaps, her sharp fingernails slicing the matron's erect clitty and wet, pulsing slit meat.

'*Ahh!*' Rhona screamed, as Arabel's painted talons reamed her cunt.

The squid's eyes whirled madly, as her cunt flaps squirmed under their beating.

'No, no,' she pleaded, as the schoolmistress ripped her stockings to ribbons, with a loud wrenching noise; tore her skirt in half, bit and chewed it, then spat the pieces over Rhona's legs.

Rhona's fingers scrabbled feebly inside Arabel's panties. Arabel clawed her quim, and Rhona's legs threshed helplessly, come streaming from her harrowed cunt, as she shrieked in agony. Drool cascaded from her mumbling lips, and her eyes were flooded with tears.

'Oh, no! Please!' she said, sobbing, as Arabel seized her clitty between her thumb and fingernail, and began to slice and pinch the erect pink nubbin.

Rhona's hand was at Arabel's buttocks; grimacing, Rhona lunged, and Arabel shrieked, her bottom springing up from Rhona's crushed tits. The matron tore down her tormentress's panties, revealing her index stuck deep in Arabel's anus. Rhona leapt up, pushing Arabel to the floor, face first, with her finger still in Arabel's anus, buried to the knuckle. She squatted on the small of Arabel's back, with her toes pinioning Arabel's neck, and her other foot squashing her left thigh.

'You fucking bitch,' Rhona snarled.

A second finger entered Arabel's squirming arsehole, and a third, until Rhona had all four fingers of her hand stretching the tender anal lips the width of an apple. She began a hard finger-fucking, slamming her hand right up

Arabel's rectum, so that the mistress writhed, drooling and babbling in buggered agony.

'No, Rhona!' she pleaded. 'It hurts so! What's got into you?'

Bonita and Sonia wanked noisily.

'Flay the slut!'

'Flense her!'

Whap! Whap! While Rhona buggered the squirming mistress with her fingers, she began to spank the exposed buttocks. Arabel squealed and wriggled, helpless to escape her punishment.

'Look at Sir's love stripes,' cooed Sonia.

'And that lust-making stiff pego.'

'Shall we . . .?'

'Let's.'

Kneeling at Luke's feet, the schoolgirls playfully tussled, until Bonita had possession of his cock, and Sonia his bum and balls. Bonita opened her mouth wide, like a baby thrush fed its worm, plunged and engulfed the swollen cockshaft in her throat. Sonia licked Luke's balls, her lips meeting Bonita's in a kiss, then sank to his perineum, where she tongued his anus, and slid her tongue over the weals of his beating.

Each girl's skirt was up, over naked cunt and come-soaked stockings, and each masturbated powerfully, as she worshipped the male with her mouth. Sonia's fingernails clawed Luke's cane welts, and he moaned, his moan turning to a gasp, as she got her tongue into his anus, and began to stab his rectum. Bonita interspersed her sucking with little bites to his cock, her teeth sinking deeper and deeper, with sharp incisions to the neck of his glans and his peehole, until he was wriggling in distress.

'That hurts,' he gasped.

Sonia sank her nails into his deepest, crustiest bum weal, and bit his anus, around her stabbing tongue.

'Ouch! Ooh! Stop!'

Luke's cries of protest mingled with the shrieks of his squirming mistress Arabel, weeping copiously, as Rhona's fingers squelched in her rectum, dripping arse grease over the matron's knuckles, while Arabel's quim spurted come all over the surgery carpet. The fellating schoolgirls groaned in pleasure, as their fingers wanked their cunts to cascades of come, soaking their stocking and panties.

'Bags I go on his cock,' said Sonia, plopping her tongue from Luke's rectum, and licking his balls, slippery with Bonita's drool.

'Mm! Mm!' replied Bonita, shaking her head, with her throat impaled on the cockshaft.

'You selfish cow!' Sonia erupted, pushing Bonita over; the two schoolgirls released Luke, and began to grapple on the floor.

'Ooh!' squealed Sonia, as Bonita kneed her quim.

'Ah! Ah!' shrieked Bonita, as Sonia clawed her nipples, and ripped off her blouse and bra.

The schoolgirls were a flurry of legs and arms, with the sounds of ripping, as they shredded each other's clothing, until they fought, glowing with scratches and bruises, and half nude, their bras, panties, stockings and skirts flapping in ribbons around their writhing naked limbs. With harsh smacks, they pummelled and spanked cunts, teats and buttocks, until their bodies glowed red with bruises.

Whap! Whap! Arabel's spanked bare buttocks, squirming under fierce buggery, were fiery red with Rhona's palm prints.

'Stop!' Arabel gasped. 'No, don't. Oh, you bitch, you're making me come. Spank me, fuck me, hurt me.'

Come squirted from her writhing cunt, as Rhona clawed her colon, making Arabel drool and dribble, her face a mask of agony, mashing the carpet.

'Stop it, you beastly sluts!' Luke cried to the fighting schoolgirls.

He seized the rattan, and began to flog the wriggling bodies beneath him. Vip! Vip!

'Ooh!'

'Ahh!'

Red stripes appeared on the schoolgirls' whipped flesh. They squealed, and curled into two separate balls, with

Luke continuing to flog the exposed bare thighs and buttocks. As they shivered under the cane, Bonita and Sonia wanked off vigorously.

'Yes ...' groaned the spanked Arabel, spurting come from her gash, as her belly convulsed in orgasm.

Rhona slapped herself on the cunt several times, then began to thumb her clitty. The tentacles of her buttocks writhed in pleasure, as she brought herself off, with little gasps and mewls, echoed by the two schoolgirls, masturbating to come, as the cane showered their bare bodies with savage licks.

'Ooh!'

'Ahh!'

'Yes!'

'Yes!'

The carpet was a pool of come and arse grease.

'Just look,' wailed Rhona.

'It's all *his* fault,' spat Bonita.

'The dirty beast should clean up,' agreed Sonia.

Arabel slammed her slave in the belly, and he doubled up; she delivered a hearty kick to his buttocks, which sent him sprawling to the floor. Vip! Vip! Vip! Each brandishing a cane, the two schoolgirls, their faces scarlet with rage, lashed his bare arse.

'Lick it up!' hissed Bonita.

'Every drop!' said Sonia.

Whimpering under their cane strokes, Luke obeyed, sucking the girl come from the carpet. He continued to lick, as hot streams of piss cascaded over his arse weals, then his face and back, until he dripped with the golden steaming fluid of all four females, who were squatting, as they bathed him in their scorn. Sobbing and crying, he swallowed come and piss, while the girls' canes striped his arse raw.

Rhona and Arabel embraced, tongue-kissing, bottom-stroking, and wanking clitties to new comes, as Arabel's slave toiled in his shame. Sonia and Bonita panted, teeth bared, as each masturbated her own cooze, dripping come onto Luke's wealed bum. Only Luke noticed the tall shadow of Miss Tupper obscuring them.

'Headmistress ... thank goodness you've come ...' he gasped.

'Not a moment too soon, it seems,' snapped Miss Tupper. 'You will pack your bags, report to my office before breakfast to collect your arrears of salary and depart by the noon train, Mr Redruth. There is no room at Licks for such a degenerate master. Goodbye, sir.'

She turned, and strutted from the surgery. Luke rose, rubbing his wealed bottom.

'You fucking bitches!' he blurted.

'Insolence?' hissed Arabel. 'You shall be punished for that, slave. Report to my room tomorrow morning, *after* breakfast. Before you depart, I shall give you a painful and permanent reminder of your slavery, in *addition* to your whipping.'

'Yes, mistress,' Luke said with a sob.

# 12

# Pierced Punishment

Luke's knees trembled, kneeling on the stone floor of Arabel's dungeon. He was naked, his arms strung above him by two ropes, anchored to the ceiling, so that his trunk leaned forwards at a slight angle, comfortably displaying his bare back, as well as his buttocks, as a target for Arabel's cat-o'-nine-tails. His ankles were clamped well apart by pinching metal cuffs, embedded in the floor. A chain was wound tightly at the base of his balls, tautly anchored to the floor, yet his cock throbbed stiffly erect. Arabel swished the nine knotted leather cords, tipped in steel buds, and kicked his glans with the sharp steel point of her boot.

'You verminous wretch,' she spat. 'What gives you the right to stiffen when your mistress is about to flog you raw?'

'Your beauty, mistress,' he blurted.

'Impudent, abject swine!'

Arabel wore skintight black leather knee boots, over fishnet stockings, fastened by garter straps to a black satin basque, whose back swooped to her buttock cleft. Beneath the garter straps gleamed silver crotchless panties, matching her bra of twin metallic cones, with razor-sharp points, which cupped her huge domed nipples, leaving her back and teats naked. Her swollen red quim lips bulged naked through the vent in her panties, with her erect moist clitoris peeping through the gash folds, and her long blonde tresses cascaded freely over her breasts and shoulder blades.

Behind her stood the other staff members: Joly, Irena and Liliane, in their pleated skirts and cream nylons, looking flushed with excitement, and Martin Morton and Tim Playfair staring shyly at the floor. Arabel traced the gouged weals on Luke's bottom, making him wince, with a deep groan.

'Bum's almost ripe for cuts,' she murmured.

She silenced Tim's and Martin's murmurs of sympathetic protest, with a flick of her scourge. 'We shall commence with a whipping. Some say a male squirming with cuts to his back feels greater shame. So, twenty-four strokes on bare back, slave.'

The female staff clapped their hands in glee.

'Oh,' Luke whimpered. 'I came here to impose discipline, and I find myself in thrall to a cruel mistress. Publicly flogged. It's all gone so horribly wrong.'

'Submissives of your sort drool to whip schoolgirls' bottoms,' drawled Arabel, 'when you really crave the lash on your own skin.'

'You did disrespect a lady, old chap,' said Tim. 'Best take your stripes like a man.'

'I'm afraid punishment unwitnessed is no real punishment,' said Martin with a sigh.

Arabel lifted the whip, and it landed, smacking loud, on Luke's back. Thwap!

'Uhh,' he groaned, jolted forwards by the force of the lash, and his wrists jerked against their ropes.

Nine livid red welts appeared on his skin almost at once. Thwap! Luke's gorge rose, as the pain seared him, and his shoulders wriggled against their bonds. Thwap! He began to weep, panting hoarsely, with his whole body squirming, and his tethered feet thumping on the flagstones. Thwap! Thwap! Each stroke of the cat covered his entire upper back, the knotted leather thongs deepening his existing welts, and gouging new ones. Thwap! Arabel varied her strokes, leaning to one side so that the weighted tips lashed Luke's nipples, bruising the flesh with red weals.

'Ohh,' he groaned.

The scourged victim's cheeks were wet with tears. The two male teachers gazed, ashen and trembling, at Luke's whipped back, while Joly, Liliane and Irena giggled, their skirts rustling and thighs twitching in a slither of moist nylon. Their faces were pink with excitement.

'Look at his cock,' Joly whispered. 'Aren't you feeling juicy?'

'So wet making. And such lovely welts!' gasped Irena.

'Let's wank,' purred Liliane, her skirt already up, and her fingers delving inside her white cotton bikini panties.

Her two colleagues joined her in blatant masturbation, swaying their cunts in the rhythm of Arabel's scourging, as the nine thongs rose and fell, thudding with a dry slap on Luke's flogged back. His erect cock shook at each stroke. Thwap! Thwap!

'Ohh!' he squealed. 'Ooh!'

'Silence, whelp,' hissed Arabel. 'Your insolent erection disgusts me. Can't someone do something?'

Joly raised her skirt fully and slid out of her panties, sniffing them and making a face, for they were wet with wanked come. She wrung the panties over Luke's head, dripping come onto his back weals, then squatted, as if to dung, over his rigid cock. Lowering her spread fesses, she nuzzled his helmet into her stretched anus bud, then dropped hard, engulfing the tool in her rectum, right up to his balls. Arabel did not break the rhythm of strokes, but Luke's wriggling was now suppressed by Joly's buttocks rising and falling on his tool, with sucking squelches.

She raised her distended anus to the tip of his cock, teasing his peehole, before plunging down again, to slap his balls with her quivering fesses. His stiff cockshaft gleamed with the girl's copiously dripping arse grease that rapidly covered his balls. As she buggered herself on his tool, Joly masturbated vigorously, with the come from her wanked cunt trickling down her thighs and perineum to enrich the arse grease from her anus.

'Buck me, sir,' she panted. 'Fuck my bum hard. Stuff me with that big tool.'

'I'll make the lazy brat's arse buck,' snarled Arabel.

Thwap! She began to flog his buttocks, smacking them, clenched and squirming, to plunge Luke's cock into Joly's hole, right to his balls.

'Yes!' Joly gasped. 'Fabulous! Cock at my tripes, how it hurts! Ooh! Ahh! I'm bursting! Come on, Luke, fuck me to pieces, and spunk up me. I'm going to come . . .'

She wanked furiously, then gasped in long, shrill ululation, as come sprayed from her gash, and her belly heaved in spasm. Liliane and Irena demanded their turns, and the panting Joly sullenly plopped her bumhole from Luke's cock, which was promptly engulfed by Irena's anus. Thwap! The cat rose and fell over Luke's wriggling buttocks, slamming his cock into Irena's arse, with the girl pumping up and down on the tool, while frigging her spread quim lips.

'Ooh! Yes!' she gasped, 'I'm nearly there. Luke, why won't you spunk? Ahh! I'm coming!'

She threshed, drooling, as orgasm clenched her; come spurted over her thighs, and Luke's balls, glistening with juice. Liliane pulled her off Luke, and squatted, plunging his cock into her rectum, in a heavy thrust, then squeezing him with tight movements of her sphincter.

'I'll make him spunk,' she gasped.

For two minutes, Liliane's buttocks bounced on Luke's cock, impaling her rectum, while his shuddering bare arse crusted with dark purple scourge welts. At last, she could hold back no longer, and exploded in a braying, gasping come. Thwap!

'Ahh!' Luke bleated. 'No more, mistress, I beg you.'

Smiling grimly, Arabel ripped down her panties, dripping with come, and bared her arse. She squatted on a porcelain chamber pot, and peed noisily, her anus plopping a little string of dainty dungs, then rose, thrust her buttocks to Luke's face, and ordered him to lick her bum clean. Whimpering, he did so, while Arabel lazily frigged her clitty; then, she raised each boot in turn, and thrust her toecaps into his mouth, with the command to polish them.

188

This was done, and the soles of her boots were licked clean, the spiked heels stabbing his throat, until her boots gleamed.

Arabel squatted and sank her buttocks onto his erect tool, kneading and squeezing his cockshaft as it slowly disappeared into her anus, all the way up her, until she gasped at the impact of his glans on her colon. She began a vigorous buggery, wanking her clitty hard, and, in only ten seconds, he spurted his cream so powerfully up her that it dribbled from her anal lips to glaze his balls. Arabel masturbated herself to orgasm, then frowned, as she withdrew from his softening cock.

'You went off like a rocket, you swine,' she complained. 'I suppose *that* was my beauty.'

'Yes, mistress,' he whimpered. 'I adore you. Your body *is* orgasm! And your arsehole squeezes so tight, I couldn't hold my spunk in.'

'Happily, the memento of your slavery shall serve as a cure,' she said, leering.

Arabel emptied salt and chilli sauce into her chamber pot, swirling it, to dissolve, then splashed her piss generously across his flogged back and buttocks. Smiling at his screams of pain, she rubbed the liquid deep into his weals. As Luke hung from his ropes, sobbing and squirming, the mistresses held him still, while Arabel fetched her surgical kit. Luke's eyes widened.

'What . . .' he gasped. 'No! please!'

'It will only hurt a little,' purred Arabel, 'and then you'll be proud and pretty, my slave forever more. It's all the rage here at Licks, you know. The finest cocks sprout them.'

Pale-faced, Tim and Martin looked away, while Luke sobbed and groaned; after fifteen minutes, his cock sported the gleaming brass ring of a Prince Albert, pierced through his peehole and frenulum. After swabs, soap, lotion and gauze, he was unstrung, and allowed to hobble to his feet.

'Which side do you dress?'

'The left, mistress.'

'Just like the original Prince Albert. His wife Queen Victoria invented the ring for him to restrain his big tool, so that he would look decent in his breeches.'

Arabel buckled a garter around his upper left thigh, and fixed the cock ring to the garter in a small steel loop in the garter.

'There, now! You will be obliged to remain decent, until I choose to free you – whenever *that* shall be. Mabel Otrifice, whom you have so cruelly abused, tells me you are to work for her family firm in Brazil. I have just caned her two-dozen licks, which impelled her to inform me.'

'Yes, mistress. She was kind enough to arrange employment.'

'The saintly girl! While you are there, your cock is my prisoner, except for peeing. There will be no depraved conduct. You must suffer full balls, without spurt. Have I your word of honour?'

'Yes, mistress.'

'Then you are dismissed.'

The three mistresses fondled their cunts.

'He does look pretty with that super ring,' cooed Liliane. 'Doesn't he, Mr Morton?'

'I . . . um . . .'

'Mr Playfair?'

'Well . . .'

'*You* would look awfully pretty, too, gentlemen,' purred Joly.

Luke hobbled out of the door to the groans of anguished protest and the sounds of two males stripped and subdued. He made his way to Miss Tupper's chamber to collect his cheque, and found the headmistress cool, but without her angry disapproval of the day before. She sighed, and said she was sorry to lose such a virile young teacher, but such males had an unfortunate tendency to overstep the bounds of discipline and stray into depraved sensuality.

She noticed the bulge at Luke's thigh, and asked what it was. When Luke explained, she demanded to see. She held his cheque, fluttering between her fingers, and Luke had no choice but to obey. He bared up below and Miss Tupper gasped at his cock, restrained by the big brass ring and fastened at his garter. She reached out to touch it, her fingertips caressing his naked glans and peehole and the shiny brass adornment. His cock stirred and began to stiffen, straining against its bonds.

'It must be awkward to pee,' she said.

'It is, a bit. I'll have to sit down, like a girl.'

'And if it . . . you know . . . gets stiff?'

'Well, the ring is big enough, headmistress.'

'But so cruelly restrained. Let's see, shall we?'

With a few deft flicks to his glans, Miss Tupper had Luke's cock straining and erect, bent grotesquely against the restraining clasp, and with his cock ring wrenching his glans flesh.

'That looks awfully uncomfortable,' she purred.

'It is,' he groaned, wincing.

Her fingers unfastened the clasp, and his cockpole sprang free.

'No, miss. I mustn't . . .'

She put her finger to her lips, even as her skirt descended, rustling, to the floor. Her panties followed, baring her dripping twat.

'You are still in my employ,' she whispered. 'Before your train goes, you have time to give me a good spanking and bumming. That is an order, sir.'


'More coffee, slave.'

Julius Puncknowle dutifully poured, wearing only a scanty pair of gym shorts, with the deep weals on his buttocks glowing through the translucent cotton, and the heavy lump of his Prince Albert bulging at the front. Severe pulled down his shorts and scanned his weals, then poked them with her fingernails. She said he was ready to take a birching, which his sloth and insolence had royally earned. Julius trembled, licking his lips, and his cock stiffened.

'As my mistress pleases,' he said.

191

She struck the cocktip with the handle of her rattan cane, with a scowl of annoyance, but that only made his tool rise fully.

'You are incorrigible,' she murmured, staring at the throbbing stiff cock, as come began to ooze in her panties.

Severe found that possessing a slave, the willing Julius Puncknowle, had its drawbacks. For one thing, a slave was so demanding, always seeking the marks of her favour, meaning a bare-bottom caning or birching, and quite wearing out her already over-exercised caning arm. Even when she used his own arm to cane the buttocks of malefactors, for their extra shame, he seemed to become twice as vociferous in demanding caning for his own. No humiliance, whether pissing into his mouth, obliging him to lick her bottom clean after dunging, or to clean her boots with her tongue – even sucking the fluids from her soiled panties – seemed to dissuade him from wanting more.

His cock ring seemed to keep him permanently, and painfully, erect, itself an impudence demanding chastisement. In addition, more and more fellows oiled up to her, smirking and coy, to suggest that they, too, longed to be her slaves. What was it with boys that the scent of a dominant girl made them turn to fawning, submissive jellies? Apart from their pegoes, which seemed perpetually rampant at the prospect of thrashing on the bare. She wondered if Julius blabbed about 'special service': Severe nude and straddling the boy's ringed cock to plunge it into her bum for a glorious buggery, making her twat gush with come, as the Prince Albert slammed her sigmoid colon.

They were always sniffing her scent, as she passed, as if the swish of her stockings, moist rubbing of her vaginal lips, squelch of her perspiring nyloned feet and bouncing of her bubbies in their skimpy bra sprayed the air with mysterious perfume. Severe thought that, as matron, she must have a sort of medical smell, but, whatever it was, it apparently aroused the boys, who became especially excited when she passed, all sweaty and stinky-toed and ponging at her twat, on her way to bathe. She didn't find *their* grubby smell attractive!

A male smelled nice if he was freshly washed and shaven nice and smooth, all over, and exuded that aroma of sheer power, which made a girl tremble at the knees. Coz had it, in his hairy naval way; Justin had it. You could almost smell the sperm in his balls – gallons of hot cream, fragrant as chestnut flowers, and piping hot for her hole. Blast Justin, the cheating hound! She caressed her cane. If only he was a boy at Crushards, she would enslave him till he squealed! In the meanwhile, she must ensure that no boy's arse was free from welts. Severe owed it to herself.

She glanced at her roster of punishments for that day and smiled, with a little thump of glee in her heart: at long last, the arrogant lout, Tremaine Duddy, was due a caning on the full bare! Should she order Julius to effect the punishment for Duddy's greater shame? No, this pleasure was to be all hers. She might even incite jealousy in her slave, by her evident pleasure in caning another boy naked. She frowned, mentally correcting herself: it was not her concern whether a mere slave was jealous or not. She ordered Julius to await her morning's victims, and tell them their punishment was deferred until the afternoon – all except for Tremaine Duddy. At last, Julius ushered in the smirking miscreant.

'Well, Duddy,' Severe said, 'it seems you are really in hot water this time. What was your offence?'

'Why, nothing at all, miss,' he swanked. 'It was a fit up.'

Severe glanced at her notes. 'Interfering with a scullery maid,' she said, 'groping her – assaulting her improperly – scarcely a laughing matter, sir.'

'Sally was giving me a Dutch fuck, miss,' protested Duddy. 'A tit-wank, with those gorgeous golden melons, almost as sweet as yours, miss, if I may say so.'

'You may *not* say so,' rapped Severe, slamming her desk with the cane.

'I gave her a pearl necklace,' Duddy continued, 'and she swallowed half of my spunk. There was too much for her to swallow it all.'

Severe's clitty tingled and stiffened. 'Enough!' she cried, rising from her desk, her thighs rippling and breasts heaving in anger, yet with a squishy wet seep quickening from her gash lips. 'You have dictated your own correction: two dozen licks of my cane.'

Duddy shrugged.

'*On your naked buttocks*,' she said.

He whistled. 'I see, miss. Well, it shan't be anything, compared to my whippings from my governess, Miss Esmeralda, back on the pampas. I used to poke her, up the bum, you know, and then she got all weepy and virtuous, and whipped me for it. In Brazil, all the girls like anal, for then they can remain virgins.'

Severe blushed.

'Worth a flogging, though,' he drawled, 'for she had the tightest, most succulent arsehole you can imagine.'

'I do not wish to imagine, you vile brat!' Severe cried. 'You will strip everything off, sir. I'll take you in the full bare.'

Duddy nodded at Julius. 'What, in front of your panty slave?'

'Assuredly.'

Leering, Duddy stripped to his shorts; Severe had often seen his rump, caned through cloth, but now the boy twirled to face her, and she gasped. His cock was clearly visible, half stiff, through the fabric, and was truly monstrous. *Bigger than Justin, or Julius, even bigger than Luke Redruth.* As if guessing her thoughts, he murmured that even Sally's massive titties had trouble enfolding his cock.

Slowly, teasing, he slipped his shorts down, inch by inch, until the giant crimson knob of his glans sprang out, almost pushing the garment down by its sheer size. He stepped out of the shorts, and stood nude and erect, with his hands on his hips. His cock towered like an oak over the muscled slabs of his belly and, to Severe's surprise, he was free of hair, the balls and massive tool gleaming razor

194

smooth, and insolent in their unashamed nudity: the arrogance of a buck subduing a doe with his power. Severe gasped at the fierce flow of come, soaking her panties.

*Well over ten inches, even when limp. And now, erect, it's too frightening to compute. Damn. I'll have to change panties. But then, the new pair will get wet, too.*

Insolently, Duddy asked where she wanted to take him, and Severe wordlessly commanded him to assume position over the sofa.

'We have a nice long morning, Duddy,' she said, 'so I'm going to take my time blistering your arse to ribbons.'

As he positioned himself, she could not take her eyes off that giant of a cock, and trembled, for despite the insistent juicing of her cunt, she could not imagine fitting that tool into her bumhole. *You're going to flog him, not fuck him, Severe. You are in command.*

She lifted her cane over the boy's taut, slightly quivering buttocks. The cane trembled; she scanned his broad, rippling back, the tightly muscled croup, free of blemish, and saw Miss Esmeralda – whoever *she* was – whipping the boy's skin to shreds, after that obscene cock had pleasured her anus, squirting sticky hot spunk up her horrid South American bumhole, and over her beastly South American thighs, in the middle of the blasted South American pampas. Severe *hated* Miss Esmeralda. Duddy twisted his head to peer at the bulge in Julius's shorts.

'Nice Albert, Julie,' he drawled.

'Don't call me that!' spat Julius, flushing.

'Come on, Julie, everyone knows you are a panty slave to the matron. Doesn't she dress you up in your knickers?'

Severe flushed.

'You beastly whelp,' she hissed. 'I have the power to inflict a further dozen cuts for that insolence, so three dozen it shall be. If you persist in this insolence, I shall order my sla – Mr Puncknowle to flog you.'

'That pussy-whipped goon,' sneered Duddy. 'He's a proper baked chicken, as we say in Brazil.'

'Right, sir. You've asked for it,' she snarled.

Vip! The cane lashed him hard across the arse plums, which quivered, clenching only a tiny bit, as a vivid pink weal spread across his flesh. Duddy's face wore a pained look, as if a gnat had surprised him. Vip! His balls and fesses trembled, as the second cut took him on the upper buttocks, just below the spinal nubbin, laying a stripe of harsh red on the thin skin. Duddy swallowed, with a little sigh of annoyance. Vip! Severe's cunt spurted come, as his buttocks noticeably squirmed and continued to clench, after the cut, which left a satisfying red gouge across his underfesses.

'Oof!' he gasped.

The massive cock showed no signs of detumescence; if anything, the cane strokes had firmed it. Vip! Vip! As her strokes fell, Severe panted hard, her teats rising and falling, and her cunt a lake of come, for the flogged naked buttocks commenced a slow, sensuous rhythm of squirms, jerking in their own dance of secret pain, even after the stinging wood slid from the boy's wealed skin. Duddy's face was reddened, and his lips drawn tight, with his brow creased in a frown. Julius gazed on the boy's thrashed croup, and his face, pale and fearful. Vip! Vip!

'Uhh!' the flogged boy panted, his buttocks wriggling quite fiercely. 'Ooh! You aren't half laying it on today, miss.'

'Did you squirm so much for Esmeralda?' Severe asked.

'More,' he replied.

'I bet your cock didn't stand so stiff for her.'

*Damn! Why, oh why, did I say that?*

'It did, though. She'd string me for flogging – that is, tied, hanging in suspension from my wrists – or else tie me like a calf for branding, and whip me as I wriggled on the grass. My stiff cock was my only means of defiance, reminding her that I'd just been up her arsehole. When my whipping was over, she'd suck me off and swallow my goo, so she knew who was master. But *you* don't need telling why a boy's cock stands when a beautiful lady whips him, miss,' he drawled.

Vip!

'No!' Severe pouted. 'I declare that I don't.'

Vip!

'Right, miss. He's thinking of revenge – *her* arse, caned bare.'

'You cheeky brat!'

Vip! Vip!

'Ahh!' he groaned, his bare glowing with stripes, and squirming frantically. 'Oh, that hurts.'

Severe lashed him to the full three dozen and, though her cuts drew sharp gasps of agony and his welted bare bum wriggled awfully, he did not cry out again, not even at her frequent uppercuts to the arse cleft, which, on purpose, nearly singed his balls. His back muscles rippled in time with the clenching squirm of his buttocks and his legs jolting rigid, in a dreadful harmony of suffering. Severe's nipples, clit and whole skin tingled with desire, and she longed to wank off.

His cock stood as rampant at the end as at the beginning of his chastisement, and, when, panting, she lowered her cane, his rictus of pain changed to a haughty leer. She gaped, mesmerised, at his huge stiff cock, and her come-soaked panties squelched at her tiniest movement.

'How ... dare you!' she gasped. 'That thing ... so insolent. I suppose you are going to ... to pleasure yourself, squirt the sperm from those bollocks. How disgusting!'

'Want to look, miss?' murmured Duddy.

'Yes ... I mean, no!'

Duddy pulled back his prepuce, exposing his massive shiny glans, and began to rub the glistening skin.

'Stop,' she blurted. 'I forbid you. I mean, no, go on, I'm ... I'm fascinated. It is horrible, what boys do. Show me; do it properly.'

Duddy waggled his cock at her, like a javelin. 'You need company to do it properly, miss,' he drawled. '*Female company*. Especially with big titties for a Dutch fuck, or a gorgeous arse like yours for the chocolate cha-cha. There's nothing like ploughing a juicy mot's bumhole.'

'Wait! No!'

It was too late. Duddy seized Severe's hair and grabbed her blouse, at the titties. He tore it from her, then ripped off her bra, leaving her bubs to spring free and naked. Duddy licked his lips.

'Stop! This is an outrage!' Severe shrieked. 'Julius, do something.'

Julius stood petrified, trembling, swallowing nervously, and with his cock swelling, as he watched his mistress humiliated. The naked Duddy, cock swaying in monstrous stiffness, slammed Severe on the sofa, lifted her skirt and ripped off her wet panties. He paused to sniff them, and called her a dirty, lustful bitch. Her skirt came off, then her nylons were shredded under clawing fingernails, until Severe was released, to stand sobbing and shivering, in the nude, save for the ribbons of her stockings and skirt.

'Oh ... oh ... you brute,' she whimpered. 'I've never been so shamed. What do you mean to do with me?'

'You hurt my arse, miss,' he hissed, 'and I'm rather cross with you.'

He picked up her cane.

'No,' she wailed. 'Julius, help!'

Julius tore down his shorts, sprang naked to her side and pinioned her by the hair to the back of the sofa, which bit into her cunt, as her legs flailed behind. Her bare buttocks shivered helplessly in the air, as the cane rose above her squirming bum cleft, her anus winking at Duddy, and her writhing cooze flaps dripping come. Vip! The cane thrashed her across the middle fesses.

'*Ooh!*' she squealed, buttocks clenching fiercely, as a thick red welt flamed on her naked skin.

Vip!

'Ahh!'

Vip!

'Ouch! Oh! You're hurting me.'

'Shut the slut up, Julie,' snarled Duddy.

Still twisting Severe's mane, Julius pushed his stiff cock in her face, and prised open her clenched teeth. Her tongue flopped out, dripping drool.

'Suck on that, bitch,' hissed her slave.

Severe fastened her lips on the boy's massive pego, and began to lick and caress his glans, then swooped to mash his balls with her mouth, pressing her lips along the cock's quivering stalk. Vip! Duddy's cane lashed her quivering croup, as she drooled and sucked on the slave's cock meat. Her tongue tickled his peehole, and Julius groaned, then a bead of spunk crept from the hole, followed by his furious bucking, and a flood of sperm, spurting into the back of the girl's throat. Sweat dripped from Severe's bouncing titties, mingling with drooled spunk from her lips, as she swallowed the boy's full load of cream. Vip!

'Urrgh!' she gurgled, spitting sperm over Julius's balls.

'You insolent bitch!' he cried. 'I'll punish you for that.'

'Good thinking,' said Duddy.

Vip!

'*Oh! Ahh!*' screamed Severe, her squirming bare bottom growing ever more livid with stripes. 'No punishment could be worse than this. And beaten completely naked. It's such dreadful shame.'

She began to weep.

Vip!

'Ooh! Please, please stop! My bum's burning! I've never known such agony.'

'Just wait,' said her slave.

'Come on, Julie,' snarled Duddy.

Severe lay snivelling on the sofa, rubbing her caned bottom, groaning dreadfully, as her fingers sliced one crusted welt after another. Her belly slopped in the pool of come, fed by her dripping cunt, writhing softly on the slimy leather.

'I . . . I don't know,' mumbled Julius. 'She is my mistress . . . I got carried away. I must be in awful trouble already.'

'Are you a mouse or a man?' spat Severe. 'Go on, you brutes, do your worst. I can take it.'

'The bitch is juicing,' snorted Duddy. 'She wants it. These haughty cunts are all the same. Esmeralda was no different. Took it up the bum, flogged me raw for my crime, then slobbered over my cock, and drank my spunk. Do you know, Julie, one day she flogged me so hard, I was well annoyed. I took the whip to her own arse, then buggered her senseless. She came in fucking buckets, the cow. This one's arse is bigger. That means she's filthier. She'll come like bloody Niagara.'

'No,' Severe groaned. 'How can you be so rude?'

'You'll find out,' said the naked boy, waving his cock in her face.

# 13

# Café Flagella

Severe wept, but offered no resistance, as her body was tightly bound in surgical cords, pushing her titties to bulbous white sacs of flesh and framing her bare buttocks and cunt basin. She cried softly, as the cords bit into her belly and thighs, then bound her ankles and wrists. She crouched on the sofa, helpless to move, head down and buttocks up, with her wrists straight behind her, lashed to her feet. Duddy retrieved her ripped panties, and stuck them into her cunt, reaming her slit, until the panties were soaked with her fluid.

He wiped the soiled panties all over her face, breasts and hair, until they glistened, then tied the sopping cloth around Severe's nose. He rummaged on her desk, until he found a large metal document clip, which he fastened on her cunt lips, clamping them tight. Severe moaned, tears flooding from her eyes. Duddy explained that the clamp was to stop her pissing, while he flogged her. He took two smaller map clips, and pinned them on her nipples, making her howl.

'Ooh! That hurts! You're cruel!'

Bright-eyed, Julius fetched the birch.

'*Mm! Mm!*' squealed Severe, her eyes rolling wildly and her head shaking from side to side. 'No . . . not *that*!'

Duddy smiled, and lifted the birch over her naked buttocks. Swish! The twigs crackled on her skin, leaving a fan of tiny red weals. Swish!

'Urrgh!' she squealed, squirming helplessly.

Swish!

'Mm!'

Swish!

*'Nngh! Ohh!'*

Her whipped bottom glowed red, like a Hallowe'en lantern, shaking and clenching and writhing, with her whole trussed body aquiver, as if to escape from the birch cuts. Tears poured from her eyes, as she squealed and moaned, gasping uncontrollably. Come spurted from her clamped cunt and, at the tenth cut of the birch, her belly heaved, as she tried to piss. She groaned, as her belly and cunt ballooned with trapped piss, unable to escape from her closed gash, save in a fine hissing spray.

Swish! Swish! Duddy continued his savage bare-birching, until his cuts denuded the instrument, and, after thirty strokes of the birch sheaf, Severe's bare was a glowing mass of deep-gouged red weals, crusting to black. He paused to scratch her wealed bottom with his nails, making her sob and shudder, then nuzzled his swollen glans between her wealed bum cheeks. He teased her winking anus bud with his cock, while she shivered, moaning: 'Don't tease. I'm so wet. Do me, fuck my bum, plough me.'

With a single thrust, he plunged his cock all the way to her rectum, and, on a second thrust, sank to his balls, with his peehole mashing her colon.

'Oh! It hurts!' Severe squealed, gulping air through her sopping panties. 'Fill me up, fuck my hole, split me, you filthy brute. *Possess me.*'

Duddy enculed her for several minutes, while the birched girl squirmed and screamed, tears streaming down her face and over her shuddering titties; the boy's cock stretched her anus to the width of her fist. Come sprayed from her clamped cunt, with the remains of her pee gradually dribbling down her thighs, and her buggered belly swollen anew, with the thrusts of Duddy's huge cock.

'Uh! Ahh!' she groaned. 'You're bursting me! I'm going to . . . to come.'

Her thighs slapped together, squelching with rivulets of come spraying past her cunt clamp, as her belly heaved. Julius's cock was stiff, and he gazed, red-faced and licking his lips. Duddy ordered him to wank off and spurt in Severe's hair; the boy slave wound his cock in her tresses, and began to frot.

'Yes, Duddy . . . do me harder,' Severe whimpered, 'fuck me, fuck me, fuck my bum . . . I'm there . . . Ooh! Yes!'

Severe shuddered in violent orgasm, as Duddy grunted, and his spunk filled her rectum, dribbling out over her anal lips, to wet her rippling thighs. Julius relinquished Severe's hair.

'It's not right,' he moaned. 'I can't . . . she's my mistress. Her hair is so lovely, it seems wrong to spunk in it.'

'You fucking wimp,' Duddy snarled.

He seized the rattan cane, and pinioned Julius over the sofa, with his buttocks up and spread. Vip! Vip! The cane began to lash the boy's bare, while Julius squealed and wriggled. Vip! Vip!

'Ooh! Ouch! Stop, you brute.'

'Give the whelp what he deserves,' gasped Severe, her mouth inches from Julius's tormented face.

She raised her head, burying Julius's stiff cock amid her flowing tresses, and began to wag her head back and forth in pigeon style. Vip! Vip! The cane lashed the boy's helpless buttocks, while he sobbed and squirmed, his cock frigged by his mistress's mane. After twenty cuts to the bare, Julius's buttocks were a mosaic of wealed, blotchy flesh, and he groaned, as spunk beaded at his peehole, then erupted in full creamy flood from his cock, spraying through his Prince Albert, to soak Severe's hair, bathing her face and head, and dripping from her earlobes.

'Please, Duddy, let me go,' she begged. 'I've got to frig. I need a come. Please.'

'Call me "master",' he sneered.

'P-please, master. I need to wank so badly.'

'I'll make you come, bitch,' he snarled.

Upending the cane, he lashed her between the legs, the cane tip knocking aside her cunt clamp, then thrashing her

203

erect clitoris. Vip! Vip! The wood squelched in her sopping wet slit.

'Ahh!' she howled. 'Yes!'

Vip!

'Ooh! Ooh! I'm coming!'

Vip! A third cut sliced her anus bud and cunt together, sizzling in the wet gash, and Severe squealed, then whimpered long and loud in high, staccato gasps, as her tits, cunt and belly heaved in come-spurting orgasm. Duddy cut her loose from her bonds, leaving her naked body wealed raw from the tight surgical cords. She sobbed, rubbing her birched bottom and the purple bruises of her whipped cunt.

'Dr Crushard will hear of this,' she gasped. 'You'll be expelled . . . *master*.'

Her lips twisted bitterly in a sneer.

'Then I've nothing to lose,' he said. 'Lie down on your back, with your legs apart, slut.'

'How dare you give me orders –'

'Do it!'

Trembling, Severe obeyed. Duddy looked through her surgical cabinet, and returned, with gauze, hydrogen peroxide, scalpels and a handful of shiny steel rings.

'These curtain rings will have to do,' he said. 'Hold her down, Julius, like a good chap. It may hurt a little.'

'No!' squealed Severe. 'This is an outrage. I absolutely forbid you.'

Julius squatted with his bare buttocks on her face, and her tongue flicked out to lick his balls, while her lips enclosed his ball sac, sucking and caressing. Duddy menaced her with the cane, and she subsided into snuffling sobs. She groaned, squealing occasionally, as he worked, but, throughout the operation, her tongue was busy on Julius's balls, while her fingertips delicately rubbed his glans and peehole, so that, as Duddy put the finishing touches to his work, Julius spurted fresh cream all over Severe's naked breasts, to drip from her stiff nipples.

'Oh! You disgusting rude boy!' she said, sobbing.

Invited to inspect herself in the looking glass, she rose, wiped the tears from her eyes and stared at her new body. Glistening amid her weals from birch, cord and cane, were two rings through each of her nipples, four rings linking her cunt lips, one through her navel and a ring through the hood of her clitoris. She wriggled her body, making the rings tinkle like bells, and a wave of electric pleasure surged through her clitty and nipples.

'Oh, Duddy, my own Prince Alberts – how fabulous,' she said. 'But won't I have difficulty peeing?'

'No,' drawled the boy. 'You'll spray, that's all, but you'll keep your cunt virgin, like a good Brazilian bitch. I always ring my bitches. You're my slave, now.'

'V-very well,' she murmured.

With her master's permission, she caned the whimpering Julius a further two dozen cuts on the bare, then knelt, panting in obeisance, before Duddy's huge tool, took it in her mouth, and sucked him to another massive spunk. His ejaculation filled her throat, and overflowed her lips to drip onto her titties. She squeezed her teats up to her face, and licked the spunk from her breasts, taking the nipple rings in her mouth to tease and tickle herself, upon which her fingers flew to her cunt, and a few flicks of her swollen ringed clitty brought her to a groaning, come-spurting climax.

'How I wish I'd been ringed ages ago, master!' she cried. Her face grew sombre. 'I . . . I will never do without my rings, but I fear I cannot stay here. The other mistresses will see me, nude in the showers, or somehow, and Dr Crushard will know of it, and . . . I'll be fired. Ooh!'

She burst into tears.

'Don't worry, slut,' said Duddy. 'I'm not just a schoolboy, more of a talent scout. There's a job waiting for you, in South America.'

Luke wiped his brow. Clad only in shirt, shorts and sandals, nevertheless he sweated profusely in the sultry Brazilian air. There was a cool breeze in the uplands, where the vast coffee plantation stretched, yet, when the breeze calmed, the heat engulfed him.

It was the same for his Brazilian colleagues, even the girls; their short skirts stuck to their croups, outlining the big sensuous peach, frequently unpantied, while their braless breasts trembled under thin, clinging pastel-hued cotton, which soon soaked to transparency. Luke's ringed bell end tingled, as he watched the cane-wielding girls pad to and from their arduous work at the whipping range. Some wore laced-up boots, others went barefoot, their dainty brown feet sparkling with mauve or turquoise toenail polish.

He sipped his coffee, lit a Dunhill and looked at his watch; only a few more minutes left of his mid-morning break. The work at Finca Flagella was well-paid, the air-conditioned living quarters first rate, the food free and plentiful, with copious Brahma beer to wash it down. The *flagelladores* had plenty of reason to be grateful to the Master, as the Finca Flagella's distant owner was referred to, in awe. They were discouraged from leaving the estate, partly for security reasons – Luke was uneasy at his lack of a Brazilian work permit – but mainly because in the wild upland fringes of the Matto Grosso, there was no entertainment, and plenty of danger from human or animal marauders. Therefore, the estate resembled a golden cage.

Miss Esmeralda, his supervisor, joked that he could not possibly be feeling fruity for cunt, given the nature of his duties; he knew her well enough, after three months' service, to reply that cunt was what he most certainly desired, relationships amongst the *flagelladores* being strictly forbidden, though he did not admit he had never sampled a girl's cunt.

The young woman was a magnificent Afro-Brazilian, with skin of the purest, gleaming ebony, long, coltish legs topped by massive buttocks and huge, jutting breasts, with bulbous brown nipples, which quivered as she spoke in her soft contralto. She had welcomed him with a full-body inspection; a cluck of delight at his Prince Albert, and a moue of sympathy at the chain restraining his glans to his ball sac, preventing him from full spurt.

It was the work of a moment to remove his thigh clip, allowing his cock to spring to full stiffness, and to be milked of pent-up sperm by Miss Esmeralda's deft fingers. She raised her skirtlet, teasingly, and pulled down her panties to show her bare arse, tattooed in crimson with a sumptuously writhing squid's tentacles, with the beast's mouth her anus bud. Under the delicate pressure of her fingers on his glans, and entranced by her wriggling black buttocks, Luke spurted his cream in pale globules over her rippling bare ebony thighs, while she dazzled him with her smile. Somehow, under the languid Brazilian sun, it seemed quite normal.

Relations with the lowly shellers, huskers and roasters were equally off-limits, and those girl slaves lived in their own compound, impossible of access to the lordly *flagelladores*, although Luke had heard rumours, from his fellow expats, of late-night trysts with the vivacious black and creole girls who processed the precious *café arabica* beans into *café flagella*, the most exclusive and expensive coffee in the world. As for forming friendships with the indentured 'sphincter maids', mostly foreign, with many apparently English (though conversation was forbidden), that was quite unthinkable: first, by the rules, and, secondly, because of the nature of their professional duties.

The rules were enforced by the whip-wielding security police: all female Brazilians, sleek and menacingly superb, in their tight brown uniforms and shank-boots, and never smiling. Luke's cock often rose at the sight of their buttocks languidly swaying under those tight skirts, the bare brown legs gleaming like chocolate and the fists clutching wicked leather whips; yet to approach a *policia* signalled expulsion, or (he gulped) worse.

At first, obliged to be nude for the performance of part of his duties – most *flagelladores* choosing to remain nude throughout, like their victims – Luke was embarrassed by his Prince Albert. However, he discovered, to his surprise, that many of the boys had similar adornments, and that cheerful comparison of cock rings was quite a common practice in the communal shower, or over draughts of Brahma. It did not surprise him that most whippers' cocks had been welcomed to their duties by the nimble fingers, lips or even bare breasts of Miss Esmeralda.

There were some English boys, along with those of most European nations, but the English boys were not the most friendly, and Luke sensed an embarrassment lest the nature of their work become known back home. Female whippers performed their task precisely and even daintily, of necessity leaving the harder work of 'cream closure' to boys, who, it was no secret, were chosen for their youth, muscles, stamina and size of cock. Luke found his nine inches commanded respect, but not astonishment.

The welcome shed was staffed only by uniformed girls, considered crueller than soft-hearted males. There, newly recruited sphincter maids were subject to shock treatment to accustom them to their new submissive role, so that they would greet their daily beatings and anal penetration with equanimity after the rigours of basic training.

He drained his coffee cup, extinguished his cigarette and made his way back to the whipping range. The coffee no longer enchanted him, simply because the entire estate reeked with the delicious perfume of coffee. He doffed his clothing in the locker room, and went out into the range: a long expanse of grass, like an archery butt, which echoed with the squeals and groans of flogged or buggered maidens. Luke's cock was already half stiff. Nude bodies, male or female, glistened, rippling with sweat, and buttocks pumped, before the anguished squirmings of their subjects, whipped and bum-fucked naked.

A police girl gave him his chit, stall 23, and he made his way to it. He found a toffee-brown maid already chained to the whipping post, her bare buttocks upthrust towards him, and her face twisted in tear-glazed fear. Forbidden to speak, she put all her pleading for mercy into her big brown eyes, but Luke smiled grimly at her, his cock hardening, as always, at the prospect of the painful humiliance of a luscious nude girl.

He recognised most of the boys at work on either side, but decorum forbade any contact or acknowledgement amongst whippers at work. In 22, a tall blonde German, or Scandinavian, was taking a bare-bum caning, in silence, with gritted teeth, and her big bubbies bounced frantically, as her reddened buttocks squirmed; in 24, a giant, jet-black African maiden writhed on her superb long legs, her firm titties quivering like big dark plums, as the boy scourged her bare arse with a nine-tailed rubber quirt. Beyond, another black girl was squirming under buggery, emitting little squeals, as her bumhole was penetrated by an enormous tool.

Buggery before or after correction was the only area of freedom left to the whippers. Luke glanced at his chit, and learned that number twenty-three must receive forty strokes of the cane on her naked buttocks. She was a sumptuous, long-legged creole, Brazilian, perhaps: it did not matter, for Luke was required, and ready, to consider her as just another packet of succulent young girl meat. He selected one of the tamarind rods from the rack of canes, quirts and whips provided in every whipping stall, and went to work on the superb bare croup presented to him. Vip! Vip!

'Ohh!' she gasped, her buttocks clenching, and face wrinkling in pain.

Vip! Vip!

'Ahh! Oh!'

This girl was a squealer; her bound wrists and ankles rattled their cuffs, and her bum squirmed madly, as his cane lashed the naked skin, while her titties slapped and her long shiny legs jerked rigid at each canestroke. Her belly was heavily swollen with ingested raw coffee beans, giving her the aspect of a pregnant sow, and the distended stomach swayed in harmony with her big flapping breasts. His erection throbbed to painful rigidity as he flogged the girl, her shrill voice adding to the chorus of anguish resounding through the whipping range.

Her buttocks, already scarred from previous correction, opened up a new mosaic of deep cane gouges under Luke's beating. He saw wide trickles of come from her gash flaps – shaven, like all the sphincter maids – which made a pretty rainbow glint on her rippling thighs. Vip! Vip! The dry crack of his tamarind cane on bare girl flesh joined the busy clatter of canes and scourges all along the whipping range.

'Ooh ... ahh ... please, no,' the girl whimpered, by the thirtieth stroke, her screams of agony having dulled to hoarse gasps and sobs, as tears streamed down her weeping visage.

Vip! Vip!

'Ahh! Ohh! Stop, stop!' she said, sobbing, yet with come spurting fiercely from her cooze, under her bouncing swollen belly.

Licking his lips, Luke brought the girl's caning towards its conclusion, lacing the beating with painful uppercuts to the bum cleft, his cane striking her quim and anus, with a deep purple welt forming between her bruised arse cheeks. Vip! Vip!

'Ahh!' she screamed, come gushing from her cunt, 'Ahh! Oh! Oh!'

Her titties and belly heaved, and the girl's entire body shook, as she orgasmed. Luke licked his lips, as his cock throbbed. It was normal for girls to orgasm under his anal penetration, thanks to his cock size, and the Prince Albert punishing their colons, but it was a matter of extra professional satisfaction for a *flagellador* to bring his victim off by whip alone.

At the fortieth cut, he lowered his cane and stepped smartly forwards, clasping the wriggling girl by the hips. Drool cascaded from her lips, as she turned to face him. He nuzzled his ringed glans into her cleft, and caressed her anus bud for a few seconds. Her mouth was slack and gaping, her big pink tongue flapping, fishlike.

'Uhh ... uhh ...' she moaned, thrusting her arse up to part her cheeks and clasp his cock.

He drove his Prince Albert into her anus, and she squealed, trembling, and panting very fast; a second thrust plunged his cock into her rectum, to his balls. Her squirming brown bottom slapping against his balls, he began to fuck her in the rectum, while she drooled and gurgled, her sphincter squeezing his cock in her bumhole to milk him. He clasped her belly, feeling the hard nodules of the coffee beans swirling inside her; pressing hard, he drew further groans of pain.

Her whipped brown fesses glowed red and puce, as they squirmed under buggery; in less than a minute, Luke spermed, pressing her full belly hard, squashing it right to her backbone, and making her squeal, as come sprayed from her cunt. He shot a copious wad of cream into her colon, with spunk overflowing down her silky thighs and buttocks, and the buggered girl whimpering in a new orgasm.

He withdrew his cock with a squelchy plop, leaving her hole to drip sperm and arse grease, and handed his chit to the watching *policia,* who marked it, the hint of a smile creasing her firm lips. He saw the girl led off to the dunging chamber, where she would squat to excrete her load of shelled coffee beans to be roasted. Then, they might be ground in the girl's cunt or anus, specially distended by the special *molidor,* toothed like a trap, and shipped to one of the global connoisseurs, who requested the savour of a particular female type, specifying details of hair, lips, breasts and buttocks, or perhaps even one particular girl.

That was the secret of *café flagella*: each bean passed through the intestines of a young girl, to enhance the brew with a nonpareil flavour, brought to perfection by the whipping of the naked buttocks to release endomorphins and pleasure hormones; while vigorous buggery and copious sperm at the arse root stimulated her bowels, enhancing her production of more pleasure hormones and scented arse grease. Groaning, she would excrete her coffee dungs into the mouths of servant girls, whose saliva moistened them, before the roasting furnace. The optional grinding

211

process was for those customers who preferred an added saturated fragrance of the girl's come or arse grease.

Luke strutted back to the changing room, rather proud that he managed his duty of three copious spunks a day, in addition to numerous unbuggered beatings. It was time for luncheon and cold Brahma beer. It was accepted that boys needed beer, although the girls, who formed the majority of the estate's population, drank just as heartily. The sphincter maids, in their secluded corral, received beer as a prize for special achievement in passing coffee beans or fortitude in taking their canings.

Nude at all times, save for permitted piercings with jewellery, the girls were sometimes called cows, while boys were jocularly called bulls, which, Luke liked to think, was affectionate rather than derisive, especially as a favourite whipping intrument was a massive Brahma bull's pizzle. The boys were uneasily aware that their position, pay and perks depended on their strong whipping arms and big cocks, with plentiful sperm in the balls.

He nodded to his colleagues, already seated in the cafeteria, and sat down amongst them. A waitress, prettily dressed in a frilly French costume, hobbled up on her stiletto heels, and set a bottle of frosted beer before him, then took his order for steak. Some of the males had girl slaves to attend them: sphincter maids who were 'rented' from the estate, for an exorbitant sum; a girl who became a bull's personal slave must be replaced by another. Her life as a girl slave was arguably less onerous, although Luke knew the slave-owners treated their girl slaves as currency, wagering, swapping or selling them, and obliging them to service other males, for a fee. The girls crouched nude at their masters' feet, their breasts held on chain leashes, fixed to their dangling nipple hoops.

The pretty waitress brought his steak, hovering, and wiggling her pantied buttocks, almost bared by her high skirt and skimpy thong panties. She was a tall blonde Swiss girl, long of leg, with full ripe teats and arse pears.

'How nice it would be to have your own girl slave, sir,' she purred. 'Me, for instance. Wouldn't you like to own my nude body? I would truly make you my king. You can whip my bum, piss on me, bugger and humiliate me until I cry, and I will promise to obey my master.'

He waved her away, frowning, and joined in the small talk of the table. Most of it was anecdotal, about a cow, or 'unit', who had responded amusingly to her treatment, either orgasming very soon, pissing herself, or excreting her stomach of coffee beans prematurely.

Luke's waitress plied him with beers.

'Why don't you tup that bitch?' nudged his neighbour. 'She's hot, and does it standing up, for a few dollars.'

'I might get caught,' Luke blurted. 'I don't relish a punishment from the *policia.*'

'Nah! You won't get caught. I've been up her dozens of times.'

'Then I'd scarcely want to, would I?' Luke quipped, causing laughter, which saved him further blushes.

Why, when there were sultry girls aplenty, did he shy from a relationship, even the easy, brutal one of master and girl slave? He thought of Arabel, and his former mistress, Severe. He was betrothed, or enslaved to two stern mistresses! He looked at the waitress, imagining her towering over his trussed body, her thighs and breasts rippling, cane in her hand, and cruelly lashing his bare buttocks, with a sneer of contempt on her lips. He sweated, as his cock rose, bursting his shorts, and his neighbour noticed, along with the girls who sat nearby.

'Ooh!' pouted a girl, in mock dismay. 'You really do fancy that bitch as a girl slave, bull! Reaming her wet slitty with your cock!'

Luke blushed; how could he explain that, although an expert bugger, he was technically a virgin, his cock a stranger to cunt?

'He is stiffpizzle, wanting to poke her big arse,' chimed another girl. 'She'd make a luscious baked chicken!'

Now, the laughter was at Luke's expense. Baked chicken was a shameful position, where a maid lay with her thighs up and buttocks spread, clutching her knees, while she

213

took buggery from on top, obliged to look her swiver in the face; her stretched thigh backs provided a convenient rest for the belly of her *enculeur*.

He smiled wanly, finished his food and drink, and left the table. Checking out of the compound, he strolled along the dusty track to the river bank. All around, in the plantations, nude girls sang, as they picked the coffee beans. Some winked at him, waggling titties, showing anus and rubbing their buttocks, as an invitation to discreet coupling.

His cock unstirred, he looked away, catching sight of the overseer, a lissom *policia* girl, bare thighs rippling under her swirling miniskirt, who swished her long cane in the air, at which his cock swelled. What if he fucked one of the inviting maids, and was caught? Extra-compound, the overseers were empowered to inflict summary chastisement on anyone. He would be stripped, bound and flogged by a lissome girl in uniform, while the nude bean-pickers laughed, masturbating at the sight of his flogged, squirming buttocks . . . his cock rose to full, throbbing stiffness.

He came to the wide, sluggish river. Beyond, shone the ochre rooftops of the village of Bonafeita, a dusty, fly-blown affair, by all accounts, although some bulls hinted at secret vices to be enjoyed in shady tavernas. Sweating in the high sun, he stripped off to plunge into the cool muddy water, hoping that the shock would soften his throbbing cock. The fish at this altitude were benign, unlike those in the jungle lower down, where there were blood-curdling stories of native women who would tether a stranger naked between poles, his legs spread, for the piranha to gobble up his balls and cock.

Luke shuddered, lay on his back and floated lazily. Life was not really too bad. He daydreamed, seeing Arabel and Severe together, smiling at him, as they lifted canes, made from the reeds thronging the river bank. In his reverie, the girls brought the stiff reeds down on his naked bottom, in sensuous slow motion, lashing him with sharp strokes that seared him with pain, and he joyously thrust his croup up, begging for the privilege of licking their boots as they thrashed him. His cock rose once more to full throbbing erection.

He started, as something brushed his side. He had floated all the way across the river into a clump of reeds. He extricated himself, dripping, and clambered onto the sunny bank. There was his clothing, awaiting him on the far shore, which seemed a long way. He prepared to plunge in, and swim back, when a steely grip fastened his arm, and another fist clamped his erect cock. He whirled to stare into the twinkling eyes and cruel white smiles of girls in brown uniforms, yet not those of the estate *policia*.

These were Bonafeita village police, teenage girls scarcely out of school, wearing uniforms that hung sloppily on their tautly muscled frames. Their blouses were unbuttoned to the ribs, affording a glimpse of big caramel breasts. Their skirtlets were tight on unpantied bums, and rode high over the gleaming bare thighs, revealed almost to the crotch. As their haunches swayed, they showed a glint of cotton panties, snow white against the rippling brown thigh skin. Their nipples, like huge brown berries, stood high over the teat flesh, each nipple being pierced by a heavy golden hoop. Their long raven manes glistened, glossy as silk, and cascaded around their shoulders. Canes dangled from their belts, beside coiled leather whips.

They spat at him in Brazilian dialect, then slowed down, until he could understand their proper Portuguese. One, wiry and slender to her colleague's ripe figure, wore sergeant's stripes and a name badge identifying her as Manca, while the constable grasping his cock was Minca; both girls were proud of buttock, their peaches swelling under their clinging brown skirts, moist with sweat between the legs which emerged long, rippling and chocolate ripe from their crotch-hugging miniskirts. They were barefoot, the slim feet beaded with moisture from the grass.

Luke stared at the bare legs: the flesh shimmering in the sun, the soft brown skin a rippling mirage of dainty strength, the thighs sleek and bulging firm and the shanks smoothly taut with powerful muscle. Their long naked toes, on slim bare feet, painted in rainbow hues, dazzled. The girls' impossibly long legs glimmered before him; his cock throbbed harder in Minca's grasp. They wanted to see his papers; he had none. Gesturing to his clothing across the river only made them laugh.

With a thunderous frown, Minca squeezed his cock, and accused him of coming to ravish the innocent village maidens. She seemed fascinated and disgusted by his Prince Albert, pulling hard on the the cock ring, until he squealed, which made them laugh in sweet girlish melody. They chattered gaily, deciding that he was a foreign pervert, without papers; his protestations of his employ at Finca Flagella made them spit on his breast. Their big sloe eyes flashing, and their dazzling white teeth cruelly bared in leers, they said they hated the plantation. Luke's cock throbbed to bursting.

'See that filthy pole – he *is* a pervert,' sneered the sergeant, holding his arm; she twisted it into a half-nelson, while the other bound his balls and cock in her leather whipthong.

Like that, he was frogmarched the mile into the dusty village, with his bare buttocks stinging from occasional, lazy cane strokes, after which the police girls erupted in gleeful giggles.

'Please,' he said, 'where are you taking me?'

'To the police station, where you will be publicly punished. Public indecency, trespass with intent to corrupt, unlawfully travelling without papers – enough for a public whipping.'

'Without trial?' he blurted.

'We have already tried you,' snapped Minca, tugging his balls on her leash, so that he whimpered, as the leather tightened around his shank.

'Please,' he groaned, 'let me go. I'll do anything, perform any service.'

'As you service our innocent Brazilian maidens?' hissed the sergeant. 'Brute, you deserve more than whipping.'

'Please, no! I cannot stand pain.'

The girls smiled, tickling their breasts and making their nipple rings jangle.

'For your insolence, we shall increase your punishment,' said the sergeant, smiling sweetly. 'You shall be flogged until you scream, vermin.'

Her naked brown thighs quivered, as if agreeing with her cruel sentiment. Luke's cock throbbed rigid, threatening to burst its leather thong, as he hobbled towards his punishment.

# 14

# Tamarind Switch

It was terribly hot in the tiny police barracks and, despite his shameful nudity, Luke was dripping with sweat. Minca and Manca led him through a walled stone courtyard, shaded by jacaranda and tamarind trees, and blossoming with bright bougainvillea. In the centre of the yard stood four thick poles, waist high and a few feet apart. At the yard's end was a small pool, with a fountain, where two luscious brown girls splashed in the nude, their uniforms neatly draped on the stone flags. Like Luke's captresses, they had long sumptuous legs, leading to perfectly swelling taut bottoms.

The bathers leered, as Minca led Luke by his cock into the musty squad room, where two more girls in uniform looked up from their desks, beneath which their bare brown legs were bunched, seemingly skirtless, but with a sliver of uniform skirt tucked up below the crotch. Sgt Manca spoke in rapid dialect Portuguese, and these girls leered also. A battered typewriter clattered, and Luke was given a document to sign on aged paper. When he tried to read it, Minca tightened her whip on his balls and, wiping away tears, he signed. The seated girls smiled, rising from their desks and rubbing their hands. Orders were barked; the nude girls emerged dripping from the pool, and Luke was led to stand, trembling, amid the four posts.

On Manca's order, he leaned to place his hands on top of two posts. The nude girls seized his wrists, binding them in stout, painful cords to the shaft, then they lifted his feet, and stretched him, binding the ankles too. Luke was spreadeagled, buttocks up, from all four poles, his erect cock swaying two feet from the flagstones. Over him stood the six police girls, two nude and all barefoot.

Minca was despatched outside the compound, while Manca began to strip off her uniform, taunting Luke with the gradual exposure of her naked body, The hard brown pearls of her breasts, the flat muscled belly, the shaven bulge of her creamy brown cunt hillock and the long silken flanks of her thighs rippled provocatively to his gaze. His cock throbbed; one of the nude bathers kicked his bell end with her big toe, and they all laughed. Luke panted hoarsely, as her colleague brought a soft rubber cup, and clamped it over his balls, drawing it tight, with a cord at his stem.

The ball cup was anchored by a rope to the bolt between the flagstones, so that Luke's slightest movement would tighten the fastening on his ball sac. Manca was completely naked; a uniformed police girl brought her a pair of shoes, fashioned from rock – granite or basalt, Luke thought – in a monstrous parody of a girl's fashion shoe. Manca purred that these were her whipping boots.

They had high spiked heels, and spiked toes, but were not really boots, more court shoes. She explained that the heavy boots afforded a firm stance for a whipper, then showed him her quirt of bound tamarind rods, explaining that while foreigners had their birch, the Brazilian tamarind switch was far more painful on naked buttocks. Luke whimpered, and began to cry, for he knew the weals of the tamarind on flogged girls' bottoms.

Minca returned, leading a gaggle of smirking, tittering village girls, all barefoot, skimpily attired in bright pastel-hued shift dresses or frocks, clinging to their bodies, with no sign of any panties or bras. Their dresses were as short as the police-uniform skirts, showing shiny brown expanses of long leg, rippling toffee thighs and shanks, and dainty, painted bare feet.

Among them were scattered nearly naked Afro-Brazilian boys, smiling coyly, with big cocks bulging in their tight, snowy-white shorts. Some of the long-legged girls had arms around boys' waists, tenting the boys' shorts at the crotch, as their silken thighs rubbed the boys' legs and bottoms. Luke groaned, as his cock throbbed to bursting. *Every girl in Bonafeita has show-stopping long legs.*

Manca raised her booted foot, and suddenly kicked Luke's arse hard, her toecap stabbing his anus. There was a giggle from the audience.

'Uhh,' Luke groaned, tears flooding his eyes.

She kicked him again, several times, until his balls and cock were shuddering, as his body swayed, jerking his tethering ball pouch. Minca now stripped, and donned her own whipping boots, the stone shoes clacking noisily on the flagstones, as her nude body shimmered towards the trussed male. With a little whoop. she sprang up, and jumped onto Luke's back.

'Ooh,' he groaned, as her spiked heels ground his lower spine.

The audience clapped. Manca raised her whip. Thwap! While Minca danced on Luke's back, the sergeant began to lash his naked buttocks. The heavy tamarind switch flogged his mid-fesse, with its tips snaking across his haunches to nip his ball pouch. Luke groaned, as his buttocks clenched. Thwap!

'Ohh.'

His whipped arse could do no more than squirm very tightly, for any wriggling or shudder would tighten the noose on his ball shank. Thwap!

'Ahh! Ahh!' Luke cried.

The searing weal of the switch was agony, tongues of fire streaked his bare buttocks. Thwap!

'Ahh!' he shrieked, as Manca's rods took him straight in the stretched arse cleft, whipping his anus bud.

The stabbing of Minca's spiked stone heels, crushing him with the girl's full weight, seared his bare back with pain. Through tear-blurred eyes, he could see the throng of village girls, their pretty pastel skirts up and bare quims exposed, for they were masturbating at his distress. Bright pussy juice glistened on their rippling brown thighs, which shivered and swayed, like swans' necks, below the swollen bare cunt flaps, oozing clear sparkling come, at the dainty motions of the girls' wanking fingertips. Thwap!

'Ooh.'

Thwap!

'*Ohh!*'

With each lash of the tamarind to his bare, Minca jumped, ramming her spikes into his back, at the moment the branches fell across his buttocks. The nipple rings of both whipper and dancer bounced, jangling, as they tortured the helpless male. To the cheers of the audience, the other police girls sprang forwards to deliver sharp kicks to his swollen glans, swaying on the end of his cockpole, their toes catching his cock ring, to jerk it, with excruciating pain.

'The foreigner thinks we girls of Bonafeita are going to open our long legs for his tool,' panted Manca.

'Or our virgin quims!' sang the crushing Minca. 'We don't need cock in our cunts, for our clits are so big, from frigging. We shall soften his filthy cock with lovely sharp tamarind rods.'

The scourging continued for nearly an hour, with the weight of the stone-footed Minca crushing him, while her spiked heels and toecaps gouged his back flesh. The village girls masturbated profusely, with melodious gasps of orgasm; some knelt before the naked Afro-Brazilian boys, whose shorts were pulled to their ankles, allowing the girls to take huge black cocks in their mouths for a vigorous sucking.

The fellating girls moaned in pleasure, masturbating hard and coming, as a boy ejected creamy spunk in her throat, or over her nose and lips to trickle over her nipples. Almost all the girls, skirts lifted, showed multiple nipple rings and also cooze rings, some with a shining armoury of metal guarding the entrance to their cunts, so that their wanked come sprayed in myriad shiny droplets from the swollen flaps.

Luke's crushed, kicked and flogged body was raw. Loosed from his bonds, he sank, weeping, to his knees. His welted buttocks were too painful even to rub for solace. The girls jeered and spat at him; one big-titted maid, her bared breasts glistening with spunk, lifted her tattered dress, and squatted to piss over his face. Her cunt rings split the piss into a fine rainbow, soaking his head. As she drew apart her cooze flaps, Luke saw that pierced through her clitoris was a thinner, golden ring.

When she had finished pissing, she crouched before him, and a smiling black boy inserted his massive stiff cock into her anus; he began to slap her buttocks with his hips, as his tool pierced her rectum, with only his tight balls visible, as his dark cockshaft swived the groaning, quivering girl. She sank lower and lower, until her face, twisted in pain, pressed the flagstones. The police and village girls cheered, frigging openly, as a powerful jet of sperm sprayed from her buggered anus to trickle down her thighs, and soak her twitching bare soles.

Minca dragged Luke by his hair to a line of girls, masturbating, with their skirts up. His face was pressed into a shaven wet cunt and, after several tamarind lashes to his back, he began to lick the girl's erect ringed clitty, his tongue poking through the chain of cunt rings to penetrate the slit, oozing come over his face. He tongued the girl to orgasm, then was obliged to suck, kiss and lick the next girl's cunt, swallowing her copious come; and the next girl, and the next, until his tongue ached, and his stomach was bloated with girls' pussy juice.

Manca had her whipping boot strapped to her groin, so that the spiked heel stuck out, in obscene parody of an erect cock. Minca forced Luke to the ground, and he lay, whimpering, on his back, while she knotted his wrists together at the back of his knees. His thighs were up on his chest, baring his balls and anus. The black boys stood around him, laughing; the boys were naked, with hands on hips and their swollen stiff cocks waggling. Luke gaped at the monstrous organs.

'Wait,' he said, sobbing. 'not . . . oh, please, stop my torment, I beg you.'

Manca laughed, then dropped on his body, in a wrestler's slam.

'Ooh!' he gasped.

Her stone dildo nuzzled his spread anus.

'No . . . please,' he whimpered.

She thrust; the dildo penetrated his anus.

'Ahh!' he screamed.

Cold stone plunged into his rectum, and began to encule him with fierce, slapping thrusts.

'*Ooh . . . ohh,*' he moaned, his tears spurting. 'Please, no! It hurts . . .'

Slap! Slap! Manca's hips smacked his buttocks, as the hard, striated stone slammed his colon.

'God, no,' he whimpered, 'you're fucking my hole raw.'

'You are baked chicken,' said the buggering girl, panting.

The masturbating village girls cheered. At each thrust, Manca's bare belly squashed his stiff cock and balls, the tool ramrod straight and erect to bursting. Luke gazed up into her fierce, sensuous face, her white teeth bared in a rictus of savage glee, as she gazed down at his tears and blushes, with the thrusting stone cock impaling his anus in a spear of agony.

Panting, after several minutes of tooling his bumhole, she withdrew the dildo, and slapped his stiff cock with the spike. Glistening streams of come trickled from the girl's bare, beringed slit, in which her massive pierced clitoris bulged erect.

'Filthy swine,' she hissed. 'I'll teach you. You'll bugger my arse, and I'll fuck you raw. My rectum will rip that cock ring right off.'

Squatting, she bared her anus.

'No!' cried Minca. 'It's my turn.'

'Why, you bitch,' Manca snarled. 'I'll fight you.'

'Agreed,' spat Minca. 'I'll rip your clit to ribbons.'

The girls rose, and faced each other for the clit fight, with bared quims out-thrust, and their hands folded behind their buttocks. Each slit glistened red and wet, festooned with shiny cunt rings and, inside, with golden clit piercings. Manca lunged forwards with her hips, her cunt slamming Minca's and scraping savagely; Minca gasped and staggered back. Recovering her poise, and her teeth bared in a snarl, she slapped Manca's cunt with her own. Their clits, erect and swollen, poked monstrously amid the jangle of cunt hoops, squelching, as the giant ringed nubbins slapped and raked each other.

Come spurting from their gashes, the girls squealed and panted. Tears sprang at their eyes and their bare titties were a furious jangle of nipple rings, as their cunt basins clashed in slippery, come-soaked combat. Thwap! Thwap! Manca held her cunt lips against Minca's for longer and longer at each thrust, her buttocks churning, as she reamed her opponent's split gash, and the girl howled in pain. Minca herself, seizing advantage, roiled her cunt against Manca's, her tongue hanging out of her drooling lips, titties heaving with hoarse pants and her flat belly grinding. Thwap! Thwap!

'Ooh,' Manca cried, come streaming down her rippling thighs.

Minca thrust harder, her beringed cunt grinding Manca's, and making the sergeant squeal repeatedly.

'Oh . . . yes . . . Minca, don't stop.'

Still churning Manca's cunt, Minca forced the sergeant to a crouch, then slammed her cunt to her mouth; Manca eagerly licked the distended clitoris of her tormentress, until Minca's come sluiced her face in a glistening torrent. Manca lay on her back, and Minca straddled her, kissing her, lips pressed to her mouth for deep tonguing, while her cunt ground Manca's buttocks to the flagstones, in a squirming, squelching clit-fuck.

Quims and silky brown buttocks writhing, the girls gurgled in pleasure, as they rubbed bare titties, and kissed

– Minca's tongue deep in Manca's throat. Minca's buttocks squirmed, as her cunt squelched against her tribade's, and her distended clit poked Manca's gushing slit to ream her victim's clitty.

'Mm,' gurgled Manca. 'Plough me, fuck me ... Ooh! I'm coming! Oh! Ah! *Ahh* ...'

Her bucking cunt slammed her tribade's loins, as she jerked and writhed in a come-spurting orgasm. The two girls' clits rubbed, jangling with rings, and Minca, too, squealed, as come streamed from her cooze, over Manca's belly, while she exploded in noisy gasping spasm. She slid from Manca's dripping body, and plunged her nose between the girl's buttocks to smell and lick her anus bud, getting the tongue an inch inside the pucker.

Manca groaned and, as Minca crushed her face with her own cunt, her tongue found Minca's bumhole, and she began to suck and lick the tender wrinkled bud. Her tongue poked inside, and the two tribades writhed, groaning, bumholes distended by the sleek probing tongues.

'How long since your colon tasted spunk?' murmured Minca. 'Your hole is awfully dungy.'

'Ages,' said Manca.

'Me, too.'

'Shall we?'

'You first. No, please. I want to watch the dirty foreigner bugger you.'

'Thank you, darling Minca.'

Manca grabbed Luke by the balls, and squatted in submission, her face to the ground, directing his swollen cock towards her spread buttocks, where her anus bud pulsed, winking at him. He snarled, baring his teeth in vengeful rage, and thrust his Prince Albert into the girl's bumhole. She squealed, as the cock ring penetrated her, fully stretching the anus lips, then howled, as Luke's bell end slammed into her anal elastic.

'See how you like this, you slut,' he hissed.

In a few thrusts, his cock ring was slicing her colon, with the shaft of his tool stretching her rectum and buried in her

hole, right up to his balls, which slapped her bottom, as he
fiercely enculed her.

'Ahh ... ooh!' Manca squealed. 'You're hurting me!'

Smack! Smack! Luke began to spank her silky smooth
brown buttock meat.

'Ahh! Stop!'

'Will you shut up, bitch,' he hissed.

Smack! Smack!

'Ooh! *Urrgh!*'

Manca was silenced by Minca's bare arse crushing her
face, so that the buggered girl's squeals were reduced to
muffled gurgles. Minca writhed on the girl's face, her
thighs apart, to show Manca's tongue eagerly licking her
beringed cooze, flowing with come over the prone girl's
face. The audience of girls were bare cunt, masturbating,
or bending over to take the black boys' cocks in their own
arses.

Luke buggered hard for several minutes, with Manca
squirming and sobbing under her friend's crushing bare
arse, until the buggered maid squealed loud in orgasm,
with come spraying through her jangling cunt rings.
Minca's cunt drenched Manca's face in come, with the
crushed girl sucking Minca's erect clit, until Minca orgasmed too, her beringed bubbies bouncing, as she pinched
her swollen brown nipples. Luke grunted, as his cream
began to spurt, filling the writhing girl's bumhole.

Panting, he withdrew. Minca leapt from Manca's come-
soaked face, and crouched, with her face between the
buggered girl's thighs. Her lips pressed to the distended
anus, and her tongue penetrated the spermed elastic;
masturbating her clit, Minca began to suck and swallow
Luke's spunk from Manca's buggered bumhole, with loud
gurgling slurps. The cream trickled down her chin, as she
wanked herself to a new orgasm, and then, having drained
Manca's anus of spunk, she patted her belly, beaming at
Luke's cock, already stirring half-stiff.

Minca crouched to lick his balls, and his cock stiffened
fully; Manca rose, groaning and rubbing her buggered

arse, then knelt, to take Luke's bell end into her gaping mouth for a fierce sucking. The two police girls licked, tongued and sucked Luke's cock and balls, until, after minutes of eager fellatio, he spermed again, into Manca's mouth. Manca's lips met Minca's in a squelching kiss, and the two girls exchanged Luke's sperm, squirting it back and forth between their lips, with loud gasps of pleasure, until each girl had swallowed her fill.

A uniformed police girl padded to Luke on her sultry long legs, and ordered him to sign a paper, demanded by Brazilian law, recognising his guilt.

'And if I refuse?' he blurted.

'Then we must hold you as our slave, in protective confinement,' said the girl sweetly. 'I hope you refuse.'

Sullenly, Luke signed. 'Am I free to go?' he said.

'Not quite,' said Manca. 'We must brand you as an offender, so that any Brazilian police girl will know how to deal with you.'

'Brand!' he gasped.

Manca smiled. 'Not quite,' she murmured. 'Seize him, girls.'

Luke squirmed helplessly, pinioned to the ground, with Minca's naked bottom crushing his face and Manca's buttocks squashing his balls. He writhed and whimpered, but to no avail; an hour later, a groaning Luke Redruth clambered naked on the far bank of the river, with shiny brass hoops dangling from his pierced nipples.

Severe simply loved the Finca Flagella estate, the balmy sunshine and cooling upland breeze, the flowers and parrots, jacaranda and tamarinds, the sultry bodies of the nude girls labouring amid the coffee shrubs. She was so lucky that good-natured Tremaine Duddy had got her such a super job.

'Basic training' sounded a bit ominous and military, but she was sure Coz would approve. She was rather nervous at having to remove all her clothes for she wore a pretty white dress, brought all the way from London, and sweet matching leather slingbacks, but she complied, assuming she must have a medical inspection. She shed both dress and shoes in seconds and, since she had no underthings, stood meekly nude before Zula, the tall, sensuous *policia* captain.

Her lieutenants, Bomfim and Aleis, equally long legged and full of croup, in their skimpy brown uniforms, stood behind the big-breasted captain, smirking rather unpleasantly. They carried canes, with rolled whips at their belts, and once Severe was naked, they pointedly uncoiled their whips. Zula reached down and stroked Severe's quim rings.

'You are a virgin, then,' she said with a smile.

'Yes, as it happens,' said Severe, blushing hotly.

'So – almost a Brazilian. We Brazilian girls take cock up the *cu*, and pride ourselves on tight bumholes, so as to preserve our virgin treasure. We masturbate for health. Do you masturbate, English maid?'

'Well, yes, of course I do.'

'So, your training shall soon make you one of us.'

'I know about training,' Severe blurted, 'but for an office job?'

The police girls laughed.

'You are a slave, not a clerk,' said Zula. 'You are to be broken in as a sphincter maid.'

Severe's jaw dropped. 'I don't understand,' she blurted.

Thwack! Bomfim's whip cracked across her naked breasts.

'Ouch!' Severe squealed.

Thwack! Aleis's whip lashed her thighs. Thwack! Zula's cane cracked on her bare cunt, making her rings jangle.

'Oh! Ahh!' Severe shrieked.

As the whips lashed her naked body, she sank, wriggling and squirming, to the ground. The three police girls lifted their skirtlets to expose their unpantied cunts; each squatted and pissed long and copiously over Severe's face, belly and teats.

'Now, I think you understand,' said Zula.

That had been only the beginning of Severe's submissive ordeal. She knew it was to break her, and, as Zula had explained, in her gentle voice, her breaking would continue until she *wanted* to be broken. To become a sphincter maid was a supreme honour. Every girl, even the *policia*, had to undergo basic training, at the command of the Master, whose feet Severe might one day be privileged to lick. Severe was to forget about clothing. Girl slaves were nude at all times, whatever the weather. Thus, the Brazilian landscape would seep through their pores and perfume their innards.

'Just think,' Zula had purred, 'distant connoisseurs will be sipping their coffee and savouring *your* body.'

Her nights were spent in a dank solitary cell, where she slept fitfully on caked dirt; the day began with a bucket of tepid water and a caning on her bare bottom, taken groggily, to bring her to waking. Then, hard physical jerks, press-ups, jumps and running under whip, with a mouthful of pebbles, before a breakfast of gruel. She had no solid foods, for her real business was swallowing mountains of tiny pebbles, which swelled her belly, with dreadful pain, until she managed to excrete them, in an equally painful process, as the hard stones ripped her anal canal. Sometimes, she was led to the river, with a padded meat hook on a rope inserted in her rectum, and obliged to dive to pick up pebbles from the river bed in her mouth, and be hauled back by her anus, with her mouth full, to swallow her treasure on the spot.

Corporal punishments for laziness were numerous. The very least was to take an enema of her own urine, filling her night bucket, which was injected into her anus and colon by a painfully wide clyster; then, with her anus stoppered by a cork, to do all her physical jerks, including diving for stones. Zula caned her bare bum with a tamarind switch, at least once a day, and enjoyed watching Severe's helpless wriggles, as she took stripes, with the big stopper sealing her anus, and her belly swollen in agony with piss and pebbles.

She had to kneel on a floor covered in stones, till her knees and elbows were raw, and pick up every one with her cunt flaps; when she had mastered that skill, she had to perform the same task with coffee beans, squeezing with her sphincter, to pick them up with her anus. Amid the ordeal, she had to crouch, holding her cunt and anus full of the fragrant pellets, to take a tamarind thrashing on the bare, trying not to slide and topple on the sea of beans. Sometimes, she squatted, strung, with her arms stretched up behind her, and whipped on the bare back, while obliged to pick up the beans and transfer them to her mouth, using her toes.

Every third day, she took a bare-fesse beating with the full tamarind switch of fifteen rods. She had to crouch, bum up, with her head clamped between Zula's bare thighs. Zula sat regally, skirtlet up, and unpantied shaven cunt exposed, with Severe's blonde tresses bobbing helplessly between her thighs, as the girl slave's naked buttocks reddened and purpled, under the flogging branches.

When Severe's flogged bum was blackened, and squirming frantically, with her sobs and shrieks cleaving the sultry air of the barracks, Zula would cease masturbating and push Severe's head to her cunt, so that the tortured girl could tongue her to several orgasms, while taking her tamarind cuts.

Perpetually sobbing, Severe experienced few moments when her naked buttocks, back or bumhole did not burn with welts or buggery, for the guards often made her their baked chicken: the English girl, helpless on her back, took an enculing from a giant dildo, with her thighs up and spread, resembling the outstretched wings of a chicken. One girl, skirt up, would sit on her upturned face, with her anus or cunt pressed to Severe's lips, for a vigorous tonguing, while Severe spluttered under the torrent of girl come filling her throat.

A second would cane her naked breasts with a single tamarind rod, while the third, wearing a strap-on dildo of imported granite or basalt, would bugger her squirming anus, until the elastic was ripped raw. The buggery threatened to split her swollen belly, heavy with its cargo of stones and throbbing in agony, as Severe helplessly squealed and sobbed. Zula said she must learn that *girls* were the cruellest of creatures, so that she would be grateful for the vigorous attentions of the Finca Flagella's male whippers.

'As long as you don't get Mr Redruth,' Zula said. 'He is a vicious one, with a hatred of girls, punishing their bottoms with his whip and their bumholes with his huge sex organ.'

Eyes brimming with tears, Severe nodded dully. Redruth was a name that seemed familiar, from an irrelevant age ago. Nothing could be worse than basic training, no one crueller than these luscious, svelte brown Brazilian girls. She was flogged in the 'four-poster': her nude body strung between four poles, with her anus speared and bum raised by a meat hook, hung from the ceiling. Spread and strung, she took licks from the tamarind, rattan cane or sjambok cattle whip on the back, legs, buttocks and soles of her feet, sometimes with all three girls flogging her, using a mixture of instruments.

At one session, three weeks into her training, she was squirming, after fifty lashes of whip and cane, and crying helplessly, when she felt the meat hook jerked from her anus, and saw two Afro-Brazilian boys approach in the nude, coyly smiling, with their huge cockpoles swaying menacingly erect before them. She gasped, as a massive tool invaded her mouth for her to suck; mechanically and obediently, she did so, her tongue licking the fruity black glans, rubbing the frenulum and peehole, until the tool was rigid. She repeated this treatment to the second cock, which she stiffened fully.

Then, her buttocks were parted wide, and she felt hot cock meat clenched to her bum pucker; two stiff tools were nuzzling her inner thighs and her arse cheeks. She groaned, as her anus was wrenched open by a massive black helmet, then screamed and screamed, as the second cock joined it. Both black boys were inside her rectum, powerfully enculing her, as her naked body wriggled, strung helplessly, and her mouth gaped in a scream, washed by floods of tears. At last, the cocks spurted in her swollen, tortured belly, filling her tripes with hot spunk, and she exploded in an orgasm of unbearable intensity, her beringed cunt squirting floods of come.

Later, she broke into frequent uncontrollable weeping at the pain and shame of her double enculement: a signal for Zula to flog her bare at once, with the tamarind switch, and turn her sobs to screams of agony, as her fesses purpled. Zula explained, soothingly, that pain of the rod was the only cure for despair, for a girl would forget her vague unhappiness, when her bum was seared with the far greater pain of stripes. Deep down, Severe knew she was right.

As the weeks passed, her sullen misery slowly turned to pride. She trained with real coffee beans, not stones; she was radiantly happy when Zula praised her for licking clean the *policia*'s stinking feet, quims or bumholes, for taking an extra quart of urine for her enema, for submitting to a bare-bottom flogging of a hundred cuts, without whimpering, or for excreting her stomachful of coffee beans in record time.

Obliged to masturbate several times every day and show her pot filled with come as evidence, she was thrilled to be complimented on a brimming come pot, and allowed to drink her own cunt juice. She came to know the black buggers, whose names were Rodolfo and Herberto, and learned to take the twin cocks in her anus with lip-smacking glee, her distended arsehole squeezing the massive tools, and milking them, relishing the copious spurts of cream up her writhing colon.

They were frequent visitors, sometimes bringing friends. Severe became accustomed to kneeling before a row of twelve black cocks, sucking them all to spurt, and swallowing every drop of their copious cream, before being spread

233

and strung, for a naked caning from a dozen cruel hands, and enculement by twelve freshly stiffened cocks. Her rectum seared with pain, she would masturbate, filling her pot with juice, as she watched squatting *policia* girls service the boys' cocks with mouth or anus.

Severe *needed* to be buggered and whipped and laved with steaming piss from girls' cruel cunts; to clean girls' bumholes, armpits and feet with her tongue; to feel the lovely tickly coffee beans, working their way through her tripes; and, the ecstasy of utter, humiliating submission. Yet only a male – a brutal, cruel, stinking male, armed with a tamarind switch, and muscled cock meat springing between his thighs – could achieve the real, delicious work of a girl's total humiliance. She couldn't wait for her basic training to be over, and her work as a sphincter maid to begin.

# 15

# Sphincter Maid

The weeks became months, and Severe Compaigne blossomed as a sphincter maid of Finca Flagella. Her body ripened with muscle, her bottom and breasts putting on firm, jutting weight; her toes became as prehensile as her fingers, her limbs so supple as to seem double jointed. The sphincter maids shared a huge dormitory, patrolled by *policia* with canes, to enforce the ban on speaking; nevertheless, the girls communicated by smiles, fluttering eyes and blown kisses.

Many, tired of officially sanctioned solitary masturbation, risked a whipping to climb onto another's rough straw palliasse, and writhe nude, kissing and frigging, their cunts soaking the straw in moonlit come. The food was better for sphincter maids, with one solid meal per day, usually of beans and fatty bacon. They got chocolate, too – a treat which had the girls bouncing with glee. Mere girl slaves, picking coffee, got none – not even the favoured crew of bean-swallowers: girls placed by a sphincter maid's anus, to take and hold the excreted coffee beans, slippery with precious arse grease, in their mouths.

Many bean-swallowers hastened the excretion by making a sphincter maid's belly heave, by means of artful licks and kisses to the cunt and clitty, often bringing her to orgasm, and swallowing her spurted come; the practice was connived at by Miss Esmeralda, the gorgeous black overseer, and her whip-wielding staff, for a girl's come, added to her arse grease, was thought to enhance the aroma of the coffee.

Miss Esmeralda knew and relished her stunning ebony beauty. She was an exhibitionist, and a cruel one; sometimes, she would lead Herberto and Rodolfo, the two naked black boys, into the dormitory, and allow herself to be buggered by both of them at once, with the tentacles of her grotesquely tattooed crimson squid writhing across her buggered bum flans.

It was to taunt the maids; Severe shuddered at the pain of her own double buggery, and assumed all the other sphincter maids had endured the same. Yet Miss Esmeralda gurgled with pleasure, as her anus was cruelly stretched by two massive cocks, and seemed to relish her humiliation. Quivering at her remembrance of pain, Severe could not help masturbating vigorously, as she watched. Girl slaves were encouraged to masturbate to increase their lustful ardour for bulls' cocks.

After their morning run to the river for a cold dip, then a thin breakfast, and supervised dunging, it was time for the ingestion of the precious coffee beans. The girls swallowed mechanically, groaning and grimacing, as their bellies swelled horribly with the cargo. The process could take hours; when Miss Esmeralda judged them full, they padded, head down and wrists at buttocks, to the whipping range, their grotesquely distended bellies wobbling in time with their jutting bare breasts.

Then, there was the ordeal of the lash, the experienced bulls careful to sear every inch of a maid's naked buttocks and to bugger her, before or after her whipping, with expert cruelty, until she groaned and wept, bursting with pain. It was the part Severe liked the least, or so she told herself; yet on the way to the range, her pulse always quickened and her cunt oozed come, as she thought of the whip and tool awaiting her.

This morning, the hundredth – or three hundreth? – of her servitude, she allowed herself meekly, as always, to be trussed to the flogging post. The police girls seemed to bind her more tenderly than usual, with little clucks of sympathy. One of them mentioned 'Senhor Redruth', and Severe's heart pounded. That boy – that submissive worm – a whipper, here? It was impossible. When the nude bull padded to postion behind her, and raised, not a cane, but a sheaf of tamarind rods over her bare, exposed buttocks, she twisted to look, and paled: it was Luke Redruth.

'You!' she gasped.

The boy sneered, standing lazily, rods raised, as his cock swelled to hugeness, his leer showing his joy at her fright.

'You fucking bitch,' he hissed. 'Look at you – a fat sow. I'm going to enjoy my work today. I'm going to ribbon that haughty bare arse of yours.'

Suddenly, she *did* feel fat, with her belly swollen by beans. That was more awful than the pain of the cane, and she started to cry.

'Stop your fucking tears, bitch,' he snarled.

Vap! The sheaf of rods lashed her full across the bare, jolting her, and Severe howled, as her fesses clenched, with the fire searing her naked flesh. Vap!

'Ooh!' she squealed.

Her nipple and cunt rings jangled harshly, raking her teat and cunt skin, as she squirmed; this flogging was worse than ever before. Luke's nipple and cock rings swirled, as his rods scythed the air. Vap! Vap! Severe's naked body squirmed and wriggled under the lash, drawing scornful stares from the whipped girls on either side, who bore their punishment with grim determination. She heard Luke's panting, as he flogged her, tears streaming down her face and bathing her twitching nipples; her bum burned with molten fire, yet a copious gush of come soaked her cunt lips, and dripped onto her rippling thighs. Her clitty throbbed, swollen stiff, as the beans churned inside her belly, their weight a sensuous, painful caress. *Hurry up! I need to be buggered.*

'Luke,' she panted hoarsely. 'Darling Luke ... I know we've had our misunderstandings, but surely we can come to some arrangement?'

Vap! Vap!

'*Ahh!*'

Her bottom squirmed, as he lashed the tamarind rods squarely between the fesses, on her anus and cunt.

'Oh, Luke ... you are so masterful! And so sweetly ringed, like me! We are one of a kind, Luke. Let me be your slave.'

'Buy you? After the way you shamed and whipped me, and treated me like dirt?'

'Precisely because of that. I'll pay you back, I promise, for one day, Poldipple will be mine. You can do anything you like to me. I'll bend over for you, tongue you, suck your cock, take you in my bum ... anything. You can humiliate me each and every day.'

'Shut up, cunt,' Luke spat.

Vap! Vap! The whipping continued, with Severe sobbing and wailing, as her upper thighs, buttocks and quim flaps glowed with burning welts. Weeping, she scarcely noticed the whipping stop, but whimpered, as the cock ring pierced her anus, then shrieked, as Luke plunged his ramrod stiff cock into her tripes, and began to fuck her, with hard vicious thrusts, his cock ring slamming her tender colon. Her belly was full to burst.

'Ooh ... you're splitting me,' she groaned.

Come spurted from her wriggling cunt, as he pounded her arse root. Severe felt her belly heave, in the onset of a come.

'Oh ... yes ... do me, plough my hole,' she panted. 'Fill me with spunk, split my guts, fuck me to ribbons ... Ooh! Oh! Yes!'

She wailed, drooling, as her cooze sprayed come all over her thighs and shanks, and Luke's feet.

'You filthy cow,' he hissed.

His cock began to spurt cream, filling her rectum with the hot spunk, which dribbled down her thighs, as Luke clawed her cane welts with his fingernails.

'Oh!' she screamed, as the nails dug into her wounds; at once, Luke's thighs were washed in a steaming hiss of pee from her writhing cunt flaps.

'Dirty slut,' he snarled, sinking his nails deeper into her open welts, and clawing savagely.

'Ah! Ahh!' she screamed, tiptoes dancing in agony. 'Oh, no . . .'

A string of coffee beans poured from her anus, clattering at her bugger's feet, until her belly tightened to flat firmness.

'No, no . . . I'm sorry,' Severe said, weeping.

'What is this, sir?' demanded Miss Esmeralda. 'You've let the slut waste her cargo. She must pick them up.'

Severe was untrussed, and lowered to the ground, to pick up all the spilled coffee beans with her toes, while Miss Esmeralda, breasts and buttocks bobbing, whipped her back with her quirt of short rubber thongs. Thwap! Thwap! Severe groaned and wept, as she scrabbled for the beans, raising her foot to her mouth, and swallowing them anew, coated with her own arse grease. Thwap! Miss Esmeralda's rippling black thighs strutted around the sobbing girl, as the overseer whipped her breasts, while Luke leered at the sobbing Severe, his arse-smeared cock swelling to new erection.

'Useless, disobedient whore!' snapped the black girl. 'You're not even fit to be a slave.'

'Oh! Ooh!' Severe wailed. 'I'm sorry, honestly.'

'I'll take her as my slave, Miss Esmeralda,' Luke blurted, 'and I promise to crush her. Only, there is a question of price. As a prime specimen of girl meat – a blonde, tall English girl, with big buttocks – she might be beyond my financial means.'

Miss Esmeralda's eyes fastened on Luke's stiff cock, and her eyes gleamed. Licking her lips, she tugged on his nipple rings, making him wince, then fingered her crotch, through the wet stain on her skirtlet.

'We can arrange a discount,' she purred. 'Follow me to my office, Mr Redruth.'

Luke obeyed, and, no sooner had Miss Esmeralda locked the door, than she ripped off her uniform skirt to reveal her gleaming hairless cunt, the black flesh split by glistening wet pink, dripping with come.

'You may have the slut for free,' she panted, 'if you pleasure me. Basic training is expensive, and I cannot afford to break her again. The Master is due to pay a visit of inspection –' she shuddered '– and if he finds any flaw, he will ribbon my bum. I've just taken delivery of another English bitch, one of those haughty, big-bummed sluts, who fancies she's a princess, and perhaps she will fill Severe's place. Meanwhile, your cock must fill my arse, and your spunk my tripes.'

She crouched, presenting Luke with her bare buttocks, spread, to expose the squid's mouth of her anus, winking at him. His cock throbbed, and he plunged it into the squid's mouth, penetrating her rectum in two savage thrusts, to begin vigorous buggery. Her crimson squid's tentacles writhing on her black bum flans, Miss Esmeralda squealed, drooling, with come spraying from her cunt, as she masturbated. He fucked her for minutes, while she wanked herself off to three successive spasms, and her long bare legs were swimming with her spurted come; at last, Luke delivered his spunk to her sigmoid colon, and she howled, squirming ecstatically, as she masturbated to a fourth orgasm.

'That is your first week's rent for the girl slave,' she drooled. 'I shall expect payment every week hereafter. If you don't fuck me hard-cock, and fill my bum with spunk, I'll flog you, and make you my baked chicken.'

It was not difficult to enslave the haughty Severe; her spirit had been well broken by her basic training, and she feared the threat of field slavery, or swallowing coffee beans from other maids' bumholes. Severe's sullen hatred even made the task more pleasurable. Luke kept her chained to his bedpost, when not at her tasks, such as licking the floor and bathroom clean, with Luke caning her bum lightly, as her head was immersed in the toilet bowl; or serving him in the cafeteria, leashed on all fours, where the bulls complimented Luke on the obedience of his doggy.

She obeyed his every order without question, yet pouting, as if she did not understand, and required a new phrasing, or a flurry of cane licks to her bare, to shuffle grudgingly into action. At first, he did not intend to bugger her every night, drained as he was by his daily duty, and the requirements of Miss Esmeralda's thirsty arsehole; yet her punishment, by ever more subtle and shaming means, brought Luke's cock invariably to stiffness.

He strung her for back-whipping, suspended by her hair, and her nipple and cunt rings, with her toes wired painfully tight, and roped to her clit piercings; forced her to hobble with a 'montgolfier', a thick rubber balloon, grotesquely inflated in her anus; subjected her to enemas of her own urine, with her bum stoppered by a cork, to hold the fluid in her bursting belly. The bulls would assemble, over Brahma beer, and Luke would sit on Severe's stretched breasts as a cushion, with her nipple rings nailed to one side of the chair, while she crouched at the other, her teats distended to pale white envelopes of agonised flesh, and her bared buttocks crouching, upthrust.

The bulls would play at inflating a montgolfier in her anus, and another in her mouth, monstrously gagging her. The anal balloon stretched her hole to grotesque dimension, as she groaned and wept, then was pricked with a pin, so that the air rushed out with a loud farting noise.

Afterwards, four or five of them would encule her, still gagged with the huge mouth balloon, until her anus brimmed with spunk. At last, she was permitted to bite through her balloon gag, but at once had to suck on a long rubber tube – its other end inserted in her anus – to swallow every drop of spunk from her buggered bumhole.

A galleon constructed from matchsticks slid into Severe's anus, and was expanded to full size with a tug on the string; hogtied in tight cords, Severe spent the whole evening wriggling and grimacing in pain. Luke masked her, gagged her with panties she had fouled and wrapped her in rubber sheets, until she almost drowned in sweat.

Bound helpless, and caned on the buttocks, she had to suck and swallow for Luke and any other bull, sometimes servicing ten cocks without pause. When severally enculed, she had to suck the spunk from her rectum, with the rubber sperm hose. As a spit-roast, lashed to a pole, and pouring with sweat, she was turned over a dainty but scalding fire, the embers sizzling with her dripped sweat and come, while one bull poked her anus, and another fucked her brutally in the mouth. The tighter and more elaborate her bonds, and the more she writhed in pain, the greater Luke's cruelty, and replenishment of spunk in his balls.

When Luke and his guests were sated with pleasure, Severe was obliged to masturbate without cease, thighs bucking and spread, and clapping her come-filled palm to her mouth, to swallow her own pussy juice, bringing herself to spasm after spasm, to rekindle their lusts. He had her buttocks, cunt and anus tattooed with a squid, like Miss Esmeralda, and faraway Miss Cluster, and stubbed out his Dunhills, with a sizzle, in the squid's eye.

Alone with his slave one morning, several weeks into her slavery, Luke bound Severe more cruelly and tightly than ever, criss-crossing her whole naked body with ropes studded in pins, pricking her hard; a dildo of jagged stone filling her rectum, and taped at the anus. Severe took a deep breath.

'Now I'm totally helpless, you vile, disgusting worm,' she murmured, fixing him with steely eyes. 'Strip, or I'll be cross with you.'

'What? I can't believe . . . Severe, you forget you are my slave.'

Their eyes met; Luke's cockpole swelled.

'That is an order!' she snapped. 'You filthy boy, erect at a girl's distress! Henceforth, you will call me "Mistress Severe".'

Trembling and blushing, Luke obeyed. He stood, nude and erect, as, at Severe's command, he dialled Miss Esmeralda.

'Yes, Miss Esmeralda, an emergency . . .' he blurted.

The overseer arrived, in crisp laundered uniform, breasts and thighs rippling angrily under her skirtlet, tamarind cane dangling, and accompanied by Rodolfo and Herberto, in their own smart new uniforms, with baggy shorts.

'Well?' she snapped. 'What emergency?'

'This beastly swine has me in bondage, and is not competent to undo me,' rasped Severe. 'A master must know how to take care of his slaves.'

The Afro-Brazilians deftly released Severe from her bonds, and she rose unsteadily, rubbing her bruised bare flesh.

'You pathetic worm,' hissed Miss Esmeralda, swishing her tamarind switch at Luke. 'You shall pay the price of failure.'

'No, please,' Luke begged, but too late.

Herberto and Rodolfo had him pinioned to the floor, and Miss Esmeralda ripped down his shorts, baring his arse for the tamarind rod. Luke heard the dreadful swish, the whistle of the cane, then jumped, as the heavy wood seared his naked buttocks. Vap!

'*Ahh!*' he shrieked. 'Please, no.'

Vap!

'Oh! Oh! Don't!'

Vap!

'*Ooh!*'

His whipped buttocks squirmed frantically, the fesses clenching tight, with cruel red weals striping his helpless flesh.

'I always knew you for a worm,' panted Miss Esmeralda.

Vap!

'No, no, please!' Luke said, sobbing. 'It hurts so dreadfully.'

He twisted to look at the imperious black girl, flogging his helpless bare buttocks – her rippling thighs, and huge, bouncing teats, below her white teeth bared in contemptuous rage. At once, Luke's cock sprang to full, painful erection. The caning continued, until Luke's naked fesses writhed purple; licking her lips, the nude Severe masturbated in his full view, taunting him, with her jangling ringed cunt, open to show the pink slit meat gushing come, as she thumbed her erect clitty. Vap!

243

'Ooh! Ouch!'

Luke took 35 strokes on bare, at which the panting Miss Esmeralda thrust her boot in his mouth, and ordered him to lick. Severe glowered, the squid tentacles rippling on her arse.

'He's *my* slave,' she hissed. 'I am his mistress, and always have been.'

'You? Insolent, for a sphincter maid,' sneered Miss Esmeralda.

Severe sprang at the overseer, toppling her, and straddling her belly, while ripping off her skimpy uniform. Herberto and Rodolfo exchanged coy glances, their cocks stiffening, while Luke groaned, crumpled on the floor. Miss Esmeralda squealed in protest, as Severe's fists began to hammer her naked breasts and cunt.

'Stop! Stop!' she shrieked, her belly and cunt writhing in agony, under Severe's pummelling.

Come spurted from her battered cooze, with the bud of her clitty peeping swollen between the squirming slit folds. Miss Esmeralda's frantic wriggles succeeded in toppling Severe; the black girl leapt on top of the prone girl slave, and fastened her teeth on her cunt. Severe howled; Miss Esmeralda had her own quim grinding Severe's face, with her bared black buttocks crushing her.

Come sprayed from the black girl's gash, all over Severe's lips and nose. Moaning, Severe lapped up the pussy juice, as her own pulsing slit gushed heavily under Miss Esmeralda's bites and licks. Miss Esmeralda spanked Severe's jerking thighs and buttocks, as she tongued her sopping slit, and Severe moaned, pressing the overseer's head into her groin.

'Yes ... yes,' she gasped, tonguing Miss Esmeralda's writhing wet cooze.

The fight turned to a slippery, slurping gamahuche, as the naked girls tongued each other's cunts.

'Lesbians!' snorted Rodolfo.

'Let's teach them,' said Herberto. 'Baked chicken!'

The black boys dropped their shorts, and wrenched the gamahuching females apart, by tugging their hair. Squealing, Miss Esmeralda and Severe had their bottoms slapped to the floor, and their thighs forced open and up, with their anus buds exposed. The black boys' massive cocks wedged in their come-soaked arse clefts, as both girls whimpered; Rodolfo split Severe's anus with his tool, while Herberto buggered the squealing Miss Esmeralda. Their bottoms thumped up and down, glinting with sweat, while the massive black cocks squelched in and out of the writhing girls' arse-greased bumholes.

'Ooh! You're hurting me!' Severe squealed.

'Stop!' Miss Esmeralda groaned, yet her buttocks pumped powerfully to meet her bugger's thrusts, and to slap his balls with her quivering thighs. 'You're bursting me in two!'

'Luke! Slave! Do something!' said Severe, sobbing.

Luke clambered to his feet, grasped the tamarind rod, and began to lash the bumfuckers on their jerking bare buttocks. Vap! Vap! Pink weals striped the black skin, but only increased the strokers' ardour.

'Stop it, you swine!' he bellowed.

'Ahh . . . ahh!'

'Ooh! Yes!'

The enculed girls panted, bellies heaving, and bums jerking, as they approached orgasm; Miss Esmeralda wrapped her long black legs around Herberto's back, urging his cock into her come-soaked hole, as Luke's cane lashed the boys' bare black buttocks in a flurry of welts.

'Fuck me,' Miss Esmeralda drooled. 'Plough my arse . . . yes!'

'Yes! Spunk in me! Rip my bum! Oh! *Ooh!*' howled Severe, as come poured from her cunt, and she joined Miss Esmeralda, convulsing in spasm.

The boys' deturgescent cocks plopped from the girls' buggered holes.

'Well,' said Severe, springing to her feet, 'you gentlemen have some explaining to do. Spunking in your mistress without permission. Get down, and bums up.'

Sullenly, they crouched. She snatched Luke's cane, and began to whip the upthrust bare buttocks of the black boys. Vap! Vap! Their cocks rose again under her savage lashing.

'*Mistress?*' gasped Miss Esmeralda. 'I think you are getting ideas, sphincter maid.'

Severe turned to her, with flashing eyes. 'Let's ask them. Whose slaves are you, gentlemen?'

Vap! Vap! The naked buttocks squirmed, wealed deep with crimson stripes.

'Yours, mistress.'

'Beat me.'

'Whip my wicked bottom.'

'Let me worship you!'

Severe smiled grimly, nodding at the huge cocks, rigid under chastisement.

'We'll see who's mistress,' growled Miss Esmeralda, licking her lips.

She grasped Luke's balls, and forced him down to the floor, beside the flogged boys. Miss Esmeralda parted her glistening bum cheeks, to drop on his cockpole with a thud, and engulf his cock with her anus. His tool sank into her squid's throat, all the way to his balls, and she gasped, as his glans slammed her colon, beginning to squirm and thrust, with her ebony thigh flesh slapping his balls, and forcing him to a gasping, slippery arse-fuck. The groaning, whimpering black boys wept, as Severe, their new mistress, ribboned their bottoms with her cane. Seeing Miss Esmeralda triumphantly squirming on the groaning Luke's cock, Severe threw down her cane, and crouched, with her buttocks spread.

'Pleasure me, slaves,' she ordered.

Herberto's cock cleaved her winking anus bud, while Severe brushed aside her sweat-dripping hair to take Rodolfo's swollen black glans between her lips. The boy moaned and wriggled, as her tongue traced the neck of his glans and his peehole, before gasping deeply, as her head swooped to engulf his whole cockshaft in her neck. Squeezing his shaft with her throat, she caressed his balls with her lips, while her body shook with the force of Herberto's cock pounding her colon.

'Ahh,' groaned Miss Esmeralda, masturbating her clitty, with come spraying from her wanked cunt, over Luke's balls.

'Ooh! Ooh!' squealed the buggered Severe, as she fellated her boy slave; both girls shuddered in climax, as spunk from the two cocks spurted to their colons, and dribbled from their squirming anus lips.

The door opened to admit a blonde girl, nude, and hobbling on all fours, with her huge bubbies swaying beneath her, big arse plums quivering in the air, and both bubs and buttocks decorated with fresh cane weals. Her neck was on a dog leash, held by a tall, saturnine male, who sauntered in, holding a short, whippy riding crop, and smoking a cigar.

'They said I would find Miss Esmeralda here,' he purred, then affected mild surprise. 'My, my! What are we up to?'

The tethered blonde gazed at Luke, and gasped, while Severe turned pale, staring at the male newcomer.

'Master!' gasped Miss Esmeralda, springing forwards, to kneel before him, and lick his boots. 'It's his fault.' She pointed to Luke. 'He allowed himself to be enslaved by this worthless sphincter girl!'

The tethered blonde's eyes flared. 'He's *my* slave!' she spat.

'Mine!' snarled Severe.

Luke's jaw dropped. 'Miss Arabel . . .' he blurted.

Arabel sprang from the floor, ripping her leash from the Master's hand, and smacked Severe on the breasts, toppling her, to gouge her titties and knee her cunt, with vigorous punches to her face and belly.

'You fucking bitch!' she squealed.

Severe fought back, and soon the two nude girls were a cloud of dust, spitting, biting, gouging and clawing, as their slippery limbs writhed in fierce combat. The Master puffed on his cigar, his face wreathed in smoke and smiles.

'What a surprise,' he purred. 'Darling Severe, still the hellcat. Cousin Tremaine Duddy did say I'd find some interesting new bodies.'

'Ouch! Ooh!' Severe squealed, getting the worst of it, and struggling, as Arabel straddled her, ripping at her nipples and cunt rings. 'Oh, Justin, help me!'

Justin lifted his riding crop, and delivered six sharp cuts, lightning fast, to Arabel's back.

'Ahh!' she screamed, falling to the floor, to lie, huddled and weeping, with six fresh red stripes on her bare flesh.

'I am Justin Otrifice, by the way,' the cigar-smoker said to Luke. He prodded Arabel's cunt with his boot. 'A nice piece of squirt,' he drawled, 'and a schoolmistress, but temperamental, like all girls. I had to dump dear little Sonia for that reason. Have you met her? Schoolgirls are so possessive, aren't they? However, I think someone must be punished for this indiscipline. One always needs a scapegoat.'

'Him!' blurted Miss Esmeralda, licking Justin's boots.

'Him!' cried Rodolfo and Herberto. They pointed quivering fingers at Luke.

'I think it must be you, sir,' Justin said.

'No!' gasped Severe. 'He's my slave.'

Justin tapped ash from his cigar onto Severe's heaving titties, then stubbed it out, sizzling, in her dripping wet cunt. She grimaced silently, as tears sprang to her eyes.

'Talking back, eh, Severe?' he murmured. 'You rebellious bitch, that makes *two* scapegoats.'

The next day, at noon – the punishment hour – Severe began to cry.

'You have no right to treat me so, Justin,' she said with a sob, breasts quivering. 'I've finished with you.'

'But I'm not finished with you, my dear,' Justin purred. 'We shall rearrange your cunt, and then you can take the superb, shaming punishment I've devised for your horrible arrogance. When my whippers have licked you both clean, you, with your fancy boy, shall return to Poldipple, shamed forever as a slag, a whore, a trollop, your precious virginity in ribbons. The disgrace of Cornwall.'

He rubbed his hands, puffing luxuriantly on his cigar.

'No! Justin, please!' she wailed.

Luke crouched sullenly beside her, naked also, and his feet in a hobble like Severe's. When Miss Esmeralda's scalpels and tweezers had finished with the sobbing, shuddering Severe, she bore a single huge hoop piercing her quim lips, as well as her nipple rings. Miss Esmeralda clipped chains to Luke's Prince Albert, to Severe's cunt hoop, and to both prisoners' nipple rings. The chains were fastened to a cart, drawn by two nude girl slaves in harness, bit and bridle, with the Master, Justin Otrifice, sitting in the driver's seat, whip in hand. Miss Esmeralda clambered beside him.

Crack! Justin lashed hearty strokes to the pert bare bottoms of the pony girls, who jumped, squealing. The cart moved, drawn by the puffing pony girls, and dragging behind it Luke and Severe, stumbling in their hobbles, their flesh wrenched by their tethering rings.

On either side of the cart ran Rodolfo and Herberto, their balls, in a latex cup, held by Miss Esmeralda's leash, and Arabel, her nipples fastened to Justin's leash. Unhobbled, the slaves ran eagerly. Luke and Severe groaned, tears glazing their faces, all the way to the central plaza of the Finca Flagella, where the gibbet stood. The sultry air was fragrant with the perfume of *café flagella.*

The nude slaves – the black boys and Arabel – pushed Luke and Severe up the steps to the whipping frame: a tall wooden rectangle. Miss Esmeralda tapped Luke's limp cock with her whip.

'Tickle his balls, Severe,' she said pleasantly. 'I want him stiff for his correction – and yours.'

Severe reached down, and caressed Luke's balls, until his cock stirred. Miss Esmeralda stroked his bell end with the handle of her whip, and he stiffened to throbbing erection. Miss Esmeralda licked her lips. The pair of naked victims stood, with bodies almost touching. Miss Esmeralda grasped Luke's cock, while Rodolfo split Severe's cunt, and the black girl forced Luke's cock through the cunt hoop, to penetrate Severe's juicing slit. Severe moaned.

'No, please . . . I'm a virgin.'

'I promise not to disrespect you, mistress,' Luke panted hoarsely.

'It's too late!' she wailed.

The pair were bound with copper wire at the waist and under the armpits, squashing their naked bodies together. Beneath them, the assembled slaves, bulls and sphincter girls cheered lustfully. Luke's and Severe's arms were strung high, lifting them to tiptoes. Behind Severe stood Rodolfo and Herberto, holding cattle whips, while Miss Esmeralda positioned herself behind Luke, and caressed the hide of her nine-thonged scourge.

Leashed by her nipples, cunt and neck, Arabel crouched sobbing behind the Master. Hobbled and strung, the victims were helpless to move, with Luke's stiff cock lodged halfway up Severe's hot wet cunt, which was dripping her come over his balls, tickling them. Justin gave the signal, and their whipping began.

Luke tensed, expecting the scourge to lash his back, but Miss Esmeralda's first stroke seared his naked buttocks. Severe's bum, too, jerked, under twin strokes from the black boys' cattle whips. Jolted, Luke's cock slid up the come-oiled cunt, but he strove to withdraw it, until another whipcut rocked him, slamming his peehole against Severe's hard wombneck. She screamed, as her own bottom began to wriggle under the whip, driving Luke's cock, trapped by her quim hoop, deeper into her gash, until his balls slapped at her writhing cunt flaps.

Thwap! Thwap! The thongs lashed naked flesh; tears streamed down their faces, with the crowd of lustful girls openly masturbating, as they cheered each cruel stroke. Thwap! Thwap! Luke's arse began to dance and squirm, his cock poking hard in Severe's cunt. Her bum, too, jerked, squeezing his tool, and sucking it inside her pouch. As the whipping continued, Luke ceased to resist the warm wetness of the squirming girl's cunt; cruelly whipped, he was vigorously fucking his mistress.

Severe wept, screaming and sobbing, as the whip thongs etched red bruises on her buttocks, thighs and back, and Luke's massive stiff cock tooled her cunt.

'Ooh!' she squealed. 'I'm not a virgin any more. You'll pay for this, you bastard.'

Thwap! Thwap! Their bellies slapped; Luke's cock gurgling in Severe's gushing come, as he fucked her hard.

'Ooh! Oh! Don't stop . . . you're so big . . . fuck me, fuck my cunt.'

Thwap! Thwap!

'Oh! Yes! I'm coming! *Ahh! Ooh!*'

Luke's sperm spurted to Severe's wombneck, and he squashed her mouth in a kiss, as both whipped bodies squirmed under orgasm and the lash.

'I promise to pay for my crime, mistress,' he panted. 'For as long as it may please you.'

'I shall never forgive you,' she said, sobbing.

'Then punish me forever,' he gasped. 'Take me as your slave to Poldipple, shame me, bugger me, cleanse me with the licks of your cane, milk my spunk with your divine bumhole, make me squirm and weep and scream with pain, as you whip my flesh, for my crime of worshipping you. You are my only mistress, and I adore only *your* cruelty.'

Thwap! Thwap! The pitiless whips hissed, flogging the trussed boy and girl. Their squirming nude bodies squelched together, and Luke's stiffened cock returned to his mistress's cunt. Severe began to buck, squeezing the tool, and milking him, her cunt spurting come over his trembling balls. Severe smiled, a cruel smile, as she fucked her slave.

'All right, worm,' she said.

**nexus**

The leading publisher of fetish and adult fiction

## TELL US WHAT YOU THINK!

Readers' ideas and opinions matter to us. Take a few minutes to fill in the questionnaire below and you'll be entered into a prize draw to win a year's worth of Nexus books (36 titles)

Terms and conditions apply – see end of questionnaire.

**1. Sex:** Are you male ☐  female ☐  a couple ☐?

**2. Age:** Under 21 ☐  21–30 ☐  31–40 ☐  41–50 ☐  51–60 ☐  over 60 ☐

**3. Where do you buy your Nexus books from?**

☐ A chain book shop. If so, which one(s)?

_____

☐ An independent book shop. If so, which one(s)?

_____

☐ A used book shop/charity shop
☐ Online book store. If so, which one(s)?

_____

**4. How did you find out about Nexus Books?**

☐ Browsing in a book shop
☐ A review in a magazine
☐ Online
☐ Recommendation
☐ Other _____

**5. In terms of settings which do you prefer? (Tick as many as you like)**

☐ Down to earth and as realistic as possible
☐ Historical settings. If so, which period do you prefer?

_____

☐ Fantasy settings – barbarian worlds

- ☐ Completely escapist/surreal fantasy
- ☐ Institutional or secret academy
- ☐ Futuristic/sci fi
- ☐ Escapist but still believable
- ☐ Any settings you dislike?

_____

- ☐ Where would you like to see an adult novel set?

_____


## 6. In terms of storylines, would you prefer:

- ☐ Simple stories that concentrate on adult interests?
- ☐ More plot and character-driven stories with less explicit adult activity?
- ☐ We value your ideas, so give us your opinion of this book:

_____

_____

_____


## 7. In terms of your adult interests, what do you like to read about? (Tick as many as you like)

- ☐ Traditional corporal punishment (CP)
- ☐ Modern corporal punishment
- ☐ Spanking
- ☐ Restraint/bondage
- ☐ Rope bondage
- ☐ Latex/rubber
- ☐ Leather
- ☐ Female domination and male submission
- ☐ Female domination and female submission
- ☐ Male domination and female submission
- ☐ Willing captivity
- ☐ Uniforms
- ☐ Lingerie/underwear/hosiery/footwear (boots and high heels)
- ☐ Sex rituals
- ☐ Vanilla sex
- ☐ Swinging

☐ Cross-dressing/TV
☐ Enforced feminisation
☐ Others – tell us what you don't see enough of in adult fiction:

_____

_____

_____

8. Would you prefer books with a more specialised approach to your interests, i.e. a novel specifically about uniforms? If so, which subject(s) would you like to read a Nexus novel about?

_____

_____

_____

9. Would you like to read true stories in Nexus books? For instance, the true story of a submissive woman, or a male slave? Tell us which true revelations you would most like to read about:

_____

_____

_____

10. What do you like best about Nexus books?

_____

_____

11. What do you like least about Nexus books?

_____

_____

12. Which are your favourite titles?

_____

_____

13. Who are your favourite authors?

_____

_____

## 14. Which covers do you prefer? Those featuring: (tick as many as you like)

☐ Fetish outfits
☐ More nudity
☐ Two models
☐ Unusual models or settings
☐ Classic erotic photography
☐ More contemporary images and poses
☐ A blank/non-erotic cover
☐ What would your ideal cover look like?

_____

## 15. Describe your ideal Nexus novel in the space provided:

_____
_____
_____
_____

## 16. Which celebrity would feature in one of your Nexus-style fantasies? We'll post the best suggestions on our website – anonymously!

_____

## THANKS FOR YOUR TIME

Now simply write the title of this book in the space below and cut out the questionnaire pages. Post to: Nexus, Marketing Dept., Thames Wharf Studios, Rainville Rd, London W6 OA

Book title: _____

### TERMS AND CONDITIONS

## NEXUS NEW BOOKS

*To be published in November 2005*

### PUNISHED IN PINK
#### Yolanda Celbridge

Sultry ebony beauty Nipringa, and innocent blonde Candi Crupper, are both English girls living in Brazil, and studying at Dr Rodd's Academy, with its traditional English regime of bare-bottom caning. They escape to Rio for romantic adventure, but find the boys there just as enthusiastic about spanking them. Fleeing to the comfort of a seaside villa in the far north, they find themselves in thrall to the whip-wielding master, who enslaves them on his tulipwood plantation. Groaning naked under the lash, they discover who Dr Rodd really is.

£6.99   ISBN 0-352-34003-7

### SILKEN SERVITUDE
#### Christina Shelly

Pretty she-male Shelly has had her secret dreams of domination and feminisation fulfilled by Aunt Jane. Yet her willing slavery has taken a new and even more kinky turn with her induction into the Bigger Picture, a secret society of female dominants dedicated to the worldwide subjugation of the male. In this intensely erotic and exciting sequel to the *Company of Slaves*, we discover a plot to turn the entire male sex into helpless sissy slaves and follow Shelly's final journey into a realm of total silken servitude. This wicked, highly erotic tale is a must for lovers of female domination and forced feminisation.

£6.99   ISBN 0-352-34004-5

# RITES OF OBEDIENCE
## Lindsay Gordon

Lindsay Gordon's classic debut is finally available again. Featuring the most intense erotica at Whitehead Academy: an adult school responsible for producing an unusually high number of successful corporate executives. Cub reporter, Penny Chambers, is sent to investigate. Once there, it's not long before the strange syllabus, lascivious students and stern staff awaken a dark sexuality she has always denied herself. A glamorous dean, a haughty Prussian doctor and the peerless Celeste twins all help her to explore new realms of sensation. Like every other student, Penny's education consists of a wide variety of specialist erotic training – in both submission and domination – under a strict regime of discipline. Will Penny expose the bizarre institute, or will she learn to accept the pleasure of fulfilling her most perverse fantasies?

£6.99   ISBN 0-352-34005-3

If you would like more information about Nexus titles, please visit our website at www.nexus-books.co.uk, or send a stamped addressed envelope to:

Nexus, Thames Wharf Studios,
Rainville Road, London W6 9HA

## NEXUS BACKLIST

This information is correct at time of printing. For up-to-date information, please visit our website at www.nexus-books.co.uk

All books are priced at £6.99 unless another price is given.

| | | |
|---|---|---|
| ABANDONED ALICE | Adriana Arden<br>0 352 33969 1 | ☐ |
| ALICE IN CHAINS | Adriana Arden<br>0 352 33908 X | ☐ |
| AMAZON SLAVE | Lisette Ashton<br>0 352 33916 0 | ☐ |
| THE ANIMAL HOUSE | Cat Scarlett<br>0 352 33877 6 | ☐ |
| THE ART OF CORRECTION | Tara Black<br>0 352 33895 4 | ☐ |
| AT THE END OF HER TETHER | G.C. Scott<br>0 352 33857 1 | ☐ |
| BARE BEHIND | Penny Birch<br>0 352 33721 4 | ☐ |
| BELINDA BARES UP | Yolanda Celbridge<br>0 352 33926 8 | ☐ |
| BENCH MARKS | Tara Black<br>0 352 33797 4 | ☐ |
| THE BLACK GARTER | Lisette Ashton<br>0 352 33919 5 | ☐ |
| THE BLACK MASQUE | Lisette Ashton<br>0 352 33977 2 | ☐ |
| THE BLACK ROOM | Lisette Ashton<br>0 352 33914 4 | ☐ |
| THE BLACK WIDOW | Lisette Ashton<br>0 352 33973 X | ☐ |
| THE BOOK OF PUNISHMENT | Cat Scarlett<br>0 352 33975 6 | ☐ |
| THE BOND | Lindsay Gordon<br>0 352 33996 9 | ☐ |